By Fielding Dawson

Stories & Dreams:

Krazy Kat/The Unveiling (1969)
The Dream/Thunder Road (1972)
The Sun Rises Into the Sky (1974)
The Man Who Changed Overnight (1976)
Krazy Kat & 76 More, Collected Stories 1950-1976 (1982)

Novels:

Open Road (1970)
The Mandalay Dream (1971)
A *Great* Day for a Ballgame (1973)
Penny Lane (1977)
Two Penny Lane (1977)
Three Penny Lane (1981)

Novellas:

Thread (1964)
The Greatest Story Ever Told/*A Transformation* (1973)

Memoirs:

An Emotional Memoir of Franz Kline (1967)
The Black Mountain Book (1970)

Essays & Criticism:

An Essay on New American Fiction (1963)
Entelechy One (1969)
The Yellow Cab—An Essay on New Fiction (1981)

Poetry:

Delayed, Not Postponed (1978)

KRAZY KAT
& 76 MORE

COLLECTED STORIES 1950–1976
FIELDING DAWSON

Black Sparrow Press Santa Barbara 1982

ACKNOWLEDGEMENTS

Thanks to the editors of the following magazines and anthologies
where some of these stories originally appeared: *Adventures in
Poetry, Art & Literature, Big Sky, The Black Mountain Review,
Blue Grass, The Boston Phoenix, Burning Deck, Caterpillar, El
Corno Emplumado, Ear in the Cornfield, The Falcon, The Floating
Bear, For Now, Granta, Grossteste Review, Harper's Bazaar, Imago,
Jargon, Joglars, Lines, The Moderns, Mother, The Ontario Review,
Outburst, The Promethian,* The Shortstop Press, *Signal, Silo,
Sparrow, The Story So Far,* Supplement to Now *(Neon), Tabloid
Story, Thrice, Tribal Press, The White Dove, Wild Dog* and *Yugen.
The Greatest Story Ever Told* was originally published in 1973 by
Black Sparrow Press.

Cover collage by the author.

LIBRARY OF CONGRESS CATALOGING IN PUBLICATION DATA

Dawson, Fielding, 1930-
  Krazy Kat & 76 more.

  I. Title. II. Title: Krazy Kat and seventy-six more.
PS3554.A948K7 1982   813'.54   82-14641
ISBN 0-87685-564-8
ISBN 0-87685-565-6 (lim. ed.)
ISBN 0-87685-563-X (pbk.)

Table of Contents

Introduction

To write these words is an honor and a fulfillment of consistent completion, a wonder, a glimpse of glory and an admission of humility in the face of the tremendous experiences these pages embrace. It would be easy, and natural, to recall the frustrations, hated limbo, the long, vain reaches, triumphs, surprise successes, speechless failures, self-conscious loneliness and the isolate bitterness that nags and deters all writers who see, or think they see, lesser work praised while their own goes ignored, yes, except when hard at work it all *poof!* vanishes. There is much to say.

Well.

A little.

Going through these seventy-seven titles, getting them in their proper sequence—at last—I saw amazing reflections, as shifting pieces of colored glass form patterns. In a surprise meeting at a publishing party at Gotham Book Mart, not long after *Krazy Kat/The Unveiling* (the first Black Sparrow collection of my stories) appeared, Zukofsky, after we'd shaken hands and said hello, gave me a pointed look, and in reference to *Krazy Kat*, said—"It's a book."

With that look and his words in mind, I arranged this book.

I had discovered, in putting together the second Black Sparrow collection—*The Dream/Thunder Road*—that *Krazy Kat* had been incomplete, for I found stories that should have been in it, a first most durable realization: I wrote so much the books couldn't keep up, for the next collection, *The Sun Rises Into the Sky*, was still of that indeed *Krazy* flow. Don't believe that in my eagerness to be published I dug through the bottom drawer to fill the books. I sent the publisher the best I had. That's why the books are rather

7

short, and perhaps why *The Man Who Changed Overnight* has an autonomy the others, each apart, seem to struggle toward. In short, *Krazy Kat* embraces the two collections that followed, from which *The Man Who Changed* breaks free (into the *Penny Lanes*). Last year (1981), however, after a bad fire, I found two short stories in first draft, written in 1957 and '58, that should have been published in *Krazy Kat*. The *Kat* still around! And I'd thought *The Sun Rises* was the end of it! So, in a further consideration, one of volume and density—tip of the iceberg image—if the stories in those four books were a selection of what I thought my best (think of the boxes of bad ones), know that for every story there were from two to five (or more) rewrites, plus clean copy and carbon (my habit is to correct the carbon and transfer the corrections onto the clean copy)—that *Open Road*, the *Kline Memoir*, *Black Mountain Book*, *Mandalay Dream*, *Great Day for a Ballgame*, *Greatest Story*, *Tiger Lilies* (unpublished), plus an almost overwhelming amount of criticism, essays, poems and dreams, each re- and re- and rewritten toward final clean copy and carbon, to be given final corrections on the final galleys while I wrote these stories.*

In other words, this collection surrounds a pure center of my life and work. The landslide of poems and stories I'd written in high school (as I dreamed of this book), crystallized in the first story in this work—*Father* (which should have been in *Krazy Kat*)—written in 1950 at Black Mountain, when I was twenty. *Krazy Kat* itself was written in the fall of the following year, 1951. The two stories that end this collection, found after fire, today are as new to me as the *Kat* for sure, and in memory of Zukofsky, I decided to let them end it, as the second in particular seems a fine microcosm.

So.

In my introduction to *Krazy Kat/The Unveiling* I thanked the editors of magazines who had published the stories, and also thanked "John Martin, for this book."

Let me again thank John Martin. For this book.

---

* I have no one voice. Every final manuscript, including this introduction, has to please all voices—we don't please easy.

Let me thank Jonathan Williams, who published the original—*Krazy Kat and One More*, and Andrew Crozier, who first published *Thread*. Thanks as well, long overdue, to M. C. Richards, who as editor took *Father* for the original one and only edition of *The Black Mountain College Review*. And here, I mean right here, these final words, for another dream has come true.

To thank my readers, a dream of thanks.

Your letters, words and notes let me know my narratives made contact. Without you there would be in me a terrible and disconnected innocence. You gave my discipline—without which there can be no freedom—space. You made a tough, often desperate continuity harmonious, your encouragement gave to my commitment a freshness and conviction that writers need like blood. Here, from all the way down the line it is you that gives this book its character of response, which is rare, and to me sacred. Believe me, I love it as I love little else, for I am the most selfish writer—thank you.

You know who you are.

This book is yours.

FD
April 22, 1982
New York

I had a funny feeling as I saw the
house disappear, as though I had
written a poem and it was very good
and I had lost it and would never
remember it again.

—Raymond Chandler
The High Window

KRAZY KAT & 76 MORE, COLLECTED STORIES

1950 – 1976

Father

BECAUSE BECAUSE BECAUSE because because be space began this morning when that little girl woke up time began this morning when that little girl drew stick figures in the half dried mud what time is it is is nine oclock well i am going to sit here and wait to see what is to happen happen because because because there is nothing but a scent from the empty bottle of turpentine there is no scattered sawdust as a remainder to remind she has taken all there are no more tears she has taken all tears all laughter all anger all misery all disgust all falsehood all pride all greed all hunger all time all space all blood all life all rot all thirst all sight all hearing all meaning all taste all touch all smell all children all people all pleasure pride heat cold names numbers books lamps clothes sensations everything from me i am alone and alone and alone and alone sitting waiting for that which is to happen to happen but i know it wont because there is nothing to make what should happen happen because i am that which is left between wall and peeling paint sitting here in this chair waiting for him my son to return to me to give me that which is mine which should have been mine from the beginning which she knew i had but she knew that i knew that she couldn't get it but she tried and she tried and she tried tried tried and got not what she wanted but enough of what she wanted to satiate her titanic lust for that power that she couldn't meet but she tried and she took me my life my children my wife myself and she used all she took not against me but used to feed her children children to grow grow grow grow into the next days tomorrows and years years but in doing so she made a colossal mistake that says the children grew up just as she wanted

15

them to grow up but they couldnt grow up because they didnt know how i have ruined their lives by not giving every bit of myself that i could give she was right in taking from me what she did take because she knew that she could use it better than i because i did not know how while she did so she took all of me she could take and left the echo of the crash of hammer on nail which is to me to exist but she made that mistake which is beginning to ruin their lives right now which she did not plan on nothing is perfect not even the earth is perfect she expected me to be the sun energy in their bloodstreams running and flowing freely through their bodies to give them a spontaneous action and movement through the time and length of their lives without giving any-thing to ME but that did not happen it will not happen now and it will not happen never ever because she failed she failed she failed she failed she has ruined their lives she has left me dead she has died herself agamemnon never left home and that energy which she took from me and gave those children was MY energy coming from HER body instead of MINE it did not it could not possibly work because MY energy is not for her to use she did not know how to use it and she never would have learned because the energy which is in mans blood is his and is not to be touched by woman and that which is womans is not to be meddled with by any man but she did not realize that in time so it was toooo late when she saw it beginning to ruin their lives and so she began to wish hope pray dream of death as both an escape and a substitute for the agony which she would have to go through when she watched her children grow (in the end she took the coming of death in the flames of that house she was building with not plea-sure but with pride because she had taken death for granted a long time ago and had nothing to do but wait for it to come but she was crazy to die too because she knew and she watched me writhe she knew that when she died the earth would die and when the earth will die nothing will be left). in the beginning when she first started to drain me of my life she hoped to give the children all not all of me or all of herself but all all that the earth and the sun could give but she knew she could not but her pride would not let up not for an instant because it couldnt because when she started creating those boys in that way she couldnt stop she couldnt stop

16

because (not because of her mind or her pride alone which did that) it was her blood it was her natural intrinsic life which did it and going on towards the end she knew she knew what was happening just as well as she knew that death was coming to her very soon it was just a dream away and she knew how she was going to die she wanted to die too because she was afraid which never showed because when she had drained me of everything except the paint which clings dry to the empty can she was afraid that those two boys would have nothing to live with but just suppose it would have happened earlier just suppose it would have made no difference what so ever because she was moving so fast then that she couldnt stop but at or just about the end she became afraid for another reason she was over there building that house living with a workman she had picked up in town and paying that man terrific wages nothing ever happened between the two of them because she was too proud then too proud for that too proud to lay down for any man then tooo proud but one day she was working on that frame house building the house because she had to do something and perhaps it was then she realized her mistake and then she became afraid then she became terrified and then she began to hammer because there was nothing else to do then but hammer there was no sense nor reason for any other act of life she prayed with those clamped jaws and rock teeth for death to strike but she knew it wouldnt because she knew it wasnt quite time for death not quite she had to go through a chain of memories and a broken and mangled chain of thoughts about the lives of her children in the obtainable future which made her cringe and tremble and which made her drive that workman double time with doubled wages until the building was finished she was driving herself past fury past insanity into the motion of hit hit hit hit sinking nail after nail after nail into that roofing with the precision of the animal who knows neither taste nor smell nor touch who neither hears nor sees but who goes on and on and on and on and on until that moment she hit and drove hammered herself and those nails into a mechanical rhythm that that workman could bear no longer local woman dies in burning house and on that day as those flames danced around her she knelt nailing nails into the flat roof with the workman now completely mad mutter-

17

ing beside her doing nothing and so she sat back on her heels and watched the flames come to her and maybe then with her death seconds away a dream come true she realized her mistake maybe then that she began to cry maybe then she cried for the annihilation of all her life and maybe then she cried for my life and maybe then then still there then she cried for the ruined lives of her children ruined past present and future future the will not ever be future of them because neither boy will ever know what is woman but then the fire did not speak to her it was the workman then who spoke who said our father who art in heaven hallowed be thy name thy will be done on earth mud dirt as it is is because of fire in this my househeaven give me this moment the painbread and forgive us her earth as is like myself and lead us not from evil but from her and deliver me unto the power and the glory of the kingdom of hot sunblood and gulping blooddirt forever and ever amen

Krazy Kat

STOP IT. You are absolutely and irrevocably out of order. Speak only when you are spoken to.

The children moved uneasily in their seats.

Then the rain stopped.

Now, he said, smiling, the rain has stopped. How now, he said to himself, that when I ask for order, the rain stops.

Then he said loudly to his class.

Repeat after me. They nodded.

This is a lovely day.

This is a lovely day.

Mary Lou raised her hand.

Yes, he said, what do you want?

Why do we have to say that?

Because I want to impress upon you the tremendously activated force that nature has. Mary Lou put her hand down.

Then the bell rang. They sat very still and he smiled.

19

Now, he said, you may go.

They all got up and the girls went out first, one by one, and then the boys did the same.

He wondered why Mary Lou always asked that and why she kept her hand in the air until the question was answered and then put it down. He looked at his watch and he felt fine that the class had gone so quickly. He began to put his desk in order. He went around the small room and placed the chairs properly, in their before class order. Then he went back to his desk and sat down and began to read. The assignment for today was Blake. He loved Blake. There is no one, he said once, who can write with such profundity, and make it seem so simple. It was Wednesday. I'll have them reciting by Friday, he thought. He walked across the room and picked up a piece of paper off the floor. It had some writing on it. He crumpled it and then uncrumpled it and read it. This is a lovely day, it said. Then the bell rang and he threw it into the waste can and went to his desk and sat down behind it. As the boys came in he smiled at them. As the class went on he was pleased. Everyone read his assignment, and read it well. There were no mistakes as yet. There were only eight boys in the class, but they were all intelligent and capable. They were quiet and they paid attention. They dressed well and had manners. It is a good thing, he thought, to have them here; it is a healthy thing for the younger children to have them near, else there might be more difficulties. He watched them write what he had said. He had them write often, and he gave them things to write—he didn't care for the word dictation, it seemed too secretarial and not quite formal. They were close to him and he would rather not call it anything. So he told them to write down what he said, and they did. He told them only twice. It is enough, he told his wife. It gives them discipline and they need it. Then he got out of his chair, as they seemed to be finishing writing, and he walked out and stood in front of his desk, facing the semi-circle of chairs in front of him. He asked them one by one which poem they liked most. Six said *The Tiger*, and two said *The Little Girl Lost*. Well, he thought, two fine poems, but he wondered quickly why six had liked *The Tiger* best. He cared very much for *The Little Girl Lost*, and he was quite pleased when those two had made that their choice. He walked over and sat down in an empty desk at the end of the curve and he asked the boy next to him, Sam, why he had liked *The Little Girl Lost* the best.

It's lonely, sir. The girl and the Lion. Real lonely.

I think so too, Sam, he said.

Sir?, said one of the boys across the room, sir?, may I say something?

Certainly.

I liked Tiger because I think the Tiger's God, and I think that it's a putting, that it's a making one God, the other God, the real God, but that both Gods are the one only different.

What do you mean?

Some of the boys looked out from their desks to look at him.

Do you mean that The Tiger, as man, and as the saying of Man and God alike?

No. I mean the great God. Only Two Great Gods like one. Like I hold the sort of Godness in my own hand.

Do you mean that you are God?

No. No, sir. Sir, I mean like I hold the whatever I am which is even the thing that I am visibly, in my hand. And rather that I would be invisible so that I could have my real visibility in my hand—even though it's more invisible.

I am becoming more and more confused.

21

I think I understand, sir, said Sam, as the teacher shook his head.

He's talking like taking a mirror reflection and having that as the Tiger—like the Tiger is the reflection held in the hand of God, and even though God is invisible as a single order, He remains real in the image of The Tiger, who is also invisible because He is only a reflection, but nonetheless, the reflection of God.

Is that correct. Is it right what Sam says, he said to the boy. I think I am beginning to understand.

No, sir. That's not right. It's not a reflection. I can't say it. The mirror's wrong because even the mirror is too visible. Like the making of the Tiger. What hand could do so. God. But the hand of God, in making the Tiger, made his own exact kind of thing, which might be a mistake, I don't know, but when God made the Tiger, the Eye, and the Symmetry, the Tiger turned out to be too visible, like the mirror a little, and even the Tiger, I think, would wish to be more—it's a division—it's a dividing one into one. Cutting God unevenly, having two real visibles but having only one reality. And so the invisible part is worth more than the visible part and the other way around—

Do you mean the *Tiger* is the creator?

I don't know, sir. In a way I do. Not then, sir, but he is now.

Sir, Sam said. I think he means The Father, Son, and Holy Ghost, like three being one, but still remaining three.

No sir, no sir, I don't sir, no I don't. I mean that if I chose to make the most wonderful thing that I could make, I would make whatever I am, and it would be invisible, because it would have to be invisible, because what I would make would be whatever it is that makes me make a Tiger, and it would be a mistake because it's more of anything that I am, and, I would rather be invisible so that what I have made would have to stand out but it couldn't, sir,

22

because it would have to be invisible too, because it's the whole order of what I can do, and to make it obey what I can do, it still remains visible and worthwhile and dangerous and more important than me but it can't be because I made it and the reason it's dangerous is because it's visible and it burns and I don't burn, sir, because I can't because I'm God, and it's a Tiger.

Because you're *God!*

Yes, sir.

Well, he said sarcastically, how do you like being God!

I don't, sir.

And why not!

Because I made a mistake.

WHAT mistake did you make!

I made a Tiger.

At the Farm

THE SERIES WAS OVER. The Yankees beat the Dodgers. It began to rain and Barnes came across the field till he got to where I was standing. He said it's raining and I said, Yes, it's raining but I was thinking what Joe would say at supper. I was laughing to myself about Cleveland. I told Barnes the Yanks won and he said Oh really? and I said yes and he didn't care because I was thinking they won The Series: The Yanks Have Won The Series like in a story the name the title but like it was them winning The Series in headline I could smell that paper and Barnes said as he held out his hand with his palm up he said it's raining but doesn't it smell nice and I grinned and said Yes and then he asked me what we should be doing and I pointed at the rows of plowed up potatoes and said

We should be picking those up.

With what?

Our hands.

Where do they go?

In baskets.

Baskets? Where are they?

At the end of the field. I pointed. Over there. He got some. I saw Jines drive the tractor into the shed. I thought he looked like Floyd, a little, but different because Floyd looks more loose on the tractor and comfortable. Jines came walking out and went to bring the cows down to be milked.

Some of the potatoes are little, some are big, they grow in clumps and like Barnes said you can walk ten feet and not find a potato and then find a dozen. It was not Barnes who said that it was Gus. Barnes picked up a basket and so did I and we began at one end of the row and we picked up potatoes and put the full baskets up by the road so

24

they could be picked up with the truck and then we began with new baskets on a new row and we got them filled too, and then Barnes asked me what to do next and I said,

Now we rake.

What is that?

At the end of the row there's a potato fork and you get that. There's one missing. I'll get another at the barn, Dole said there's one around somewhere. You rake at the side of the furrow, you just rake the loose dirt, break up the clumps and look for potatoes. It's not hard but it's something.

Okay.

I'll go and try and find the fork now. You go ahead. I'll get back soon.

He went to the end of the row to get the fork that was lying there and I went to the other end of the field to the barn awhile and couldn't find it so I went down the road and turned by the fence by the ditch and I looked under Dole's house and then, by the trees, I saw a long handle. It wasn't a fork it was a hoe and I thought that I would use that as well and I took that and cut across the field from the house to where Barnes was standing raking and he was doing it all wrong so I showed him how to do it and he said,

Oh yes, that's a good way, too.

It began to let up a little but then rained harder. Barnes said that it was raining harder than before and I said, Yes, it is. Dole came down the road in his Ford and turned into the yard in front of his house and he stopped. He got out and came to where we were working and asked me if I found the rake.

No, I said.

Barnes said it was raining.

It sure is, Dole said. He looked at me.

Ain't it. I said,

It sure is. Dole said,

How much you done?

About two and a half rows.

That's good. Tomorrow we'll bring in some tobacco.

Then he went across the field to the house and Barnes and I watched him. I said that it must be near six and Barnes said he didn't know and I said, Well, when we finish this row, we'll quit and

Barnes didn't say anything. He began raking potatoes and I did too and a little while later we put the hoe and fork under the house and walked down to supper and Barnes asked if this kind of weather keeps up for long down here and I said it sure does. You get used to it. It stays like this and when it's different it's snow and gets colder and after that it gets windy and blows out doors and windows. After that it gets hot and then like this again. Barnes frowned and said Jesus. He was from Boston.

THE NEXT DAY

The next day it was raining again and Floyd jumped up on the tractor and yelled TOOT TOOT and the tractor began to move ahead. Dole and I stood on the wagon in back. It was loaded with tobacco. Dole and I laughed and so did Cleary's father and Gus. Barnes walked up ahead to pull the threaded tobacco stakes up to put on the wagon to take to the barn where we would hang them and wait until it stopped raining. When the tobacco was cut the stalks were pushed over the gav which is a metal tip on the end of a stake, and when there are five or seven or eight stalks, the stake is pulled up, loaded on the wagon and taken to be hung in the barn to dry and later the shriveled leaves are taken off the stakes and graded. But the tobacco barn wasn't finished yet and Dole was hanging the stakes full of tobacco in the cow barn, the beef stall and in the barn where I saw Buck given an injection for his bad eye. Floyd held Buck's head and they tied a rope around his neck and brought it around a beam and held the end of the rope and Floyd said, Buck's a good bull.

The wagon jerked a little from side to side as it went through the mud. Up ahead Gus and Cleary's father had a stake ready for us when the wagon slid to a stop. Floyd and Gus shouted at the tractor because it was still skidding on even after Floyd stopped it. But finally it stopped and Gus and Cleary's father handed the stake up to us and Dole told Cleary's father to be careful and Cleary's father sort of smiled, we took the stake with all the tobacco leaves threaded on it and we laid it very carefully like a tablecloth over the other stakes of leaves and we did it very carefully, not to injure the leaves. Then Barnes gave us a stake and then Cleary's father and then Gus and then Barnes again and Floyd got off the tractor and helped and so on

26

until the wagon was piled high and we went to the barn. We sat in the doorway of the barn and looked out at the rain and big dark clouds hanging over the mountains that surrounded the valley. Dole said that turkeys are crazy. They follow you around and get in your way because they walk around in the rain. I could see Floyd looking out from the doorway across fields and he said to Dole,

You got company, Dole.

A car came skittering up the road pretty fast and slid into the yard in front of the house. I wondered if Cleary was there, the man was knocking on the door and then he quit and got in his car and we watched him back out and turn and drive up to the barn and stop in front of us. He got out and came toward us and nobody said anything. Then he said he was looking for the man that ran the farm for the College and Dole said,

That's me.

Floyd said at the same time, pointing at Dole, He's right there. Dole and the man talked a little, after the man introduced himself, about some custom work that he had to have done would Dole send somebody down sometime soon. Dole said that he would and smiled at Gus. Gus here would be down Tuesday morning. Then they squatted down on their haunches in the doorway of the barn and one of the turkeys got up and walked around on the hood of that man's car and Dole went over and it flew off and we laughed and Dole said they were ignorant things they always got in your way. Dole and the man talked about plowing and how hard plowing had been a few months before because of the drought and I watched the man roll a cigarette. He had blonde hair and a white shirt. Floyd was inside the barn tapping his hand on one of the steel bars that separated the cow stalls. He was back in the corner and I wondered if Floyd knew the blonde man. Floyd was all loose, tapping his hand on the steel bar waiting for Dole to stop.

The sun came out and the chickens and turkeys and guineas and bantys were walking around and Floyd rattled a chain on the bar and Dole said that field out there had been hard when they had plowed it and he asked Gus if he wasn't right and Gus said yep that was right and after the man had gone and when the tobacco had been put in and we were finishing up cutting corn and the sun was shining bright and the shadows were long across the floor of the valley I asked

Floyd if he knew that man and he said no that he didn't know him, I don't know many people around here, I come from California. I thought of that bent license plate on his old Dodge as I looked at him and Floyd said he sure thought that man talked a lot.

Urbana, Illinois

A DOCUMENT OF THE 1950S

THEY HAD RETURNED from their stroll.

He said, Thank you for making me come out.

She said, I charmed you. She laughed. She rubbed her head with the towel and bent over the open door of the oven.

He drank coffee, watching her. Funny, I think, he said.

What is?

How you are.

Oh.

Do you know what I mean?

I think so. She looked at him and smiled. Said,

But it's different to really know me. She paused and said, I'm being brainy again. I know what you mean. I do. More than that, I think I'm funny, too; I don't mean like intrigue, I mean like I am.

She wrapped the towel around her head and sat down at the table with him.

I want so much, she said. I want nearly all of it; that and control, and to be right. I don't like being wrong. That's not sly, it's very conscious and known. I don't have any idea what it is, but it's something I know, only to know it all and be it all. Once I heard a woman say, and she was married and had two children, she said she imagined everyone had a secret idea they really wanted. But she made her secret idea a paradise and it makes me laugh because that's stupid, particularly in her case because she's a very intelligent person. Aren't those funny words? Intelligent and person. Very odd I said them. Not like me. Perhaps it's because she said them.

She leaned across the table and touched his arm.

I think you're intelligent. And kind. Don't forget me. Please.

He smiled.

29

She went to the oven and took the towel in her fingers and rubbed it hard on her head, feeling her senses rock. The interesting lie she had just made. In sunshine. It was a real daytime lie. You couldn't lie like that at night.

She took the kettle of water off the stove and waited until he put the teaspoon of instant coffee in the cup. She filled the cup, put the kettle back on the stove. He stirred the coffee with the spoon, thinking what he was doing stirring the coffee. She caught herself standing looking blank. She glanced at him. He was watching her. He was sitting back in the wooden chair. She went to the cupboard and got a cup, came back, put it on the table, made herself some coffee, sat down and looked at him; he dropped his eyes. She rose and went to the icebox and opened it and looked inside.

Would you care for something to eat?

No. Thanks.

How had he said that? She felt everything slide away.

She closed the icebox door and rubbed her forehead, pushing her fingers into the skin. She went to the table and sat down beside him.

Why does it always have to be this way?

What way?

This.

He looked at her. She looked in his eyes and put her meaning in her eyes.

I don't know, he said. Drinking the coffee, she thought he was avoiding her. She clenched her teeth. She caught her breath. His lie!

She stood up but he took her wrist.

Sit down.

She sat down and folded her hands on the table: I am an actress.

After he had gone to his class she stacked the dishes in the cupboard and took the rag off the faucet and began wiping the table. She swept the crumbs into her hand, went around the table and then shook the crumbs into the wastecan and washed her hands, emptied the dishpan and hung the rag over the faucet, wiped her hands on the dishtowel and straightened it on its rack by the edge of the sink.

Then she went out on the porch and sat down on the swing and looked at the lawn, the garden, and the Urbana street.

30

She walked along the front walk and looked up and down the street.

She went inside the house and into his room and looked over the books. She couldn't decide which. She went out of the room and out on the porch again. She sat in the big rocking chair and looked at the lawn.

A bird flew to the first step and hopped up on the porch. It fluffed its feathers, spread its wings and then stood still, looking. It tilted its head and looked at her. It looked at her; the one eye, on her.

She laughed to herself. Yes, I see you too.

Not much later it flew away.

She knew it would, and when it did, nodded.

She laughed because she knew it would fly away just as surely as it had come.

Why not?

The little girl, three, from next door, came up the steps.

Hello, she said to her.

The little girl smiled.

Come. She patted her hands. Come and sit on my lap.

The little girl went to her and she pulled her up and sat back and pulled the little girl against her, and made the chair rock, the girl would like that.

Where is your mommy?

The little girl didn't answer.

Is she at the store?

The girl moved her head. Yes.

That's very nice. And untrue.

Then she leaned forward, picked the girl off her lap and put her on the porch.

You must come again.

The little girl looked at her vaguely, and went away.

She sat back, curled her legs up, frowned, wondering.

Well, she said.

She got out of the chair and went inside, to his room again.

I will sew, she said.

She laughed, looked at herself in his mirror.

She sat down at the desk, opened the drawer and took out her gold lipstick, put a little on her lips, bit them together, looked in the

31

mirror again and put the lipstick away and closed the drawer.
Well. She watched her face in the mirror,
I believe that is enough.

The Nature of the Universe

dedicated to Gene Reid, 1930-1956

WHERE I WENT TO COLLEGE was pretty great, though—well, it was. It's where I met most of the friends I still have now: Leo Kelleter and Gus Kell. Two really great guys. But it's where I met some girls: too. That was pretty great. I remember once I got sick. And I was sick: too. When I get sick I really do a good job of it. Boy. But she used to come and see me. She'd bring some soup or something, on a tray with a cloth over it. There'd be toast and some grape jelly . . . I'd eat it and she'd stick around most of the afternoon and read to me and all. You know. We had a pretty good time. She used to read Gertrude Stein to me. I had a little trouble understanding it but now and then something came through and sounded good. She was crazy about Gertrude Stein. She used to say Gertrude Stein was the greatest woman writer that ever lived. I can't say as I haven't read much of her. I like detective stories myself. But I admit some of it was good. Gertrude Stein sure kept it up!

I went down there to school because I thought I could paint pictures. But I gave it up at the end of the first year. I draw a little now and again. I used to paint pictures of ships from photographs. I like the black and red on the hulls and smokestacks. Tugboats are great. That's another reason I like New York so much. When I lie in bed at night I can hear them going that low boooo. Pretty nice. Then in the afternoon in the summertime I lie on my roof, tar beach, and get some sun. And listen to the big ships coming in and the distant boooo sound in the air. I guess I gave up painting because that's what I really want to paint. Boooo.

There was a lake at school and an old rowboat. I was going with a girl then that later came to New York and married a guy. She was a pretty good sport. A little too moody for my taste, but sometimes it was a lot of fun. We used to go out in the rowboat together and drink home brew. We made our own there and drank it while it was still going. Gus and I. Leo Kelleter had come from New York and was getting ready to go to Spain. And Gus and I would dip quart jars into that big crock of home brew and go off and drink it. It looked like bean soup and didn't taste very good because the yeast was still pretty thick. When you make it don't dip in too soon. Give it a chance. Then cool it. It isn't bad and it's very cheap. Actually, it's very strong. We had a farm at school and the farmer said it was fifteen per cent. The home brew. That's thirty proof beer, which isn't bad. German bock beer is more but you have to go to Germany because their export beer is lousy. You don't have to go. You can make it at home. If you want. It's not bad. You ought to try it. Sometime. That girl and myself would go out in the rowboat. At night. About ten. We'd take a half gallon out with us and row around the lake, talking and drinking. We even sang. She used to know a lot of songs. She was a blonde, had really beautiful hair. Sometimes in our room she'd feel spooky and put a sheet over her head and come at me. I always knew it was her though. We used to get all tied up in that sheet. It was nice. In the boat was nice, too. The stars and all. They were so clear. Like you really felt you were with them. Clear and nice, up so high and far away but right there. The sewer line ran parallel with the lake and it leaked and nobody could swim in the lake but we used to anyway. At night. I'm not a very good swimmer but we used to anyway, row out to the dam and tie the boat up and jump in. Or not. Just us. With the frogs going, and the crickets and insects. Bats, too. They had bats down there. You could feel them pass close to you. In the dark. It was so dark you couldn't see where to walk. But the bats never hit you. They have that radar thing. They can tell you're there and they avoid you. But they come pretty close.

I used to stand on the dam in the afternoon and look down in the lake. It was something. There must be layers of water. It has that feeling. I mean kind of tone layers. Like you know there are layers of air. I saw some diagrams in *Life* once where they showed air layers from the edge of the earth up to the top of the page. Infinity. It must be like that with water. It looks like it. Feels like it. And then when fish come in that's great. Fish are great. Swimming around without a

34

care in the world. So if some girl asks you why you're so irresponsible you tell her you're a fish.

We made a raft, nailed a bunch of boards together and put big empty oil drums underneath, lashed them on with ropes. One of the drums filled up though and the thing kind of listed. It was big. Bud White and his girl and my girl and me would go out on the lake. Sometimes we'd go out after lunch. All hop in swimming suits and shove off. They had a pole about fifteen feet long to maneuver the raft around as it was pretty clumsy. I liked the rowboat better. I got so I could handle it pretty well. It was no Chris Craft but it was a lot of fun. When I got very loaded and felt a little down I'd go out by myself. At night. Sometimes I fell asleep and would wake up just as dawn was coming up. The college was in a valley and the mountains were all around. Like in the bottom of a cup. The sun came up and as it came over the mountains on the east, the west mountains would blaze with color. Especially in the fall. Blueridge October. Those trees shouted color in the morning and the mist came curling up into pale blue air from the tree sap and there I'd be waking up in the bottom of my boat that was bumping up against the rocks at the foot of a dirt embankment. I'd look over the side and there would be a big bullfrog sitting on a rock, about a foot away. Looking at me. I'd look right back though: we'd be looking at each other, his throat going in and out a little. He was probably breathing. Watching me breathing. They're big, too. Bullfrogs. Some as big as a grapefruit. Bigger. Not much though. That would be too much. Bullfrogs are great. They're terrific when they take off. Their toes spread. Must feel nice to hit the water and have it rush between your toes.

I killed a bullfrog with a BB gun. When I was a kid. Out at my uncle's place. I remember it. That old frog floating in the reeds over by the edge of the pond: dead, his long legs spread slack, hanging in the water. I began to walk away feeling like I was going to vomit. I headed up towards my uncle's house but it seemed so far off and everything got dizzy like curved silver lines moving around everything, making it glisten, like everything glistens and gets blurred when you cry. The tears in yours eyes seem to cover the sky and the blueness gets like far away sheets of ice.

35

It was snowing. Hard: the wind whipped around corners and met the other wind straight on: confusing the direction of the snowflakes so that they jumped and fussed around in the air like excited barflies. The sky was a mottled gray sheet: a truculent parent above blanketed Manhattan. Forecast: snow. Forecast: cold. The forecast. Tomorrow it would be cold: and snowing. Please. I have spoken. You can't take the king of kings away from the nature of things (Kline said): There's so much space you'll drown in it. Jack Powell tucked that curtain in around the sashchain absent-mindedly. He looked out the window: hands folded behind him. Traditional with thinking people. Two bundled men headed towards Third Avenue with alcoholic certainty. One foot: now: there: in front of: easy: there, the other. Thinking of all the things they have done which they should not have done and things they have not done which they should have. Done. They began across Third Avenue. They did not look at the traffic light. Jack looked at the traffic light. It was green. Oui. The positive of power drinking. The window pane was cold. Jack felt a slight breeze. In that sequence he thought of weather stripping. The two men were across Third: going towards Second. Tinker Chance? It was still snowing. A yellow taxi crawled downtown like yellow & white Kafka. Klee? No. Driver hunched over the wheel? No. A bum stopped by a Third Avenue Puerto Rican grocery store and looked up at the sky. Who knows what goes on in that poor neglected mind. A bottle of wine as big as summertime. Do you have a dime—hey. Do you have a dime? No. Reasonably enough. I don't. For the lack of a dime two birds out of hand huddled under snow covered stoops and made intricate plans. Frobenius. Articulate. A partridge childhood in Manhattan. Time stops. A.P.M.E.N.D. A lute. Christmas in 21 days. Last night she said tonight should be Christmas. Jack nodded. The bum looked down from the sky and around Third Avenue: began up towards 14th St. A blue Chevy and a blue Plymouth ground uptown: passing by. Unheeded. A plump man in plaid overcoat and snowshovel in hand stepped out of a hockshop doorway. The bum stopped. They looked at each other. The bum held out his hand. The man looked at him. The bum stank? The plump man began shoveling snow like it was something SHE COULDN'T STAND fast off the sidewalk into the gutter. An allegory. A fart in bed.

"What is the MATTER with you! Phew!": she snarls, rolls over and faces the wall.

"Aw you think I love Arrid, you're nuts." The man went on shoveling snow. Fiercely. Oh yes. Jingle bells, too. The sons of bitches expect it! God, think of it. They probably live above that hockshop in a shabby flat with a quarter million bucks under the floor. Wake up in an old brass bed with your husband farting. Wrap it up. Dear. Save it for Christmas. Put it under the tree. A little something wee Santa brought in the night. Dear: a new pair of trousers from Robert Hall and a pink fart. I love you. My darling. A whole armada of cars crept downtown like stalking a terrific idea. It was winter in Manhattan. No dice. No furs. No violets. Tee dum. No sir. We'll build a stairway to the stars. In the spring. Sputnik infatuated. Stendhal last night. On love. Kline and his girl went to the movies. The RKO on 14th St. Jack finished painting and cleaned up. Sat down and read until they came back. That was nice. They made a fire and sat around drinking coffee laced with good whiskey. And talked. Tonight should be Christmas: she said. Jack nodded. Kline grinned. Later Jack walked home in the snow. He woke early in the morning: made a fire in Mr. P. Belly Stove No. 212 and instant coffee as bad as fast as you taste it. He smoked cigarettes and looked out the window. Christmas in 21 days. It was snowing. You are there. A bus went uptown: backfiring leisurely. All covered with snow. It should see a doctor. A bus doctor. Now there's something. Give it something to make it go. Sort of an oil base Allbran. Then downtown again. Perky. The wind sent swirling snowflakes against the window. An old woman bent inside an enormous black overcoat, with her head wrapped in a purple shawl crept across Third Avenue slowly: heading towards Fourth. Cane in mittened right hand. Belle vieille femme dans la neige. Bonjour. Oh oui: Mother: sweet snow. He's done shoveling. He stands up: arches his back: breathes deeply—coughs. Slams the shovel on the clean sidewalk brutally: looks up at the sky and frowns. A great cloud of vapor leaves his mouth: vanishes in the cold air of the street. He turns and goes into the doorway: opens the door and disappears inside the building. Up a stairway to a warm flat. Something to be thankful for. Time goes by. See you around. In the snow. 21 days. People change. It was snowing. I remember you.

37

My Old Buddy

for Leonard

PEOPLE ARE ALWAYS TALKING, you know about how great Christmas and New Year's are. I get a little sentimental, myself, around that time and if it works out ok, it's all right. But it always seems to be a little confused. With me, I mean. You know how people always talk about things. I got a letter from a guy I've known for years and he says he's married. I think it's pretty great but really I don't. Or there's something wrong with the way he told it. If you get married there isn't much to write to anybody. In the ways of like how really great she is, and all, but there was a way he told me about it that sounds like he thinks maybe I won't like the idea, for one, and for another, he doesn't exactly know how to break the news. That's more than ok. That's wonderful. But I suspect. I do. I have a hunch that—well, it leaves me a little uneasy. Boy. People are always talking about how great girls are and they are, no question about it. They are. I could tell you a couple of stories about girls I've met. You'd get warm all over. So maybe he thinks he's done for. You know, they get married and all the fun is over. Fun. Then it's Christmas and you want to forget about all of it. I do. Even Saroyan. Anything. Especially myself. I know that guy pretty well and he was nutty about girls. I remember once he was in a bar outside St. Louis and I came in and saw him sitting with a fine looking girl, over there in the corner by the mirror near the window. I've always liked the place. But it's funny because the mirror is right in front of you before you turn left to go take a leak. Like you look at yourself before you go in. He was near there, by the rear window with this girl. Well I joined them. I had a little money. Not very much. But I was so crazy about him. He was really great. He'd get so excited by thoughts of girls he'd

38

begin to cackle. You know what a bird dog is well that's when I'd try to make out with his girl while he was off pissing. Which I did. Birddogging they call it. Anyway he got sore at me, not really, but a little, and I left, went around back and got in the back of his car, fell asleep with six cans of beer in my arms. He thought I had gone home. Well later he comes out with her and gets in with her and we all drive away. I woke up to hear her ask about me and he says that birddogging bastard and she laughs. I decided to cool it. I fell asleep again because I was pretty plastered, drunk, you know, but at a sudden change of the light he crammed on the brakes and I was thrown forward on the floor. He turned and saw me, got sore and she began to laugh. I was laughing and offering everyone some beer. He began to laugh and soon we were stopped in front of her house. He went in with her, he was gone about an hour. I stayed outside in the car and drank beer. He came out disgusted and we drove home. I picked up about twenty bucks I had from my unemployment check and we hung one on for three days. We drove all around Missouri. I came back with no shoes and my ma was out of her head. But I had a terrific tan, had spent an afternoon in a pasture sleeping and drinking cold beer. So now my old buddy's married and it's a little tough I guess, to tell me. For him. To tell me apropos of nothing, now he's married. In the letter he said he had hoped to make it down to New York (the Big City, he called it), for the holidays but couldn't because he was married now. That's how he broke the news.

Classical Symphony

for Laubies

HE STOOD BY THE LINOTYPE watching its action while the operator typed. An old fascination. One of the girls came down the aisle saying Truman ought to be in any minute. "You going to see Harry?"

"Yeah." Jack closed one eye slowly: "Him and Mack Arthur."

"Aw—no," the girl said. "Harry Truman's coming in on the three seventeen, taking a limousine into St. Louis."

"How come he doesn't get off at Union Station?"

"He's coming in from Kansas City, Globe says he wants to see some friends along the way."

Jack said: "Probably has 'em from Clayton on."

The man at the linotype tipped his head back and muttered oh yeah.

He went back to typing, saying, "Harry Truman." Then he laughed. The girl grinned. One of the Jones boys angled between presses and tables covered with type, some proof sheets in his hand, said hello to Jack—

"Going to see Harry?"

Jack laughed. "Wouldn't miss it!"

About five after three the man turned off the light above the linotype keyboard. He shut off the machine, stood up and stretched. The girl who had spoken with Jack finished distributing type, and the Jones boys, the janitor, the editor and Jack went through the front office and out the street door, crossed the asphalt street, cut between a line of trees and walked a narrow expanse of grass that ran parallel with the railroad tracks. A few people had gathered, and were standing around talking and smiling. The group from the town newspaper joined them.

The railroad station was on their left, about fifty yards away,

40

and on their right, just their side of the bridge which was almost opposite the newspaper office, was the cabstand, and cabs pulled in and out, and at three twelve a shiny black Cadillac slipped into the parking area, a man at the wheel cut the engine and another man, beside him, rolled the window down and looked out. A man in the back seat took off his hat.

A distant whistle sounded; they looked west towards the bridge and heard another whistle. A moment later the big Missouri Pacific engine roared in under the bridge and ground to a stop in front of the station. Two men got out of the Cadillac. They were dressed in black, they were smiling.

A few people got down from the sparkling Pullman cars, handed luggage to station porters while men and women and children greeted each other, moving over the brick walkway toward the station.

But two men separated from the passengers and began crossing the grass towards the group of townspeople. The two men in black likewise moved away from the Cadillac, toward them.

"Hiya, Harry!" somebody yelled, and the people parted for him. He smiled and nodded, touching the brim of his hat.

"You're all right, Harry!" a man exclaimed. Truman was talking to the man at his side, and then greeted the two men in black who had come to him, and the four moved to the Cadillac. Somebody asked Truman what he thought of Ike now. Truman grinned, people were walking alongside him now, looking at him and smiling, as Truman talked with the two men in black. He walked briskly, his arms moving, and he talked to the men in a knowing and reasonable but altogether friendly manner, inquiring about friends, using first names or nicknames, as he was walking through the grass, and when they reached the car the door was held for him and Truman got in the back seat, the three men got in, there was a pause while the engine started, and as people waved, the black Cadillac pulled into the street, Truman looking out the window pleasantly, smiling and making a gesture a wave in departure, before he sat back in the seat of the moving machine.

Paris lay under a fog. The Eiffel Tower looked like a nail, its tip

41

just visible above the fog. From the foot of the rampart orchards lined off into the distance. Tall, evenly spaced poplars lined the promenade. Her fiancé stood by the poplars; a darkhaired man, a critic in his late thirties. The American soldier on leave from Germany stood beside Mirielle, and they looked into each other's eyes.

She asked him how he liked Paris, how he felt about America, and what the difference was between them. "We don't have your wide open spaces," she said.

"They're all wide open," he said.

He turned his back on Paris, she followed; they leaned against the wall, facing the poplars. "How do you like Germany?" she asked.

"Fine," he said flatly.

"Oh, tell me."

"It is like great paintings in the past that seem to sleep in a dying present; I feel it wherever I go here."

She said she didn't understand and he said, "Well, I resist myself, and Germany and Europe seem like they can get along with the old art."

He sighed at his density, but said, "Listen to me, Mirielle. America has the brightness and glitter of someone who is big and rich and powerful who is trying to skip what can't be skipped, itself, using everything it has to avoid itself, it doesn't glitter inside, inside it's dirtier and more neurotic than it dares believe, it's soaked with guilt and fear for its unsatisfied viciously related hungers which are *never* satisfied, causing a friction sending up great showers of sparks for the whole world to see, and the world cries, 'How wonderful!' "

"You are serious," she said gently.

And oddly, he was flattered. She watched him, and after a silence asked him where he was from. Missouri brought a confusion to her and he smiled, watching her looking into herself; she was involved in a little mystery. Then she looked at him, her broad face bright. "Truman!" she exclaimed.

He wanted to be alone with her, in a quiet room alone with her. With her, as in her eyes he saw the straightaway yes, to extend that day, sexually into sexual night, together in arms.

But the breeze along the promenade brought a premonition of no more than that instant precisely remembered—then the outcry of her name from the darkhaired critic, "Mirielle!" She turned. The man called to her in French, adding in English, "Come on! We go back to Paris!"

The Highwayman

for Tonio Kroger

HE SAT ACROSS THE TABLE from her; they drank, smoked, talked. To the right of his plate was the little package. White paper and light blue ribbon. A card was tucked under the bow.

Supper was delicious; the rare steak supreme. Fresh piping hot string beans and fluffy mashed potatoes were wonderful and the after supper coffee was superb. She rose from the table and went in the kitchen, returned with the small round cake in her hands and her face was angelic in the candle glow; she put it in front of him and told him to make a wish.

"May I tell you?"

"No. It won't come true," she said. "Blow 'em out."

He blew them out and she helped him take the candles out and he cut two small slices.

"Open your present," she said.

He read the card.

"Happy birthday, my darling," she said. It was what the card said. He smiled and opened the package, not tearing the paper or spoiling the ribbon. It was a lovely edition of Joyce's *Chamber Music*. "Lean out of the window, golden hair, I heard you singing a merry air."

"Thank you, sweetheart," he smiled.

His eyes were bright. He read the poems to her while she did the dishes. After that they locked up the house and drove down the street towards the highway to St. Louis.

The movie was clever and relaxing and afterwards they had a few drinks in a favorite tavern; the drive home was lovely. Early summer nights are beautiful in Missouri.

"It seems like the air is humming," she said. The wind rushed through her hair and she spread her arms high and wide and brought them down in a windy laugh: "Oh! How happy I am!"

The stars were bright and high and far away. She looked up at them.

"Do you think there is noise in the universe?"

"Sure," he said.

"I mean—without any reason. Just noise . . . you know?"

"Um hum."

"I'm in love. I guess that's it."

He didn't reply.

"It must be terrible if you're lonely."

"It is."

"Were you lonely before you had me?"

"Yes," he said.

"Are you now?"

He smiled.

"No."

"Are you happy?"

"Yes."

"Just yes? Nothing sensational."

"Yes."

"Is that all you can say?"

"Yes," he smiled.

The car glided around a long turn and a distant bridge loomed up. They shot under and it slid away behind them like a great stone dog.

They turned in the driveway. He opened the garage door and drove in. She got out; she went in the house.

He pulled down the garage door and she called out from the kitchen:

"Would you care for a nightcap?"

He locked the door and dusted his hands.

"Very much."

"What."

"Rye and soda."

"Ok."

"Do you want to watch TV?"

"No. You?"

"Not if you don't."

"Fine. We won't."

"Do you think I'll ever be as old as you are?"

"Not at the same time."

Her laughter was lovely and as she sipped her drink she looked over the rim at him. Something like something marvelous.

"I love you," she said.

He turned the glass around in his hands and looked into it, watching the cubes stay in the same place. She lowered her drink.

"I was cruel to you, talking like I did in the car."

"No you weren't," he said. "It can't be helped."

"Will you tell me about her? Again?"

He turned on the sofa and looked at her and smiled.

"Your voice is like your mother's," he said, "and when you said you loved me, it was her again."

"Did she say it often?"

"Not very."

"Are you still in love with her?"

"More with the dream, darling. The way I'd want her."

"May I ask—What way?"

"Sure. She's beautiful. I'd like her to be as beautiful as she is."

"Change of subject," she smiled. "Bob and I are getting married next year and—what will you do?"

"I don't know," he said. He cleared his throat and finished his drink. When she returned she asked him as she handed him his drink:

"May I ask you something personal?"

He answered the personal question:

"I don't know if I'll marry again. Probably not. And yes, there is a woman."

" 'I hear an army charging out of the sea . . . ,' " she quoted. She recited it all. It was the last poem of *Chamber Music.* " 'My love, my love, my love, why have you left me alone?' "

There was a pause.

"Did you like that?"

"Very much."

"Why do people fall out of love?"

"I don't know. They do."

"Why were you and mother divorced?"

"Well . . . there were problems."

"What kind. Please—I want to know."

He raised his eyebrows and sighed.

"There were sexual difficulties . . . and that's . . ."

"What kind of difficulties?"

He looked at her pointedly. Not unkindly.

"She remained aloof. Took a distance from me. She wouldn't come to me."

"I see . . . I guess." She looked at the floor. Then she ran her hand through her hair. "Bob likes you very much—if it helps."

"I like him too."

"Do you think we'll be happy?"

"I'm sure of it."

"You are?"

"You've inherited (that is true), your mother's beauty and I hope some of my best qualities. Bob seems sure of himself and that's important. He wants to make his life his own and you fall into that. That's very good. Your mother would never include herself in my life; we fought over that. She liked being a wife but wouldn't accept me. I think a woman is only happy when she is within the life ring of her man."

"I love you so much."

He smiled.

"Well," he said. "Why don't you have another drink?"

"May I?"

"Of course. You're—how old now?"

"Twenty-two."

"Then have a couple."

She made the drink and returned.

"Have you seen mother since last time?"

He sighed. "I did. It was strange. No. Not strange. I saw her drive by. I was coming out of the office onto the street. She drove by."

"Did she see you?"

"Yes. As I watched her, she turned. Our eyes held for a time and she smiled and waved. Then she was gone."

"And you were in love with her all over again."

He sighed quietly, nodded his head, sipped the drink. "I sure was. My golden ex-wife." He looked in his daughter's eyes. She said,

"Do I look like her?"

"Yes. But more."

"That must be something. Her pictures are terrific."

There was a lull and he finished his drink.

"Would you like another?" she asked quietly.

"No. I think I'm going to bed. I'm very tired."

He stood up and smiled: "You can stay up. Finish your drink; have another; leave the things out. Sadie will clean up in the morning."

"Ok."

"Goodnight sweetheart."

"Goodnight, daddy. I hope you had a nice birthday."

He turned in the doorway and came to her, kissed her forehead.

"I did. I had a wonderful time."

She turned on the radio and put her feet up on the coffee table, lit a cigarette and laid her head back listening to the quiet dance music and letting her thoughts go free. It was like a movie with dimension and another sound. A throb. A fierce hum. Like the mandolin passage in Bartok's 6th Quartet, or a wind—or James Joyce. She snubbed out the cigarette and finished the drink, yawned and laid her head back again and the moving reel of vision unwound around her mind like gauze around the brain. The future with Bob was bright and real and she felt she could hear his voice. He wasn't speaking but it was his voice . . . her father appeared before her, walking, as he walked every day, and his phantom loneliness seemed to make her sympathetic, wise and womanly . . . she felt and saw her life rise before her almost in awe of itself and there was that music, too, of her oncoming life, superimposed over the giant outline of the great mystery of her mother. Did James Joyce know her mother? The drawing of him by Wyndham Lewis took shape and spoke of the translated ex-wife: the words? Her father's voice rose into the volume of her vision pronouncing THE LIFE YOU ARE ABOUT TO LEAD

A silhouette against the first streaks of dawn. Then he began down the highway. The credits read like an unusual verse line; their meaning was hard to understand. But now they were over. The plot was taking shape.

School Days

THE TWO GIRLS introduced themselves and began unpacking. They chattered nervously, asking each other obvious pleasant questions.

Jody Haller was slender, about five feet seven. She had light brown hair and yellow and brown eyes, a turned up nose and a small taut mouth. Her ankles were a little thick. Her slender arms flew through her bags and put things out on the bed and away. Now she was a little embarrassed at some of the things she brought from home like the picture of that crazy Hank Whaler at the party at Peeler Stone's house when everybody drank and got sick and where Hank said such wonderful things. But she quickly tucked it between a blue cashmere sweater and a white oxford cloth shirt; she knew Hank was a part of all that had gone before because now things were going to be different.

Ann Meyen was about two inches taller than her new friend and roommate. She had long soft yellow hair that just missed having a dyed look. Her face was narrow and her lips were wide and very thin. She had high cheekbones and her green eyes were almost slanted; arched eyebrows gave her an Oriental look. Her neck was long; in contrast with Jody she had small breasts and long attractive legs. She dressed plainly.

Whereas Jody—as Ann noticed—had brought many little things of sentimental value, she had brought only one along. This she laid on top of all her clothes. It had been a gift from a very nice but tiresome sweet boy named Harold Tyndown and on the flyleaf it read:

The Four Quartets

for Ann
in hopes that she will
read and admire these
as much as I have.

Sincerely,
Harold Tyndown

in his sloping thin line writing. Ann smiled and ran her hand over it. She had read it—and re-read it. In the middle of it was a letter Father gave her that was not to be opened until the day you arrive. She smiled at that, too. It'll be a lovely note with some money. Money was no problem. At least not now. She would keep it.

Both girls finished and sat on their beds and looked across the room at each other, smiled and began to laugh. The next day they registered and got supplies and the next day school began. The first day of four long years at the University!

Jody was depressed because she didn't get in a sorority but Ann reassured her:

"We'll look around together for the first year and then next year if we want to belong, we'll make a real effort. Anyway, I'm not really anxious. It seems a little silly to me. Too easy to be worth it."

At first it was all right for Jody but as the weeks passed she became lonely and began to think she was no good.

"They don't like me," she said one night as they were going to bed.

"Who?"

Jody gestured and pouted.

"Anybody."

"Don't be silly. It's always lonesome at first. You're away from

51

home and meeting all new people. Just because bright clean boys are in fraternities and sweet lovely girls are in sororities, it doesn't mean a thing. They're lonely too. Maybe even more lonely. Clean haircuts, nice clothes and white teeth doesn't make good men and women, it just makes them more anxious."

Jody frowned and sneered.

"Aw you're just jealous."

Ann sat back and pulled her legs up under her, lit a cigarette and narrowed her eyes.

"Oh?"

Jody bent her head.

"Well, I am," she whispered.

The days went by rapidly and Jody found herself changing. It certainly wasn't like it seemed and once you were on the inside, what it looked like before was long gone compared to what it looked like now! She discovered she couldn't do anything really good or successfully all the time, that she worked in streaks. Like she would be terribly lonesome for a few days and good old Annie always pulled her out of it; then she'd forget it kind of and really buckle down to work. Then that would pass and she and her buddies would go out by themselves and have fun. Then it would be Ann and the two of them would talk and talk and that was swell but then she would be lonely again. The idea of almost being able to chart her emotions wasn't pleasing at all and she became a little bitter. Ann and her damned level head. Jody *knew* Ann was lonely. And Ann had more dates than she did, only Ann didn't talk about it. Then Jody's mind became confused and a whirl of jealousy and loneliness tangled up and she lay awake in her bed, looking out the window at the campus, wanting to kill herself.

Thanksgiving came and it was great, just GREAT to be home again. The second day, though, as she had breakfast she missed something. And as Mom was scrambling eggs Jody realized she didn't want any eggs; all she wanted was to have coffee and a bun in the Quad Shop with Ann.

Ann was at the game with Leland. Leland brought along a pint of bourbon and they sat arm in arm in the stands and watched and cheered but the school lost and Ann laughed and Leland kissed her and they realized they were getting a little looped and they told each other so and laughed. They left the stadium and walked the streets of the University town in the November chill holding hands and scuffling leaves. They drove out to a nice roadhouse Leland knew about and the place was crowded with people from school and Ann and Leland had a cheeseburger supper and then danced a little and drove slowly home. They made a date for the next night.

Jody was glad to see Hank again and they went out a little and she kept running into people from school and at first Jody was afraid to say anything so only smiled and waved but then she finally said hi to Jocko Wheeler and after that was anxious to say more but by then it was school again and she let Hank kiss her more than usual and promised to see him when she came home on Christmas vacation.

The two girls were glad to see each other. The first two days were exciting like the old days. The third day Jody was still very happy and couldn't wait to get back in their room to talk with Ann. She ran in and threw her books on the bed and plopped down.

"Hiya Annie!" she laughed.

Ann grinned and they began talking. Then they went out for supper. They saw a good movie and came home, talked some more and went to bed. Jody had a dream.

"You were standing in my back yard at home," she explained in the morning. "I can't remember what happened. You were just standing there. You seemed so far off and in your hand was a camera. And then you walked away from the garden, towards me. You seemed so real, so alive."

Christmas vacation was a week away and Jody noticed something different about Ann. Jody came home from a date with Phil Alden and when she opened the door the lights were out and that was strange because they always left one light on. When she turned it on she saw Ann was in bed, asleep. Jody quietly undressed and got in bed not knowing why she thought anything was wrong, if wrong was the right word, or different because it was different, somehow. She turned off the light. It was a long time before she fell asleep. Before she dropped off she had a hazy sensation of hearing Ann speak but it was as if Ann was saying things that hadn't been said before, as if she had been keeping something to herself.

In the morning when she awoke there was a note from Ann on the desk, held down by a prism paperweight. Specks and elongated shimmers of color spread over the sheet of notepaper.

> Dear Jody, why don't we have lunch together at The Alligator. I had to do a few things so got up early. Meet you at twelve—or two after.
>
> Ann
>
> P.S. Have a surprise for you.

Jody couldn't find her. She sat in a booth and waited until twelve twenty. Then she got up and walked around the place again. It was pretty crowded by now and she went in the back. She saw a couple seated across a table from each other. The fellow had a messy dark brown tweed suit on, a matching vest and mussed up dark brown hair. He was very casual and had bright gray eyes. He glanced up, took the cigarette from between his lips and came over to Jody.

"Excuse me, miss, are you by any chance looking for—"

"Ann," Jody blurted. "Annie Meyen."

The man smiled and touched her elbow, stepped back for her to pass in front of him.

"Here," he said. "Right back here."

Ann came out of the booth and faced Jody, standing, not five feet away. Jody's lips parted.

Ann's hair was bright, gleaming yellow; radiant yellow. She wore soft eye shadow, rouge on her cheeks, softly reddened lips, a new beige suit with a soft belt at the waist, three buttons, two of which were open, the collar turned deliciously against the nape of her neck. Ann spun once and stopped. Jody held her breath. Ann grinned.

"Do you like it?"

Jody couldn't take her eyes away. They had eaten tuna fish sandwiches, had milk, and were now drinking coffee. The man

54

was a fashion photographer from New York, was making the rounds of schools in the midwest. He had seen Ann and talked with her; they had gone into town with the money Father gave her on the first day and she had gotten the suit, had her hair fixed and that afternoon was going to a studio to be photographed. If nothing happened from his contacts he would give her recommendations for modeling agencies in New York. She could go and try her luck. She seemed to have a chance. A terrific chance. But it still depended on the pictures. Ann's Oriental eyes held little stars in the centers.

Jody tossed and turned, clenched and clawed the mattress, kicked sheets and blankets awry, cried into the pillow and saw distant puffs of color, and a few hours later, exhausted, she fell asleep just before Ann came tiptoeing in. Ann shut the door and crossed the dark room wondering why the light wasn't on. She put on pajamas in the darkness and got in bed, pulled up the covers and folded her arms under her head and stared at long rectangles the streetlights threw across the ceiling. Ann daydreamed and realized she was really tired. Moments later she fell into a happy slumber and strange funny dreams of magic New York.

Christmas came and went, the New Year began and soon the new semester. Jody moved out in silence, Ann discovering it after having returned from a date. In the following days a new girl named Mary Ann Porteron moved in the room. She was short, sweet tempered and very quiet. She read movie magazines and was crazy about Stan Musial.

February moved into March. March, the tenth day, brought a letter from Donald Peters who lived on East 58th Street in New York. Ann read it. It said she had made an impression on editors; he thought she had a very good chance. Mr. Peters suggested she make plans to come to New York as soon as possible. She answered impossible now but spring vacation would be all right. Before he got her letter she had another from him saying come immediately, three possibles and one sure job. She packed a bag and left that night for Manhattan, asking Mary Ann to watch her things, telling her she was going to New York for a few days.

Jody couldn't sleep. She wept and prayed forgiveness for the terrible things she felt. Bitterness and guilt fought in her heart. She dried her tears and got out of bed, dressed in silence and crept from the room. Annie! Annie! She went along the hall to the stairs, went down two flights and turned left. Room 210, 209, 208—207. She tapped on the door. A sleepy voice said just a minute and soon the door was open. Jody slipped inside.

"Mary Ann, where's Annie!"

"She's gone, Jody. She went to New York tonight."

Jody backed out in the hall. Mary Ann closed the door and went back to bed. Jody stood in the hallway, mouth open, eyes fixed on the wall where the dormitory colors, dark green met light green. She began back to her room, stumbling up the steps and finally through her own door and back into her bed where she lay awake until the sun came up. Classes began. She fell asleep, her roommate not bothering to wake her as they hadn't been compatible. Shirley didn't care. Lunch came and Jody slept. Supper and evening, night time and curfew and late at night and early morning and the beginning of classes. And Jody still slept.

That afternoon she woke when Shirley came in and Jody asked her if she would bring some coffee back with her when she returned from supper. Shirley agreed reluctantly. Jody fell asleep and woke when Shirley handed her the container of coffee. Jody drank it, showered and went back to bed and slept all night.

Spring vacation came and Ann's brother Harry came for her things. He left a note for Jody.

A really swell apartment in Manhattan . . . wonderful time . . . if ever in NY drop by, the address . . . keep in touch. Love. Ann.

Then it was almost the end of the year. Then it was in the summer and no school. Jody stayed home mostly, swam a little and went to movies with girl friends. Hank joined the Army and then it was September again and Jody felt panicky at going back.

The same old people, the same old rooms, desks, chairs, places and people, people, people. Boring students, boring teachers, boring books. The pointless sorority now: pointless boring girls. And

56

the dreadful absence of Ann who was not at the University anymore.

The same old routine and the same old days and nights. Thanksgiving came and was followed by Christmas. She went home and went to a few parties. Hank was home on pass from Fort Leonard Wood and on Christmas Eve came over to Jody's house and spent the evening telling about the Army. Then he left. She let him kiss her passionately on the porch and saw him walk down the steps and cut across the snow covered yard, across the street and get into his father's Chevy and drive away. Those footsteps in the snow. Same old Hank. She closed the door and went into the kitchen and made some coffee, took it out to Mother and Father by the fire, put the coffee pot on the stone in front of the grate. She went across to the table and returned with a flask of brandy, poured some in her coffee, handed it to Father who refused, as did Mother. Jody sat on the rug with the cup in her hands, sipping the hot liquid and staring into the bright dancing flames.

The Big Story

HE WALKED DOWN the dark street. It was a long way to the next streetlight and that light was a dim saucer on the black asphalt. A few houses were scattered back from the street. He crossed the railroad tracks. It was about nine and he was going over to a Sunday School party at Mrs. Schillinger's house. Mrs. Schillinger was like an old European cloud. Her ancient breath. He thought about that and walked towards the light, through it and was then enveloped in the darkness beyond. The next light looked about a mile away. He held onto the present. It was a small box of peppermints wrapped in blue tissue with a white ribbon around and a big bow and a card which said thanks for being so swell Mrs. Schillinger. He wrote that. Mother did all the rest. Even shined his shoes. Well.

A block past the next light was where the colored people lived. Crystal Park wasn't big but it had its Negro population too, just like any town. He walked on and began to be afraid. Black people are spooky on dark nights. You can't see them. Glad to be out of that part of town and around the corner where Mrs. Schillinger lived. Everybody would be there and even Kitty. Kitty was advanced for her age. At fourteen girls don't have chests like that. She had big ones. He thought about that and when the hand stroked his shoulder he gasped and dropped the package.

"Keep walking," the voice said. It was a colored man.

"My my my—" he stammered.

"Yeah," the voice said. Someone picked up the package. He

was nudged on both arms and he was so scared his legs felt like ribbons.

When they reached the streetlight they surrounded him. They were tall and very big. The smell of their flesh and sight of their blackness almost made him faint.

"White boy," one of them said. "Where are you going?"

He said he was going to Mrs. Schillinger's house.

"Who's that, boy?" The voice was patient.

He said she was his Sunday School teacher.

"Your Sunday School teacher," the fellow said. He was standing in front of him looking down at him. They all looked down at him.

"Your Sunday School teacher."

Did he repeat it or was it an echo?

He nodded

"Mrs. Schillinger," he said. "A party."

Soft laughter.

"A party . . . well now. Suppose we come along . . .?"

Tears were in his eyes. "Oh no," he said. "Please."

There was a soft swift sound like a wooden matchbox being closed. A big fist held the knife in front of his face. For a long time no one said anything and finally he gathered enough courage to ask for his package. There was no answer. He was too frightened to look around and he knew he was surrounded. They were waiting for him to make the move.

He sat by the piano with the cup of punch and a napkin in his hand. The others were singing but he couldn't join in. He had told Mrs. Schillinger he had forgotten her present and the words came out so fast and everybody laughed so much he became very embarrassed. She was crazy about mints. She had about 18 boxes of mints on the table. One was from Kitty. Kitty was on the other side of the piano, singing like wild. Kitty's mother said Kitty was a natural soprano and every time Mrs. Huntar talked about Kitty men nodded and didn't say anything. Kitty's mother had a bigger pair than Kitty.

He had waited outside before he had gone in. He stood in the bushes and looked through the windows and saw them sitting

around with Mrs. Schillinger busily setting things straight and all
. . . he had waited until his head cleared. He had a story, he had
the big story. Then he went in. And couldn't tell it. Then his
embarrassment over the mints. Mints. Mother had laughed.
Mother had laughed the whole time she wrapped the box up.

"Billy! You look terrible!"
That was what Kitty whispered to him after he arrived. So he
went to the bathroom to pee. To look at himself. Bad? His eyes
were sunk in his head and he was as white as Mrs. Schillinger's
underarm. He splashed water on his face and used her old comb.
It didn't help much, but the face in the mirror wasn't quite so
bleak . . . he went back in the living room and drank some punch
that tasted like hydrochloric acid his throat was so dry.

"Let's go this way," Kitty giggled. "Niggertown's spooky."
"No no," he stammered. "We'll walk down the other way."
"Oh Billy! I want to go this way!"
"No."
He looked at her angrily.
She took his arm and held tight. "I want to see some niggers at
night."
"Don't use that word!"
"What: nigger?"
"Once again and you go home by yourself."
"Oh—you," she minced. "All right, we'll go your way."
The main street was well lit and refreshing. He held her hand
and they walked home. It was near ten o'clock. When they turned
up the walk she took his hand and put it on one of her breasts.
"Billy? Do you love me?"
"No," he mumbled.
"Scared?"
He didn't look at her. What a night.
"Billy? Will you kiss me?" She tugged at him. "Come up on
the porch now," Kitty whispered. "Now."
She pulled him along.
The door was shut, they were in the swing together. It creaked
and the ends of chains rattled.

60

"Billy?"

"What," he said.

"Kiss me, silly. Let's be in love."

She put her arms around him and kissed him on the mouth, nipping and pecking at him. He pulled away and jumped up.

"Don't you want to feel me?" she cried.

"No! I'm going home. Goodnight."

He opened the screen door and began down the steps. She took his arm and pulled him around.

"I'll never speak to you again," she said.

He shoved her back until she hit the doorjamb. He held her straight up. Then he let her go.

"Big tits don't make *you* so smart!"

He ran down the front walk and across the street.

He lay in bed looking up at the ceiling. Then he rolled over and looked out the window. The lawn stretched to the street and was eerie in the moonlight. Grandma was snoring again, like she was at war with Germany or something. A car went by and the headlights swept across the ceiling and down the walls. Pictures and toys sprang into view, then vanished.

They waited for him to make the move. He did. He put his right hand out, took a step forward, he touched the Negro's stomach. It was hard. The soft warm pulse ran up in his arm like a river. The Negro stepped aside. He looked up into the Negro's face. It was black and implacable. He walked away from them.

At the top of the hill he stopped. He was perspiring. It was running down his neck.

He sat on a grassy bank. He didn't think. He stared at the dark shape of a house across the street. He gripped his arm.

He stood up. He looked down into the Missouri valley at all the colored people's houses and shacks. Smoke curled up in the moonlight and distant music filled the quiet evening air. He turned and looked down the street. The pale white disc of light on the asphalt street was empty. The Negroes had gone.

61

The Morning News

"YOU'RE NOT BAD LOOKING, why don't you get married?" he always said. Sam was a sweet guy but a real dope. Honestly. His breath smelled bad and he had lousy teeth. And he was nineteen. Nineteen.

"I've told him but it hurts his feelings," she said.

"Poor boy," mother said.

I'd like to have my chest wet, she dreamed. I'd even do it with Sam, she said. She looked at the moonbeams coming through the window. She spread her legs and took a deep breath. No children. I want romance. I'd like to get wet all over and be bloody. My hot body. I'd like some big thing to cut me where it would hurt with some hot blood. Her heart began to pound. Hate him, she thought. Hate him just right. Ecstatic murder. He would kill me. Her breath whistled. The room was brightly etched.

She caressed the tip.

NOW!

She ground her teeth and writhed on the sheets: listening, again, to the silver bells.

"Hiya Peg. Look, I got a couple of tickets for the ballgame tonight. Like to go?"

"Oh Sam," she said. "Golly. I have to help mother."

He sat on the corner of her desk and looked at her. She sorted through the drawer for some paper clips.

"What," asked Sam, "do you have to help her with?"

She didn't answer.

62

"You know," she said then. "Ironing . . . we got some new curtains," she said, thinking of new curtains.

"Yeah," Sam said.

Sam was half tight by the sixth and he grabbed her in the seventh and said for Christ's sake, stand up, it's the seventh inning stretch. They stood up and Sam belched and laughed. He had a nice beery smell. She laughed. But nothing happened. Even Musial couldn't tie it up. He had gotten two out of three, two singles hit so hard against the right field wall they bounced back good for only one base each.

In the last of the ninth the Cards needed two to tie and three to win. Sam was excited and Peg was—too. She felt clean all over and the fresh air of the ball park was cool and nice. She even liked the male smell of cigar smoke and hot dogs.

"Sam," she said. She took his arm. "I hope they win."

He looked at her and winked.

"Hiya baby," he said.

A faint puff exploded near her heart.

Musial doubled down the right field line and was on second base with his hands on his hips, one foot on the bag and his head down, looking at the batter and then to the coach on third.

"I like him," she said.

Wally Moon walked from the on-deck circle to the plate.

"Wait a minute," she said. "There's a stick under me."

Boy there's something funny about this, she thought. She turned her head and looked towards the infield. The old chicken wire backstop loomed up in the distance and the small crescent moon shone through making it look like a web against a part of the night sky. His hands held her firmly and his body bore down on and in her and she thought it was something that it was so comfortable. She looked up at the sky, searching for stars; not finding any she moved her hands on his back, tenderly, patting him. His skin was wet and the little bumps and moles distracted her and she discovered she was looking for more. His cough was an explosion in her ear and she jumped but he held her so tight so suddenly—his teeth ground and a low angry growl came from his

63

throat. He trembled violently; his hands and body were clenched onto hers. She was afraid. What was happening? He coughed again, almost in a shout, and buckled, hurting her hips—in that moment she felt some liquid down there. A pleasure and warmth circulated through her, to seem to gather somewhere. His face was buried in her throat. His jaw ground against her collarbone. His heart pounded. His hands held her more gently. She felt almost suspended.

"Don't stop," she said.

Five dates, two weeks, later, nothing had changed except Sam didn't laugh much. Each time they made love he always stopped just when she was beginning to feel something. One day she saw him with another girl. She froze with jealousy. She saw Sam introduce the girl to Mr. Piercy, the boss, and Mr. Piercy smiled and rubbed his hands together and he and Sam had a big laugh. Sam was the best doggone office boy in Missouri, Mr. Piercy said.

Invaluable.

Peg sat at her desk, the typewriter a blur in front of her.

"Martini," she snapped: "Dry."

Chris nodded. Peg noticed a young man at the end of the bar in a light blue cord suit. She looked at him until their eyes met.

"Gee," she murmured. "What a swell place."

Jerry smiled and shrugged. "It's okay."

"Christ, Arthur don't stop," she pleaded.

"Busy these days, eh?" Sam asked.

"I saw you with—that 'sister' of yours . . . you with your stinking breath and bumpy back—I've had a lot more—"

"Too late," he interrupted.

Her angry expression changed into puzzlement. She frowned.

"What?" Then she sneered:

"What do you mean by that?"

Sam shook his head: no.

She sat in the crowded bar and looked at the array of bottles; they weren't very clear. But hell, it was Friday night. She sighed and opened her purse, laid the dollar bill on the bar.

"Same?"

"Please Chris," she said. The words were a little slurred.

A man came in the door wiping his forehead and muttering about the heat. After a time he sat next to Peg and ordered a beer and a shot of rye. He drank quickly, ordered another.

"A secretary?" he asked. "Yeah?"

Peg nodded and grinned.

"Just around the corner . . . my office. My office is just around the corner. From here. Isn't it, Chris?"

"Sure Peg," Chris said.

Out beyond the ball park. North St. Louis. Four flights up.

"Hey baby," the man said, chuckling. His hands were trembling. She pushed them off her breasts.

"Watch me now. Stand over there," she pointed. The man stepped back and grinned, watching her undress.

Her mind was the color of mud and she knelt on the floor and touched her knees with her forehead and began to hum. The man began to laugh, his expression almost tender.

"What the hell are you?" he asked. "Do you mean that?"

She stood up and looked at him. She has a nice body, he thought, and it's bruised so she does mean it.

He walked towards her.

"You better get outa here. I mean what I say. I mean what I say."

"Why?" she murmured. "Why?"

"You don't want to make headlines tomorrow. I mean it too."

The cabfare took about all she had and when she got home she took two aspirin and undressed and lay on the bed naked. She couldn't sleep. It was turning clear. She listened to the bells again. The tingling silver bells. A far away roar.

Captain America

(AFTER FROBENIUS)

WEBSTER GROVES WAS SHORT and stocky, well dressed and his bushy mustache gave him the air of someone different which he mildly enjoyed and the gestures of his hands and fluidity of manner made him seem to be a plurality rather than something the *avant garde* might regard as vaguely singular, or parenthetical, for which he seemed grateful, although he understood what that, in turn, might well signify. So he kept to himself, and accepted it. He hadn't really made the team in school and didn't pretend he had. But he could tell wonderfully amusing stories about The Bench. His large mustache was a shade darker blonde than the long light blonde hair on his head, but it, the mustache, it was wonderful, gave him a forward quality that kept his head up. He worked in an art supply store in downtown St. Louis and was indifferently happy selling canvas, tubes of paint, brushes, turpentine, stretchers and such. Often his friends, casual or close, dropped in, "just to see Webster." There was something charming about him.

He was twenty-nine, soft spoken and unpretentious. His manner held a flair for light sarcasm. He didn't have many really close friends . . . few do—certainly not in St. Louis. But those that were, were distinct—as distinct as Webster was from them: they were not really like him in either habit, appearance, desires or detail. They had the quality of what most friendly people really are: dull.

Kirk, Ferguson, Craig or even Manchester—Clayton, a mild mannered Impressionistic painter who sold reasonably well but never really got too serious had a nice studio on the fringe of the city and from his wide windows you could see the distant Hotel

Chase and the Park Plaza above the trees, overlooking Forest Park. When Webster went over to see Clayton after work they'd smoke Clayton's favorite Cuban cigars and drink espresso in little cups and look out the window in friendly silence. And then, pleasantly bored, Webster would leave. Go to Tony's—or home and eat supper; maybe take in a movie. Or read.—Or call up Valley.

Valley was tall and slender with soft round breasts and narrow hips; her green eyes were set far apart and under her slightly upcurved nose her lips were thin and soft. Her hair was dark brown and long and thin and when let down reached her waist. But mostly she piled it on top of her head—almost, as Webster noticed, in the fashion of the Gibson Girl. She was twenty-two and an inch taller than Webster. And his closest friend. They got along very well; they were very much alike. She was the only real friend Webster had. They had been just friends in school and it wasn't until a few years later that he discovered, and became intimate with, her. He'd stop off in Maplewood and pick up a fifth of bourbon and call her up to say I'm coming out now. She was always there but it always startled him when she answered the phone. Sometimes it would be days before he'd call, to make the long bus ride out there.

Valley lived in a made-over garage in back of a vacant lot that was really all weeds and tangled thorny bushes full of old rubbish and rabbits and burrs. A narrow footpath ran from the corner of the street through the lot up to her door and Webster walked it, stepped up on the log and knocked on the door. When she opened it, he said,

"Hi."

And went in.

She had a pleasantly messy studio: clothes on the easel and doorknobs as well as the bed and floor; on all the walls and stacked in all the corners were the many varieties of surfaces she painted her little Bauhaus landscapes on: pieces of wood, old window panes, slate, rocks, sheets of metal, etc., and even, when they had been drinking one night, they went out in the lot and hauled it in: a railroad tie. She did a long pale green and white landscape which took her two weeks with her palette knife. In the corner to one side of a window was a yellow icebox and above it were red shelves with patient black Greek meanders on the edges. She went to the icebox and got out a tray of ice, took two glasses from the shelves while Webster opened the bottle. Then they began to drink.

When Valley got drunk things became larger and she more capable of handling them. Webster usually got very quiet and remained unmoved by whatever happened to be going on, but was attentive—. If they got very drunk, hardly ever, they might fall asleep or gaze at each other and chatter dreamily. Or if something really ugly happened, remote chance! he'd rise and silently depart. He might not. Who knows? But as Valley became a little tighter, and more expansive, Webster grew quiet and might gaze at the Feininger-like painting on the railroad tie which now hung over the little fireplace.

"I can wander in it forever."

When they made love she took over and it was a quiet moment in which the attenuation became a yellow flame and banished her from name and face, became a fine and soft warm reality of his body being in and on and later there beside her for her to caress until the time when they fell asleep, he with his fingers on her wrist, she knowing he was there beside her.

Their making love was never exactly the same. They were able to lose themselves in the presence of each other and it became what he regarded always as the one moment in his life as virtually invisible as the palpable sense of despair real as the act for it always followed, like an unknown soldier or a dusty shadow or introspective déjà vu. With his fingers touching her wrist he'd lie there listening to her breathing regularly and almost see and hear the footfall of something as wide as all space and long as all time, a shadow like the pale mother in a jar of vinegar only this: spread over the imaginative face of his seeing existence. Singing a song in a prehistoric language, a long unending tune of death, loneliness, despair, forever.

Valley was forever. And when he went to see her he knew he was literally walking across a field into the valley of eternity, forever, death, in a sequence of no pattern at all. She was like a magic place, a glade within the great fulcrum of the universe—he knew it. Knew that. And knowingly entered it. It was like walking into an invisible dimension and losing himself. In that world, in that room, in that bed, deeply burrowed in that woman and without identity.

During breakfast the next morning they ate and drank coffee in silence. And if they didn't go for a walk or she didn't make some drawings of him or they didn't listen to the radio or read or talk, he would leave her. Dazed, he walked out of the door and across the vacant lot to the street. The sunny day.

Back now, in the world again to sell tubes of paint and talk with people, read and maybe go to a movie alone or with friends, or simply be and listen to the ideas and noises of life in the city, to go to sleep—wait for the return, the inevitable scent in time and space to carry him across the vacant lot to that little house of hers.

That was what that was. He didn't count on it. Her. He never tried to make it anything. It was right. There. Wherever he was, whatever he was doing, when the great Anything happened, he knew her reality existed within it, identically off from him, for him. Never waiting but always there. Eternal. To occur. Then—anywhere, anytime, no matter what was going on, the reality of Valley would appear into his life in substantial form. Like the dream sound of a distant trumpet, clear and keen, existent but untouchable, she beckoned. So now, at work, on a bus, home in bed, at a movie, a party, out walking or while over in Clayton's studio, smoking those Cuban cigars, drinking espresso and looking out the windows at the Park Plaza Hotel . . . some thing from outside himself, between which he saw nothing, off from himself spanned the space and distance like a bridge, like a weird reflection-bridge from out of a prism, magic and shimmering, came to his eyes and within the invisible glitter a form appeared to make whatever he was doing cease to exist. And rather than quickly phone her, he woke slowly, let her fill the air so when he called, it would be his hand on the instrument and his lips speaking words and the reality of her voice surprising him because all the rest was already fulfilled and what remained to be done: was. So he walked and talked, acted and gestured, spoke mildly of school or art—letting the sound of her flesh fill him, slowly, on wings, until he was on his way to her.

Then there was no time. The distance between himself and Valley did not exist. He bought a bottle. The bus ride was accomplished and he walked across the vacant lot on the footpath to her front door as the nearing sea of her reality rose to drown his identity. Gone when, after he knocked she opened the door, he said,
"Hi."
And went in.

She broke ice cubes into glasses while he opened the bottle. They drank and talked and she became expansive and he listened. Then they made love and then she fell asleep, he with his fingers touching her wrist, she with the knowing sense that Webster was there beside her; he listening to her breathing regularly and wondering if it might come from another thing, the thing from the old world—or a more knowing world where the dream sound of a distant trumpet call and the invisible presence of the unknown soldier were the flesh and blood, the universe, the stuff of reality within which men and women existed. The hum, like the tune of doom—of despair and loneliness and death, the language of an unknown man who fell in an unknown field in an uncharted time.

Bloodstar

You bet. Not till Tuesday. Okay.
He hung up, stepped out of the telephone booth.
One.
He sat at the bar and thought.
Thoughts and images: her guitar and singing voice. Embraces all the rest: in importance, in fact. That need not lead to other facts; that did lead to other facts. Get receptive. Stuck there, like a burr in your hair. Maybe it was most of her; there's a fact.
The bartender put a beer in front of him. He paid.

Lesbians.
After the Kodachrome photographs

> On the Swiss alps: skiing with a handsome man. Sun spar-kling on show-white, red ski clothes, snow; gleaming ac-coutrements.
> On the Caribbean with another fellow on a yacht. Glisten-ing, spanking white; bright green stripes, red stripes. Col-ored flags.
> Along the beach in Nice: arms linked with another man's, running into the water laughing: hair flying behind her tan body. Photographs in color: blonde hair blonde, golden body golden, white rim above white breasts, white line around white waist, between white thighs; white line of sea foam, flurry of waves. Silver white beach: dazzling in that sun. Blue, ultramarine, blue, green sea. Invisible winds: soft sweep across flesh, water, earth. Photographs, color, sound. Hold it—great—another? Laughter. They kiss. Hey!

Take one of me like that! Two men trade places and he kisses her as the other shoots. Then they lift and carry her wriggling body into the sea

were passed around, held against the light of the lamp on the table, she stood up, finished her glass of beer and touched the snout of the police dog who rose with her; she passed into the other room. He refilled her glass, his own and the beautiful girlfriend's glass while she sat at the other end of the table, handsomely sullen in the glare of the lamp as the shade had been
tipped, the light flayed out.
fix the shade why don't you.
okay.
He straightened it and they waited in silence; drank beer. She returned to the room with her guitar and sat down. She took a drink. She tightened the strings, tested their tone; finally she began to sing.

Three years before, when he had been in school, he received a letter one afternoon. It read:

my dear sweet friend,
i have met the most beautiful woman
you could see. if you ever come to
n.y. i want you to meet and know
her. i have told her very much
about you. when you come, phone.
if i had a flower, a violet, i
would send it to you; however,
it is winter in n.y. and bitter
cold. there are no flowers. there
is hope. i have found hope. i
send some of my hope to you. a
gentle hug, a small kiss.

Time passed.

. . . sure it's late . . . yes of course I'm drunk . . . no I don't

72

have a job you do? In forty-five minutes? Just time enough . . .
yes me. I want some hope too. Never mind. Too long ago . . . sure
I understand, tomorrow, okay, tell your beauty hello . . . years
. . . right, no, Army. Kilmer . . . till Saturday evening . . . at
noon? Tomorrow at noon . . . right. Promise. Carny Taylor? Nice.
See you.

He came down Broadway in the early morning snow. It was
near eight. He crossed Union Square and later Fourteenth Street,
headed down University Place towards the bar, AWOL bag in his
hand and dressed as he was in the olive drab of the U. S. Army: in
one month, Germany. The Atlantic Ocean Crossing: February,
1954. But his feet were getting wet. GI low quarters weren't made
for snow. He crossed Thirteenth, looking in a bar with a glance,
seeing opening preparations just as the clocks struck 8 in the
churches: on Fifth Avenue, Twelfth Street, Tenth Street and
Broadway. Eight o'clock. Up too early. A mild hangover. The
snow felt good. He leaned his head back and closed his eyes,
letting the flakes hit his face.

Tuesday, two years later
he called her:
Yes, Miss Taylor, Fourth Floor. You will? Thanks.
He lit a cigarette in the phone booth and waited, the receiver in
his left hand. He watched the bartender serve a man a beer. His
own stood on the bar, waiting for him.
Miss Taylor—
Carny? I'd like a large hopechest—
You! How are you—are you out now?

They talked about Europe, things in common, and even got a
little loaded at lunchtime; she confessed she was high and didn't
know how she would finish out the rest of the day.
He realized as she talked: I put in my life. Without photographs. Over the rim of my friendly glass, I see you. He laughed
out loud. A puzzled look came over her face. She had been explaining her job to him.
What is it? she asked.

73

Nothing, he said.

Nothing? Tell me, I'd like to share it with you.

No, he said. I'll tell you something else, though. I'll tell you a story about Germany. It's to the point.

I'd like to hear it, she said.

I met a girl in Heidelberg who was bright and attractive, he began, sitting back in the chair, offering her a cigarette; she took it, he took one for himself both of which he lit; he exhaled and in the smoke: even in the eyes, but like a clouded or filmy thing, just behind the front transparent part that I took to be withdrawal at first, from lack of confidence, all of which was true enough. But as it later turned out, you can never be sure about what is something else when first you encounter it. So she was full of doubt. You want to go faster? We talked, walked, drove, danced and laughed around Heidelberg. She had an old yellow Mercedes convertible which could scarcely run but which we drove everywhere. So what was it, I kept asking myself: that thing, like a burr in your hair, a nettle, refusing to let loose of you. She asked if I believed in the stars telling things. We were out walking, then, one night, up near the Schloss, the Castle, and there was a tall stone tower which rose into the dark sky. When she was a girl, one night she had wandered into the tower, gone up the circular flight of stone steps to the top, come through a trap door and there, in the tiny circular topmost cubicle was a giant man: beard darker than night and as thick as hands clung to his jaw, eyes like luminous blades, revolving, slowly whirring, covering her. He did drawings of her, told her of her past: of a sunny day in Rotterdam when she had gotten on a streetcar; of her future; of the art and magic of the universe and revolving galaxies spangled with stars like all seeing eyes. When she returned the next night he was not there. She returned again and again to the old tower. But he had vanished. Years passed. She grew up. The war came and she idolized Nazi fliers like Americans idolized movie stars; every German girl kept photographs. When the war was over, she went to Belgium, rented a room in a boarding house; she met a woman of her age, they became fast friends. They swore in blood to always love the other: it was in the stars for them. They separated for a time; she returned to Heidelberg. What was it, she kept asking herself, about this woman that so fascinated her. One day she passed the tower: suddenly she knew! She knew! She wrote to her friend, told her everything. The friend wrote back; they were to meet in Berlin. She went. Gladly! Her heart happy in anticipation. They met, made plans—she had known an old friend in Dresden and they would go. An adventure into Communist Germany! They went to Dresden. The friend was gone. The city was in ruins, streets bare, skies grey, overcast; Russian soldiers paced guard in their ugly and unkempt uniforms. The two women wandered over the city, exploring the ruins. They discovered a restaurant she had known as a child, long before the war. They went in, sat in a booth; the waiter came and they ordered. The waiter said they could go in the back, if they wished.

What is this? they asked each other.

They went in the back.

The room was bathed in blood red light; couples danced to cool American jazz records; moving figures, faces and shadows were murky red forms. They sat at a table. A woman approached them, sat down and smiled and other women joined them, talked in many languages and drank with them. Across the room, through red smoke, over the rows of liquor bottles and large purple mirrors behind the bar, a mask hung on the wall, a glass mask whose blue red star shaped eyes bubbled. Under the mask, red neon said: BLUTSTERNEN

A decade later she ascended the long flight of steps to the Heidelberg Schloss for the last night of Fasching festival, she, in costume, a princess in her gown. It was late, approaching midnight. At midnight the Queen of Fasching would be chosen. The party would last all this night as it had lasted for four days. As she went up the dark steps she noticed a figure descending, far above: a shadow had moved. It is nothing, she told herself, someone coming home early from the party. The figure came closer—they met, a hand took her arm and the voice apprehensively questioned: Dresden? and the eyes glowed and whirred like bloody stars on revolving blades and the beard, darker than night, the beard like claws on a jaw moved as the voice repeated: Dresden? like a wind come clanging out from the craters of the moon: *Dresden? Dresden? Dresden?*

Soldier's Road

THE TWO MEN DRANK COFFEE and faced each other over the table in the train station. German civilians and American soldiers streamed in and out and the repeatedly opening door brought in the freezing Deutschland winter.

Phil grinned and sat back, rubbed his chest with his hands, then stretched his arms wide, yawning, finally falling forward in a burst of laughing breath.

"I'm goin' home!" he exclaimed.

Nat smiled. Phil breathed and looked at his watch, then at his friend.

"Home to U.S.A. By God. American women again!"

He laughed and waved his hands.

"Hey girls! Look out! Here I come!"

Nat grinned and fiddled with a teaspoon.

"It sounds fine," Nat nodded.

"Well . . . in seven months, we will. It'll be summer in America, summer . . . in Terre Haute . . . I'll go home first," Phil began dreamily, "and then I'll travel a little. I'd like to see my old Stateside U.S.A. again . . . you know, make out with some nice young pussy and take it easy . . . swim a lot, play some ball . . ." Phil rambled, eyes already seeing it. His smiling lips and staring eyes seeing the great plains and mountains of the United States, the huge cities, the vast unending dreamlike vision of America, full of hope and security and young women freshly turned from girlhood with bright sparkling blue eyes and perfect teeth; and the swell big houses and lawns and a kind of controlled violence, gentle perversity, possible loneliness, habitable streets and highways, charm, delightful backyards . . .

Phil swung up on the stool and smacked both hands on the bar and laughed and yelled at Old Hank and Hank asked him how he had been and how come he didn't come around any more and before Phil could answer, Hank was serving a customer at the other end of the bar. Phil had a few and then a couple more and went home a little dazed and drunk. He had waited for the gang to come around but nobody showed.

"If they haven't got jobs, they got a job keeping a wife and kids," Hank said. "Come by this weekend."

The next day Phil went downtown. Gasoline Alley had gotten married and sold out. Bingo had moved up to the Sinclair station and nobody knew where Hi Hat was and the man, a Mr. Grien, said now and then boys stopped by and asked . . . he was sorry . . .

Phil called up the old boys he hadn't known well but—but nothing. And in the following weeks he only saw a few of them.

Girls, you know, some young hunk and have a ball. He flipped the cigarette out the window and wondered what to do next. He turned out into the street and drove downtown. Terre Haute wasn't very large.

"It's good to be home," he told Hank. One afternoon.

"I guess it is," Hank said.

He had remembered Betty and didn't want to see her at all. But he called her up and she said Oh Phil sure, come on over and by the time he got there he wanted, really wanted to see her after all. She used to have terrific boobs and if she . . . he stopped the car and got out, walked up the driveway and across the lawn to the front door, rang the bell.

She opened the door and grinned.

"Don't stand there, silly, come in!"

"Oh Phil—please. No, I mean really."

The TV set sang like Eddie Fisher. Phil put his hand on her breast again.

"Phil," she breathed harshly: *"don't."* She took his hand away. He was perspiring.

The next day it all seemed like a bad dream. He tried to remember some more of the other girls he used to date. He couldn't. He had tried them all. He told his mother so long and she watched him get in the car and drive off. She was standing in the doorway, living room lights behind her.

He drove a long way down the highway and stopped in a roadhouse and ordered a beer. He looked around and in the corner were two girls, talking with each other. He thought for a long time and had a few shots to brace himself, went over and asked them if they'd like a drink.

"Well," Red said. "What took you so long?"

"Sit down," Blondie said.

They were college girls originally from Chicago on their way to Mississipi and were staying over a couple of days to visit Red's aunt. Phil got pretty looped and hot and was kissing them both and remembered he'd heard of one guy making it with two girls but he never believed he would. He laughed a lot and they teased him and he said he was just back from Germany and the three of them chattered like a bunch of old friends.

Their little cottage was nice. It was set back from the highway about a quarter of a mile and there was a note pinned to the front door from Red's aunt saying she had gone into Terre Haute and would be back on the weekend you need some bread, cigarettes and magazines pay you when I get back. Phil slumped down in a chair and laughed, sighed. Blondie told Red to make the drinks and she sat on Phil's lap, took the cigarette out of his mouth and had a drag herself.

"C'mere honey," Phil said. He pulled her down and kissed her, fondled her breast. No resistance.

"Just a second," she said.

She went into the kitchen and Phil waited. He was very drunk, then, and he waited what seemed a long time. He read an old magazine and time dragged by. He went in the kitchen. It was empty. He went into the next room, empty, crossed it and opened the door and stuck his head in. It was dark. He reached for the light switch.

The owner found him naked, tied to the bed, spread-eagled. He wasn't hurt. They had taken his mother's car, his wristwatch and money and had left. It took a while for him to get his normal weight again and when he was able to be with people he was offered a job as salesman in a department store downtown. It was good to be with people then, and the best part he met a girl one day who insisted she return the curtains her mother bought yesterday. "Second floor," Phil grinned. She laughed and persisted. Point blank he asked her for a date. "Okay," she said. He took the curtains up. She was terrific. She had short, fashionably cut blonde hair and her eyes were brown. She had a light slender body and her name was Jeanne and there was something about her he loved. They dated a while and one night she asked him if he was that boy who was in the papers and he blushed and said he was and she asked him what happened. They were parked at a drive-in drinking Coke and he saw her hardening eyes asking him what had happened.

"They robbed me."

"What happened next."

He told her how he had met them and everything. He left out some.

"That's not all, Phil," she said. "What else happened."

It wasn't easy telling her but he thought she took it pretty well: it was embarrassing.

"How do you do *that?*" she asked, frowning. She had her head on his shoulder and her fingers were playing with the knot of his tie. He kissed her and her lips were like fiery little animals; he began to sweat, remembering how. He kissed her again and they drove away fast and parked. She couldn't speak right.

"Show me."

What's so wrong about it? Phil thought. He was worried. Jeanne was coming around the store every day now and making it a little obvious. One day she was laughing. She leaned on the counter. As he told her to take it easy she said she found out what they called it.

"What," Phil said.

"Ride the horse," she said. "That's why the two girls tied you down."

Phil frowned and cleared his throat.

"Why tie me down?" he asked.

"Oh Phil," she said, pursing her lips, "don't you know?"

"No."

"They wanted you to be almost dying and still want to make love like that. See? They wanted to drain you."

"Yeah, but why?"

She looked at him.

"Some people like things different."

He got sore.

"I'm not different," he said. "I'm like everybody and Hank said it's normal, people do it all the time. There's nothing wrong about it. Nothing."

"Those girls did it real different," she smiled.

He was silent.

"And you liked that, *didn't* you!"

He didn't answer. Then he said, "What you've heard is nothing to what happened. It wasn't sex, Jeanne, it was like food, puked food, to them." He paused. "It was like being tied in a trough of filth. No one . . ."

He stopped and lowered his eyes, said softly.

"We don't—we're not wrong. We aren't."

She frowned in thought, then said: "That's right. But I like you to think so. You know I do. You like me to think that way, don't you?"

"Who's who," he muttered.

They didn't talk for a while.

"Why do you want me to please you to make me make it dirty?" he asked, looking at her.

"I like it that way," she looked back: "If I didn't you'd be a dull boy."

"Thanks," he murmured.

"Okay."

Barbara had sweet lips and though her nose was too sharp, she was swell. He bought her a drink and watched her brooding eyes; now and then she widened them and they seemed to come out of her head.

In a furious sweat he told her all about Jeanne; Barbara understood, she said she would cure him and she told him a few facts that were really dirty and said Jeanne's way was as common as any other, position never got so different it changed sexual intercourse, it gave it a little variety, that's all. Phil took Barbara to a movie that Friday night. When Jeanne had called before he had told her his mother was sick and Jeanne believed him because she had no cause not to and she told him that, too.

"Barbara baby blue-eyes," he said.

"Let's go for a drive," she said.

She dug long nails into his back and he winced and gasped; she was drawing blood.

Her voice was rising,

"*Faster, faster, faster, faster—*"

He quit the job, began to use his savings. Barbara loved it. He began to drink and when so drunk his last act of consciousness was entering her he could go as fast and as long as her splintering voice could last and on every date he had a six can pack and a pint of rye.

"You drink too much, darling," she said, "Why?"

He didn't answer; he didn't look at her.

One day Jeanne came to his house and asked him where he had been. His mother was at work at the drugstore.

"Come on in," he mumbled.

She followed him inside noticing his stumbling walk. He had a bathrobe on; his eyes were bloodshot. She watched him make a drink. His hands trembled; he drank it quick, made another.

"What's the matter with you? Where have you been?"

He didn't answer. She went close to him.

"I miss you honey . . ." she whispered, her head on his shoul-

81

der. She rubbed his back and he cried out, twisting away.

"Don't do that! Don't touch me!"

She drew back.

"Well," she sneered, "this new lady must be something. You're getting the jitters."

Phil finished the drink and eased back on the sofa and closed his eyes; he opened them a minute later and looked at her.

"Beat it," he said. "Now."

"Huh?"

"I got a head."

He looked at her. His eyes sagged but his face was lined and hard. "Out!"

She began to cry and left. He closed the door and locked it, sat down on the sofa, made himself another drink and sipped it, looking across at the wallpaper. The large pink flowers seemed to move, slowly, with an odd and almost ominous purpose.

They parked on the edge of the highway.

"You're too drunk. You can't even stay awake," Barbara snarled. He began to paw her and she shoved his hands away—he grabbed her throat and jerked her head up, looked in her eyes. His eyes were crossed, her face was double. He fought to see her clearly, not hearing her choking cries that he was strangling her. He saw her, finally, and released her. She fell onto him and put her arms around his waist and began clawing his back—he straightened up and groaned, choked and hit her on the spine as hard as he could; she made a sharp cry and slithered across the car seat away from him, opened the door and got out, straightening her back with difficulty. She looked at him. Her eyes were bulged, bright with excited fear—he lunged across at her and she slammed the car door: it smashed into his face. He yowled in pain, opened the door and threw himself at her, brought her down and began tearing her clothes off; she dissolved into tears and made herself helpless and he embraced her, saw her brittle, breakable like a glass straw; he made love like a demon, like hatred inflamed and she began to cry sharply and urge him on, fingernails cutting through fresh wounds, splintering voice shouting faster, faster and he tore into her like a human jackhammer, to finally kill her with it, to finally murder her, be rid of her and had it, came, rolled off, body folding up in pain and conflicting realizations his mind fought to save or slam down unrealized, the voice through it all, gentle now, full of tenderness and grateful tears, thanking him, loving him and murmuring soft childish tones of adoration and sobbing affection and her hands caressed him as his churning mind tried to waken him, called with dissonant trumpet notes to get him clear, bring him up in rage and smash that voice, break that glass spine, crush that life. He couldn't. The ringing nightmare of whiskey ran around in his brain like a chariot of Walt Disney lightning, seething through all parts, inflaming them pointlessly, calling to him to awake in the cause of all, attainable or forgotten, yet remembered . . . but the greater body of sleep drove all else under and Phil gave in and the din of the rest of the clanging universe fell away and in a fan-like motion he was asleep.

He came out of the hospital a sober and cured man, moved to Columbus, Ohio and got a job through an agency as the night man in an all night coffee house. He tried not to do much thinking and to put his attention to the job. He did all right and six months later was given a raise. He had saved his money diligently and planned, one future day, to go abroad, maybe visit Germany again. He wondered what had happened to his old buddy, Nat. Now and then he saw movies that took place in Europe and he was sad and full of memories and made a real half hearted promise to someday return. He came out of the theater and looked at his watch and thought he'd go back to the hotel and write his mother a letter—something he hated doing but it would kill time and get that worry out of his mind. He turned the corner thinking what he would eat when he got back to work, unconsciously calculating the time: 55 minutes—

"Excuse me," she said—she looked at him.

He stared back.

"Sure," he smiled.

She walked by.

"Wait!"

She turned and her eyes were direct; he caught up with her and looked at her again. He said,

"You're beautiful. I'll—"

Memories rocked him. He took her arm, holding softly "nkyou . . . my husband . . ." and she was gone, gone down the street. Phil felt his legs go; he stumbled against a building and swallowed, closed his eyes, fought for control, fought for this discipline which he had fought for all this time: he opened his eyes and the bright night of the city, the busy city was there, real and itself. It was clear. Suddenly she left his mind and his self collapsed in a wave of thanks. But then, obliquely, like an ax edge of experience: she returned. He cried out and ran down the street, turned in the doorway and signaled the man: said,

"Double rye and beer chaser," the twenty dollar bill on the bar in front of him.

The first time, he thought. He said it.

"For the first time?" she asked.

He grinned.

"In too close to always," he laughed. She laid her head on his lap and he stretched his legs, put feet on a footstool and swished the whiskey around in the glass and ran his hand through her hair.

"Hey honey," she said. She wasn't very young and a little fat, and she was smiling. Mac had given him the night off. Phil yawned and laughed. He leaned down to kiss her. She met him half way.

While she (Laura), slept, Phil sat naked by the window and looked down the street; it was almost dawn now, the first streaks showing on the horizon as if they were full of future hope. He wove his way to the kitchen and returned with soda and ice; across the room she was in the big bed, on her side, facing the wall. She breathed heavily and he knew it wouldn't be long before he would begin to loathe primarily himself. He sat down, thought how depressing it was . . . there, in her apartment, thinking. And he liked the apartment; it was lived in. He poured a good belt and put the bottle back on the sill of the open window. He added soda and ice. There was another bottle in the cabinet and more in stores: he had plenty of money; he had saved it all. And now, he thought, watching the long dawn streaks leisurely brightening, developing color, now? At last this is it. My life. Old pal Nathaniel, goodbye. Now my life.

He finished the drink slowly, yawned and lit a cigarette. A moment later the warm tightening and elongation of muscle overcame him easily. He put out the cigarette and stood up sleepily, looked across the dawn-filtered darkness at her bulky form tangled in the sheets. He crawled in beside her, he her young lover man, as she had said, and he took the sheets off her carefully. When she rolled over and opened her eyes and put her arms around him, his consciousness went away and left him with her.

Air Trails

HE MET HER IN THE LOBBY of the building where she worked: a handsome laconic blonde, secretary to some business man. They took a crowded bus across town, transferred at Fifth Avenue, rode down to the Square and got off and went along Thompson Street and down the steps into Fellin's where they had a quiet Italian meal with wine; then they went to a movie; the Eighth Street Playhouse.

After the movie they walked out on the street. She was really tired; she had worked like hell all day. Inventory. He persuaded her to stop in at that place around the corner, down a couple of blocks on Sixth Avenue where they'd have a cup of coffee. She smiled thinly.

"One cup."

Afterwards they took a cab to her apartment. She lived with her mother. Her father was an Army doctor stationed overseas, in Stuttgart.

They kissed at the glass door; he went back across town to Barry's, had a couple of drinks and went home, took off his clothes, put on pajamas, turned on the radio and got in bed and listened to soft music and looked at the room and smoked a cigarette. Then he put it out, turned off the radio, set the alarm, turned off the lamp and went to sleep.

One night he met her as usual.

"I have to be home early," she said. "I have to get up around six; I'm going out of town for the weekend."

"Who with?" He was a little jealous.

"A friend."

"A friend?"

She nodded.

?

They went to the Vanguard and dug Stan Getz and had a few drinks and left. He tried to kiss her in the cab but she said she didn't feel like that tonight. He sat back and listened to that a while. He looked at the back of the cab driver's head. He looked at her out of the corners of his eyes. She was looking out the window.

The following Monday he saw her again. But she had to go uptown with her mother. A party. Friends of the family. They walked across town. On the way he began to count the weeks; in so doing discovered poignant facts:

1: She hadn't said anything since he had met her except hello, details concerning her arrival or departure to or from a place or inevitable situation with which he obviously wasn't concerned. And in that frame of thought, in answer to a question her typical response was,

A: A nod, or corresponding gesture

B: Yes

C: No

2: He had spent a good deal of money and time, and thought, on her, and had at best tasted her chapped mouth. But the real thing he missed was not knowing what she enjoyed. She always seemed to play along.

He called her the next afternoon and she said she had a hangover. She said her stomach was upset. Maybe he shouldn't see her. He frowned. It was strange, *maybe you shouldn't see me tonight. See what?* Her upset stomach? He listened to the hanging sentence. *Maybe you shouldn't see my stomach tonight.* They talked and hung up. Her stomach. Tonight?

He called Sunday afternoon to see if she was feeling better. Her mother answered and said she had gone to New Jersey with an old girlfriend. New Jersey? Her mother sounded pleasant, and formed a new corner on the already geometrical paradox.

He met her after work Monday and they went to Pete's on Irving Place, had supper, caught a cab and went downtown to a poetry reading. The large room was packed with dirty bearded poets, dangerous looking characters and Picassoish girls with smoky blue eyes and black stockings. It was hot and uncomfortable; at the first intermission they left. He went in the street for a cab, his hand in the air. He spoke over his shoulder to her:

"Did you like any of it?"

She smiled: "A little."

His hand dropped and he turned and stepped back up on the sidewalk beside her.

"A little," he repeated. They crossed the street, heading north. She smiled distantly.

"Did you?"

He looked at her and grinned.

"No."

He made to kiss her. She drew away and shook her head slowly.

"Not tonight," she said. "Why don't you phone?"

He helped her out of the cab, walked her to the large glass door and opened it; she slipped inside and he walked away. Par.

His voice kept saying goodnight, goodnight, goodnight as she rode up the elevator; she smiled and nodded her head, liking him because he said such strange things. A pleasant young man for a change. "Isn't it about time?"

He rolled over. *Why don't you phone?* What did it mean? At a time like that. It sounded—and kept sounding. Over and over, echoing away senselessly.

He didn't call her all week. Uneasy days. Out of the blue, Fred came through with a party that Friday night. Old hopeless Fred!

He met a tall airline stewardess and they talked in Fred's kitchen. After a few drinks they cut out and took a fast cab across town.

They made it that night and the next; Sunday afternoon he went to the airport with her. He stood behind the fence and watched her fly into the bright sky. He would see her in three days. He laughed. Wow!

The Man in the White Raincoat

It was early in the morning, and quiet. Three stools to my left, a man in a white raincoat was looking through a magazine; he and I and the bartender were the only ones there.

I ordered another glass of beer. As the bartender gave it to me, I paid him and lit a cigarette, and looked across at the rows of shining bottles against darkly stained paneling; prints of old New York.

The bartender was cutting a lemon. He cut off both ends and sliced it vertically around fourteen times. Then he peeled off thirteen pieces of lemon. I could hear the sound; a soft rip, as each piece came cleanly away. He put them in an oldfashioned glass and began cleaning shotglasses. The man to my left asked,

"Do you think it'll be a busy day?"

"Maybe," the bartender said.

"Well, it's a nice day," said the fellow.

"Yeah."

The magazine was open in front of the guy and he looked down at it, but before he did he looked at the bartender and then at me. I wasn't looking at him but there is a way you know.

He was pretty tall, and thin. He had a narrow skull and shortly cut light brown hair. He had an angular clean cut face and a long neck. When he laughed, the grin split his face and laugh-lines came out. But he stopped quick. Then he was the calm clean cut guy again. He wore what looked like a brown tweed suit under a white raincoat. White shirt, narrow tie, brown shoes. He sat at the bar in a pleasant long legged way, like a big bird, all folded up. The raincoat hung on both sides of the stool and the belt dangled.

A couple of neighborhood building superintendents came in

89

and sat down. Rye and beer. Down. Another, down. They left, stopping at the door as a woman came in. She was in her late forties and she sat near the door and two colored men came in, followed by a fat, sarcastic looking guy who sat next to me and breathed, "Harper's and water. Mixed."

"Bartender?" It was the guy on my left. The bartender nodded. "Same," the guy said.

The bartender filled a shotglass with gin and added tonic and a piece of lime to the glass but did not mix in the gin; he took money and gave change.

I had another beer and put out the cigarette. The guy mixed his drink, stirred it, looked at us and then at the magazine, turned a page and looked up. He drank a little, lit a cigarette and glanced at me. He looked down at the magazine and then looked up.

"Hey. Excuse me," he murmured.

He meant me; I turned.

He stood up. "Would you—um, watch—" He gestured at his articles on the bar. "O.K." I nodded. "I'll be right back," he said, and passed behind me.

He walked like the tall bird he was; the raincoat billowed in his long strides. His arms swung and when he reached the open door he stopped. He looked down the sidewalk to the left, and right.

He put his hands in his trouser pockets and rocked back and forth on his heels, looking straight out front. Then he looked to the right again, and to the left. Then he walked out of sight.

I looked at his stuff on the bar.

It was a transient hour. The city was opening for business. On a clear September morning around nine o'clock, New York can be beautiful.

The bar was almost empty. He came back in, walking those long steps, passing me and sitting down. He had gotten another magazine, one of those men's things, I thought, and a paper. The *Times*. He put them on the bar and looked around.

A little colored man sat up front, in a patch of sunlight, with a glass of beer in front of him; he looked out the front window, a big plate glass with a curtain behind it and a kind of dusty display in between, potted plants and a poster for a benefit dance. The sun streamed in the window and traffic tooled by.

The bartender was taking cherries from a gallon jar and putting them in a drinking glass. The radio was on then, and Frank Sinatra was singing "I Won't Dance." The bartender hummed along; I sipped brew and that guy to my left read his new magazine and looked at us. A building superintendent came in and sat beside me. We said hello and he ordered rye and beer. He got it and he and the bartender talked a little and after he finished his drink, he left. The bartender moved down the duckboards and stood in front of the tall guy and began dipping olives into a glass. The guy looked up from his magazine.

"Whatever happened to those guys in the 44th Division?"

The bartender looked at him. "What?"

"Those guys. In the 44th—"

The bartender glanced down and went on with what he was doing. "I don't know," he said. The tall guy cleared his throat: "Where were you?"

"Through France."

The guy nodded. "Airborne?"

The bartender looked at him. "No, I was in the Infantry."

"The Infantry."

The bartender capped the gallon of olives and put it in one of the closets down in back of the bar. Then he began cutting sheets of Ballantine notepaper into small pieces. He folded and cut them with a knife.

"Another, please," the guy said.

The bartender made him a gin and tonic again, like before, not mixing it. Another building super came in and sat next to me, said hello to me, and began talking with the bartender. Quietly. One of his tenants had done something. Then the tall guy said, to me,

"Just a minute."

He walked out again, striding along, arms going and the rain-coat billowing. He paused in the doorway, then went out. The bartender began wiping the bar and talking with the building super. When he got to where the tall guy had been, he said,

"Hey! The guy didn't put the gin in!" He grinned and held up the full shot of gin. "He was just drinking tonic."

The little colored man up front began to cackle.

The building super said, "Some guys are funny."

The bartender began to laugh. "He didn't even know it!" The building super laughed and the little guy up front cracked, "Didn't even know!"

The building super began to tell a long story about a guy he saw do the same thing. He kept repeating himself. Halfway through it the bartender began taking inventory. Just as the super finished the story, the bartender smiled, nodded his head and said,

"Yeah. Ha ha, I know."

"Maybe this guy's a little nuts," the super said.

The bartender was bending down, looking through a closet, counting bottles of wine; he nodded, said, "Maybe," whispered, "two red." He stood up and wrote some figures on one of the pieces of paper he had cut. Beside the figures were colors. Red, white.

"Just a second," he said.

He left the bar and the tall guy came back in, unwrapping a pack of cigarettes. He sat down as the bartender went into the back. The building super finished his drink, touched my shoulder and left. A young colored couple came in and asked me where Bethune Street was. I knew, but while I was trying to tell them, the little guy up front began to cackle again. "Naw," he laughed. "That's all wrong. You go west on 8th Street until you run into Greenwich Avenue. Follow it until you come to Christopher Street; go down Christopher until you come to Hudson. Turn right there and go about five or six blocks. It'll be on your left."

The young guy and his girl went down to the little man and they straightened everything out. Then they left.

The bartender came back with several bottles of wine. He glanced at the clock and went behind the bar. He began distributing the wine.

The tall guy had a smoke lit and was reading his newspaper, going through it pretty easily, now and then looking up. People came in and out of the bar. He put the paper down, poured the shot of gin into his glass and mixed it, drank and set it down. He crossed his legs and bent foward and picked up a magazine and opened it and folded the cover under and held it. His right arm was lazily on the bar; cigarette smoke curled up. He began to read.

Then he closed the magazine, put the cigarette out, finished his drink and put his cigarettes in his shirt pocket, folding money in his left trouser pocket, slid change forward for the tip, gathered the two magazines and the newspaper together and stood up putting them under his arm. He stood behind the stool, looking at the bartender, at me, and at the little colored man up front who gazed out the front window. Nobody moved. He tucked his papers under his arm firmly and started walking out. He strode along, left arm swinging, right arm holding his literature. As he approached the doorway, his left arm went into the air and he waved his hand behind him.

"See you," he said over his shoulder. We nodded.

He went out without stopping.

The Next Turn of the Wheel

The next turn of the wheel.
what do you think
about the next turn
of the wheel?

CHARLES OLSON

EVERY MAY THE AMERICAN LEGION carnival came to town; one evening I went by myself. I had been to ball practice and my glove stuck out of the back pocket of my Levis. I wandered up and down the midway looking at the ferris wheel and the spinning number wheels and the prizes, listening to the noises and looking at local girls. I played the penny toss and lost, I drank pop and wondered what to do with myself. I didn't see anyone I knew, so around nine, as it had gotten dark, I decided to go home.

Halfway, I missed the familiar bulk of the glove against my ass, and with sinking heart I touched my back pocket. The glove was gone.

It was a Rawlings trapper model, dark brown, almost black. It was heavy and stiff, waiting to be broken in. When Uncle Essex had given it to me I had quietly looked it over and that spring had begun to try and play first instead of the outfield. Right away it was wrong, it was as if something dark and heavy in my hand became mine to handle. I was afraid of it, and I felt a kind of fear and awe of other guys who played first base much more elegantly than I did, which meant I was supposed to assume a look that they had without trying. I was not cut out for first base, I belonged in the outfield, I was an outfielder and I had needed a fielder's glove. I liked it out there, with the whole action in front of me. I imagined myself playing infield, even shortstop. But not first.

94

Shortstop was a tense charged place which I always wanted to bring into action, my action. My style. The oblique and powerful style at first base was glamorous to me but it wasn't mine—I wasn't anywhere in the infield. As happy as I had been to get the glove, with its first feel I had been numbed by the apprehension of first base. I had daydreamed about backhanding a liner, stepping on first, firing to second, but with the glove in my hands and my Uncle Essex watching for my reaction, my heart froze. I was no first baseman, and worse, I had needed a fielder's glove.

I went back. I walked through the mobbed carnival street and asked older people and other kids and men in charge of booths. They hadn't seen it. I looked under chairs and around the baseboard of the penny toss and soda booth. It wasn't along the curb or under the bushes. I didn't know what to do.

I started home. If only I had told Uncle Essex, he would have understood. He could have exchanged it—I could have traded it, sold it or given it to someone I knew. His unspoken generosity and belief in my desire! To simply drop the glove for anybody to find at a carnival was the severest irresponsibility: a carelessness coming from self-consciousness, nervous loneliness and a terrible knowing what I could get by with, and as I went up the walk to the front door I opened the now old scar for the first time, and the persisting claw of my ancient knowing self came into the daylight of my consciousness, gouged my safekeeping and slid back inside my skull. I had lost a glove that had held darkness and a power other boys made graceful, the glove had held me, and I had been myself to become. And since then the darkness and power has taken the more strict form of myself, clawing and hurting and forcing strength into me. Strength! For the fateful moments of purpose without accident—when I destroy and proceed to the fearful time when the moments will not be accidental or constructed, but fact!

The High & the Mighty

I MET HER IN A CUT RATE STORE on Highway 66. She was buying a pack of cigarettes and I was waiting my turn beside her. She turned and glanced in my eyes. I saw what you see when you're looking out at the ocean. I got some cigarettes and walked out of the store close to her, and asked her what her name was. She had a steady expression of surprise around her eyes and mouth. She said, pretty coolly, I'm engaged. She got in her convertible and looked at me. I was standing by an outdoor coke machine. Cars raced along 66. She said I could call her, if I wanted, and gave me her name and number. The next afternoon I called, later caught a bus that dropped me off in front of her house. She was on the doorstep.

We used her car, and drove around, had something to eat and then I rented a car and we ended up out of town in a hotel. Our names and faces focused and wound around us; we breathed the air of it until it was finished and we returned. She to her familiar fellow, me to my familiar world in the rain. She got out of my rented car and ran to the city garage where she had left her own car. I watched her go from me into the color of the city. Somewhere in the traffic I imagined Gershwin's Concerto in F. Goodbye, goodbye. I drove away. I returned to my job at the pool. I was a lifeguard. I sat on a high seat under an umbrella, wearing white swimming trunks, dark glasses and a whistle and watched pretty girls all day long. They had a good time, it was great to them, and while I fulfilled my appointment I also wondered what

I was doing from one minute to the next, sitting up there looking over trees at farm houses.

II

It was a small town in the lower left hand pocket of Missouri and I got hung over there longer than I expected, starting by going to a movie instead of catching the next bus. I left the station and walked along the street. It was one of those midwestern evenings when you don't feel like going on with the trip, around seven o'clock, an hour before things start to get light blue. In June. I should have been in New York. As I walked in the movie house the first show was just ending. I went in and sat down wondering why the manager had chewed on his hand and looked at me like he had, why the flowery woman who took my money and slid me the pink ticket was drunk, and why the boy in the dirty gray suit gave me the popcorn saying,

"Sho. Why not?"

It takes my eyes a little while to get used to darkness and main features, but I sat down on the aisle towards the back of the theatre and watched previews. I began on the popcorn. A while later the hair on my neck was moving around as if there was a sudden chasm behind me. I turned and looked behind me. Nobody there. Nobody was sitting behind me, and in fact nobody was anywhere: back front, either side.

The theatre was empty—except for me and a young blonde usherette who stood by the exit, off to my right. She stared at the floor. That painting by Hopper. Then she looked at me. The music was loud. It was about an airplane and whistling pilots. The point of no return. Something moved in the corner of my eye. The blonde came up the aisle and stopped beside me and said,

"May I sit down?"

"Sure," I said. I moved over a seat and she sat down.

She had a maroon uniform on. In the painting the girl has a maroon uniform on. So my blonde had a maroon uniform on. Her breath smelled like lipstick: strawberry. A young blonde. My breath smelled like popcorn.

"Um," I said. I put my arm around her and she laid her head on

97

my shoulder and sighed.

"What will I do?" she asked. "Nobody comes to the movies."

"Except us," I smiled. I felt her lips on my neck; her cheek moved. She was smiling.

"Except us," she repeated.

"Why don't you quit?" I asked.

She raised her head and looked at me. The movie house wasn't dark at all. From the light of the screen—the bright lights from the interior of the airplane and music—her face was pretty clear. She had an ordinary face that was pale and in good light her eyes would probably be soft blue and they would seem resigned. I didn't find out the facts. The three days that followed saw us together but we didn't talk about our lives. We hardly talked at all, except what flavor ice cream she wanted, or me answering her questions. Like the time we were swimming. It was the next afternoon at the pool in the next town. We hitchhiked over. My suitcase was on its way to New York but the travel bag was still in the locker in the bus station, and hands empty we stood on the road in the hot afternoon and held out our thumbs. A pickup truck was the ride all the way. We got off and walked through town to the pool and I rented suits for us and we went in. There were a lot of people, it was a small pool, and after swimming in between them for a while we had iced coffee at the refreshment pavilion. We sat in wicker chairs and held hands across a sticky roundtopped table the color and scale of a candy lifesaver.

"Where are you from?" she asked. She was so still it seemed like the words came from someone in the pool. On a hot day like that, beside a swimming pool a thousand miles away from Manhattan, the question was almost unreal.

"New York," I said. I felt like I was lying because she was so silent. Nothing in her face changed.

"Let's go back in," she said.

"Jobs are hard to find," she grinned.

"Then give it up," I said. "Look." I was from New York so I tried to talk that way. Instead I kissed her.

"OK," she said. "Oh baby, I quit."

We cut out through the theatre exit and walked through town.

I bought a half pint of cheap bourbon and we walked the highway until we got tired. At a turn we stepped over the crash rail and went down an embankment like Indians, into an orchard. By now it was dark and we were having trouble walking. We sat under an apple tree and I lit a cigarette that lasted three drags. I undid my tie, she unbuttoned her maroon jacket. The orchard slanted off and the smell of green apples was as fresh and keen as the sound when you crack one in half: it lies open: two halves, one in each hand, dark teardrop seeds in the centers.

On a sunlit wall of a tractor factory I wrote our names big, and to the right of my message she made an x and an o, smaller.

After walking in fields and wading in creeks, we were exhausted. Wednesday night we rented a room in town. The next day we went swimming again, getting there in two rides via the route we had taken Monday. We lay on the duckboards by the pool. Quietly, in the hot sun. That night the bus station was full of people waiting to go places. I took my travel bag out of the locker and we sat on a bench and waited. Outside it was getting blue.

"Goodbye baby," she said.

The bus pulled in noisily and about four people got up and began getting on. We were at the end of the line. When it came my turn I gave the driver my ticket and he tore the bottom part off. I had my travel bag in my hand. I didn't know what it was for or what to do with it. Where I was going or why. I put it on the bottom step and glanced at the driver. He got on the bus. I looked in her eyes and we kissed goodbye. I got on the bus, went in back and sat near a window, slid it open. She stood below me, blonde and pale, looking up. Her light blue eyes were still and distant. The bus engine growled and barked. I shoved my arm out the window and she took my hand. We both said it but not out loud. I got my arm back in and the bus began to move. She walked across the street with it and then began to run. GOODBYE BABY. The bus gathered speed and smoked out of town.

The last I saw she was standing on a street corner in her maroon uniform, in the blue Missouri twilight.

99

The Photograph

A DREAM TO REMEMBER

Shy Cleo

Across the room for Cleo to see, even after Cleo sailed home.

Almost sly, smiling out
  But a little bored. Careless.
  Unsure; thoughtful; selfish.
  Spoked irises winced in sun at zenith glistening silver white, silver gray and glossy black photo paper, and until the paper began to turn brown and start to crack, the photograph was a temporary eternity of Cleo smiling forever for a while, scotch-taped on that wall locker door in the WAC billets.

His third day on the Army post in Germany, the WAC Sergeant showed him around the Special Services office.
  "This is your desk," they crossed the room and she opened a closet, putting her hand on the large shelf: "you can store your drawing equipment here."
  They had a smoke. She briefed him. Her nametag said SGT. WILKS. He looked at it and at her stripes, then at her face. Around 37. Rimless glasses, thin lips, narrow nose, watery eyes. Her manner was defensive and self-conscious.
  They went downstairs; she went on talking, at a flat clip.
  "You'll get all the things you need in the next few days."
  He nodded. They went to chow.

A month and a half later he was dismissed from Special Services and was sent to the gym to distribute basketballs, sneakers, box-

100

ing gloves, etc. At night, in the little office at one end of the empty gymnasium, he wrote letters and listened to Parisian quiz programs on the Halicrafter set.

Now and then he saw Sgt. Wilks.

"Hi."

"Hi."

In the summer of that year he was transferred to another job, still on the same post, as clerk typist. Then a week later he was a cook, and the first time he was on duty he was serving oatmeal and making toast. Sgt. Wilks came along the mess line, he gave her some oatmeal and toast and she smiled sleepily, a little wryly, he thought, and she made a quiet wisecrack of some kind, like what next.

Gradually he began spending his free time in downtown Heidelberg.

He also walked and drove around the German countryside, doing sketches of trees, carts, animals, houses, peasants in fields, children and street scenes. Now and then he did watercolors; Impressionistic, he thought, but then, Europe was.

He met a German girl and they went together a few months; at first it was great, but later she turned angrily pale, he began to drink too much and they fought continually. Then he met and fell for another German girl, Maria, and lost both.

It was a lonely winter.

The following spring a group of WACs arrived fresh from the States; Sgt. Wilks showed them around. A WAC named Cleo was among them, and one day, as he served her broccoli, he asked her if he could take her around Heidelberg. Ok, that evening they had dinner in a German restaurant and later went dancing; they walked around Heidelberg. He showed her a few famous statues, the Castle, and the river, and then he brought her back in a cab, and said goodnight at the door to the WAC billets; she was lovely.

But then the other soldiers began to date Cleo. He ate dessert and looked out the window feeling moony—saw Cleo go out the gate with a Corporal.

"Why didn't you go out with me?"
"He asked me first."
"A ha."
She nodded. "That's right." Then she smiled shyly, almost slyly. They were walking across the parade ground. He walked her to her billet, and asked her at the door, if she'd like to go for a walk the next day. "Sure," she said.

They gazed at the panorama along the Neckar River. He showed her his new camera, an Agfa Silette he'd bought at the PX: he explained how to use it and let her take a couple. He took several of her, posed in front of boats, picnickers, children and refreshment stands. In the background across the river, Heidelberg spread before them.
Around 5 they took the strassebahn back to post.

It had been a lovely day.

The next day she was with the Corporal again; he watched them, hand in hand, walk across the parade ground.

A few days later he got the prints, and the pictures came out pretty good; they were the first he had ever taken; he didn't tell Cleo. He would wait. If she asked—twice a day she came along the mess line, following the Corporal, who held her tray. At first she smiled when he served her, broken hearted behind the counter—a few days later she didn't bother to look, she passed along, lovely eyes front, as if the food would appear there, on her tray, which it did.

In April of that year he went to Paris for fifteen days. He had a good time and saw a lot. He wrote Cleo "a long wild letter," and included a selection of postal photos of Paris. But he also inserted the pictures he had taken—and the photograph of her that he liked best, from his wallet, the really good one he had taken during the afternoon they spent by the river.

Cleo thanked him for the letter and said everybody liked the photograph, and on the following day he was back on duty, she spoke to him, but a couple of days later, once again, didn't, now with a different soldier each time. He couldn't forget her, and he felt a pang every time she appeared. He even felt bad not awfully, for the Corporal, who kind of slouched around, pink and blonde. But—in the meantime—his overseas time was running short! Back to the States! A month later he packed to leave, and on the afternoon of the next to the last day of duty he was out on the deserted mess line, cutting pies for supper and thinking about home. Sgt. Wilks came in the mess hall, walked up to him and abruptly leaned across the row of pies on the serving counter.

"Hi Sarge," he said.

She looked a little blurred: "Do you have another copy of the photograph you took of Cleo?"

He shook his head. "I only had one made. Sorry."

"Could you give me the negative?"

"Aw Sarge," he said. "I got hundreds of pictures; I'd have to sort through—they're not marked—all that crap is packed."

That night he unpacked his stuff remembering her face. "She wants, she gets," he murmured, taking out paint brushes, watercolors, drawings and books and little souvenirs. He began going through the seventy odd rolls of film.

The following morning the cooks brought the griddles around, unpacked the eggs and arranged bowls with little opened boxes of cereal inside; the troops came in, and he went to work. When Sgt. Wilks was waiting for her eggs, he looked in her angry eyes and handed her the small celluloid negative wrapped in tissue, watching her eyes change and become grateful, hearing her husky thanks and understanding the long sad Army days in front of her, every morning and every night, even after Cleo had sailed home, an invisible kiss, a caress, to celluloid.

Movietone

THE YEAR THE GOOD EARTH won the Pulitzer Prize, Dinah's college boyfriend ran off with another girl; that summer Dinah met a woman in a drugstore who asked, "Have a Coke?"

They took a taxi to the woman's apartment; downtown Cincinnati. Dinah was afraid.
But they drank gin and Coke, and she let the woman play with her. Say!

Sure! Swell! And she was good! Drove her wild!
Tickle that thing. Get next to it. 1935

Hurt it
Laughs   1941   Chicago,
Aw, come on

                          1946
                          Pittsburgh

"Great song," Philly said; she took a toke, and passed the joint to Dinah, and Dinah made it, and slowly leaned back against the wall.
"Billy Stayhorn," Philly exhaled.

                          Miami Beach
                          1951

Dallas
1956

New York
1960

Dinah wandered around the Village, and met Shirley. They went
in a bar and Dinah saw the guy who had been the best friend of
her old boyfriend, the fellow who had split with that other chick.
Dinah said,
"Ben."
Ben smirked and got off the barstool. "Dinah," he said. She
grinned and a little of the old feeling came back. Dinah softened,
and embraced him; Shirley put on black gloves and moved towards the door.
"Well, man, how have you been?"
"It's been a long time, Dinah."

Dinah was sore.
"That hoople," Shirley said.

Dinah stood on the sidewalk snapping her fingers. A year later,
in the winter of 1961, outside San Francisco
Late At Night
the car she was driving skidded & ripped into the back of a
slowly moving truck. Dinah was badly cut, and bruised, but her
twenty-five year old girlfriend was in shock, dying against the
dashboard & smashed windshield. Dinah climbed out and stood
on the highway with the truck driver. They stopped the first car,
gave the people orders, and directed traffic until the police arrived.
The girl in her twenties died on the way out of the car. Dinah
went to Southern California to live with a group of women her
age, occupied as secretaries and private nurses. Years and years
later, Dinah died too; in bed, in a bad mood.

105

The Source

ON APRIL DAYS IN 10TH GRADE I exchanged notes with a 9th grade girl who sat in front of me in study hall. We looked in each other's eyes.

One afternoon after school I embraced her and then we fucked. That was the first time, for us together and she laughed at me; it was like a rewarding scream.

The second fuck was at night. We sat by a stream, naked, on a mossy hillock. We talked about school and drank in cigarette smoke. Then we fucked. Afterwards we talked and then we fucked again. We dressed and I walked her to her bus stop. A month later I met her again, at night, in the same place, for the last time. I was not cool. The last fuck was wild.

There was a boy, before that. We skipped school together, and fucked by a river. And much later, another boy, in highweeds in a field, at night.

In a game, I was on the pitcher's mound. There was a runner on first. I bent for the signal, got it and straighened. I put both hands on my chest and held the ball in the glove. I looked over my left shoulder at the runner on first base. He took a lead.

It was around three and the sun was at that hot point in its drop. I saw the sky. I saw myself standing on the pitcher's mound. I saw other teams on other diamonds in St. Louis slanting towards the horizon. I saw it all.

Five years later on a road march in Germany I saw it again, and four years later was reminded of it by the movie *La Strada* as a girl turned off a road, to be in a room in a house on a European plain.

Uncle Brent came up on the porch.

"Hello, Seabiscuit," he smiled to me. I shook his hand. Those death defying summer afternoons of 1942.

"Hi, girls," he said to my aunts. Then he said hello to my mother. "Hello, Kerra." He sat beside me on the swing. He asked my aunts, in turn, how things were. They nodded and said fine, things were fine. Aunt Mil grinned, "Not s'young as we used t'be."

Then he messed my hair and asked how I was and what I had been doing with myself. I shrugged and smiled and I asked him how he had been, he wasn't my uncle, and he looked out through the trellis of morning glories and said, well . . . he had been behaving himself. His collar was frayed and I was intensely aware of his heart, beating away beneath the thin white shirt.

I saw Seabiscuit and POST TIME in his eyes. The roar of the crowd and volume of dollars won and lost. I saw him, surely with a woman in a yellow dress; a pint in his coat pocket and some folding money in his wallet. I saw America in his eyes, his sad light gray eyes. I saw so much. I saw my father before he died; alone in New York.

My mother drank coffee and Uncle Brent sat beside me on the swing on our front porch in Kirkwood, Missouri, not saying a thing but telling me the history of a time that had failed. And when his sad gaze fell on me, and our eyes met, it was confirmed, and my twelve year old heart went straight, and altogether, out to him.

Delma Ciminello

THEY WALKED TO THE TOP of the hill, crossed the street and walked down the other side into town.

He watched her, conscious of her straight back, her womanly figure and her silence. But he was self-conscious: she would graduate in June and he was yet in 9th grade. Every day he looked to see if she would be walking home alone. She was very popular. But she liked to walk home alone.

He loved to walk with her, along that silent mile from school to her house and say goodbye at the end of her front walk.

At moments she looked at him with an uncontrived directness, and his answering look seemed to please her, but then a distant thing in her eyes seemed to deepen, and he felt she saw him as if in seeing him he became himself to her and so she admitted him, giving him freedom but whitening it by her reaction to the implication she had allowed—he saw she was looking into herself and a hardly visible mist was cast between them.

One day she asked, with her introspective smile, "Why do you like to walk home with me?" The words "walk home," and "me"—the evenness of her meaning made his mind into planes of light and dark consciousness, and he was a little frightened of his own passion and awed that she had seemed to speak to it; showing a hard to explain confusion.

When he saw her going home alone, he ran toward her, and within a distance not to disturb her, he would call her name, trees and lawns—her figure floated down the sidewalk, hearing him she turned, and seeing him, smiled; he caught up with her. "A 9th grade boy," she would describe him. "He walks home with me."

He stammered and laughed while she smiled; he brightened towards her. "Delma," he smiled. "I did a drawing of you today."

She looked along the horizon and laughed. "Of me?"

"A profile," he said seriously, "in study hall."

He slipped it from his notebook and they paused on the sidewalk; he held it in mittened hands while she looked.

The drawn line had captured the straightness of her forehead and nose, the clean edge of her chin and the graceful descent of her throat. He had had trouble with the profile eye and lips but he had caught the attention of her expression and the total drawing looked like Delma with her face up and her eyes lowered.

"Does it look like me?" and she let him hold it.

"Yes," he said. He put the drawing back in his notebook and they walked on in silence. She looked in front of her as they crossed a street; she said, "I don't know how to draw, but it looks good. You're good."

They stopped at the foot of a high embankment. Branches of great trees reached over the quiet asphalt street.

He looked at her. She looked in his eyes, then seeing him rise within himself and become himself, he held her in his life beside his own life, he held her in his heart and his spirit stirred and made his body strong, his spirit sparkled in his eyes and on his lips. But a pale mist appeared before Delma and bid him stay away; it was the whiteness of the unbegun. He stood in the street as Delma withdrew from him.

He took her hand. She was over the trees following the sky, he held her walking body's hand leading her home, and at the end of the front walk broke the silence to murmur goodbye. She removed her hand from his for the last time, whispered goodbye and walked silently into her house.

Early in the Morning

THE OUTDOOR GAME YARD of the Catholic nursery school was empty. Chairs were stacked to one wall beside a row of brightly painted tricycles. Blocks and balloonsize balls lay around.

The janitor sat on a kiddy chair facing her. The girl, a teacher, stood not two feet away, throwing a ball above his head against the brick wall behind him. She threw, just missing his head; it bounced and she caught it.

They were talking. She threw the ball girlishly, awkwardly but surely. The ball bounced above his head; she caught it with both hands and held it on the palm of one hand.

He sat in the tiny chair, hands clasping it between his legs. He was an old man with white hair and pink skin and bright blue eyes. She threw and caught the ball and then popped it in the air, just a few inches, caught it and did it again. Then she held it by her side, arching her hip so that the pleats of the skirt moved. His shoulders sagged; she shrugged. He grinned. She threw the ball over his head; it bounced against the wall and she caught it and threw it again. She caught it and popped it in the air like before. It hung in mid-air. Her fingers spread and the skin of her palms stretched tight. As the ball came down her hands jerked, she caught it; she popped the ball into the air again and she caught it. Each time she threw the ball, either in the air or against the wall, she took her eyes away from his. Each time she had the ball she held her eyes on his while they talked. When she threw the ball, she stopped talking. When she had the ball, she talked. She talked and smiled and shifted her feet and swung her skirt and moved her arms, talking and not talking, throwing the ball in the middle of a sentence, taking her eyes away from his, catching the ball,

110

holding it, toying with it, looking at him and then throwing it, either in the air or against the wall, breaking a sentence, catching it, talking, throwing, catching, talking, playing with it and talking. She threw it over his head against the wall. She caught it, moved her hips and threw, catching it. His mouth was level with her navel. She threw the ball and it bounced off the wall above his head and she caught it.

The door opened and screaming children rushed out, anchored by two laughing nuns. The girl threw the ball, caught the ball, and slipped inside the building.

The Invisible Glass

AFTER HE MARRIED JEANETTE, it was easier to let—her—he went along with her. He was thirty years old, six feet tall, and a little fat. He had a good job, good enough, not as good as, he was sorry, he could do better, maybe, but Jeanette was pretty, their little home was nice, it might be—she had difficulty getting things in place, pictures, furniture—that magazine table, where she wanted, if she could find where she wanted it like Joan, Joan had a wonderful sense of—those drapes, did you ever see anything like those—oh, Dick, do you want—

The car ran fine, it wasn't—but got him where, the office where he worked was large with bright colors and modern furniture, Richard had a desk by the window.

"Dick," Sally said. She was a secretary. "Here's the report; Mr. Winters said bring it in before you go to lunch."

She dropped it on the desk. He glanced at it. "Thanks, Sally." He looked out the window. Horace sat on the edge of the desk. Horace grinned. "Good morning, friend."

Richard turned. "Hi—hey, could you give me a hand with these figures? I—this morning, I—"

They worked it out.

Richard parked the car, got out, closed and locked it and went up the walk, he saw the dog barking behind the window. He went inside, patted the animal and looked toward the kitchen. He called.

"Hi. I'm home."

"Dick?"

"It's me."

He went in the kitchen, she glanced over her shoulder and said hello; as she said hello he crossed the kitchen to the refrigerator. She turned, as he opened it.

"Coke?"

He scratched his neck, nodding, looking and finding it in the refrigerator. He took out the bottle, some ice and made the drink. He went in the living room, sat down in his chair and unfolded the paper. The dog barked, crossing the room to him. Dick patted the dog. The phone rang. He rose, and answered it.

"Hello?"

"Dick? This is Nan. Busy now? Leland and I thought maybe you'd like to come over."

"Wait a minute, here's Nettie," he said, feeling Jeanette slip in behind him. He handed her the receiver, quietly saying, "It's Nan."

"Nan?" Jeanette asked, face bright. Listening, she nodded. "Um hum, well, let me ask Dick."

He had sat down and unfolded the paper and was looking at the television listings. Jeanette said,

"Dick?"

He looked at her.

The first martini made him giddy. "Let me have some more potato chips."

"Dick, you're already overweight!"

"I hate fat young men."

"I know," he laughed. "Leland, the cheese dip!"

They were talking about the Jackie Gleason show. Leland was imitating that comedian and Nan and Jeanette were egging him on. Richard sipped from the second martini and apologized: he had fallen asleep while the show had been on.

"Hey—where's my glass?"

They burst into laughter. "Glass?" Leland mocked. "It seems to be in your hand, kind of around your drink!"

"The other one!" Richard said angrily. "It was right here."

The girls were in hysterics. Leland chuckled. "What kind of glass, dad?" They all teased him.

On the way to the car he rough-housed with Jeanette. He was

glad to be outside. Jeanette laughed and told him to stop, she pushed him away. They got in the car and he felt anger and confusion, he took the wheel, raised his shoulders, raced the engine, the car lurched into the street, where he stopped it.

"Why are we stopping?"

He glared out the windshield.

"*Drive*, Dick!"

They drove home. They had supper, watched television a while and went to bed early.

He woke feeling an urgency. He looked around the dim room, and after a moment the feeling paled and shifted into a necessity to know the time in which he was—he was ahead of himself, yet almost stopped in the middle: he looked at the clock. The indicated numbers said he had another hour to sleep. His heart sank and rose at the same time hurt and delighted, and in the odd polarity he looked at Jeanette beside him, and seeing her awry in her sleep, he also saw himself and felt a strange regret which was then halved by a necessity to move ahead and away, but to also backtrack and catalog feelings to return to the mood of the urgent awakening, and figure out what was significant in a dream which he must have dreamt that had awakened him as it had.

He backtracked through necessity and regret to the time in which he was, trying to figure out how the waking sensation had seemed important and why it had occurred with its particular evasive identity, and as if someone had then touched him, he distinctly remembered the waking feeling, and in the order of what was familiar to him, he felt out of place, and he tensed, knowing he would never know . . . he had felt the character of the dream, and now he was losing it by being aware of the self that tried to summon the self that knew. He pulled the covers around himself meaningfully: placating the safekeeping mind which was alarmed.

He felt he was dwindling, as though he had once been large and all of himself.

He lay back despairing, staring out of his shrinking skull, watching running images and hearing himself breathing in a growing panic, realizing his metaphorical time of one hour was

moving away from him, and his time-keeping consciousness fla-
grantly slanted into it, counting fifty-eight minutes fifty-seven
seconds fifty-eight fifty-nine snapping into sixty, fifty-nine minutes, one second, two seconds and three going. He closed his eyes,
counting, really exhausted.

And then an altogether understood sense of time seemed to
direct him towards the activity of busy streets which included a
superior sense of other things going on elsewhere. Possibly his
time was part of another story, as accepted as it also seemed to act
out another potential, as if his longing for completion was even
originally incomplete, and that dimly envisioned world seemed
nearly *thus* X *and* familiar, young and old at the same time, and
confounded by a painful necessity to begin quickly.

Remember Pearl Harbor

for Ed & Jennifer

SHE OPENED THE DOOR of the refrigerator and took out the lettuce; she took out the mayonnaise; she took out the butter and milk, and she closed the door and took out the peanut butter from the cupboard and after taking the breadloaf from the breadbox, she made a peanut butter sandwich he would like, and eating it and drinking the glass of milk she looked out the window.

The lawn sloped like a long backyard to the neighbor's backyard; they were forever sitting in their backyard; her little hedge hadn't done much good, and she looked at her sloping backyard lawn a nice lawn and she looked into the living room where no television set stood.

Her husband sat on that sofa every Sunday and read *The Post-Dispatch;* she missed him there.

Out of the corner of her eye a figure—at ease in a humorous way—stood on the lawn, and as she smiled and turned, realized no one was there. She looked in again where her husband would be if it were Sunday and saw the figure out of her eye on the lawn. It looked like, smiling as the man was, curiously, like Gatsby.

Her son lay beside a beautiful captain's wife on the beach in Hawaii, and they necked; her son felt he had made a conquest, it surely was a form of something that he could go in and out of Headquarters Gates with her driving her car, and then, having her there, must be something, too, yet, he postulated, if she wasn't a captain's wife it wouldn't mean what it did, she would be what she was without being a captain's wife and he would be a guy.

In the mind of the man on the beach beside the other man's wife she and he strode differently; what was extraordinary about

116

it they were their own experience as well away as at home; mis-understanding was across the water.

Boyishly he grinned: "Let the rest of the world—"

"Yeah," she murmured. "Go by. I believe."

"What's the matter?" he asked.

She looked at him. She didn't love him, but she loved to fuck with him, and she turned to him, and confusing him, said,

"Hold me."

He held her and gazed at the Pacific.

The man just stood there, smiling. Where had he come from? She munched the sandwich, wondering.

The sunlight streamed as if forever, through the windows as they rose and fell, like sex in a slick magazine he wondered about her intense pleasure, and not like a hammer; she was purely delighted, and the man, the other man, who flew hundreds of miles away thought of her in the sky, of her face. How he yearned to love her! He would take her to the dance this weekend, and blinding lines crossed his face, and the enemy planes were by them even as he wheeled, wheeling looking at them and the holes their 30 caliber bullets had made in the cockpit. He saw his were four, and theirs were six.

She was gone as he worked the machinegun on its pivot, and yelled over his shoulder to the pilot, "Get 'em Charley!" yet seeing the ships below.

"*You* get 'em," Charley snapped back, and he moved around seeing the Zeroes coming in just under the sun, and firing, looping his heavy 50s out watching the enemy planes' wing guns spit lines at him he saw his shells strike and strike again, the belly of the enemy plane zoomed over, another, and Charley banked and 30 caliber shells tore through the housing, and he saw the third Zero had them—

Charley yelled—"Heads up!"

Frantically, furiously he swiveled his guns as the plane banked, and suddenly dived, the Zero was out of sight and then he saw it zip underneath, but underneath was up above, and the enemy plane twinkled away, his plane levelled, the sea and sky and clouds fell into place and he saw two Zeroes come in like ten to twelve, towards him, the sky was so bright behind their approaching crisscross he sighted under them firing above, looping a crazy lateral figure 8 clothesline of bullets and as Charley dove very fast to the right the Zero coming in on 12 blew up, and the plane on ten to was beyond them so close overhead, and so quickly gone he only realized he was in a panic crouch fighting with the guns to get them around pointlessly because one plane was down and the other was gone by, and he remembered him and Charley yelling "There's one! There's one!" hysterically, the housing smashed and shredded from shells, and his skin crawling with fear, and the Zeroes hung on, rising and coming at them again, riddling the torpedo planes, yet the torpedo planes hung on too, and went in low, into the meat of the broadside destroyer fire, Charley letting the torpedo go while the Zeroes chased them from above, while the inverted gull-winged Grummans chased the Zeroes, the man at the guns doing his part altogether angrily, there wasn't anything else to do, and there they were, and so he fired at them, and saying hey Charley, and the old plane for some reason was all by itself over the Pacific, and the ships and fighters way behind, Charley, and then he saw a torpedo plane to his right, climbing, and then another was on its way up, too, and he said, "Hey, Charley," and twisted around in the wreckage, "What happened?" Charley didn't know, Charley had been hit.

"Can you make it in?"

Charley hated him. Boy did he hate him. And Charley made it in. He was afraid of Charley, even with the planes—the Zeroes, the destroyers, the cruisers—firing at him—what he was really afraid of was Charley; he sat at the table, looking a little haunted as she made coffee, and when she served it to him, her hands trembled.

Man Steps Into Space

for Martha

AFTER WORK THE BIG BLONDE SALESGIRL from Texas sat on a bar-stool beside Thomas; he had gone to the bank to make the evening deposit and she had crossed the avenue gone into the bar and ordered two large steins of Ballantine, and as he entered she pulled the stool out and he joined her, both murmuring hello hello to each other touching the steins hoisting and drinking.

It was seven o'clock on a hot summer evening New York girls had come from work eaten washed up and were walking with friends to and from the department stores and Thomas and the salesgirl from Texas talked and Thomas watched the parade as evening turned into night a particularly pretty girl passed, and for a moment looked Thomas's way. The charm of her face and sweetness of flesh in summer clothes touched him, and yet took him into another consciousness, she disappeared in the crowd and he was puzzled; the blonde salesgirl watched a slow frown darken his face and she loved him because he was funny and brilliant; they supplemented each other's need for friendship side by side selling furniture everyday and week and when she saw the pretty girl look at Thomas Thomas double-crossed the girl from Texas by going into his mind and closing the door. Okay; she winked.

"What is it?" she asked. "I saw her."

Thomas looked at her and shook his head.

She said bitterly, "You're real fun."

He nodded and moved his hands as if searching through smoke, "I hear voices," he said and she nodded, "You're crazy." "Yes," he nodded; he told her a different story.

She was disgusted; his story, she thought, didn't have that much in it, Thomas looked at her and said, "It does and it doesn't, depending on where you're sitting," and he smiling flicked the switch: sitting.

Sounds of laughter.

It was yellow face again, sitting to his left as the girl appeared—and as Thomas was startled by the masked figure in the corner of his eye the girl went away in the crowd Thomas's heart yet following—cherry lips in yellow said,

"Put her face before your eyes."

Thomas did so, and as red lips opened and closed Thomas nodded in a comprehension of grief and loneliness, and the harlequin man, the fellow with the yellow face and blue plume of hair gazed sternly at him.

Surely, behind her pretty face I did see misery of loneliness and an unknown despair of existence and I knew her attractive body would not be resilient; that she would be in fact vague in all ways. You are right. Her eyes were fearful and I saw their deep dullness; the dull smokecenter covering what she was afraid to be. Red lips moved again.

Look—but then let her go by! Lean toward the wife whom you fear—who is different from you. And what is a pretty face, and a body seeming in summer clothes? The wrong dream, only you lead you to your own art, where your face is, she is; do you see you, my Thomas? Yellow laughed a savage amusement. Why don't you be me? I'm not afraid of your wife.

Around a year later Thomas had a dream.

He was walking down that avenue; the rain had stopped, bright colors of neon signs reflected off cars, wet asphalt and glass windows; the air was fresh, sharp and though it was summer he was chilled, although warm as if his wife were within him—he sensed his friend the blonde Texan girl near him in a knowing way and his feet were bare.

He pushed open the swinging doors of the tavern and went in but the bar was old in a different way, a hollow way, and Thomas stood in his feet tracks on the floor saying to the owner, "Where's the familiar bartender Ireland?"

"Ireland doesn't work here anymore," the owner gravely said. Thomas frowned and experienced sorrow. He turned, and the food counter, which had been just inside the door, was without the usual refrigerator and stove, and pots and pans—"Where's Pop?" Thomas asked. The owner shook his head, his rimless glasses glinted sharp: "Gone," he said, and Thomas trudged up and down the wet avenue looking in and out of stores for his shoes.

That was the year Thomas quit selling furniture, he got a new job working with an importing firm and one day he sat at his desk by the window on the sixteenth floor looking out at the city with the telephone in his hand, he was dialing the number of the old furniture store, sitting tipped back in the swivel chair running his eyes up and down the Empire State Building; the switchboard operator's voice said the name of the furniture store, Thomas said um hum and asked for the uptown branch and the operator fondly said hello to him. He grinned across the city to her; "Hi sweetheart; how are you?"

"Fine," she smiled, and he saw her face before him. She paused—"How are you?"

"Fine. I have a new job—are you looking?"

"Yes I heard—not yet," she laughed, "though I ought to be." Then she said softly, "This dump."

Thomas chuckled, "Amen."

"Here's uptown," she said, and the big blonde girl—Texas voice said the name of the store—"Uptown." Thomas said hello. She cried "Oh God, how I miss you!"

After work he took the BMT uptown and met her as the furniture store closed, they crossed the avenue pushing open swinging doors to two large steins of Ballantine at the bar, toasted and drank and lit cigarettes; the owner smiled and asked Thomas if he had a new job, yes, how was it, fine, and Ireland came on duty pulling his white apron around by the string and tying it across his waist while he treated himself to a shot of Scotch with icewater chaser and inquired if Thomas had a new job yes—pay better? Sure, Ah, and the health of the blonde from Texas—while at the same moment a different figure with flat cheeks and thin lips sitting beside Thomas leaned and touched shoulders with him saying out of the corner of his undertone imitating a shadow a thumb appearing by Thomas's cheek the figure pressed close, "Did ya notice?" Thomas looked where the thumb pointed—the

121

food counter was without the usual refrigerator and stove, pots and pans, "I had a dream," Thomas said, his eyes on those eyes of the figure which darkened in cynicism; thin lips moved, "Whaddya mean a dream—" "I mean a dream," Thomas said, "the food counter was closed." The figure nodded bitterly and Thomas turned to the blonde girl: "I had a dream."

"A dream," she smiled. "Thomas Crimmins had a dream."

He told her the dream. "Okay," she said, "and thanks." He told her to look, she did, she didn't get it. Look carefully, he said: the refrigerator, the old stove and all the banged up pots and pans old Pop used were gone and so was Pop. She looked at Thomas carefully, and slowly a fine perception came into her eyes, she touched his hand, "Thomas Crimmins," she whispered; "you are fantastic."

The Pride of the Yankees

I GOT A LINE SINGLE to center which scored Mantle and sent Maris to third yet Dickey was waving me to take second. I had come in from center a little too fast, the ball hit my glove wrong, it bounced off my wrist and over my shoulder and went into center yet I had come across from left and covered as I came at the ball seeing me go into second, I picked the ball up with my webbing but of all things dropped it, I picked it up again and furiously fired it to second, my throw was to the third base side of the bag, but I caught it and pivoting with a kind of leap not to get spiked I slapped the glove across as I came in hard, knowing I was safe I made the traditional umpire gesture of safe which irritated me as I knew I had made the tag. I was wild in the stands. Maris had scored and as I came to bat I looked down to Yogi for the signal.

"Boy," Mantle later teased me, "it's lucky you goofed in center, you never would have made second."

Red Impact

I WAS DRINKING BEER in a bar on lower 3rd Avenue and idly staring at that Miller High Life anxiety gadget, as its brightly colored lines wove and looped and twisted in an endless-seeming pattern.

The bartender, Jimmy, a patient goon type, was wiping the bar and in a sense I had the eye on him which he knew, and he seemed carelessly pleased, we had a relationship of sorts, a waiting one; after I'd had a dozen or two he generally gave me one on the house.

It was a dull night. I was sitting near the door, and as the bar was small, when the door opened and the man and the girl came in and stood at the end of the bar, they were almost at my side, and the handful of people at the bar looked.

He was about five ten, and slender with a flat face and careful little ice gray eyes, and I hated and feared him immediately. He was dressed in a gray double breasted suit, pressed neat, a white shirt and pale gray and red diagonally striped tie, and as he looked along the bar at Jimmy, I saw his nails were manicured. He was at least forty-five.

The girl was as tall as he was, but young, not over twenty, and the American prototype: long light brown hair, beautifully modeled face on a skull that rose in back, like an Irish setter's skull, she was slender, poised, and beautifully dressed, yet there was something dog-like in her expression as she stood beside him; with her eyes down like that, she was having an effect on the bar.

Jimmy ambled down and stood in front of the man, and pleasantly smiled, Yeah? as the man looked Jimmy directly in the eyes without hardly moving his lips, the man put his right index finger on the bar square in front of the girl, and then moving his finger and putting it on the bar in front of himself, he said,

"Two Johnny Walker Red on the rocks."

He had an accent.

Jimmy made the drinks, and set them on the bar as directed and the man paid him, Jimmy rang it up and began wiping shotglasses and watching as the man turned to the girl, he turned completely, and facing her, with his glass in his hand, but very casually, he said,

"Drink."

She took a sip of her drink. So did he.

I lit a cigarette in a muted alarm, put my head in my left hand, stared at the bar, took a drink of my beer, like he had told me to, and cleared my throat and glanced at Jimmy. Jimmy had moved to the far end of the bar and stood in a shadow, watching. He glanced at me. I glanced at the girl and the man in the gray suit; at his flat face. He was a foreigner, and his gray eyes swung from her face and gazed directly at me with a touch of amusement, though his lips were tight, but he was completely at ease.

She, however, stood as a fine creature with lowered eyes, her lovely hand around her drink on the bar, standing beside her master. Her shoulders were slumped a little forward. Her hair had fallen a little, following the forward tilt of her head so it framed her face in a very fashionably sad way and I couldn't bear it any longer. I got up and offered her my barstool. She didn't move. The foreigner said, softly to her,

"Where are your manners? If as this gentleman has, someone offers you a seat, you accept, and you sit. *Sit down.*"

Most subtly she shook her head. No. He made a faint smile. And firmly:

"*Sit.*"

She sat down.

Then the foreign man looked at me. His gray eyes became hammered and angular, oblique, and my heart froze as his smile spread, and then I went rigid—as his words,

"You are very kind," vanished in the collective gasp from the others at the bar, as his dense gray mica eyes sparkled above a spreading stainless-steel-toothed grin.

125

The Dancing-man

for Guston

HE CAME TO WITH A CHILL: 10 years and an even thousand miles away he saw his drink on the bar; remember her. It is a man's memory. He stood by the bank. She passed with a look of hate. He jumped away from the tree.

She was coming down the street toward the bank.

It was just turning into summer, and on the evening of the day he had reacted to her on the sidewalk by the bank, he walked across town and stopped at the end of a street. He leaned against a tree and looked at her house, hungry for her.

She was coming down the street towards him; he stood by the bank.

"Hello again!" he cried.

She passed with a look of hate.

"Remember me?" she asked.

She said his name then; the way people do after a long time; his heart jumped. "Do I remember *you!* Of course! Ann Fisk!"

She laughed and nodded. She bought a pack of cigarettes and they stood away from the drug counter; people elbowed through the noontime crowd. She asked,

"Where have you been all this time?"

"Away at school four years and then the army. I got out two weeks ago."

"How do you like being home?"

"Pretty well, though I'll probably take off for New York later—"

"How was the army?" she grinned.

"Haven't you heard?" he teased.

She laughed.

"Well listen," he grinned, "how about a little cup of coffee? We can stand in line like anybody else." He laughed at himself.

"Oh I can't," she said. "I've too many things to do."

A woman elbowed between them. They stepped aside.

"Sure?" he asked. He cocked his head and smiled. "Positive?" The charm. Ann laughed. "Really," she said. "I can't."

"Aw come on." He thought he saw her eyes narrowing.

She shook her head. They stood for a moment, and then spoke in unison.

"Well, I—"

"Sure, I'll see you—"

She smiled and made a little wave. "Bye," she said. She moved into the crowd.

"Right," he said, and left the drugstore. He stood on the sidewalk for a moment, and then went down the street to the bank. He pulled on the handle of the glass door but it was locked and he stepped back perplexed. The bank was closed. He turned to go home and saw her coming down the street.

There you are in front of me, you swine, by the bank. I'll have to pass you. Back!

"Hello again!" he cried.

AH!

He leaned against a tree and looked at her house. The ground floor windows were lighted.

But the upstairs was dark and like looking into himself. She was out on a date; he envisioned her in one of the rooms in bed, her

127

body on the open sheet, her head on the pillow her eyes staring out from within, so pretty, so vehemently herself like a pool of desire in the distance beyond her mind, across a slanting field, poplars grew in perpetual night, and dark grass twisted on a gently rising hillock. Little amphibians whispered on grassy banks. And leaning against a tree on his side of the field, his monster stirred. The hackles went up, it growled and shook the dust off its back and peered angrily through the mist to the shady hillock. His monster cried out to her, and began to sing a gutteral tune, earflaps wide for her first resonant response, a beckoning hum to draw him across the shady grass to her boiling pool, grapple and slant in while she craved him arching against him in the grip of his claws to the rhythm of his buried dance.

Color of Sienna

HER FLESH WAS MYSTERIOUS under her clothes, and the paradox of frailty and determination darkened his already shady desire. But the woman in the flesh was apart from the woman as she behaved, and the woman she thought herself to be made three conflicting actions.

Knowing, she loved to know: she acted out her life in a moving complicated texture of decisions: the day began with color. What color was shimmering on the curtain by the bed? It was yellow, but what yellow? Yellow with a vertical innuendo of—was there a whisper of gold? A whisper of gold.

But what to wear?

And to have for breakfast!

He frightened her. He fascinated her, he amazed, surprised, confused, delighted, confounded and angered her.

"Oh I know *you*," she laughed. Almost a sneer. Her joke. "I know all about you!"

He sighed, "Yes," and the woman under the dress moved.

"Yes!" she exclaimed. She laughed and laughed. The heart of the woman under the dress beat fast. "But I have to be careful!" she cried. "Yes, I do!" The remote woman laughed, how right she was! But one was aware of herself thinking—the woman under the dress stiffened towards a strangely colored and excited mask: dark eyes, passionate eyes, eagerly flexing eyebrows, sensitive nostrils, anxious lips, and ah! her delicate ears.

They had a cup of coffee in the hotel drugstore and now they

129

were walking in the park. It was a hot day in July. He held her hand.

They had argued in the drugstore. Now they argued in the park. They always argued; yet there was hardly an argument, and each time she was more tensely beautiful. She was a splendid woman.

"You think you're my first! You think I've never done anything!" She smiled mysteriously. "I've been with lots of men!"

His unusual silence irritated her. They walked on. "I know you," she said angrily, "you're nothing but a—" she burst into shrill laughter, her mouth a grinning grimace, "shit!" She laughed and laughed. He threw his hands in the air.

"What does that mean!" she demanded.

He started to speak, but didn't. She thought he had steeled himself against her.

"Say it!" she sang. "Come on! Speak, child!"

They emerged from the park onto the boulevard. Traffic rolled by. The park lay behind them. Hotels rose into the sky.

He looked up at them.

They crossed with the light, walked by a crowded hotel patio swimming pool, and down the secluded street to her apartment.

Of several rooms. A front room, a bright sunparlor faced the quiet street that entered the busy boulevard. The park lay beyond. Hedges and walks angled into the distance.

They had tea and cookies. But she was angry. They hardly spoke. He left at five thirty, and took the long bus ride home. A few days later, as he had told her, his visit to St. Louis was coming to an end. He called her, and said he was going back to New York. She said she was sorry they had acted the way they did during his stay.

"As my life is complicated," she said, "I should be more"—she thought—"cool."

He said he would write, and she said that would be fine, she would answer, and he said goodbye.

He did write, and she answered. But later he stopped. But she continued—each letter in scarlet ink, lengthy and curious in introspection; her language was biblical in its rhythm, dark and sexual in its imagery. Executed in a thin and exquisite feminine line. The last letter ended, "I'm coming to New York. Don't meet me at the airport, I'll call you from the hotel."

She talked about herself. He drank coffee and smoked cigarettes. Her face was passive, but she spoke continually, telling how she had improved, she was a whole woman now, she could do things now, she—her analyst approved the New York move. The man said it would be good for her to get a job and work on her own.

She had lost weight. Her face was drawn and the shady erotic color that had settled under the eyebrows and above the cheekbones, was becoming pronounced from ear to ear. Her cheeks caved at the dimples, thrusting her shady mouth forward hungrily, drawing the lips flat. The woman under the dress was losing ground. The woman at the job watched close, but the woman in the distance had come to take her name. A confused two-legged ladycat with sienna colored eye cavities was determined to tempt and walk down any public street—out of the jungle of her past: her lacklustre rich parents, that animal beneath the dress was fighting for life.

A week later she called to say goodbye; she was going back to St. Louis. Would he have lunch with her?

"No." Softly.

But he would not.

She was shaken. In a closing silence she murmured goodbye. But a month later she was back in New York. "For good," she said on the phone.

She was in her slip when he arrived. He was drunk. She looked at him. He stood before her. He clapped his hands on her hips and looked in her eyes. She said,

"I don't want to do that at all."

"I do," he grunted.

"You."

He sat on the bed hopelessly. She couldn't, couldn't. He waited while she dressed.

They went to a movie and began arguing in the lobby. "I didn't want to come," she sneered, "*you* did!"

"What do you want to do?" he asked.

"I don't know! Why don't you take me somewhere, or don't *you* know what to do!" She snarled and laughed. People pushed by. He pulled her inside, down an aisle where they found seats. A moment later she said she was going for a drink of water; ten minutes later he found her sitting on the steps of the loge, a cop standing over her. She saw who was angrily coming towards her, held out her hand and sang to the cop,

"Oh here he is! At last!"

He dragged her out of the theater while she laughed. They waited for a cab. She stopped laughing. They got a cab and went to her hotel in hot silence.

They got out of the cab. He paid the driver, but she stepped behind him and the doorman opened the door. Without looking back she went straight in. She walked over the rich carpet, almost floating, arms a little out from her sides and both hands in fists, her head held high, her shoulders and neck drawn rigid. Her womanly hips swung beautifully and step by step her lovely legs moved her away.

He walked home in that same step by step; and thus they drew apart, but in the years to come he would receive a card, or letter, or a phone call, or spot her crossing a crowded room in a different city, to sit beside him and talk, and carry on the argument as if they had just parted.

Reflections of Steel

for Leser & Henry

I HAD KNOWN THE OLDER MAN as I had known Peter, in a different time, and seeing them again at that party was strange because they returned my past to me in a way that it seemed to be happening within me yet before my eyes, and as the man in the gray suit crossed the room and sat beside Peter and introduced himself, my knowing what would happen, and later did happen seemed a connection of sentiment, and in my reaction to it I realized the difference between them and myself. I was not them—seeking each other—I followed myself, I knew my stink—one day I would get me. Yet in those days I had gone with the older man because I was lonely for a sexual body man or woman, it didn't matter, I needed contact to awaken me to my routine consciousness, and in the moments before orgasm I realized who I was and what I was doing, who I was with, where, and then forgot in the pleasure—to sleep like a rewarded selfish man-girl.

But Peter thought it should mean something, and I yet see his pointed shocked face when I told him it only meant myself to me, although, at the party, so drawn to what I knew so well, I did speak to them—I told them a story—before they quickly left. How I know them! How I know it! I really felt European! I can hear the older man close the door to his apartment, and taking off his topcoat and scarf ask Peter if he would like to watch television; the same routine as with me and I am also Peter, and I remember

---

Note: The story of the young man of the ancient race is from *Bushman Tales* by W. H. I. Bleek, published circa 1895, which brought into English for the first time the folk tales and prayers of the Kalahari Bushmen.

the tall windows and the thousands of long playing records, and the sterile neatness, the rugs and the polished furniture and the soft light . . .

"Want to watch TV?"

"No."

He turned it off. "Drink?"

"Please."

"Same as you were having at the party?"

"Please."

He went in the kitchen. He put ice in the glasses and sent Scotch swirling over the cubes. He returned to the living room. Peter was sitting in the chair by the table.

"Will you play something?"

He gave Peter the drink and was thanked with a look. He crossed the room. "What would you like?"

"Something light."

"Mozart?"

"Is Mozart light? All right."

He stood by the turntable and then bent down. He looked across the room, from that position. He was smiling. He asked, "What Mozart?"

"Anything. You must know more about it than I do."

He got on his hands and knees, and as he looked through the rows of long playing records, he began to make dog sounds. He sat on the floor growling and whimpering, and took out two handfuls of records and looked through them, discarding them on the floor beside him. He took out that many more and put them in his lap and sorted through. He pushed the pile away and took out as many more, and halfway through he found a record, whimpered and barked and took it out of the jacket, dropped the jacket on the floor and stood up, put the record over the spindle, lifted and moved the arm to his right. It made a soft click, and the turntable began to revolve. He put the nose of the arm over the outside band and lowered it, lifting his hand as the needle caught and Mozart's Symphony No. 40 began. He turned one knob, treble, to his right, and the bass knob also to his right. He lowered the volume and crossed the room with his drink in his hand. He sat in a chair across from his friend. He sipped his drink, put it on the low table between them and proceeded to light a cigar.

He puffed.

"What did you play?"

"Something by Mozart. I don't know." He grinned. "Who knows, these days?"

"I don't," his friend said. He was a young man.

"Is the drink good?"

"You know it is."

They sat in silence.

"Oh," the older man exclaimed. "I bought something today. A book." He rose and crossed to the bookshelf. Four shelves high, stained oak, gold wire supports. He ran his finger along the spines of the books and then bent down.

"Here it is," he said, straightening. He opened it, riffled the pages and brought it across the room to his young friend.

"Who is it by?"

"A young poet. Boy from England."

"Is it good?"

"Why don't you read it?"

"I mean, do you like it?"

"Of course I do. Many of the poems seem the same, but—" he laughed— "they aren't. And there are interesting ideas. The title poem is on page thirty-four, I think."

He paused.

"John Wrywer," his young friend said reading, "twenty-seven years old, from Birmingham. And they go on with the jacket reviews. Doesn't sound unusual."

"No," the older man laughed. "It seems anybody can write these days. Anybody does." He puffed on his cigar. "I don't," he said.

"Yes you do."

"Do I?"

"I think so."

"When?"

"You have your secret little jokes—"

"That's not writing."

"By inflection it is."

"No, it isn't."

"Yes it *is*. The expression on your face is."

"Expression?"

"It really isn't *writing*, but the way you say the words that are on your mind, I mean, with a sneer, it—"

"Do I sneer?"

"Sure you do."

"Sneer?"

"Sneer. A little sneer is always on your face."

"Oh well, a little sneer. That's different. Nobody minds a little sneer occasionally. What's mankind to do if it doesn't sneer now and then?"

The young man closed the book and put it on the table. He lit a cigarette and soon he didn't know.

The older man finished his drink, puffed on the cigar and nestled into the chair. Then he leaned back. "Later I'll play something else. Have you ever heard *The Card Game?*"

"The title is—what is that—Cézanne's painting?"

"That's *The Card Players*. This is Stravinsky. It's good."

"Stravinsky. I like *Petrouchka* and *The Rite*—"

"They are good. But I enjoy *History of the Soldier* and some of his wind things."

"I loved *The Firebird* when I was young."

"We all did."

"I mean the augmented version."

"I do too. Stravinsky is part of growing up. A parallel in painting would be Hopper, and in writing, Cummings."

"Cummings is my favorite poet!"

"You're still growing up. And I'm not saying anything bad about Cummings, he's simply a part of growing up and entering into larger and more complicated ideas. Yeats, for example."

"I—haven't read much Yeats."

"You mean you haven't read *any* Yeats." The older man said feigning a shocked look: "You haven't read any *Yeats?*" he smiled, and then he laughed. He crossed the room and sorted through the records until he found the one he wanted. He removed the Mozart symphony, put it in its jacket and dropped it on the floor. He put on *The Card Game*, and as the music floated into the room he crossed to the bookshelf, took the Macmillan edition of *The Collected Poems of W. B. Yeats* from a shelf and carried it to his young friend. "Find *The Second Coming* and read it to me."

He went in the kitchen and took out more ice. "I think it's on page 182," he called. "Or 183. Around there." He returned with a dish of ice and the bottle of Scotch. He put them on the table and sat down, smiling and pouring Scotch and adding ice. His friend said,

"Here it is, page 184."

And his young voice began while the older man smoked his cigar and sipped his drink.

"I don't understand it."

The older man smiled. "You didn't read *The Second Coming*, you read *Three Things*."

"You don't understand either," the young man laughed. "It was around page 183."

"Yes I do, it's just difficult to explain." He chuckled then. "All three."

He rose, crossed the room and abruptly cut off *The Card Game*, starting a record by Erroll Garner. "You're a tease."

"Who is that?"

He said, "Garner," and the phone rang. "I have it," he said, and holding his drink in his left hand he lifted the receiver with his right. "Axel here," he said into the mouthpiece. "Well, why don't you?" He laughed and hung up.

"Who was that?"

"Armand."

"Who is Armand?"

"A friend of mine; he'll be over soon. Good company, you'll enjoy him."

"What does he do?"

"Nothing very honest."

"Axel, your cigars are marvelous," Armand said.

"I know," Axel said.

Peter watched Armand. Axel asked him, "How is the drink?"

Armand sipped. "Good!"

"How is the job coming along?" Axel smiled.

"Fine," Armand laughed. "It takes time."

"Well, everything takes time," Axel laughed. "I mean, what is worthwhile that doesn't take time?"

"Money," Peter said. "But it—"

Armand interrupted: "Axel baby, your young wife just said the holy word."

The two men burst into laughter.

He stood in the middle of the room, his drink in his hand. He gestured with the hand which held the cigar. "Axel," he said, "if this was my apartment—what the hell is that you're playing?"

"André Previn," Peter said. "Don't you like it?"

"Yeah! Why not?" Armand laughed. He looked across the room and then crossed to a framed drawing on the wall. "What's this?"

"A drawing," Axel puffed. "An early Mondrian."

"Oh, yeah," Armand nodded. "He did that boogie picture."

"*Broadway Boogie Woogie*," Peter said, standing. His face was flushed. "Don't be ignorant about Mondrian!" he cried. "Mondrian was wonderful. Nobody knows about Mondrian! Nobody!" He glared at Armand.

"Okay kid, I like it."

Peter sat down, hands trembling.

"He gets excited," Axel smiled. "He likes Mondrian."

"I do," Peter said defensively.

The following morning after breakfast, Axel was saying, "I'll be home around four. We can go down to the Village for supper."

"I think I'll leave," Peter said.

"Aren't you comfortable here?"

"Yes, but I'd—I'd like to do some things. Oh, well, I—I might stay a while. But not all day."

"I hope you stay. But if you go give me a call tonight."

"All right."

Axel left a key and money on the table.

Peter made a cup of coffee and took it into the living room as

Axel gave the cab driver the address.

Peter listened to the Second Brandenberg Concerto, smoked a cigarette and drank coffee. He then crossed the room to the bookshelf and casually looked at the book and magazine titles, neatly arranged in alphabetical sections, each section seeming as complete as it could be, and the names of the people on the magazine staffs, Peter was sure, were all friends of Axel's. Peter returned to the chair and sat down again, awkwardly humming with Bach. He spotted the book of Wrywer's poems and picked it up and leafed through. His eyes fell on the title poem, he settled in the chair, and began to read. He began it again, more or less skipping through to the last three stanzas:

> Came then a dream, of fantastic vision,
> Of mathematical night and superstition.
> A robèd spectre seated gazed
> Through a slender curve he raised
> Out arm's length. The sculptured bone
> Made body's edge the edge of stone,
> And sunken doorway's blackened pits
> Facade for shattered daytime wits.
> That spectre toward me turned,
> At me his endless eye-holes burned.
> A naked German whore was there
> Beside me. She saw my stare,
> My nightmare face, my deep despair.
>
> The gloomy years that daily followed
> Were then reflections, hollowed
> To a steely shallow shaft
> Of me, whose eye had seen the Deathly half.
>
> A power omnipotent, strange, severe,
> Sweeps the land with crackling fear.
> I in my state of indecision,
> Lose my faculties of recognition.
> Instead of charging army's flanks

I see retreating, staggered ranks.
Instead of rain soaked summer grass
I see lakes of blood as bright as glass.

Peter turned the page and saw another poem, turned the page back and realized the poem was finished. He closed the book and put it on the table, and was aware of silence. The record was over.

He sat in the quiet room somewhat distracted; feeling a desire for more coffee, went into the kitchen, and while the water heated he looked out the window; buildings angled together and shafts of sunlight brought out the natural color of brick, above a rooftop the sky was the blue of air travel posters and he felt it was a fine warm day in the city.

From his chair he looked across the room, and continued in the frame of his distraction, vaguely wondering why it so happened he was in Axel's apartment, what would happen next and what he was going to do in his life; he settled more comfortably in the chair. He was in Axel's apartment because Axel brought him home from the party, etc., and Peter felt that he really didn't much care what happened next, what would happen depended on Axel, probably get a job modeling for television.

Secretly he didn't like Axel and was angry at himself for letting himself be taken so easily. Memories of the party made him frown, it had been just another party, it had all taken place in an overtone, nobody knew what they were doing or even why they were there, they were probably bored. When you meet someone it should mean something.

But the story Axel told about Jack Zero was good. Columbus, Ohio. Axel had wanted and had gotten the works, violently in a gasoline alley, and Peter had at first been frightened but then laughed and they looked at him and then they all laughed, Axel the loudest. Then suddenly a dark man with a lined yellow face spoke to us about a young man, a young man of the early race, who, formerly, hunting, ascended a hill; he became sleepy; while he sat looking around for game, he became sleepy. And he thought that he would first lie down; for he was not a little sleepy. For what could have happened to him today? Because he had not previously felt like this. The lion had made him sleepy; the lion in its way had made the young man sleepy.

And he lay down on account of it; and he slept, while a lion came; it went to the water pit, because the noonday had killed it; it was thirsty; and it espied the man lying asleep; and it took up the man.

And the man awoke startled; and he saw that it was a lion which had taken him up. And he thought that he would not stir; for the lion would biting kill him, if he stirred; he would first see what the lion intended to do; for the lion appeared to think he was dead.

And the lion carried him to a zwart-storm tree; the zwart-storm tree is a large tree; and it has yellow flowers; it has no thorns; and the lion laid him in it. The lion put the man into the tree, at the bottom of it. And the lion thought that it would be thirsty if it ate the man; it would first go to the water, that it might go to drink; it would come afterwards to eat, when it had drunk; for, it would be thirsty if it ate.

And it trod the man's head between the stems of the zwart-storm tree; and it went back. And the man turned his head a little. The tree hurt the back of the man's head; therefore he moved it a little. And the lion looked back on account of it; namely, why had the man's head moved? when it had first thought that it had trodden, firmly fixed the man's head.

And the lion thought that it did not seem to have laid the man nicely; for, the man fell over. And it again trod, pressing the man's head into the middle of the zwart-storm tree. And it licked the man's eyes' tears. The man cried quietly, because he saw himself in the lion's power, and in great danger. And the man wept; hence it licked the man's eyes. And the man felt that a stick did not a little pierce the hollow of the back of his head; a stick had fallen down and lodged in the bottom of the tree, and the man turned his head a little, while he looked steadfastly at the lion with almost closed eyes to see if the lion remarked that he moved his head, a little. And the lion looked to see why it was that the thing seemed as if the man had moved. And it licked the man's eyes' tears. And the lion thought it would tread thoroughly pressing down the man's head, that it might really see whether it had been the one who had not laid the man down nicely. For the thing

141

seemed as if the man had stirred. And the man saw that the thing seemed as if the lion suspected that he was live; and he did not stir, although the stick was piercing him. And the lion saw that the thing appeared as if it had laid the man down nicely; for the man did not stir; and it went a few steps away, and it looked towards the man, while the man drew up his eyes; he looked through his eyelashes; he saw what the lion was doing. And the lion went away, ascending the hill; and the lion descended the hill on the other side, while the man gently turned his head because he wanted to see whether the lion had really gone away. And he saw the lion appeared to have descended the hill; and he perceived that the lion again raising its head stood peeping behind the top of the hill; the lion came back a little way to look again, because the lion thought that the thing had seemed as if the man were alive; therefore, first it wanted again to look thoroughly. For, it seemed as if the man had intended to rise; for, it had thought that the man had been feigning death. And it saw that the man was still lying down; and it thought that it would quickly run to the water, that it might go to drink, that it might again quickly come out from the water, that it might come and eat. For, it was hungry; it was the one who was not a little thirsty; therefore, it intended to go to drink, that it might come afterwards to eat, when it had drunk.

The man lay looking at it, at that which it did; and the man saw its head turning away and disappearing, with which it turned away and disappeared, seeming as if it had altogether disappeared. The lion looking at the man had only its head and shoulders in sight. And the man thought that he would first lie still, that he might see whether the lion would not come again peeping. For, it is a thing which is cunning; it would intend to deceive him, that the thing might seem it had really gone away; while it thought that he would arise; for, he had seemed as if he stirred. For, it did not know why the man had, when it thought that it had lain the man down nicely, the man had been falling over. Therefore, it thought that it would quickly run, that it might quickly come, that it might come to look whether the man still lay. And the man saw that a long time had passed since it again came to peep; and the thing seemed as if it had altogether gone. And the man thought that he would first wait a little, for, he would otherwise startle the lion, if the lion were still at this place. And the man saw that a little time had now passed, and he had not perceived the lion; and the thing seemed as if it had really gone away.

And he did nicely at the place yonder where he lay; he did not arise and go; for, he arose, he first sprang to a different place, while he wished that the lion should not know the place to which he seemed to have gone. He, when he had done in this manner, ran in a zigzag direction, while he desired that the lion should not smell out his footsteps, that the lion, when it came, should come to seek about for him. Therefore, he thought that he would run in a zigzag direction, so that the lion might not smell out his footsteps; that he might go home; for, the lion when it came, would come to seek for him. Therefore, he would not run straight into the house; for, the lion, when it came and missed him, would intend to find his footprints, that the lion might, following his spoor, seek for him, that the lion might see whether it could not get hold of him.

Therefore, when he came out at the top of the hill, he called out to the people at home about it, that he had just been lifted up while the sun stood high, he had been lifted up; therefore, they must look for many hartebeest-skins, that they might roll him up in them; for, he had just been lifted up. Therefore, he thought that the lion would come out from the place where it had gone, it would come and miss him; it would resolve to seek and track him out. Therefore, he wanted the people to roll him up in many hartebeest-skins, so that the lion should not come to get him. For, they were those who knew that the lion is a thing which acts thus to the thing it has killed, it does not leave it, when it has eaten it. Therefore, the people must do thus with the hartebeest-skins, the people must roll him up in them; and also in mats; these are things which the people must roll him up in, that the lion should not get him.

And the people did so; the people rolled him up in mats, and also in hartebeest-skins, which they rolled together with the mats. For, the man was the one who had spoken thus to them about it; therefore it was that they rolled him up in hartebeest-skins, while they felt that their hearts' young man he was, whom

143

they did not wish the lion to eat. Therefore, they intended to hide him well, that the lion should not get hold of him. For, a young man whom they did not a little love he was. Therefore, they did not wish the lion to eat him; and they said that they would cover the young man with the huts' sheltering bushes; they would cover the young man with the shelter of the hut so that the lion, when it came, should come seeking about for the young man; it should not get hold of the young man, when it came; it should come seeking about for him.

And the people went out to seek for !kui-sse and they dug out !kui-sse which they ate at meals; and they baked !kui-sse, they put it in a hole that is hot, they put it in the hole and they covered the hole with earth, when they put !kui-sse in the hole. And an old Bushman, as he went along getting wood for his wife, in order that his wife might make a fire above the !kui-sse, espied the lion, as the lion came over the hill at the place which they young man had come over. And he told the house folk about it; and he spoke, he said:

"Ye are those who see the hill yonder, its top, the place yonder where the young man came over, what it looks like!"

And the young man's mother spoke, she said:

"Ye must not allow the lion to come into the huts; ye must not allow the lion to come into our hut yards; ye must shoot it dead, when it has yet not come into the huts."

And the people slung on their quivers; and they went to meet the lion; and they were shooting at the lion; the lion would not die, although the people were shooting at it.

And another old woman spoke, she said:

"Ye must give to the lion a child, that the lion may go away from us."

The lion answered, it said that it did not want a child; for, it wanted the person whose eyes' tears it had licked; he was the one whom it wanted.

And the people speaking, said:

"In what manner were ye shooting at the lion that ye could not manage to kill the lion?"

And another old man spoke, he said:

"Can ye not see that it must be a sorcerer? It will not die when we are shooting at it; for, it insists upon having the man whom it carried off."

The people threw children to the lion; the lion did not want the children which the people threw to it; for, looking, it left them alone.

The people were shooting at it, they wanted to shoot him dead, before he could find the man. The people were shooting at it, while it sought for the man, that it might get hold of the man, the people were shooting at it. The people said:

"Ye must bring us assegais, we must kill the lion."

Their arrows fell short, they thought they might kill the lion with their assegais because their arrows fell short. The people were shooting at it; it did not seem as if the people were shooting at it; they were stabbing it with assegais; some threw assegais; others stabbed the lion with them. The people were all around it; but it did not bite them, because it wanted the young man whom it had carried off. They were stabbing it with assegais, while they intended to stab it to death. It did not seem as if the people were stabbing it; for, it continued to seek for the young man; it said he was the one whom it wanted.

It scratched asunder, breaking to pieces for the people the huts, while it scratched asunder, seeking for the young man. And the people speaking, said:

"Can ye not see that a sorcerer it must be?"

And the people speaking, said:

"Ye must give a girl to the lion, that we may see whether the lion will not eat her, that it may go away."

The lion did not want the girl; for, the lion only wanted the man whom it had carried off, he was the one whom it wanted.

And the people spoke, they said, they did not know in what manner they should act towards the lion; for, it had been morning when they had first shot at the lion and it was now late, and they did not know what they could do to get rid of it; the lion would not die; for, it had, when the people were shooting at it, it had been walking about.

"Therefore, we do not know in what manner we shall act towards the lion. For, the children whom we gave to the lion, the lion has refused, on account of the man whom it had carried off."

145

And the people speaking, said:

"Say ye to the young man's mother about it, that she must, although she loves the young man, she must take out the young man, she must give the young man to the lion, even if he be the child of her heart. For, she is the one who sees that the sun is about to set, while the lion is threatening us; the lion will not go and leave us; for, it insists upon the young man."

And the young man's mother spoke, she said:

"Ye may give my child to the lion; ye shall not allow the lion to eat my child; that the lion may go walking about; for, ye shall killing it lay it upon my child; that it may die, like my child; that it may die, lying upon my child."

And the people when the young man's mother had thus spoken, the people took the young man out from the hartebeest-skins in which they had rolled him up, they gave the young man to the lion. And the lion bit the young man to death; the people, when it was biting at the young man, were shooting at it; the people were stabbing it; and it bit the young man to death.

And the lion spoke, it said to the people about it, that this time was the one at which it would die; for, it had got hold of the man for whom it had been seeking; it had got hold of him.

And it died, while the man also lay dead; it also lay dead with the man.

Warm Simplicity

for Leser

NAZI PRISONERS MILLED in the snow and mud waiting to be interrogated. Inside the hut a captured Prussian officer gazed at the opposite blank wall as the American interrogation officer held the Prussian's diary, opened, in his hand, and once again asked him the meaning of a minutely scrawled sentence: "I know what the words mean, but what do they mean to you?"

The enemy officer remained silent. The American officer turned several pages, and indicating the word *wieder*, said, "All right, here you've written *again*, so that means something happened again," and the American turned a few more pages, stopping and pointing as the single words or exclamatory phrases appeared, and looking at the silent and exhausted face of the enemy officer.

What interested the American was this fellow wasn't just Nazi he was Prussian, these curiously dense words and phrases had appeared at intervals in four years of diaries which had been interrupted by his capture, and the American officer was a little fascinated—at the paradox of frenzied exclamations, outcries— and the worn out stone silent Prussian man in the chair; there was—an inner contradiction, and the evasive answer lay like a simplicity exactly unknown which seemed to glow and create a heat of its own,
January 17, 1944 *Ich schame mich!*

The notations occured between five and eight weeks apart, among weather descriptions and documented troop movements which had been written daily in a level style, but the exclamations occurred in a slanting and tiny scrawl at the lowermost corner of the printed frame for that day, now and then underlined March 3, 1944

wieder!

Another man in the room was about five feet two; he had gray hair, gray eyes, thin lips, a long nose—unusually deep furrows spread from his nostrils to the corners of his mouth. He had escaped Hitler in a real adventure, had gotten to England and then to the United States and gladly joined the Army and returned for revenge to his native Germany with American troops: The American officer asked him,

"What do you think this means?"

The little man faced the diary casually, eyes whipping over the words, pages flew, he closed it, handed it to the American officer saying, "His masturbation calendar."

The Prussian officer began to cry.

"When you do it," the little man told me, offering his experience and conviction as one gesture of love, "enjoy it, don't rush it."

Double People

THE CRIPPLED MAN shopping with his family in the furniture store was short and powerfully hunched over; he lurched forward with a bad limp catching himself on his cane by stabbing it on the floor and throwing himself on it, bringing his left foot around and raising himself and lunging and spearing the floor, he caught and raised himself and lurched between pieces of furniture stabbing and catching and raising lunging and stabbing and catching himself. His forehead was furrowed, his eyes sunk back under the scowling bone; his dense eyebrows meeting the thick snub nose above the thick wide lips made a meaty triangle based by blunt lower teeth visible when he spoke; his wife moved energetically ahead of him leading and clearing the way with their scowling son beside her talking and then screeching and screaming shrilly announcing now that or that, this! That! His little fistlike face, his boy and baby flesh, he was his father's double.

They decided to get a bistro table and three wrought iron bistro chairs. I wrote out the sales slip explaining delivery was extra, and the crippled man agreeably said, "It doesn't make that much difference."

"Tuesday?" he asked, clumsily shifting his feet. "What time?"

Salesmen weren't allowed to give delivery times, I explained, and the crippled man nodded writing out the check. I saw he was a doctor; I cranked the triple copies of the sales slip from the machine and gave him his receipt and attached the check to the white copy, put it in the Office box beneath the counter tossing the yellow in Shipping, hearing the boy screech, "I want an ashtray! I can pay for it out of my allowance!"

I walked across the floor to the glassware section where they were, hearing the crippled father murmur no no you don't need to; mother softly asked, "Why don't you let your father get it for you?"

I came around the corner, and down by the far end of a glass shelf filled with martini pitchers, brightly colored ashtrays and glassware, I saw the crippled man closely hugging his son, kissing his son's cheek murmuring against the flesh no no I'll get it for you, anything you want—seeing me, father broke free in a glance of panic, tore his face from his son's cheek, and his heavy shoulders shook as he roared,

"What color ashtray do you want!"

The boy had ducked behind his father's back and slipped around behind me to a shelf of bowls and different sized beakers, taking a small blue: crackling harshly,

"This one!"

He darted out in front of me picking up a blue glass,

"And this one!"

In the other fist: gold,

"And this one!"

"Enough!" murmured mother, "I think that's—"

Father lurched close by my face avoiding me with his eyes of panic, reaching his wife and seizing his son, patting and stroking, pacifying him, suddenly lurching away, forward, catching himself, free hand riffling clattering china ashtrays on display the words looping over his shoulders: Is this one all right? Is this? This? as the boy handed his already chosen colors to me softly snarling, "I want these," and followed me away, which motion drew mother and father to each other.

Standing at the sales counter I wrapped and put the boy's objects in a bag without yet making out a sales slip. I met his glare and he yelled,

"How much is sales tax!"

He looked at me darkly as I said five cents on the dollar. I walked across the floor and handed the bag to his father making a note of the items on my clipboard as father pointed to a rattan chair and asked how much it was.

"Ten ninety-nine," I said. "Two for twenty."

He asked his wife, "What do you think of it?"

150

She smiled brightly. "I like it!"

The boy stood close to me, almost touching.

His father asked me, "Do you think we could take it with us?"

I said sure.

Mother said, "We have a car." Raising her eyebrows, "Will two fit in?"

I picked up the rattan chair, flipped it over and explained that the wrought iron leg frame was very light, removable, and the chair shells would stack. Father decided two chairs, were they in stock? I nodded; he asked me, "How do you like them?"

Mother twinkled. "We'd appreciate your opinion."

I gave them a little pitch about cushions and comfort while watching TV.

Father exclaimed, "Just—"

"What we had in mind!" mother added, and the purchase was made.

I wrote out the sales slip telling them to wait by the door, and I went into the shipping department handing Frankie their receipt explaining the shells and frames were going separately, and I left, returning to the floor where I waited on an elderly woman by making up her mind for her. Walnut finish on the frame, rather than black, yes, walnut frames on the Shoji screens would match her parquet floor better than black, and I arranged delivery, took a deposit, wrote up the sale and thanked her, giving her her receipt, watched her leave, and asked a short lady if she wanted any help, no, she said, she was browsing, and all the while—all the while at my side the crippled doctor's son had followed me; he had gazed at Frankie and then at me; he had gone out on the floor with me and looked at the woman who had bought the screens, watching me as I convinced her of the walnut finish, and as I asked a tall man if he wanted any help I touched the boy's shoulder to let him know I saw him, but not for him to get in my way; the man said he wanted to see desks; desks, I said, and pointed across the store. The man went that way, and seeing a young couple by the sleep-sofas, I crossed to them as Frankie called my name. The rattan chairs were ready.

I walked to the boy's father to tell him, but Frankie was standing there, holding the chair shells, and father asked Frankie if he

151

would take them to the car. I stepped in front of Frankie thanking him, taking the chairs and looking into father's wavering eyes, I pointed to the boy and said,

"Let him take them."

Panic flashed in father's anguished eyes, his brows creased and he looked at the floor. Mother, startled, and the boy, angry, looked at me.

"I can't!" he shrilled. "They're too heavy!"

I held the rattan chair shells out and said, facing his mother, into his eyes. "You can."

Father shoved forward awkwardly, lunged and caught himself and lurched towards the door, leaving us; the boy asked me,

"Do you think I can?"

I held the rattan chair shells out and said, facing his mother, but talking to the boy,

"Take them."

She looked in my eyes. I held her there with my eyes.

The boy took the chair shells and passed his father going out. Mother looked at me speaking words that were far apart in an understandably wrong hope.

"Will you bring the leg frames?"

"He'll do it all."

Her face blurred. Then she saw I was looking at her, waiting for her to see that I had slightly become them. Her eyes deepened, sharpened and in the back, opened. For an instant she looked at me brilliantly, and was then gone, helping her husband down the steps. Later the boy came back; he picked up the leg frames. I was with another customer; I sensed him and turned to acknowledge his return. He held the frames triumphantly in the air, but then, in a silent thunderclap his child's face changed—scowling and crawling in on itself. It split into lined and frightened divisions of age, manipulated and torn by powerfully carved hands. His body shook, he grinned, laughed, screamed and cried there—then stumbled, turned, and lurched out the door.

No Feet

I GO ACROSS THE FLOOR towards the ringing telephone beneath the mirror that covers the rear wall of the furniture store. I punch lighted blinking seven and pick up the phone saying yes, making it clear I want whoever it is to respond hearing the main-office Special Order secretary's voice whisper yes and then begin to say my name in inner hatred and suppression of frenzy her tongue torches scorching the syllables of my name inquiring the grade number of the fabric for the R Ohio I sold to Customer Karen Seibel; I get the gold carbon copy of the receipt from the portable files to my left remembering Karen Seibel and look at the sale I had written yesterday and see the fabric grade number, the carbon had blurred yet I have the number in memory as the secretary's voice *"what is"* forms her cry of exasperation which I answer and her snarled thank and singing you brushes me off in a distant click to secure her hatred of any one that gets in her no way out of her dry dock wrecked marriage or two children, which causes me to question the mirrored store behind my mirrored face, as the telephone rings anew I punch five and the voice says she wants to speak to Mister who is the one? I am I answer, this is, she gravely announces—she is who I tell her she is: Mrs. Spies, you were expecting me to call, she says, did they come in yet? In two weeks, I answer, in two weeks in two weeks! she cries, they were promised for yesterday! I explain saying I do understand how she feels, I know you do she says, and I imaginate aloud, narrating the difficulty with the shipment, a slow boat full of chairs from Italy the Mafia raided the ship then there were problems with customs and the first load of H was powdered sugar in her soft laughter saying my name I join her chuckling promising to call her when the chairs come in that I am making a note of it and I make a note, we say goodbye I put the note in my personal file making a mental note to remember to look in the file and hold my hand in the air over the telephone which rings I punch seven drawing the pleasant feminine voice into my experience hearing it ask if that strawberry blonde saleslady is there no, today is her day off and I ask if I can and she, yes, last week, she says, she bought a chest now could she change the finish from oiled walnut to satin yes, I say, but it will mean a little delay, the phone rings, five lighting blinking and ringing, I will do it for you would you excuse me, I ask, I have another call, do it she says, Okay I will I say I mean take the time! she cries, I mean the extra time, for the satin finish! I will do that I answer, taking her name and making a note to call the embittered shipwrecked secretary to arrange it, going through the files and finding the gold carbon copy and changing the finish assuring the woman and hanging up punching five, yes, hearing a trembling tongue slide a shaky hello, it is the sexual and badly hungover elderly buyer and floormanager of the main store asking a splintering "do you have" sentence, that blue and green striped madras up there, single or double, I ask, single, he says, we have a few color combinations like that, I say, what's the code number I'll check he softly stutters the F in Fielding how, triple c in can (I) you expect (me) him a double t to know a ringing handful of nerve endings gone berserk—his eyes flutter and his lips slip across his lined face, he laughs fuck it, we'll say we don't, I laugh: jake, he gives a long butterfly sigh in middle aged distraction he wants to be hurt and be friends, thank, he says and sings you, hangs up, I likewise. I move away from the telephone to the shelving display. I am standing on the floor of the uptown branch of the furniture store, my feet are firmly planted on the floor my back is to the mirrored wall, and I statue stand with folded arms looking along the sunfilled corridor which goes straight ahead to the glass door through which all customers come from the outer world as I do every working morning in a recurring daydream my walking feet in step with feet, walking to work all over America while in lifelong darkness a dream in a lighted office or waiting room, another man stands to my left, much taller and of dramatic private eyes I gaze up at in childish awe and envy, and look over his left shoulder at the pebbled glass door—I, changing into a terrified boy witnessing a slanting shadow of death darkening the glass door I out waking cry: I: *still* the child! Will I never go to the darkened door, open it and confront the grim shadow with the tall figure of myself I invent and envy to see others as? "You can sit there," I murmur to the little boy as I would to me, I: he, were—I, "but," I make a gesture with my hand, "no feet on the furniture"; his mother pivots, glares down at him, cries NO FEET exclaiming his name, repeating the underlined order; "his feet," I say forcefully to her: "not him," watching her inner decision of what she now is as her hands waver angrily, self-consciously, irritably, sorrowfully, pleading and I regret it all helplessly remembering how my boss came across the floor of the main store downtown, towards me on the first month of my job approaching swiftly like others in day and night dreams he, with a quality of thunder and understanding, stalking sweeping in his stilted obliquity pipe in hand shaking fiercely left and right in front of his cold gray razor face his dark eyes flashing No he cried shaking his head No! No! and coming to the little girl took her feet and placed them so they were sticking off the edge of the sofa No Feet he firmly underlined in air his face smiling down on her sending me a maternal fiery eye of hatred snarling and underlining those two words to me. No Feet.

Different People

for Aram

THOMAS, BEING WATCHED, crossed the hotel lobby to the wall phone and compulsively dialed the number of his friend the famous Negro writer; the wiretone burred across the city. Thomas leaned on the desk and waited for the writer's voice—contact—feeling compulsion smack his temples, a woman's voice said hello; it was the writer's wife and Thomas' head boomed.

"Hello sweet—sweetheart, how are—you—is—"
She said hello Thomas; she said she was well; she said just a second, she would get her husband and she called his name; after a pause the writer answered. Out through the thunder in Thomas' skull, Thomas called hello—stammered hello—he hadn't seen the writer around—he hoped the writer was okay. Thomas asked him if he was okay—
"I'm okay," the writer said. "Just a second—" the writer's footsteps went into the distance and Thomas waited for his return, waited for himself, Thomas listened—
Differently, he sat in a chair across the lobby watching himself at the telephone; Thomas' different lips were red; the slightly feminine face was yellow orange and spoke in a gutteral articulation.
Speak. Me.

Mother

SHE WAS IN HER KITCHEN making eggs and bacon and coffee, the sun shone through the windows brightly and warmly, she made herself breakfast with motherly know-how yet she was unfamiliar with herself, her movements were shy, she was shy and she took the eggs out of the frying pan and put them cleanly on the plate as the toast popped out of the toaster, she was looking at her life, as she had looked at her life all her life, she saw the same things she had seen every day yet she had never commented on them, and she had never tried to remember what she couldn't, she buttered the toast and poured the coffee, a virgin world had come with her all her life, and having listened to all the bar room wise men, the living room prophets, the men of God and the husband of business-sense she had given up trying to salvage her unfound life from behind a strange shadowy wall, she looked into her life in a clear eyed manner like watching a never ending film, and scenes of her life unfolded every day, and she watched them and pronounced herself hopeless and without having lived, she could look in the mirror and say to the image "I have never lived," almost everyone had lived, she had watched them live all her life and her private movie unfolded unforgettable things in her life, private noises, private scenes, private meetings, private understanding and perception and private feelings towards herself, but as no one had spoken about that, it turned into her understanding of eternity misled by the deep sense of having missed her depth of life, her deep, cruel, savage life in a character of failure she avoided without forgetting, not thinking to bring the parallel picture into consciousness, she put her breakfast on a tray and went out into the back yard and sat at the table in the sun and ate, noting the distant bulldozers turning the woods over on their way to new houses next door, the coffee was delicious, she was without any sense of hope other than that which existence demanded, she had followed her inner sense of duty and devotion all her life, haunted by disaster, a sense of failure, reflections of grotesque mistakes and a glowing absence of love as love is known with her eyes on the grass, the hedge, the garage, the car, the sky and the table, they revealed the details and all accumulated implications in the way experience translated inner perception, she was fifty-two and she was going to live fifty-two years more, so in balance with her fate was she, that knowledge shook her, automatically she seemed bland and hopeless, her husband had died by degrees for months, he had been fifty-one, within the year her oldest son was killed in an airplane crash, her youngest son was now married and involved in life in awe of his mother, and in love with her and devoted to her, he was like her in his shyness and neatness, and he was away, and she was alone with her life and experience, the same memories returned every day and she watched them, a little marvelling at them, yet leaving them alone, and that semi-consciousness which paralleled her became an unconscious means of communication with herself, and the understanding of This Is It that came with every awakening became included in the understanding it was part of her complete existence, and in the many years ahead her life would accumulate into a total sense of its own within her, as she had lived and gotten it by living it, so too would her living son by taking it his way it would be his, of her character and he would do that in his way, she lit a cigarette and finished the cup of coffee, poured another and contemplated the dull beautiful day ahead of her, hoping the agent would call to say someone had bought the house so she could move away, knowing what would be once she arrived, today she would dress and go down the street for the party and that night was also invited to dinner where conversation would be familiar and tedious, yet she understood it must be so, and in her shy way that men had always loved, she decided, once again, to enter her day.

Aubade

SHE SAT AT HER DESK sleepily looking at the blank sheet of paper which lay before her pencil beside it, it was two o'clock in the morning; she bit her lip, she washed her face with dry hands and gazed at the paper aware of the dozens of crumpled sheets of paper on the floor around the desk, she felt separate from herself, she couldn't write the paper—it ought to present difficulties, she sounded, but to not be able to begin it—

A dull charge of electricity spun around her brain and she put her face in her hands telling herself she really must get this nightmarish thing done and the blankness of paper swam before her eyes, she lit a cigarette and yawned and ground her teeth picking up the pencil, cocking it—her hand shook—she smashed the paper and left the desk; she sorted through the papers on the floor; she selected one that was nearly unreadable for its crossed out sentences, but looking over it remembered her intent, and anger and frustration and self pity rose in her throat, and not reading what she had written she began remembering what she had meant to write, panic filled her chest and she started copying the sentences again, a fresh start on a new sheet of paper. Across the room she sat differently in the corner watching herself bent over the desk copying, noting the familiar tilt of the head, the serious expression—handsome indeed—as the handsome figure of her sleeping goddess daughter in the next room: the handsomeness in her twenty year old son; she, differently, standing by the writing woman, gazed down upon her, speaking, sending.

Let me write it, dearest.

Her hand trembled and she scowled; then she scratched out the sentence, and started again and looked at the clock, one after two,

159

returning with coffee six after she sat down, and starting on a new sheet of paper she again began copying her original intent while the tall man apart slept in another city and she watched, downward gazing at her living figure as the General Electric second hand swept toward the seventh minute.

Dawn rose over Missouri.

The sun crept across the windowsill, dropped down and crossed the crumpled sheets of paper on the floor into the invisible eye that never sleeps, and the sun crossed the desk. The sun touched and illuminated the hand, the wrist, the forearm, the shoulder and then the head of the woman asleep at her desk.

The Goddess

for Gabe Kohn

HIS HANDS OUT, reaching for her his eyes glittering the sculptor is laughing smiling talking as she wordlessly beckons he leans towards her his heart pounding he breathes sharp grins widely she stands in his mind out of reach he sighs, he sighs calling to her that she see and come to him naked in her great youthful power, ah! he cries, dozens! I had dozens! The sculptor spreads his hands casting his eyes over remembered girlhood flesh dozens! he snaps his fingers, for the taking chuckling no more m'boy, here, he says softly, have another drink, I hold out my glass he apologizes again for no ice and pours whiskey into winter New York water, follows suit with his own drink and again seats himself in the shabby chair by the small wood stove murmuring Christ shaking his head, ah, he spreads and drops his hands looking at me, they waited in bars they brought us drinks they waited tables hoping someone would see them, we would come in after work—how I see it! he cries, he sits back in his chair leaning forward intently looking at me we would go in there they'd be waiting anything anything hoping for a smile a word from an agent or producer in those days Hollywood boomed a cream colored Cord convertible I was making seven thousand dollars a week, seven thousand, he stands shaking his fists seven he screams yells thousand a shouting fucking week I burst into laughter he sits grinning chuckling nodding eyes bright yes! he says, seven thousand dollars, the sculptor looks at me thoughtfully, in those days seven grand was peanuts, and above his head on the wall I see the photo of Barrymore as Mr. Hyde and beneath it a letter to the sculptor who sits across from me beside the stove we don't have a nickel between us he is

161

turning fifty and I am in my late twenties you're a young man he says, you can get all the girls you want, but not me, and he gives me a dense and lecherous wink solemnly murmuring: this old pecker seldom stands. He drinks, looking at me from one self-amused eye over the rim of the glass and lowering the glass asks,

"Who was that girl with you in the bar?"

I frown, when? and we search hopelessly through recent nights for a touchstone I ask him what she looked like short he says young he chuckles curly hair he crookedly grins I say you mean and I say her name as he looks pointedly at me hungry dog on the threshold of every word his eyes glittering I make a gesture of descriptive uselessness laughing oh she's—ridiculous! he repeats after me, then he grins and sits back face assuming the composure of his mask as I know him, yet then he springs forward terrifically—did you—did you he cries fuck her! I did! How was it! No good! Why! She's cold! Ah! he groans, ah! Cold! He makes fists in the air and squeezes a bitter truth; I say: "With her hands beside her she spreads her legs—" but he is crouched to spring his hand angrily out and then he is sitting and then he is rising announcing there I was on her, in her working away and I opened my eyes she had her head turned, she was reading a newspaper on the chair! Reading! he cries, Jesus I whisper: what did you do, I threw her out he yells pantomiming his rising separation from her pointing to the door get out you disinterested fuck! I laugh as he sits scowling drinking remembering smiling at my fast response we are twenty years apart similarly jaded lonely childless father and fatherless child lonely in poverty and necessity for contact I gaze into the front room of his tiny loft at finished and unfinished wood sculptures wherever I look I see the evidence of his poverty and work and he talks and I listen and the cold gray winter day in the city changes to a darker color and he speaks on of brilliant destruction in paradise of set designs he made naming the films and stars in his land of sunshine where teenage goddesses swam and screwed why did you leave I ask I wanted to be an artist he answers, I have asked the right question and he steps into himself time now looking at

162

me, nodding and pointing into the other room, this is it, he is right, he is standing inside his twenty five year old understanding that after the first twenty five years his sculpture is it in the metaphorical other room, and he puts on his glasses and goes in, bending and sanding, cutting or gluing, and I a little help him, yet in the room now behind us the stove sends out heat, I see his small mattress on its wooden base, the sprung and shabby easychair in the corner and his tiny sink and toilet adjoining— his objects in his wooden time where he works, and cavorts with women a little older than *she* where he, seeing me looking at the picture of Barrymore, takes the letter beneath it off the wall and hands it to me I read the sculptor's first name prefaced by "My Dear" and my eyes follow a warm and touching note from Barrymore and then my friend speaks of Barrymore, he hails and fairly sings that name—how I see my sculptor friend now! His face his terrific awe and devotion to that outward moving outward spreading inner illusion of sensitivity and power, Barrymore! he cries, fists in the air face torn laughs deep, roars, was an ACTOR!

And then, on cue, he subsiding backs off from me looking a little furtive glancing around the room as if haunted, his head jerks, he glances at me and glances away he looks behind him as though pursued, and rising and crouching and rising crouching sips then gulps an invisible potion finishing it drops the beaker on the floor he shudders as if inwardly turning, his stature shortens and his shoulders twist his legs bend bow and distort, his head tilts his eyes glaze one eyebrow rises in terror the other tightens in hate, and possessed by pain and distress clutching his coattails with his right hand his left goes over his head as his face turns to me creased and savage its lips drawn back teeth bared its breath rattling gasping it claws the air snarling, arched fingers slice through the air and freeze, it is Barrymore transfixed by the stove, and then its arms drop and it straightens its legs its eyes adjust its lips close, its face becomes the man I know and it smiles frowning thoughtfully says it was Barrymore's greatest role, and it smiles in pain and bitterness and sits down whispering, "If only a girl would look at me the way I looked at Barrymore when I told him."

163

A Letter to Philip Guston

I HAVE A WATERCOLOR, Bill Cushner said, and he held his hands up and began putting the scene together in air, over here his right hand settled in front of him are the contours of fields, and over here his left hand waved is a road and there are trees, there is a character in oddly colored clothes on the road here, he said, and beyond is the sea.

Yet over here his right finger circled there is a color and his face changed as he said: a—he paused, there is a color there, in the field that takes my eye away. He looked at me, his eyes are gray and black and blue. Every time I looked at it I went from here to here his left hand swerved, and I, each time I, I finally took it to the right *and* left, I had it retouched so I could see it, the color I mean was a little faded, d'ya see? he asked. Even there it was just there, it was as if it was also there, and I grinned and told him how you reacted when I mentioned my interest and curiosity in that green—in the green in the lower right hand part of the one at Sidney's, in fact the day after your opening, and you yelled Let me alone about the fucking GREEN, and I also thought about Rothko, sizing the whole thing yellow—first, then starting and I remembered my own dismay at changing a painting towards the red on the left and in the end beginning all over again, after all the tough work, still the painter's problem the color calls the painting. That funny color on the right, it is a watercolor and he probably put it aside beginning a new one starting with that problem color, I would, I did, looking and looking at that color wondering where it was going knowing something was next to it, something invisible—or not there—was beside it, and away from it a little to the left and something slanted down to the right, what—as in anxiety of can you hear me? Unh huh, what color was it. Well, I went to it, and stood outside it looking at it, and I was within it, looking at it and painting it, and years later thought of you when I saw it again in the watercolor he described—this here, that there—I mean seeing you in there was great, as he talked about that color in that field.

Mirror Road

I CAN SEE HIM STILL, across the room from me sitting on an upholstered ottoman in her living room, the mixed vodka drink in his hand, and in his world brain the Kiplinger Report. I see his open collar and short sleeves, his mid-western slacks and socks that match in contrast to his loafers. He is smiling and talking and his eyes are clear they are always clear, I remember his hands holding the drink, he holds himself in place, he was any place now or then with the drink in his hands holding tomorrow and thinking and going to see her and talking and smiling in the kitchen while she made the drink on the table inside the kitchen window which overlooked the worn driveway that ran out to Highway 66.

I saw him once as I turned the corner, he was in her driveway in shirtsleeves, he waved to me.

His oval face and thinning brown hair, and his perpetually clear eyes, his intelligent look and open collar and normal figure seemed hardly without secret—I or the panicky girl in me was afraid of him and he would frighten me or the girl-boy now as I know I see him in my mind as I know I am still able to draw myself to the darkness in my configurational fantasy of his violence, his face in dark rage would freeze me, I was younger then, and I shouted at him, we had been drinking all evening and into the night, it was late and I, bleary eyed and furious almost in tears from no response and the next day's memory of a one sided persistent and irrational scream to a pithy gray or white phallus without evil: I bounced: off his irrelevant question,

"Could I have another?"

Her rising to make him a drink, her returning with the drink, her returning to her chair and sitting down, I me in my, he in his, yet he appeared, he appeared and appeared without repeating, he appeared, his nose the quality of what's his name's nose, lips like those of that guy in A Kiss Before, his eyes like Colonel— appeared appeared without reappearing he became his face again and again an eye and ear a cliff, his hands around the drink, the vacant lot next door I lived around the corner and last spring towards end of evening my wife and I went around the corner the house was for sale and the yard was full of weeds and junk, I know the lighted windows and slanting frame and I see darkness and little things lost never found, lonely midwest woman, moving toward sixty she had never—with him never she said, away in my or her mind or in Southern Missouri with her daughter and son-in-law the cheerful and deductive absent minded unsure frightened woman fearing things at hand slip away the cigarettes were right there what happened to the tonic oh here, I wanted her to need my influences: I couldn't influence me and if I knew my answers I could help myself to her, me, I needed her to find more problems, answers were my joke: if I could offer sexuality to him for his response to me I'd have her with a larger package of me: more, I drank her endless supply of vodka and usually returned the next day for more to aid my trembling hands he rose to meet me, she said my name, and his, we shook she said I was hung over, I laughed, he laughed, he was a man of her age, she made the drinks, I sipped mine, the sun came through the windows into the room where three world people talked and drank reality in the shape of themselves and I spoke to his appearing face, I had failed to reach myself I was self-conscious as I am when I am defensive about my obvious failure to reach myself in the presence of others, I gave in fell away he would step across the room and raise his fist, me-pussy said things to anger him and the eyes in his face appeared above his nose his chin his shirt buttons his hands and looked at me understanding how he felt about himself without showing what it was, again and again, repeat: he looked at me understanding how he felt about himself without showing what it was, he nodded and agreed and frowned and thought and laughed and rose to leave it was two in the morning, she was tired, I was drunk, he went out the door, I apologized, he said he would see me again we would talk some more, I flushed with resentment and was happy he wasn't angry, I asked her for two beers and stumbled home and drank them in my back yard and vanished into the next appearing sun changing and shifting from side to side to fool my need for the influential and inherent sense of mother and dead father which I hadn't let myself experience but thought I saw in other men and women, to know the male self without myself I would seize a man or me the way I would fear him as I appeared and appeared weary and frantic and frightened from my appearing face *what are you, I want to know what you are, I have no sense of what is in the face I see before me.* I washed my hands in the men's room where I work, I glanced up and saw a handsome man's face, the fellow saw me, his face was newly lined and in existence, his eyes saw mine and changed in perception—I then understood how far I was from my simple common mirrored face, lonely years and years from what I am.

Thread

I HAVE GREEN EYES, I sit at the table nervously listening to them I am watching myself listening and looking I am telling myself to pay attention, see and listen and not see and listen, my hair is a little gray, a woman walks in me, she pays no heed, I sit here and listen and look, I am myself, the others sit around me and talk, I am tired, I have not worked hard today, I am drinking, I am confused, I am restless and my mind is on other things, I am interested I am an interesting man I interest myself, I reached for her in the distance behind her green eyes she stood behind the mask of her beautiful flesh: in through her eyes I went, reaching for the distant visible woman, I was clear, hard, etc.

I listen to them, they are talking about dogs, a dog lies on the floor beside me, a cat is on the windowsill behind the refrigerator, the man gestures across the table, he is talking about movie stars, Garbo, he says, he doesn't understand how anyone can not see Garbo, he says he confused the Gish sisters, the homely one was the one he spoke to meaning to speak to the pretty, I am, neither slowly nor rapidly, revolving within insanity, my mind confuses my feelings, my powers of interpretation fail me, my sense for sequence is passé and I fear what's ahead, I am going into the darkness, I hear them still talking yet I am nervous in a current, I gather myself in an interest but I am far from myself, I am on a train, I am in darkness every moment every day nearer the farness and nearness of my self and oblivion: a thin man beside me is slightly bald, dog leash around his fist we are talking about dogs, until I got the job, I contribute, I hadn't understood so many where do I work, Joe E. Brown asks from across the table I say I work as his eyebrows go up the dog chases the cat, Joe E. Brown throws his hands in the air: pardon him for being queer but he doesn't think dogs are supposed to like cats, Joe E. Brown bursts out of his mouth, someone rises, I smile, I chuckle, I laugh, I grin, I mutter, someone says dogs aren't like they used to, I am self conscious I see my wife looking at Joe E. Brown talking to her, she sees she listens to him and looks at him and in her turn nods and responds and sees and hears, she smokes a cigarette, she's a little earthly, ancient, she is not me, she looks at him, she is moving outward in perception, she sorts through his face behind his face and hears his running mindless meanings, I am sent into myself, I lay my naked face on her naked chest and came out from within my head and adored her, and her responsive heart banged against my face—last night, now she has stepped into that chair and I yet feel her sound and touch her feminine message pounding through her important life, I want you to meet me, otherwise I am Joe E. Brown, you are reading self consciousness and emotion, myself, the pale and pretty girl says after she looked at me for answers and I gave them, my friend the host of this party asked her why she had looked away and she lied, she had looked at me for an answer, the writer writes into the dialogue of the world, she says, the writer writes the dialogue of the self in the self into the dialogue of the world: I insist on separating accumulated perceptions: no synthesis, and she agrees I say I overcomplicate things she looks at me, I look at her and know her complicated need for her within and away from someone else, love, and fear of the shadowy fearing self in her flesh without resilience, I see in darkness I see her eyes her bright strike of perception, I say to her, I hear you and like it, I like you, I say, I love the sense of her she pays no heed and I love and know her, green in my eyes, don't leave me, she says, she sees and knows she is lonely that he whom she perceives should appear before her complicated in her voice "him" her own dark eyes, pale face, her face is drawn, she has razor dimples and thin nostrils, the temples are nearly transparent and as she speaks of Russian men her face hardens her nostrils move her teeth set, her eyes flash and she invisibly goes into "his" arms in conflict and perception against the wall of windows and night, she at my side as I cast

170

my experiences ahead of myself beside her moving endlessly forward tell me a story, once again, and again, and then again I encounter myself and the shifting constructions of the selves of myself within turmoil, the man or woman on the streets of a novel are the writer and his world pattern within him, she asks, what if it's true? cars crash, when you write it, I answer: change it, tell me a story she says, I continue, to what it means as it is familiar like world cars and world people, us, I grin, self conscious, she is interested, she says, tell me, two highways spread towards her one sexually and capably bright and unending, the other sexually incapable and immediately disastrous—lonely and regretful, I met him at a little get-together at Otie's house, I begin, we were drunk in her kitchen he shot the Nazis as they came over the rise, one by one, he said, as they came over and they kept coming I kept shooting and then they stopped coming, there were tears in his eyes he gnashed his teeth he bit his lips my green eyes were contemptuous he saw them and accepted the look, he was a rich young artist a big man with big shoulders and big hands, he had stiff light brown short cut hair and perspiration spotted his skull giving him a hectic look he gave me a dirty look he glowered had I ever been in war? no, I didn't know anything about death, he said, we were in the living room looking and talking at each other and Otie's high waisted daughter sat in the big artist's lap as Otie talked about the art critic for the St. Louis Post Dispatch a good man a little naive and a few weeks later having nothing to do I walked across town to a new suburban development where the rich young artist lived, I went in through the gates passing a ranch house on a hill where the D.J. for radio station WIL lived and I went around the bend up the street to the artist's house, I buzzed the new buzzer and his wife answered she had indeed spotted me at Otie's, Otie introduced me as a young writer from around the corner who couldn't make up his mind whether to stay in St. Louis or go to New York where his friend Franz Kline lived I said I would go to New York I didn't know when, and the artist's wife, happily contemptuous, watched me become resentful, his wife said her husband was busy in his studio, she stood behind the closely woven cooper screen and smiled, the corners of her painted lips moved up her

171

face and her eyes went flat I heard an ice tray pop and his voice who was there? Invisible teeth appeared behind her felled lips she opened the door over her shoulder describing the young writer at Otie's I went in he shook my hand avoiding my eyes I looked into his to pester him I had nothing to do, I said, so I thought I'd visit she walks in me she guides me, we crossed the cork floor and sat on a long foam rubber studio couch in St. Louis earth colored batik, his paintings hung on the walls around the house we began to talk, his wife sat across the room, she was petite with big hips her pleated skirt hung down her shinbones sweeping in her feminine walk, she had smooth skin her grin was sharp up her enthusiastic face, facing me obliquely from a little behind herself feet flat another face a shark's face set in possession jealousy anger and apprehension she glittered her role in his life and he blended and sat back affluently a successful artist, young with a great future in her skyscraper eye he was leaning against himself as he had leaned toward and painted the young boys with idealistic expressions and dark flat empty eyes which yet held an inner unpainted glitter, a chemical and fantastic radiance on the painted face of the painted boy gazing beyond his outstretched hands entwined in a construction of string against a wall of criss-crossed twine, later the wealthy artist and I walked down the sloping back yard, his wife in the front, eyes burning over the grass setting up a charged field around him, one touch/instant death, he seemed glad to get out of the house, I wanted to possess influence and pester and touch him, I could touch myself but I couldn't possess me and in a while I a little stole him and understood him as he wandered in himself so aimless, distracted, young, lonely, haunted by the quick step from a vivid gutter to bewildering fame we sat on large rocks and chattered like two lovers I felt sentimental I had already become the part of me which was him, and he, still, him, so I told him a story, about a girl in New York and I left the story unfinished— after she threw it to me I looked at it lying in the palm of my hand, and then looked up at her and in the terrific glitter in her eyes I did understand it in the way I had turned into her, we plotted a murder and it failed she confessed she was glad, I was too, I didn't mind killing myself I had killed me all my life but to

172

kill someone else to strengthen the feminine bridge between myself and the girl I had become confused me and I omitted that mystery keeping my eyes on his telling him of the young man on the Tarot card who holds a large tilted figure 8 and in each loop of the 8, a world circle, and in the center of each circle, a star, one of energy the other of violence: two ships crossed the ocean at my feet. I was the young man, she interpreted, I was holding the opposite worlds which I was, a double destiny while world ships went their way as they would continue to go, being there meaningfully for me to board.

She lived on the Lower East Side in a railroad flat, and one narrow rear room was divided almost in half by a table against one wall. Two barrels supported a long sheet of plywood on which lay small collections of numbers, buttons, letters, pins, cloths, clothes, books, boxes, shoestrings, clothespins and photographs, all of which I looked at while she went into a corner, she took a little box from beneath a crumpled cloth and crossed the room towards me, she stopped, she opened the box with her head down giving me a level up from under look, she unfolded tissue paper reached inside and took out a toy gun and pointed it at me raising her head holding her eyes on mine; she put the box on the table. And then, simply standing looking in my eyes with the gun in her hand, she was a beautiful girl, her hair framed her oval face, she smiled, her figure seemed to straighten and float I saw her breasts rise and fall I was aware of her hips her shoulders her legs her power in her flesh—I then saw she was distant from me I grinned I dropped the grin she was distant from herself, my ears picked up the noises of the city I saw the muscles in her forearm change, the bones in her hand set, she was clenching the gun and squeezing the trigger for an instant I saw a distant darkness spread and like a dark cloud on the horizon sweep forward toward her eyes I was alive, vivid, she pulled the trigger, I stepped forward and the rich young artist threw his hands in the air she tossed the gun to me I threw it to him no! he cried, stumbling backward, arms over his face, we have a drink, our glasses touch I am tangential and aware, you said turmoil, I sit here nervously with my drink in my hand wanting to say the familiar variety of opposites in inner con-

173

structions in inner turmoil in the inner world darkest of all frightening invisible a turmoil to become, it is more real than this which is an integral and momentary part of us, that's good, she says, I say you are history, as you speak I hear in you: Now. Self consciousness rises and envelopes me, we, this glass, are.

I am lonely for myself I rise I fade from the end of my story towards my friend the host to get a drink I stand at the bar/ kitchen counter while he makes a drink I make a joke, at the end of the movie he gets on the bus and goes away but he will come back, children have fallen in love with him, so has Ida Lupino in my life, they are all him and he is her and them and he takes leave of himself repeatedly entering the forward moving stream of his lives. I am in a different chair and my wife is talking with the pale dark haired woman whose eyes flash when she speaks of Russian men, I have told of my life, I have departed from it into it and I am nervous, I cross and uncross my legs, I shuffle my feet, I squirm in my chair, my host glances at and sees his me, he would call me his friend, it is up to us he said when Kline died, he has said many things to me as I to him from first college days, and by entering my mind I have split and shattered me, there are many roads to follow and many lives to be, I follow them I am different from other men only in the hunger for unity within inner frenzy and I am angry that he befriends me in the way I am his friend by him, by me we are each other's experience and fate: friends. In his consideration the roads lead to deductions, answers and opinions and I follow them obediently all at once to him or not to him as he sees me, I would call him us before I would call him my friend, I love him, not our friendship. He separates himself from me in thought and contemplation and he sees his me, and in his thought I become myself as he perceives me, he blends his deductions with his attitude which omits me, but this deductive attitude is him is his personal moral development, it is his style of being sentimental, self-pitying and ridiculously in love with himself. Detective; lover of deadly goddesses; world of experience within a world of thwarted experience; he carries himself with a tough sense of humor and an attitude of deductive knowing.

An old friend of mine wrote a book about two married couples but I did not think my friend had learned about himself from his experiences which made his novel an acidly angry narrative, the frenzied rage of himself blinded by his memory of jealousy and desire and fear and failure, in a representation of sections of memory, not as they changed and/or influenced him, but as he reacted to his failure to *follow any initial reaction that made it memorable*, there is a realization of adultery in the book which changes into the vehemence he reveals by denying true action, but as he fails to follow *any initial reaction* he uses his protagonist to represent reality; he remembered the memories and overlooked the causes. The causes make fiction nearly unwritable. His hair seems longer, he rather stoops, his skin stretches tightly over the bones on his face, neck, his blouse bags forward and I see his scrawny chest and shoulders, his lips are drawn back and his teeth are bared and smeared with blood and lipstick, he will kill his experience and his life, and as his killing goes on he will naturally reach out to kill me, include me, "You can't change anything by intention," he wisely said, I asked, "Where were you ten years ago when I was concerned with that?" "I was right here," he said metaphorically.

"You were no help then," I said.

He reached across the table. "Look," he said tenderly, and a man appeared beside him looking intently at me; the other said, "I care for you. Do you know that?"

"Which does?"

He pointed to his chest and underlined I do. I nodded. I had just seen him appear apart from himself; which cared? The one there? Or that one? That frenzied hag in him didn't, she wrote a book about what she cared about—she loved him, loved to hurt him, and to haunt him with disaster and loneliness, if it was up to her she would change the world, it had been her intention from the start, and she looked gravely at me as I said to her, "I battled the compulsion of intention for ten years, I and all my selves including my witch intended to change the world. Now I intend to change into all I was and am."

175

He stepped into the one to his left and nodded drunkenly, she rubbed her hand across her mouth and drew blood, and the face of flesh which identified the man I once knew as my friend, one out of several faces of his own that did care for me, looked a little hauntedly at me as if he was seeing us together in a photograph, laughing and loving each other a long time ago, and was now condescending to me, "You'll make it," he said, yet that strange tall child clinging grimly to him for him as if he was his own son and father of same, hated and feared and loved and needed, and his face became a complicated and brilliant hostility, but looking at himself he thought he was one man.

I despise my self conscious witchness, my wary and defensive reaction to my host at this party. In him as I would build a historical fiction of him, I see Juarez vs. Maximilian von Hapsburg as John Huston made it. Maximilian's wife Carlotta could not have children, she stopped herself and turned into his Mexico and the adoption of one who would one day rule Mexico in the Hapsburg tradition. Juarez had been double crossed by one of his generals who seized the shipment of arms from the United States and Juarez was in peril—the United States warned Napoleon III that Maximilian's reign violated the Monroe Doctrine, that the U.S. recognized the government of Juarez, not that of Maximilian, the U.S. was ready to go to war with Napoleon. Napoleon withdrew his armies from Mexico just as Maximilian had Juarez wiped out, Maximilian then discovered Napoleon had sent him to Mexico as puppet, which enraged Maximilian and Carlotta sailed to France and threatened to expose Napoleon to the world, she suffered a mental breakdown, Juarez killed the general who double crossed him, gathered his armies and swept towards Maximilian. Maximilian's general told Maximilian to flee. Maximilian would not, he received word of his wife's condition, dissolved his palace guard and made preparations to flee, as Juarez's troops were at the palace gates Maximilian changed his mind, he stayed to fight, was captured, put in jail, Carlotta sat in a high backed chair facing Austria through open doors in sun and mist, silent and still in that arched high ceilinged chamber of insanity, and rose from her chair she fled out the doors screaming his name, he came over the rise the men with guns behind him the figure of Carlotta all over him

me too as I see me standing in our driveway, ten years old in Missouri, our dark brown hair and white flesh a pretty girl with flashing eyes watched the children play across the street. I was new there I was eight years old they looked at me they gradually stopped playing I crossed the street, I joined them on their side of their street of my future street of my home town later I wrote from my college to G—'s that I loved him sexually I desired his flesh his reply ended a companionship of separate destinies begun from across the street I had always, through high school and college envisioned him older he was younger I wanted to possess and influence him as I would me I did not possess me or influence me he seemed older more decisive he turned me into me turning me into a little girl yet in world life we grew older influencing each other, I desired he separate himself from his father and he argued I wanted to possess him as if I was father, he was brilliant that night I was objectively respectful but jealous that he saw me so well and then, a year later, I wrote him for his flesh and a year after that I saw him at a home town wedding and spoke to him his word was hello his eyes stated his certainty of self: a gulf between my self-consciousness and me, later, a few days before I was drafted I met him on the street and we walked hostile blocks to the main street of town where we parted and I was gone falling in step with my life and our unified separate destinies which keeps my reaction to him in my reaction to my experiences as I react to me, in outer and inner worlds my letter parted us for us to never part, I was far from myself I touched him to bring my inductive influence into view via him into me I saw our childhood play I pushed him places in a baby buggy tank in our artillery games down streets through yards I pushed gazing radiating down on him older decades older I was in a nearly tragic sense of mother yet feeling like a little girl-boy as I pushed leaning over G mother brother sister lover friend student teacher envier in every billion cornered day saturated with existence reaching into an idea of words in a letter that went out with rightness à la serendipity which he read they said, they read—I loved him, the him-ness of him I was starving for me, too late,

177

the words were I want you, just as he read them, to him sexually. I remember Fatty.

I remember Fatty was funny with girls so I felt to save him in me, me in me, sorry for him, me, I pulled him across the street to the rest of the gang to play airplanes his fat face pouted his double chin doubled the tips of his ears pointed above his chubby neck and his high voice protested he didn't want! I took tugged him the other kids looked I said He's mine! He's going to play with us! Fatty didn't want to he took the model ME-109 in his hand but couldn't bring it across the field and I said no, and I told him how to hold the plane, later we played football and he cried, I knelt beside him and later I walked him to Kirkwood Road. His eyes were dark his eyebrows arched he pouted he kept pushing me away I pulled him on I told him how to hold the plane, when you get shot down I said wetting the kitchen match, you do this, I struck the match on the sidewalk and held it against the fuselage on the side of the cowling it smoked the plane had been hit its engine smoking it winged over with G's Spitfire following it toward the trees firing short bursts again and again then banking off toward the Lizard's tanks which crossed the tennis court see? I said, the Messerschmidt ripped into oblivion at the base of the tree Fatty looked at me distracted and frightened, I came around and fired the pass he missed it I walked him to Kirkwood Road as he wept I comforted him his hands and arms had gone into the air fluttered for the ball, missed, he hated me for bringing him. He crossed Kirkwood Road and went home. I stood on the corner and watched him my hand holding my hair my skirt.

Asleep, twenty years later, in a kitchen like the kitchen in the Episcopal Parish House or the one in the army mess hall in Germany I was standing at the other end of the cutting table from G—what is it my wife asks, I open my eyes and look across our loft home—he came slanting around the corner in an angular caricature of a small western town, we looked down and saw him chase G around corners of the Hollywood cow town G fled around a corner and the other man, bent over as if to merge with himself, emerged from himself and putting on hat and pants he stepped on stilts as Uncle Sam disguised in striped pants steadied himself rose up to me very close and lurched around the corner after G with a quality of thunder and understanding, we were afraid as he bent forward and elongated, tall Uncle Sam pursued G.

Uncle Sam's hands unfolded blossoms and deep in the center of a flaring two handed single bloomed tiger lily lay G, and the disguise buried his face in the bloom.

"Run!" I cried, and G ran around the corner.

It was a beautiful day we drove along a sunny road I was young and old at the same time, the movie was continuing over my shoulder and off to our right I saw G run up a long sloping hill stilted Uncle Sam still following, so small they were against the sky going outward from us, G neared the top of the hill and Uncle Sam charged after far away and small.

Uncle Sam loomed over him, Uncle Sam reached down and his radiating downward power transfixed all that Uncle Sam was except his head, and all that G was into a slowly but quickly flowering tiger lily inside which G must have been for Death went grinning into his grimly unfolding flowering fingers, after we reached the end of the street, where the railroad tracks ran to my left a stretch of green separated it from the street I said,

"Now we get him."

We ran down the street towards G and Uncle Sam I was still young and old but now in my home town and in a movie watching myself run childishly carefree along the railroad tracks away, G seemed to have gone through a field I hit Billy Sol Estes and he looked at me for an instant young and old he seemed resigned I was the citizen in town, the cop locked the glittering handcuffs on right in front of my eyes, "Here is your man," I said to the marshal, and Billy Sol Estes and I were face to face in the newsreel, big people, and he was off to jail.

I hated the skin on his face that slick immature double chin and the way his upper lip rode over his lower and how his teeth were short, he was gone to jail I had done my duty tears in my eyes I looked across the table at G in the dark kitchen hoping he knew I had doublecrossed Billy Sol Estes for him would do anything for him, with our eyes on each other.

Captain Meyers and his date Judy sat across the table from us

179

on the terrace at the country club; Felix and Celia Clayton had invited us to the club for dinner, with Meyers and his date, Judy, and we all sat under the umbrella and the late afternoon sun and talked and drank Scotch and looked over the golf course while Judy underlined what a marvelous guy Dr. Paterson was everyone knew Dr. Paterson yet one day he suddenly moved out of town, I looked at my wife as Celia Clayton added, from her distraction, "he was really" I laughed. Judy smiled "I met him briefly at a party right away I saw he was somebody I saw it"—I was looking at her intently because I had gone to school and church with Judy's children and the Paterson's children, Judy's children were married now and Judy was divorced, Dr. Paterson had been very popular around the church, Celia gestured "When Fee and I joined the Episcopal Church we heard about him everywhere we went and finally we met him he was so striking and I was shocked when I heard he'd left town." Judy said "I've known him for years." Captain Meyers looked at her "Did you know his wife?" "She was incredible" Judy said. Judy put her hand on her drink and I asked why'd they break up? Felix answered, Felix was a preoccupied man, Paterson was unsure of himself his practice was down, Judy murmured she didn't know why, Meyers asked why would Paterson be unsure of himself he had been in practice for years, yes, Judy said, he was a very reliable doctor, my wife asked Meyers if he was ever unsure of himself although he was regarded reliable. Meyers answered yes but Paterson seemed different very sure of himself in a—in a controlled way, my wife said, Meyers nodded yes. Meyers said, Paterson kept himself in control, and Meyers became introspective and my wife looked into his introspection he saw her doing that and his face opened to himself seeing himself through my wife's use of her reaction to him. Meyers said, "A reliable doctor can be an unreliable man." "Not for long," my wife said. And later we went to Fee's house, an interesting house, the kitchen was to the left of the front door the living room was straight ahead and bedrooms and a den flanked a corridor on the right down which I walked into the bathroom at the end and got into swim trunks drunkenly holding onto the sink and then moving down the corridor passing the living room going into the

180

kitchen, I knew where Fee kept his booze, I opened the cabinet took out the Dant made a highball and went out onto the side porch down the steps across the cement and stepped into the pool as my wife jackknifed off the board hitting the water to Judy's applause. I paddled across to my wife's bobbing head in cap, she wiped her eyes, she smiled, she asked did you see me? I said, indeed I did, and we swam across to the edge I put my drink down and Meyers came into the water hands and head emerging near me, terrific, he said and Felix threw a rubber ball a duck and a raft onto the water and dived in after, bobbing up and smiling in his pool and we threw the ball around, but later when the others were partying inside the house Judy lay alone on the raft in the shadow of the diving board and I came to surface beside her and pulled the raft out from beneath her she came to the surface fuming and I angrily asked why she had said Maria Paterson was incredible. Judy sneered Maria didn't care about Pat it was the children. I splashed water in her face, no, no, you mean credible, then, because you bring out the familiar thing, Judy asked who cares but me? I answered when Paterson left town he left it all including you, how do you know? Judy asked. Because it's familiar, I answered; now Maria's dead. So she's incredible. The common *call* the dead incredible. That wasn't Pat's fault she's dead, Judy said. I said it was Pat's fault she died in his life without affecting him, and Judy asked, why ruin it? I had good times with him! Now you think it is you, I said, but Maria knew Paterson was an exceptional doctor, your sexuality was familiar stimulus to escape as his failure within himself to him oddly seemed to stimulate his success—you saw him as a success and he saw himself as—my wife later cried at me: Who do you think you are! What did you say to her! Do you have your deductive shingle out? I chuckled I told her Judy was the part of me I knew best and most despised, it is someone else's life my wife underlined, her dark eyes fiery, not yours, it's a long story I said, she nodded, and complicated like the others, yes, as the day Felix's wife Celia was telling her ten year old son Jason to sit up straight while I drew him, I said don't listen to her Jason just keep your eyes on the bridge of my nose, Jason's twelve year old brother George sat behind Jason politely watching me I had just drawn him and Celia was pleased and excited because Felix wouldn't like the drawings, he wouldn't understand them thus she was vindicated and her son Jason studied me as I looked at his face, he stood in the distance inside his blue eyes and studied me, George had done likewise both boys adept at moving their self-undergrowth over the rug through invisible mother and father life walls reflecting images of their childish faces and adult faces and figures young and old the whole family rushing into their futures. George and Felix and Celia, yet primarily Jason, so vividly American, so frenzied in his intuitive space, and like his mother's shadows behind her eyes shadows lurked behind Jason's eyes, and when I saw into the shadows his face blurred, and behind the bushes I saw a spectral soldier darkly clad in sexuality, and over his shoulder in the distance, at the end of the woods, at the start of the highway of childhood which Jason was already avoiding, I saw his young figure flying over childhood into his well dressed invisible unbearable future experience to which Jason was already reacting as I drew into his splintered spatial blue eyes—which I knew from history yearned for war— sound of march of feet confetti and music armies of children marching in time space away from distracted mommy preoccupied daddy to the phallic one-sided frenzy without opposites as the sleek man in the furniture store where I work, lines slant across his unfinished pink face that is looking to me as he is speaking to me glancing away from me he speaks, his waxen fingers strike his chest and fly in front of his puckered waxen face thrust forward his trunk tilts his hipless hips drive long legs nervously awry and an aura of pre-nascence outlines his thirty years revealing Blake's deadly conjecture this man-at-edge before me is one more child- ishly excitable sadist lusting for pain and excrement lips wrapped in a groping circle sucking and eating his pre-embryonic self suck- ing for life on the dark inner outline of existence walking on the floor of the furniture store he sells and speaks his formal and idiomatic hostility in suppressed pop-eyed rage at older women, tall pink boy of wax making out a sales slip, his childish loopy handwriting hardened and pinched and naively decorated by ten- dril scrawls hanging beneath the sloping unclosed circle-letters that curl and wriggle on a downward slant across the lined blue shadowed throat into a darkly warm and bloody place in my

182

experience begun on August 2nd 1930 by poor people in New York my father fighting to hold a job my mother disillusioned my sister five years ahead of me I began the lifelong unification of separate selves in the dark clockwork of inner and outer worlds, I drew Jason looking out of his doomed eyes, and later one day Celia told me a story, she sat in the sun by the pool, one day Jason came in the kitchen, she said, she was doing the dishes and Jason greeted her in his formal manner, she returned the greeting and he asked her where her gun was, she asked him why he wanted her gun, he wanted to do some shooting target shooting at the woodpile, he said, she told him her gun was dismantled in the shoebox on the floor of the closet in the den and Jason faced the closet door he turned the knob and opened the door he peered at hats and sports equipment his gaze lowered and focused on the box on the floor, he knelt he held his fingers over he lifted the lid witnessed parts of the gun he assembled it and loaded it and went outside by the side of the house and faced the woodpile and the soldier in the shadows stepped into Jason's brains and turned his face full of lines to the side of the house the low casement bathroom window, and from ten feet away, he fired, Celia looked at me distractedly, a pretty girl growing old with staring eyes, the bullet hit the shower tiles a few inches above the hot and cold water spigots had she been under her afternoon shower and facing the spigots, it would have hit the base of her spine, or, had she faced the window Jason would have had his revenge in her womb, the drawings are framed and on the wall, I told Fee don't try to understand them let them hang there one day you'll come home walk in here and they'll be real to you, he was doubtful, a few years later wrote I was right, and one bright day years before that I cut across the Paterson's yard on my way into town, I heard my name called I turned and Maria Paterson gestured from a chair on the lawn I went to her she was in a folding chair smoking a cigarette and drinking Coke, grey eyes looked out from her wide handsome face; she said,

"I saw your mother in town the other day, we had lunch together, did she tell you?"

I said "Yes, mother likes you."

Maria smiled and thanked me, she sat forward looking at me,

how old are you? I answered seventeen in August. She said your mother tells me you want to be a writer when you grow up, I nodded, Maria sat back looking at me thoughtfully. Your mother is a wonderful person, she said, she asked me if I knew that, I nodded, she said not many mothers would and she underlined dream, she looked at me sharply, I nodded and she said, don't be a writer. Her eyes deepened, get a job when you grow up be a ballplayer, you're a good ballplayer, find a nice girl and get married, have children, be a man like other men, okay? Our eyes met and the last look in her eyes was her reaction to what she saw in mine, she lowered her eyes, and my gaze followed her unfolding reaction, yet I then felt a little away from me, as though I stood on the lawn, away, looking at me and Maria like they were statues on the grass, am I for ever to be at such lengths from me, from the middle of me where I can look out of, to point at me and point back? I sit here nervously watching myself remembering waking just after dawn, I was six years old, in Pittsburgh, I went out of the house in my pajamas, I went across the silent deserted street I knocked on the screen door of the house across the street and waited, I knocked again and waited until the inside door opened and Freddy's father looked at me through the screen door I asked him if Freddy was up no I asked him "Why are you bigger than I am?" I am older, he said, I am a man, not what I meant, a slender man with thin face and dark eyes stood in the middle of the street behind me I peered out of my rear eyes at him while looking up at Freddy's father I turned toward the man in the street, the street was empty, I recognized him later in *The Turn of the Screw*, he comes from existence, not the grave. It was me ahead of myself. I woke in darkness in Florida hearing my mother murmur everything is all right, I heard the voices of men in violence and fear on the wind in palm trees, my sister and I sat up in our beds, or I was on the sunny seashore wading and gazing dazzled out to sea going up the pasture to the foot of the cliff of ice and wandering by rivers through forests and jungles up mountains along roads highways looking at hills all my life awake and asleep certain if I embraced my peripheral selves I would have me, I was wrong they are already mine, I am these. They are the separate unity, this face you see is the lifelong image of fate at

184

work in the middle of other lives that outwardly connect in the flesh of the one me, in existence doomed to be all that I am which I have always been as I was born begun, even as if I was someone else perceiving me watching me or him work on the drawing for the display window flirting with myself or himself his or my youth young and old at the same time I looked across at the drawing as the sketched face rose becoming a papier-mâché oval standing vertically in front of me shifting and growing larger to my left above me dots in the center of pencilled circles took life and glared down at me, and then two pairs of eyes appeared on each side of the oval shield with a white line between: black pupils corkscrewed and burned darkly out at me and violet triangles outlined in black covered the steadily darkening shield the jungle roared in flame beyond and the eyes blackly cursed me I stumbled backwards from her, animals screamed and she sent her fiery double eyed anathema down upon me I cowered growing younger starting to cry her eyes increased their savagery I fell back yet rose swiftly to my feet to furiously face that mask of Maria I cocked my arm and spear finger my face drawn in anger, I bellowed, I lunged, the letter! I sat up beside my wife, I got out of bed and crossed my loft in darkness, opened my mother's letter and read by moonlight: ". . . friends . . . neighbors . . . Dr. — is her physician, Mrs. — is a lot like Maria Paterson used to be, witty and attractive, and like her in appearance,": Henry James returned (Quint) to seize his unconscious child-perceptor of the man he would become. He would become his adult and boyhood inner companion the goddess the governess the woman Henry James was, the woman he possessed, the woman he never had, I was depressed. I grinned, I looked introspectively into Felix's swimming pool, although I don't mind when you drink, my wife said, I do mind, but when you're like this, and I felt inferiority approach my life to implicate me within my confusion, but then I saw Judy's imitation of herself as though she was Paterson's pride—characterized my reaction to me, and my sense of inferiority realizing I was seeing me across the lawn, i.e., I wouldn't let me accept my perception of Maria perceiving me, and my dream of Maria's savage mask was my dream of my savage endowment of me within her which infuriated her, and she would stare me

185

down to hell, I took my wife's hand, we walked, darling it is a long story, it is a world I will clearly see I shook my fist I must. I was close to inner rightness and violence, a deep dark volatile frenzy of true emotion, and I put my fist against my forehead and my wife touched my fist. I perceived her perceptive touch sounding a great union of our two great opposite selves. She murmured, "You will."

My friend the host knows the dark things about me, he speaks to me through angry eyes his knowing flowing out darkly, darkly as from a woman's need.

I can see her still, I sit in a chair the radio is on and she is across from me wearing her mask of control, then my dearest friend her husband comes home and we greet him and we sit and talk, we resemble three friendly world people, yet her husband walks down the streets in Brooklyn still stepping through a childhood without childhood as I do my father dead for the rest of my life yet I still stand on the porch steps in Missouri and face the sun in my mind at the morning and end of that street for the rest of my life missing my father; I miss myself. Her black-eyed husband looks out of his window at the yard, tree, garden, hedge, we love and need each other. I need him to gain me, his wife is away within us in the street with the old man she goes toward, her father, where she thrives best, but her husband and I have gone from her in our loneliness for ourselves, and in her mortal turmoil she sits inside herself with a drink in her outer hand, that afternoon a circle in the center of outer window eyes drew me across the room into her, into our adulterous afternoon as she connected with herself, I crossed the room into her turning into her and her husband step by step straight of spine and darkly black in his inviolable youthful loneliness my dearest friend whom I imitated and betrayed lovingly looked at me, sitting beside his wife in those days as if I had been some previous where in him, yes and both of us seeing his wife circling within herself, drew together with my hand out to him as she in her guilt in hand took me, killing him to hurt herself—hurting herself to death that she die again. First in my arms and then in guilt, she died in doubles, killing and dying and killing and dying, she died and then she died again loving and lusting and dying, then dying again in other arms than her husband's, than mine, on dark streets, night beaches, in and in her living room killing and dying and living and lusting and loving and dying lacerating walling her husband away from her, eyes bulging for the incestuous touch in her shadow on the wall of the older phantom, man stalked by her, the daughter of killing and dying, she was the daughter of herself, I see her still. My friend the host of this party knows these dark things, he knows them about me, he speaks to me through angry piercing crystal blue eyes, his knowing flowing, etc., this fiction is mine resembling me, not my friends, we are hardly alike, yet the bone chips on the bridge of my friend the host's nose are those I see on the shadowed father's character-face in the incestuous pattern of the adulterous wife's—I wanted to guide and influence her husband and in the living room with his wife where I saw him I wanted to be him or father in a girlish way possess him, reach up and influence the air I was with him, of him, Fitzgerald, and I was a little becoming his wife who sought her transient guilt in me as her self, young and old, experienced me in her daughter-life while I accepted, so husband wife and good friend sat and drank and talked and my life fell out of my face and eyes upon them, and her husband's tender expression seemed to see me as if I had appeared in his experience like he did, I did, and had he looked for me he would have seen me tying it, he did see me move—I met him at the big table in the back of the crowded tavern, we talked we shouted we laughed we drank I slipped thread around his ankles and then around mine I tied them together we became friends I went to dinner I met his wife she stands in my mind in the small kitchen of their small apartment, we are talking, it is evening and we have just committed adultery, I sit in a chair in the living room, the radio is on, her husband comes home, we greet him we sit and talk resembling three world lives in an air of a priceless world spinning in eternal return. We are, I am too late for what we mean, for what I mean, it is too late in experience for sorrow and I am sorry, and as he looks at me he doesn't understand that I am Judy, we have come three separate ways, inner unions formed in that living room where outer unions fell forgotten and Judy, I love a good story, later met a young man in a bar one night, she feared him she took him out of the bar into her wide hips waking with semen in her bowels she went into the kitchen and made a drink and watched his sleek silent slanting punk phallic figure cross the street she had feared his violence, she later spoke with him pretending she had forgotten, his face savage saying, *you also wanted*—in that room again, and again it is me ahead of me within me waiting teasing taunting patient to kill me, and in later years my friend and his wife greet me yet the tension of worlds in suspension is absent now, the greetings are now remote and time has passed over them he has changed she has changed I have—we have not changed, never change not now not tomorrow that suspended Pan sexual living room—gone in lieu of better things, there are no better things and that intensity of emotion and experience is in my mind as the chairs and walls are, as he is as she is as I see them they are in me, and I am in them, my dearest friends. Her husband walks down the streets of himself with thread in his hands, his wife has a character of a savage actor, and I see stars, of violence and energy, hanging before the blinded eyes of her refused entelechous existence.

My friend the host speaks through the concavities around the meaning in his blue crystal eyes, targets flanking the chipped bridge of his nose—years ago when the adulterous wife spoke how she liked him I—thought I—perceived an a priori reaction to him in her understatement then, and he had, not long after, spoken off-handedly of his liking of her with an a priori familiarity which, as they didn't know each other except by name, connected their faces—

If in his deductive attitude my host keeps me near and far to him and I am by my own deduction: Judy, is my description of him not invariably bound to overlap my description of my self or vice versa as his manner in keeping me from him closely is a similar color or tone as the unfaithful wife's keeping her realization of the form of her refused existence closely to and from herself—and isn't the experience within perception extended out from me to her, and to him, in their each's own, similar? Doesn't this similarity explain the adulterer's *sensation* of being the wife and being the husband—as then or now opaque or clear my selves

188

are near and far from me or from my host, that, without me, these people and all the relative separate selves are objective of one another, through me they appear and look at each other—

Crystal target eyes, owned by the girl (that my friend, the host, Maximilian, etc. is), that is still in my mind in the driveway in Missouri—glare in brazen contempt of me, disgust and impatience—all these are my friend my host this witch who is in my mind and feelings curses and snarls, despises me. I have mispronounced a word.

A voice says my name with a character of endearment, it is time to go, and so, in a large room with a high ceiling and high windows I am facing my frenzied host whom I have realized in my experience. Outside are the night and the silent city, inside this room my wife and I prepare to depart, we put on our coats and hats and then we go into the hall, we go down the steps and out on the street and head for home and ourselves.

Of the Dream

THE LIVING ROOM of this house is not coldly modern, it has a sense of warmth, a touch of impulsive indulgence, and character; newspapers are scattered over arms of chairs, ashtrays are full, magazines and comic books are helter skelter as if suddenly thrown down, and there are cups and glasses half full of coffee, and milk. As if they suddenly decided to take in a movie or visit someone. The room is softly lit.

The kitchen beyond is brightly lit, and cluttered.

A glass door with aluminum trim, leading from the living room to the back yard, is a shadow; the time is twilight.

The front door opens slowly, and a man enters wearing a dark blue suit and a white shirt open at the collar, black socks and black shoes. He closes the door quietly and comes into the living room. He is rather hesitant, and stands in the center looking the room over. He begins to move to the glass door, but stops, and without dramatic effect sits cross legged on the floor. There is a hardly audible sound, then, and then a murmuring sound, yet quite clear: of delighted children, which stops.

His face expresses concern. Yet though he is a serious man, his face shows curiosity and humor. It is a fact, a man's finite mask.

The glass door to the yard opens and a boy of about eight years enters and slowly closes the door. He stands watching the man. The boy is naked except for baggy underpants.

They look at each other, and without moving his eyes the boy advances to the man, stopping within arm's reach.

Muted sound of delighted children. Stop.

The boy begins to silently speak, moving his lips without sound he is talking of everyday things, and gesturing his eyes are now turned inward, in his preoccupation of telling what has happened; the man puts his hand on the boy's hip tenderly; the man lowers the boy's baggy underpants and takes the boy's penis in one hand, and smiles; the boy continues his silent narrative gesturing freely, hands wandering before the man's face, the man, using his free hand, takes one of the boy's hands, and kisses it. The boy moves his hand away in a continuity of mime, and walks across the floor in a circle gesturing and speaking in a moving rhythm, and halts in a shadow, and turning warmly gazes at the man.

The man makes an amused slightly tightlipped smile, and holds his hands out before him, beckoning, and gently, yet with strength, questions,

"Where have you been?"

The boy crosses the room, and before he goes into the man's arms, he meets the man's eyes with his own, and gravely answers,

"I have always been you."

They embrace warmly and the man whispers, emotionally, "At last."

Dream

THE ROAD LEFT THE HIGHWAY and wound between farms and hills; a small wooden fence held the name of the school and the taxi went between fenceposts up a dirt road and stopped in front of a large screened in building. Thomas got out, he had arrived at college and was immediately confused in directions, he had seen the school lake to his right and also the dam; across the lake from the dam stood old and new buildings where classes were held.

He began along a dirt road, and at the top of a hill he crossed a bridge, and after asking directions he found the registrar's office; he announced and introduced himself and the next day, again going to the registrar's office, he walked along a dirt road and something was familiar although he couldn't find the hill and the bridge he began through a field of tall grass, he stood under tall trees darkly conscious of terror and fascination and beauty, density of air—he saw a fence; then he saw the dam. Later the registrar smiled; "You went the wrong way." Thomas laughed—

He sat on the edge of her bed drinking vodka and orange juice remembering walking along the highway at night with stars overhead following a downward slope through grass into a thicket, and emerging entered woods and came upon another road which he left, going up some wooden steps into a tavern where two or three farmers drank, standing—maybe knowing and not knowing or not remembering him, for they were different men, he had a drink by himself; they continued drinking, backs to him in the dark and wooden Klondike tavern lit by kerosene lamps— warm in a sense of home, of men and experience: déjà vu vanished walking down the highway he crossed over the shoulder and descended into woods, he was afraid it was dark and the earth was moist beneath him parting heavy leaves before him he moved slowly with rapid pulse, he stopped at the sound of running water; he got down on his hands and knees; he felt ahead of him, he was on a ledge and the ground cracked downward he tumbled in a panic, landing slightly bruised in a shallow brook; he got to his feet trembling and looked around there was nothing to see in utter darkness, he began slipping stumbling through water—into a mud wall, face colliding against mud, he put his hands on it, it rose above his head; he leaned his face and body against it, heart beating in a similar density of darkness.

He felt along the embankment, fingers gently touching touched concrete and moved back again to the mud embankment which sloped up; Thomas scrambled upwards—quickly hauling himself over the top and lying flat "on my stomach on the grass beside the dam over which water trickled; and across the night lake I saw lighted windows in old college buildings, where myself and unforgotten students worked," in Thomas's dream—drinking vodka and orange juice on the edge of her bed lonely for college, lonely for—for encounter—re-encounter—he reached for it—*reaching*

WHAM!

He stepped out of the cab and heard his name spoken. He closed the door and stepped to the sidewalk to encounter Billy and Vivian Earl coming down the street, going out for the evening again; he shook hands with Earl in a difficulty, Thomas had compulsively promised to telephone and hadn't, Earl seemed to understand, though, and he and Thomas slightly talked, Earl looked at Vivian waiting for her to direct; Thomas faced them a little between them although he was a few steps away, she doesn't like although she does, a little, my eccentricity in me makes her nervous, a smile is her personal humor, I from in me see you; face involving feminine pleasure of disdain; in the distance behind her eyes I am represented as though she faced me smiling goodbye, the expression in her eyes is gauze-like—subtle—yet incredibly saying

193

hello; "We have to go; we don't want to be late," Vivian said; she took Earl's arm; they said goodbye and walked away. Thomas went home depressed and sat on the bed; his wife sat beside him and asked what was wrong. "I saw Earl and Vivian on the corner just now," Thomas said; "I'm never sure how they really react to me—and I was pissed at coming home from a hard day's useless-ness to see Earl and Vivian going out again." Thomas's wife smiled inwardly; she prompted him to look at his jealousy. "He needs people and places," she said, "and more than you he can go visiting;" Thomas said, "God they go to a movie a friend's house or the 5 Spot and hear Monk."

"He selects it," Thomas's wife said; "I don't seem to be able to do those things," Thomas said, and she said "Until you want to, he keeps himself in control so he can anytime," she said, and Thomas asked himself if he wanted to go to a movie (no) "Do you want to go to a movie?" he asked his wife, she shook her head and he asked himself if he wanted to visit someone, no, "Do you want to visit someone?" he asked her, "Who do we like?" she asked him; "I don't want to be a clam in society," Thomas said unhap-pily, and Fanta let him see him drifting along and dying. He agreed he could surely give himself away, yes you can, why I'd give me away before I'd take me, Fanta opened the door and Thomas remembered the dream conscious of a change in face, "I dreamed I was crossing the street to our loft, but at the same time I was in Earl's loft looking out the window at a convertible, I approached our loft looking out our window at a convertible with red leather upholstery and a brilliantly waiting steering wheel; do you remember we were in the bar the other night? And Earl came over with the news that Nathaniel was married?" Thomas's wife nodded. Thomas: "We invited him to join us but he said no, he said he had to go home, Vivian was expecting him, he had bor-rowed a car, he said, they were going to the beach early the next morning, and because he had to return the car that evening they wanted to get an early start. I was jealous of him because he had a car; because he could drive, but the car in my dream wasn't the car Earl was anxious to return, it was *my* car, powerfully primed and waiting for me to get in and go, but I couldn't drive it so well as Earl—"

194

"Why?"

Earl was a tall, quiet guy. He lived around the corner from my loft.

In the old dream I was young and old at the same time, peering between the slats of the manger watching Bill Earl and my wife. He lay in the straw on the floor of the barn, he was on his side looking down into my wife's face as she lay on her back yet a little awkwardly away from him with her head on his arm looking up at him; they were talking; my distress and disappointment with my wife turned into anger and agony and confusion and I went to them, I stood over them, Earl looked up at me carelessly and the cruel queen at his side was remote from me; there had been a time she had spent with me, but that was all gone, she was with him now; I had been deleted.

How could I be angry at Earl on a street corner as he and his wife were on their way to hear Monk or visit Nat's brother or have dinner with that trickster Jackson Hatfield? I was jealous—and I actually liked Earl, and Vivian, for it: it was the way they were *regardless*—of dreamy illuminatives like—me, Thomas a Crimmins meandering with Fanta, I'll—twenty years from now I'll see Earl and Vivian on their way to visit someone, no escaping it, and I'll still be jealous just as when Earl borrowed the car to go to the beach, but in my dream I parked the car in front of his loft, not mine, and when I looked out his window there it was. I fear the drive through the known—a whole geography I know awaits me, just as it keeps Earl and Vivian out for the evening, I saw them on the street—or, as I was coming home in the dream I cross the street to my loft looking out Earl's window at my car, or go to work in underground thunder and take the luxury of a cab home, and when I get out of the cab I see Earl and Vivian going out again, I say hello as I've said hello to them on the street before, or hello at the bar they are always just leaving "only stopped in for a moment," having been at Jackson's for dinner*—how can they

---

* Jackson hadn't been at college two weeks when I climbed in his bed giving him a big story to tell about my name and face in his large and small resentments, hate, envy, and lust.

The sexual guilt that had become the reaction, or, my reaction to my memory of the first weeks I knew Jackson seemed, ten years later, to be

visit Jackson so often? His right hand fights his left and his feet trip each other—but he was a pretty thing he hadn't been in college two weeks when I climbed in bed after him, which now gives him a sneering story to tell about my face and name in large and small resentments hate and envy and lust I am the same face Jackson first saw, yet as I grow older, different figures, among them him move in and out of it as if it was a stage—a fiction in fact, and he who crawled across Jackson's sheets was one individual darting between other bodies coming so close it caused friction, the chills up my spine—one of me had moved me between the others, and as the players dashed dodging around between themselves battling for the possession of my mind (he was standing on a high platform in an old building in his home town in Missouri, and he, Thomas, looked over the edge afraid he was going to fall, and he fell stomach convulsing he falling seized one of the light cords that hung from a checkerboard of hanging cords—chess strings—and hands clasped around the neck of one psyche, he gradually descended), turning me into (a machine in the sky) bed with Jackson, I reached what I reacted to in him, his boyish glamour, which forcefully pushing pulling drove me be-

---

usable in his mouth, and he talked, revealing his power to puzzle me with myself, as I refused to recognize my double sexual image. I thought there was only one image for me, like a pyramid with a large evil base and I dissolved into bed with Jackson—and men and women for a decade a certain notoriety for sexual festivity. My mind turned into an exploding star; sparks sizzled up my sides to the top of the pyramid; I was really something to see.

Thomas and his wife went to a party at his friend's apartment—the famous Negro writer's East 14th Street place, and saw Jackson there, drunk beside his wife on the sofa in front of the window; Thomas said hello to forward tilting Jackson, Jackson's lips were trembling and brimmed with saliva, and with a furious look at Thomas, Jackson tossed a half a glass of rye down his throat which came suddenly right back up and out in a stream back into the glass again; Jackson looked at it and choked; he set the glass on the table in front of him and gripping locked his hands together holding on, and looked up at Thomas. "You don't know it," Jackson said, "and in your star struck way I'm sure you don't care;" Thomas watched him swallow spit while he Jackson gathered powers

tween me, to him; united with *self*—the general in the generalized first person—I'm coming to it! Listen! Listen! Progressions! Me, mine or mine-self my (own) self, mine my-self, my-self, myself mine *I* rushed through me to possess a fixity of face—Jackson features included—a thousand male and female features in a single splash of come, out of which springs I of time in face, me and mine a child a man a feminine goddess/destroyer and creator of my impulses and fiction in a car moving alongside my train—in Jackson's boyish face; he was very embarrassed. And, nothing.

When Thomas was fourteen he loved them; he followed them around after school, they were tall and they drove their cars fast; and in his loft in New York a man Thomas was on the trail of the living child within him.

"I loved them. They liked me well enough," he wrote, "and in a feminine way I felt they belonged to me—they delighted me and I envied their older ages, their size and their nights in their cars. One fellow was big; split tooth and a lisp; one fellow was short, he wisecracked and sharply dressed and the third fellow was nifty tightlipped fascination and I used to imitate the way he walked I

Thomas had given him—Thomas's fear to own his sexual selves; Jackson took position in front of Thomas, Thomas smiled and stuttered hello; Jackson discarded the self Thomas wouldn't own—he waved it away—and leaned toward Thomas as if to lean into him, furious of Thomas's relation with himself, and others in Thomas's manner, and Jackson shook his head his eyes drilling into Thomas's, "no," he repeated, "though you are pretty, though you are bright, bright Crimmins, I think I even know why *you* don't know." Jackson separated from himself rising taking Thomas's arm leading Thomas into a corner holding his arm whispering informing Thomas that he Jackson had been uptown—had spent two days and nights with a pretty girl who was in love with him. Thomas mentioned that was terrific, stammering he didn't understand why Jackson was telling him; of all people. Thomas's eyes were bright in his combination. But Jackson's eyes *glittered*, he tilted his head back and curled his lip he was now the wise avenger with the key to Thomas's past "You don't know," he whispered; and Jackson fondled his chin, but the one man knew so much he vanished becoming teenage twins and four eyes flashed as if Thomas had captured Johnny and Josie,

197

could do it now; he could go down any world street." Thomas remembered his name, and wrote it down, *Airling*. Thomas's heart suddenly jumped! They called him—Thomas's writing hand shook as he stared at his written slip:

"A nifty tightlipped fascination and I used to imitate the way he walked I could do it now; he could go down any world street—" Robert Airling, but they called him—I gave him my love and awe at fourteen and at thirty two I give him my wife. No wonder. I am still there. I had written the following:

"A nifty tightlipped fascination . . . he could go down any world street. Robert *Earl*." Not *Airling*.

Thomas smiled in his wife's level eyes. "Still me."

She opened the taxi door and turned, smiled wanly, waved, got in. The cab lurched into the street and sped west across town.

"3C-28C," Thomas laughed, "speaks: attack the unknown." He asked Al,

"What do you think of her?" Al shrugged; Thomas said, "I saw a veil over her eyes, did you?" Al said "No," and his face

---

yet as if bearing the burden of Jackson's history Thomas saw a figure behind the twins, or a figure of two figures, both left feet joined, trudging through The Hatfield Twins—who were shrinking—as through a dark and stormy night, children spat at them, and at Thomas, cussing him, and Thomas hesitatingly yelled, "I'm not yours you fucking goofy boatload of people, I—I'm MINE!"

And she came out of Jackson walking, she recognized Thomas and for a moment they were fascinated with each other; she was young and intuitive, her eyes twinkled and as though she winked at Thomas—that he pay attention to her—she told Jackson she had the feeling she met Thomas before—at college? Jackson's face changed, brightened, as she vanished laughing at her joke, but as Jackson believed anything she said the way she said it, he shouted—triumphant—"I knew about you FROM THE START!"

"HER!" Thomas angrily cried—he pointed into Jackson's astonished expression: "THAT'S your uptown girl!"

The one Thomas had gone for, naturally.

clouded, irritated at Thomas's metaphorical nonsense. Then Al saw Thomas had seen him frown; Thomas smiled; then Al was glad Thomas saw him and felt grateful for Thomas's perception, for he loved Thomas because Thomas responded to him, but he reacted thusly apologising, "Well I just met her, maybe after I got to know her," "You would see," Thomas compulsively interrupted, "how guarded her eyes are."

Al was irritated by Thomas's lordly attitude, so, said, bitterly, "Of course." Thomas picked his nose and said, "I'm not attacking you; I'm after what it means. There isn't any veil, naturally, her eyes gaze out of her head like—" "Don't be childish," Al snapped, and began filling his pipe; Thomas said he hadn't finished "but it seemed I saw a veil—right away—which partly explains why her face is so white, the color is behind her face—is her face a veil? That sleepy look—everything happens in—under? Behind? The outer face is fixed," he concluded; he complimented himself on the sentence, yet the alliteration sounded familiar as he had the feeling he was explaining his reaction to her to himself—as if Al was somebody else—and Al was! Thomas laughed; he tapped himself on the shoulder, "At it again? Convolution? What happened to *her?*" Thomas wiped his brow, sorry, sorry, don't want to scream on, etc., and he saw himself wanting to describe her, and he answered, "It interests me. What can you expect? I have no style to speak my interest, I have me to speak and there isn't any veil, except maybe in my eyes, but it's still what I see so it seems to reveal my creation of her, which is not her, but my vision *intrigues me*, I love it and can say—I'm *fascinated* by her, I love her in a way I don't understand—I ought to, too. I'm a fool." He looked at Al. Thomas's introspective eyes sharpened and his face became the words he was about to use—Al couldn't take his eyes away from Thomas's—struck by Thomas speaking, gesturing, and Al, realizing how intensely he felt about Thomas, missed what Thomas said; Thomas had come to a conclusion, Al had just caught the last few words he clenched his teeth searched back for the beginning of Thomas's sentence, but Thomas, though not speaking, was gesturing, and Al panicked because he didn't know what the gestures meant because he hadn't heard—etc., Al searched on, at the same time frightened of Thomas because

Thomas would be disappointed with Al, and Al would almost rather die than disappoint him, suddenly Al saw Thomas get in a cab and go away, and self-conscious in Fanta's grip (Thomas's metaphor, Thomas again; Why can't the cocksucker-combination say fantasy like everybody else! Because he's a writer. Cocksucker—bad or good? Al's hands were trembling), and he had the feeling he was a whole audience between himself and Thomas—a man rose from the crowd, and cried—strangely, "Let *him* know it!" A woman screamed "NO" and a different man jumped up and called to the first, *"You're* afraid to know!" Al— feverishly—smoothed his face down working and wondering why he wouldn't let himself remember what he had heard Thomas say he set his eyes straight and fixed his lips and opened his ears he nodded fake comprehension comprehending he had missed the boat—But—!—Thomas said it—Thomas's right fist in the air! His left hand pointed to his raised right arm he shook his fist savagely, "—for her," he snarled through teeth; yet Thomas asked himself, "Which one? Thomasina or the girl in the taxicab?"

He saw her face, lips parted and eyes closed in passion against the back of his neck, his left arm behind her back his right arm between her legs he bent and kissed her navel; she kissed the back of his neck running her hands through his hair—but the girl in the taxi was moving away, his fist turned into a flat hand, he lit a cigarette smiling thinly as Al was wondering where Thomas was; Al had caught up. "No, no," Thomas said, and he shook his head translating to himself, to Al, *"If* she was mine. She isn't. She's hers, with a veil over her inwardly guarded—" What! Secret, he whispered, her secret vagina! Vagina? Woman! Woman! Thomas's lust cried out, "Rip away the veil! Pull her out of her head and deliver the hidden pussy to ME!" Al lit his pipe and grinned.

"She's got you." He puffed.

Thomas bent over laughing and clapped his hands. "She does indeed."

He added, "All my life; even before I met her—" Al scowled, "What the fuck does that—" Thomas cried out striking his chest his balls his head and pointed to the sidewalk—"As I walk down

the *street!* and now that I see her I—say—I cry—there THERE
YOU ARE MY *darling!*" But Al underrated his intuition and
world knowledge of stereotyped phrases—Al said, pointing the
way the taxi had gone, "*She* isn't yours." Suddenly he added—
with eyes in surprise and delight: "Or you!"

Thomas snapped his fingers angrily. "How damned right!
Right, and right again! A double rightness, how God damned
bitter it is, and I lean towards her! I try and bring her into my
arms—try to bring that bitch Thomasina into my *arms,* but my
arms are my arms, dearness I feel—Yie! Yie! Naked and
darling—my darling! How I desire—how I yearn to possess
you!"

"The other one went that way," Al pointed. "Your arms are all
yours."

Thomas took his friend's hand saying, "She did, you're right,
they are, she did," and stepped back casting his cigarette into the
street, face flushed and eyes a little glazed; he pointed to his
chest; he began to cry; he lowered his head tapping his finger
against his chest repeating he didn't know how to own them, he
had always given them to her, he whispered it was impossible; Al
asked, oddly,

"Do you look like her?" and Thomas muttered, "Not in fact;
only in face," and snapped his fingers again and looked up, he
thrust his index finger in the air. "There is more to this than
we—than I think—come in 3C dash 28C!" He grinned; he wiped
his eyes, said goodbye to Al, and—stumbling took a few steps and
turned, said goodbye again, winking, grinning, "Wow!" turned
away, tripped and went home.

He heated the coffee, filled the cup, added sugar and cream, sat
down lit a cigarette and conjured her pale face and figure before
him, and seeing her he warmed, yet once he looked into her eyes
he saw how fixed and troubled she was; and then her face was
troubled, and looking at that face saw she was absent from it—
lovely but not there; another figure was there—concealed within
and perspiration appeared on Thomas's forehead; a continual
searching into her eyes met the gaze of an inner woman who was
as if asleep—as Dracula in the sunlit hours; the deadly eyes were
half open, looking dully through the eyes in the face of flesh and
he realized he must separate the girl in the taxi from Thomasina

and from the inner figure he saw now, and as he studied her outer hair and dear body two things startled him—she actually did not want him—and not only did not want him, she had actually forced him out of her—head; Thomas felt a chill, remembering.

He remembered how she sat in the darkness of the far rear corner of his loft—the night she had come to supper, and after supper she had sat at his desk and made a whispered telephone call; Thomas left his wife at the table and nervously moving as in a trance into the darkness of the back of the loft—not knowing what he was doing, standing as a statue in the dark unconsciously listening to whispering—realized he was alone, the whispering had stopped, and from out of the dark silence a strange harsh hiss commanded *"Go. Away!"* which he did, yet leaning, bending backwards drawn to the voice of her sexual phantom, and that was the first. Through it came the second, like sound out of an engine, the drawings her aesthetic lover had done of her naked figure— now appearing, clinched it as Thomas remembered the darkly shaded charcoal flesh the artist had included in his attitude of his life within her, for he walked in her he walked in her, not her flesh, not terribly vital, her head without face was turned to a huge sweeping black wing, the tip of which now crossed her face as her body of flesh helplessly leaned beyond a spatial blackness at her feet; the aesthetic artist who had feared her identity had drawn the black wing of the raging creature in her outside her.

Thomas's perceptions came out of his experience and lined up within a dark voice from a far corner that had drawn him to it—why—why—seeing the great black wing cross her face in the drawing—the veil—she wanted him to leave, he left, yet he leaned towards it, her, her secret sexual configuration, he back-wards leaned, he had heard, and desiring and looking he saw the hands and arms the bodies the writhing naked bodies of the crea-ture and the whispering girl covering the telephone with her hand—go. Away—she waited until he had left—then! And then as he left leaning backward to her—pulled back by!—looking over his shoulder at her fixed and dimly white and weirdly featureless mask whispering in darkness "I'll be over soon, am leaving now" kissing and caressing the other, Thomas cried out, disillusioned, invisible—*not mine!* And he left—Thomasina pulling him back even as he moved towards his wife, Thomasina so hotly desiring to strike fire in—shadows, in space—in the pale white veil of face whispering to the girl on the other end of the line—now fiercely—a voice of scarcely controlled lust from the lips of the powerful Dracula within; utterly, wildly, awake.

Carol stood at the sink peeling zucchini; Al sat at the table nervously smoking his pipe, puffing, tamping, puffing, waiting for the knock on the door to signal the arrival of Carol's mom and dad from home—Carol was pregnant; Al rose and stepped to the sink beside her, put his hand on her rounded belly and kissed her ear, she drew away muttering his name saying "Don't"; he smiled—gazing upon her a cloud of fear crossed his heart convinced he would be a weak father; her mom and dad would come into the apartment where he feared and worried and watched his baby fill his wife in spite of his feelings.

Footsteps sounded on a flight below and Carol tensed, her hands moved up and down, and Al said her name, tenderly into her apprehension, she looked at him and smiled, her eyes filled with tears as double footsteps approached the flight below. Al went close to Carol and she put her head on his chest; Al was already seeing the father mother eyes searching his face and figure within the wooden railroad flat. A despair of poverty swept through him and the objects in their newly-wed daily existence sat raped without paint or neighbor, only the rocker had a rug in front of it and Carol's hairbrush lay on the barren dresser with no mirror; their legal match of hearts, with Carol pregnant now, formed the only union they knew in Salvation Army furniture on the top wooden floor in the sky above Chinatown; Al filled his pipe and went into the front room and sat in the rocker puffing and talking to his nervousness as four feet shuffled up the stairs, he clenched his teeth and fists and went into the kitchen, heart pounding; Carol had turned and wiped her hands, taken off her apron and was facing the door and the knock, together Al and Carol went, ushering in mom and dad with hellos handshakes and embraces.

The outcrying world of mother and father swept through and filled the flat; they stood and talked and sat talking and wanting to know, scrutinizing Al. And Carol's father sitting across the table from Al. And Carol rather shyly asked what it was *he* was eating—invisibly reaching his hand across the table, eyes blazing, holding his daughter in an iron embrace—mother made a tentative stand of affection beside Al in her habit of thwarting her husband smiling and snarling at and to him, squash, Carol said, zucchini, Italian squash watching her father inwardly snarling, smile all over his face: to Al "Writer, eh?" Al nodded, and Carol's father mentioned he, at one time, and the favorite was Chekhov and Al nodded, Chekhov, Chekhov was certainly, very good and after lunch, over coffee Carol's father asked Al what he did to make a living rubbing his thumb over his first two fingers grinning and humming, "You've got to have money." Al was a trucker's helper moving furniture and her father smiled and sneered nodding and Carol's face darkened, Al looked at her father's calloused hands by the coffee cup around Carol's body with a hot glitter of hate and time-revenge in his eyes; he's a long way from Carol's mother, Al saw, and the man and woman sat beside each other to give Carol the best life they could, withdrawing into themselves with her, Al saw that the man profoundly hardly cared about him, Al, and—Al was frightened. "I'm looking for a full time job," he lied, stammering there was an agency a good agency good meaning sympathetic to creative people—"I made a cake!" cried Carol, rising her father lightning-like beside her as Al rose shoving his chair back "It's all right, Daddy," she said over her shoulder, taking the cake from under the plastic dome; she put it on the table and cut it while Al got the saucers Carol's mother put the coffeepot on the table and Carol served cake, Al got cream and sugar and they ate cake and drank coffee; "Tell us about the ceremony!" Al and Carol burst into hysteria which they (almost tearfully) suppressed remembering Herman Katz at City Hall, the honeymoon night, a Spanish restaurant a movie and a bottle of wine at home her father's invisible hands gripping Carol's shoulders said, what they should do, if they wanted a *real honeymoon*, would be to visit *them* at home for a couple of weeks and Al and Carol brightened anything to leave the city going dark in memory of possessive oppressive rooms of home; Al glanced at Carol's doubt and their eyes met, they said they would definitely

205

visit, but not just yet, the baby and coffee and cake as Al's mother
and father appeared in Carol's father's concern—Al said he hadn't
told—his folks yet and Carol's father's face assumed surprise,
bewilderment, a shared sorrow; misunderstanding and a vindic-
tive triumph and a curiosity as it darkened and made Al nervous,
he said he had problems he had to first solve, "What kind of
problems?" her father asked, "You can't even tell your mother
you're married? That your—what & why, father would be—
what, because—" Al said he didn't know how to explain what he
meant and Carol's father said if Al was a writer, shouldn't he—Al
answered it was part of the reason, if there was a reason, why he
was a writer to enter those problems—and he said he wanted to
tell his mother and father but—first—he must first, tell himself,
Carol's father's face clouded and opened downward in an exclamation "If you're married you're married!" and he invisibly sat
beside his daughter in proof, and, arm around her waist said
"See?" Al said it wasn't—you—altogether—"It takes years for a
marriage to become real as a marriage otherwise it's two people
across the room from each other—separated—when you're *married* you can't tell yourself from the marriage," and Carol's father
heatedly said Carol's baby was real, and as Al shook his head how
was Al going to accept that—and when? in ten—? "You'd better
get a grip on yourself," Carol's mother agreed with arms around
herself as Al agreed yet explaining they had been married a week
and Carol's father said *evidently* they had been with each other
longer than, Al nodded with Carol's mother saying yes, but being
married was different than not being married, Carol's father said,
true and asked Al what he was going to do for money, money was
necessary, he had worked all his life and raised his children and he
pointed at Carol he pointed at her sister he pointed at her brother
in a line across the nation behind her slightly slapping Carol—
independently leaving him mentioning Daddy had helped her
brother's family her sister's family—showing they too lived independent and not independent still leaned to him like a secret
darkness her father conjured before Carol threatening her in his
need to turn from—*no face*—opened his hands, he had worked
hard; he had made sacrifices; he said he had raised his children
and witnessed two weddings; but he missed this one; yet he *only*

wanted to be sure Carol was secure in, Al agreed interrupting breaking the spell—yet the spell was cast, Carol was dazzled by her father's need, for Carol was the baby Al had taken away, and as Carol's mother smoothed the waves violence threw between them Al wondered how many years it would take for the man to realize Carol was out of his hands into Al's hands—on Al's side of the table beside Carol—possibly never, or almost, yet if her father did—not a day to look forward to for the man might then react, and out of the turmoil of violence Al lent to her father in that future possibility Al flashed that more lives were there than four, more than the fifth of Carol's baby, more than the sixth and seventh of her brother and sister, the eighth and ninth of their wives and the numbers of their children; there were lives in Carol's father's past that had never been lived, that stayed darkly in the distance down the undergrowth in the tunnel of her father's restless and avoided accumulated experience—did Carol represent any of those lives? The question seemed to strike true; and from out of the man's past lives rose and swarmed against the faceless glass of Al's and Carol's future—and with finality the future of her father, Al had a bitter fantasy Dear Mom & Dad I know you don't care, I'm married my wife is expecting a baby and both of us understand we are living within my wife's father's unacknow-ledged past, my wife holds hands with her father before me and her father rejected me long ago, and the feelings that pass be-tween the four of us here set sirens screaming—I siren—Al put his head in his hands. Carol's mother and father stared, "Al," Carol said. Al, to himself: All these feelings would turn us woe-fully away from the dream—as if we fight to blind ourselves from the dream Carol's father rejected in his youth, form of perception, intuition and true emotion. For three days they went sight seeing around the city, and said goodbye in Grand Central; as they talked on the platform, Carol's father seemed to separate from what he had been, he told Al to write—"your mother and father, your mother should know." "I will," Al said, and the two men met differently in a handshake of farewell, the thaw of a three day freeze; Carol's father's soft accent had fallen on "mother"— "your mother should know"—revealing Carol's stories of the closeness of her father with his mother, warmth and affection,

207

attention and trust; Al was touched. Carol's father turned, and, taking Carol's hand put it between his calloused fingers looking into her eyes, and though his face was averted from Al, Al saw what came into Carol's face and he shuddered, knowing the spell was being cast again, and the inner eyes of the old father blazed, drawing Carol away from Al—away from the world—and when her father, holding her eyes with his—softly spoke that she be a good girl, Carol's eyes lowered demurely, she smiled, nodding, and the unconscious genius the old savage king swelled and thumped his chest—his maiden daughter turned, and glanced contempt at Al: Al: stunned, and double-crossed, fell reeling across the platform in Carol's promise of a visit, home, they'd be home the first week next month.

Straight Lines

for Louie

JACKSON FROZE IN HIS TRACKS as firing broke out. A mortar exploded deep in the bushes behind him, and he ran deeper into the jungle veering to his right where Sergeant Lewis was with the other guys, and that turned out to be right. They didn't find the V.C. and the helicopter picked them up before nightfall; that night Jackson was drunk and doing the Monkey with the whores in Saigon. She was getting used to these compulsive Americans with trembling hands. He was nineteen years old, and when he finished the beer he drank the whiskey and started on the next bottle of beer, gazing at the four angry Negro paratroopers at the bar.

"Why drink so quick?"

He muttered, "Why not."

The air was tense.

Sunday morning Jackson got hit walking down a jungle road with Jacobs and Nicholson.

A poem! The V.C. did a dance! There was terrific gunfire. He went to his left fast, feeling nothing but terror. He collapsed on his knees near the trees hearing Jacobs yell that Jackson was hit. Jackson looked up at the sky, and then dared to look at the shattered bone in the hole in his shoulder. He passed out.

Woke in whiteness remembering the last lines of the poem, and hearing a roar of engines.

"You're going home, Private Jackson."

"Home?"

The poem, and the V.C. doing the dance by the jungle. Three months and ten days to get to this. How about the others?

"My buddies!"

He felt his body rise, in sheer emotion for the living and dying;

209

then he slept.

Mother and Dad were shocked at his bitterness. He had a hard time talking. He was in the backyard watching the squirrels in the trees, listening to gunfire, remembering the poem.

> "Drive, fast kisses
> no need to see
> hand or eyelashes
> a mouth at her ear
> trees or leaves
> night or the days."

Who had written it? Nobody knew. And the one guy who would was away at school, but lucky enough, in November Jackson got a letter from him. Joe had quit school and was painting in New York. He wrote saying he heard Jackson had been wounded.

"Why don't you come to New York? I can put you up."

Jackson went, and they had some good times, but Joe didn't know who wrote the poem. It sounded a little like—Sappho? No? Jackson told Joe about what happened, and about the V.C. doing the dance and Joe said a funny thing. He said he had written Johnson about it; he ought to talk with the V.C.

Joe was drunk and angry and Jackson was depressed; his shoulder hurt.

A couple of weeks later Joe invited a guy over, a skinny 4F character with acne that stammered it sounded like Zukofsky. But how do you talk to Zukofsky? You call him up. The next morning Jackson looked in the phonebook and there it was.

They met in the poet's apartment, and the poet asked Jackson to tell him exactly what happened; Jackson did, and the poet couldn't figure out how, or why, Jackson had heard his poem.

Around a year later Jackson wrote the poet this letter:

Dear Mr. Zukofsky,

Yesterday morning I remembered something; once, when I was a little boy, we were going on a trip. My father was driving, and at one point he began to drive faster, and then he kissed my mother,

210

then he kissed the top of my head and messed my hair as we approached an intersection, I saw a truck abruptly swing out in front of us, right *there*, my father swerved our car, there was no accident, but as the truck had so quickly been placed, as if put there, I sort of *heard* "trees or leaves/night or the days" but I don't think it's your poem I heard, Mister Zukofsky, I think it was an a priori perception of death, deadly stillness, and I hope you aren't angry, I like the poem you wrote, but it's mine too. (I forgot to tell you I heard it before I was shot. Not after. Like the truck in a way, dead ahead and we were racing towards it.)

It was like this:

I went down the road with Jacobs and Nicholson, the jungle on both sides of us, in Viet Nam, and a V.C. stepped right out of the jungle with a tommygun, and was going to let us have it, fast, but Nicholson and Jacobs nailed him faster, and for one lightning instant his weapon was pointed at me, and as he started to spin he fired. It happened so fast, you can't believe it until you experience it. He came out of the jungle like a shadow, and he wasn't fifteen feet away, and when he was shot and began to spin, his gun swung to me and I saw he was going to fire, I heard—"Drive, fast"—then he fired.

The Major Circle

WHEN HE GOT BACK to Philadelphia—Chestnut Hill—boy were they glad to see him! Mom's open arms, her flowers, and her speeches and Dad with tears in his eyes. His buddies cheered and shed a few tears themselves.

He was a little thin but no wonder. So the idea was to give him good food and let him rest. What he needed was food and rest, he said they treated him okay but his eyes had a glaze of vulnerability, and Mom said after a few weeks at home he would, but he didn't, he wasn't. Toward Thanksgiving nobody could figure it out. He wouldn't talk.

The story was his plane had been hit and he had bailed out over V.C. territory, and had been captured, held prisoner for a few months, and in an undercover exchange, had been freed and after a lengthy interrogation, sent home.

I knew him in high school; I used to dream about him, then. He was a great ballplayer, and even though I was his age I used to chase his home runs and bring the ball back to him. In my dreams I stood at the foot of his bed, and he—the body essence I knew from the locker room—slept before my eyes. I would have been his slave; he was so beautiful. And shy. His hair was soft, so black it glinted blue. Skin just the lightest olive, and his amused or serious eyes sparkled innocence in darkness. His lips were dearly sensitive and when he flashed his grin and tilted his head I used to laugh out loud. I used to follow him down the street and read Saroyan to him. One night at a dance I told him it was the point of life to love. His eyes were contemptuous, and he manipulated me with a smile; "What's love, Dawson?" Well.

212

His high school girl got him, and married him. She had chased after him, down hallways and streets from the Seventh Grade on, and hand in hand she went along with him after football games and summer dances, and after his second year at the University of Missouri he went into the Air Force, she always waiting at home. Then he went to Viet Nam. My mother wrote me when I was in Mexico about him being a carrier based jet pilot. He was a Major.

I came home and got an apartment in town, and continued writing. We never saw his name in the Philadelphia papers, but then we never really looked—the old gang was too preoccupied with wife and kids and money to really wonder anymore, and as they didn't come around, whatever interest there might have been faded away, and for a long time I didn't have my gang to drink with.

But when he was shot down it was in the papers; it was reported the Viet Cong had kept him in Convolution, he had been treated all right, etc., no war's over till people stop talking, and I got curious. (I saw him a couple of times. It was all he could do to say hello.)

In the following months I did some traveling, asking questions and adding things up, like a detective, until I saw it, and to make a long story short the Major had gone before this Viet Cong officer in a tent, and apparently the guy, the V.C. officer, like me, was pleasant enough, and the Major understood he, the Major, had been desired to be brought in alive, unharmed, and though exhausted and apprehensive, the Major responded with that Geneva Convention name rank and serial number stuff. The officer smiled. He said they knew that, and he asked the Major about his wife and kids; the Major said his name rank and serial number, and the enemy officer looked at him, and gravely:

"It is a dark and stormy night, the men are outside sitting around the fire," he said. He asked the Major about Mom and Dad and Philadelphia and childhood:

"Major! Tell us a story!"

Name, rank and serial number. The officer leaned forward and said persuasively,

"Tell us a story, Major."

Oh the arms and breasts of Chestnut Hill! *It was a dark.* Her

213

Flowers! *And.* Her warm voice speaking that *endless magic.*
Stormy night.

"Tell us a story, Major!" cried the enemy.

The Major began his story.

The Figure in the Sky

IN BASIC TRAINING the Corporal handed a rifle to the trainee who didn't carry any gun he was a non-combatant; the trainee flushed with embarrassment and self-consciousness and took the rifle, and standing with it in his hands the Corporal snarled,

"Now we get you."

He pushed the confused trainee out onto the porch where all the other trainees, who were policing the area, could see him.

The Corporal screamed to them all: "This Conscientious Objector holds a weapon a Court Martial offense!" adding softly to the trainee, "I'm going to get you."

The trainee later wept, and the other GIs in the platoon tried to soothe him. A Sergeant said the Corporal simply hated him, and said a Court Martial is a lot of red tape, don't worry.

Nothing happened. The Corporal waved curtly and grinned the next day.

In Korea, in the cold, they threw corpses out of fox holes and got in and froze their feet in mud and masturbated; in the days before, their company had raped four American nurses—miles back and left them gaping bloody and dead; they tortured enemy prisoners and mutilated their corpses; death on their minds they stuck in mud as the Chinese advanced machine guns cut them into a rising wall of corpses and still the Chinese came; in the thick of it a helicopter arrived and all the officers and Sergeants got in.

Sweeping upward the Sergeant looked down at the Chinese swarming over killing and mutilating the American soldiers; the Conscientious Objector saw the helicopter curve up into the night, and a moment later regretted his not having killed himself as the first enemy face met his, and without anything to save him he fought with his hands for life and all hope was gone, and when his enemy was on him in such a way he screamed, thinking, passionately, all these bodies were rushing to kill him, and dying swiftly, as he was doing, meeting someone who killed him because he was there his eyes bulged out of their sockets and he gave in, falling he gave himself to himself vanishing, and they cut up his corpse; yet they also died, and they tried to kill others first. Dead eyes were punctured by bayonets; the penis and testicles were cut off and crushed—in an upward motion where he seemed yet to wait; that man stood there for him, and he vanished into his arms.

The Vertical Fields

In Memory of C.D.K.

ON CHRISTMAS EVE around 1942, when I was a boy, after having
the traditional punch and cookies and after having sung round the
fire (my Aunty Mary at the piano), I, with my sister, my mother
and my aunts, and Emma Jackman and her son, got into Emma
Jackman's car and drove down Taylor Avenue to Church for the
midnight service: I looked out the rear window at passing houses,
doors adorned with holly wreaths, I looked into windows—
catching glimpses of tinseled trees and men and women and children moving through rooms into my mind and memory forever;
the car slowed to the corner stop at Jefferson and the action seemed
like a greater action, of Christmas in a cold damp Missouri night;
patches of snow lay on the ground and in the car the dark figures of
my mother and sister and aunts talked around me and the car began
to move along in an air of sky—at bottom dark and cold, seeming to
transform the car, my face, and hands, pressed close to the glass as I
saw my friends with their parents in their cars take the left turn
onto Argonne Drive and look for a parking place near the Church;
Emma Jackman followed, and I watched heavily coated figures
make their exits, and move down the winter walk towards the
jewel-like glittering Church—up the steps into the full light of the
doorway—fathers and sons and mothers and daughters I knew and
understood them all, I gazed at them with blazing eyes: light
poured from open doors; high arched stained glass windows cast
downward slanting shafts of color across the cold Church yard and
the organ boomed inside while we parked and got out and walked
along the sidewalk, I holding my mother's right arm, my sister
held mother's left arm (mother letting us a little support her)—
down the sidewalk to join others at the warmly good noisy familiar
threshold: spirits swirled up the steps into the Church and Billy
Berthold handed out the Christmas leaflets, I gripped mine, I

looked at the dominant blue illustration of Birth in white and yellow rays moving outward to form a circle around the Christ-child's skull as Mary downward gazed; Joseph; kneeling wisemen downward gazed; I gazed down the long center aisle at the rising altar's dazzling Cross and we moved down the aisle, slipped in front of Mr. and Mrs. Sloan and my buddy Lorry, Mr. and Mrs. Dart and my buddy Charles, Mr. and Mrs. Reid and my buddy Gene and his brother Ed—we then knelt away the conscious realization of our selves among music in the House of the Lord, I conscious of a voice which, slowly, coarsely, wandered—the I (eye) in see, hear me (I), we were on our feet singing and the choir swept down the aisle, their familiar faces moving side to side as collective voices raised in anthem I held the hymnbook open and my mother and sister and I sang in celebration of God the crowded and brightly decorated—pine boughs and holly wreaths hung round the walls with candles high on each pew, I glanced at the gleaming Cross—my spine arched, and far beyond the Church, beyond the front door, beyond the land of the last sentence in James Joyce's *Dubliners* a distant door seemed to open away beyond pungent green of pine gathered around rich red hollyberry clusters, red velvet, white/yellow center of candle flame, white of silk, gold of tassle, and gleaming glittering eternally Cubistic gold Cross and darkness of wooden beams powerfully sweeping upward—apex for the strange smoky pneuma that so exhilarated me, I who smiled and reeled in a vast cold cold gaze down at myself listening to Charles Kean's Christian Existentialist sermon in time before the plate was passed and the choir had singing, gone, and we were outside, I standing by my sister; my mother and aunts were shaking Charles's hand, I shook that solid hand warmly, and I walked down the steps, my mother and sister and aunts again, again, once again it rushed through me taking my breath, my spine arched toward trees and streets walking slowly breathing deep I moved down the sidewalk, eyes crystalizing streets yards houses and all lives within; my perception forked upward through treetops into the vertical fields of space, and a moment later, in the crowded back seat of the car, as Emma Jackman started the engine, I breathed vapor on the rear window, and with my finger, I signed my name.

The King and the Burning Boy

MY FATHER, WHOM I SCARCELY KNEW, had come home to die, and in the months following the funeral I transferred that love to my uncle who responded with an unusual strength turning me into myself in spite of me, to get me to do things he gave me myself as often as he could, and included me in the things he did in a way that. was as generous as it was thrilling, and on mornings when I was thirteen, fourteen, mornings so cold water and ink froze and I huddled close to him beneath the blankets, he spoke, awakening my tense devotion to him.

"Get up you lazy rat, get some coal and start the fire," sending a tingling chill up my spine—I, a rat?—as I doubled out of bed laughing into the cellar for the wood and coal, emerging to make a fire in the pot bellied stove, and when the room was— wonderfully—warm, my uncle emerged from the bed in his long underwear putting his salesman's feet on the shabby rug looking at me as I laughed in affection for his thin frame 1918 underwear— handing me myself in his manner of shaking his head at me with the sleepy look on his face, a heavy man-drowsiness, which I envied, was his and created a delight in me; I knew—deeply—I was some thing, some self, my self, mine, he never thanked me for making the fire, and in his understatement he would and many many mornings did remark that the room was warm enough for him, that it was time he should get up; he yawned.

One sunny Sunday afternoon in our room, my uncle, in my eyes, smashed a ladybug on the door to the cellar, I had tried to stop his hand, he shoved me to one side with disgust at my sensitivity, and killed the spotted insect. Tears welled in my eyes, I flailed my arms and stammered and he backed away face downcast, avoiding my experience with death in a semi-conscious repeat motherbug, motherbug your children will burn and thereafter I labored hysterically to suppress my reaction so my uncle and I could have our relationship again. I did, and we did, though indeed his impatience, living with the mad boy I was, brought in his swift crush of the insect, the awakening of my torment and I screamed.

In a field I found a dead cicada at the foot of a tree. I put it in a wooden matchbox and carried it with me, repeatedly looking at its crisp corpse with a combination of pride that my father was with me, and shame and guilt and loneliness that I thus carried him, in the reeling of the senses and a sense of time being endless without having yet begun, and fascination as my heavy finger stroked its dead flank and wings as I gazed upon it.

My father's favorite poem had been the Francis Thompson—but within a roar I translated—I thought I was the Hound of Heaven chasing

> down the nights and down the days
> down the labyrinthine ways

and each time I went down the cellar steps for wood and coal to start the fire I had the same fantasy. I was the captive of a king, and his proclamation was that, at any time he saw fit, I was to stand before his figure on the throne and sing to him, for my voice pleased him greatly, and so I sang—vain that he had chosen me; darkly not admitting if I didn't sing he would have me killed.

I sang, I sang I thrilled him, I sang for my life, and one night when I was in high school I stood on a chair in my mother's room, she was in bed, and I sang the hit tunes from Oklahoma, I sang until I began to yell I began to scream and cry, tears ran down my flaming cheeks I threw out my arms and the song was over, my mother patted her hands in soft applause; I stepped down, I threw my arms around her, I—wild eyed—tensely laughing, choking, weeping, kissed her.

220

Dream

In the hospital terminal looking out, with the rest of the patients transients and students, at the stormy sea that battered the promontory building "when that goes, we all go," I said, knowing it would never go, and it began to crack, the floor under my feet buckled, and I fled.

In a labyrinth below the women before the mirrors promised their change in a droning speech given by a doctor who looked like a barber. He hung up his L shaped she horn—all the face fixers did—and they proceeded, in confusion to the women who sat before the mirrors and couldn't think of a face they wanted and the mirrors stayed fogged in the blank parts. An actress was there, lipstick on the cracks, and her painted eyebrows up too high; she looked old and tired and a young face fixer waited until she made up her mirror who to be and she gestured nervously talking her angry hipster talk, she was like her, you know? Me! I am like me, Goddammit! *Me,* and she waved her hands.

I ran down the steps toward the basement running anyway as I am always running to where he is still alive and I have my schoolbooks under my arm—I opened the locker and took out my books with Mr. Hicks in my mind I am up the stone steps and the beach is crowded. I stand at the rail with the patients and doctors and students and I see the young writer and I call to him to come and he doesn't, I laugh, come up here you young dog and everyone laughs including him and I am older and up he comes—stopping half way, his younger brother gazing up at me—lonely and confused, amused, dazed.

I run down a corridor to escape the falling building seeing the stunned face of a doctor teacher executive, I race into a dark

221

elevator which lowers me onto the changing shifting steel scissor train tracks which I study and elude leaving the grounds noticing again the great windswept character of dunes—in the older dreams it was dark out there and still is, at night, but in the light of day, the figure who stands on the old wooden pier in the sand and gazes out at the universe is me from my oldest dreams, and I walk to high school, and as I get to the street in my hometown I see a man, he inquires of the disaster and I answer the building only settled, and although—I mean it had all the character of collapse, and I say, bitterly to him, a little snarling,

"You should have seen the last one."

Little Women/Lost Horizon

for Ray Spillinger

WE WERE AT THE BAR.

My wife was sitting on a stool facing me with a gin and tonic in her hand; Ray sat a little in between us drinking gin and soda water with a twist of lemon. The bar was crowded. The tables mostly empty. It was after two a.m. Men and women stood in groups looking and gesturing at each other, the men keeping an eye on the girls along the bar while their girls checked out the men along the bar. Figures moved around us shifting and glancing in and out of eyes; a pretty girl kissed a little man and he pulled her close, I watched my wife watch Ray look at the girl, and watched the girl look at Ray; my wife watched me as I watched the girl looking at Ray, I popped a wink at my wife and looked at Ray sipping his drink. The little man went away and Ray and the girl began talking to each other, and a moment before, before the editor came in, a tall bar friend in a dark topcoat appeared with an Englishman whom I'd met a few days before, we had been drunk and everything had been sparkling and funny, but the night Ray turned forty the Englishman wasn't funny, and though the Englishman and I greeted each other warmly I became tense, he was smiling and talking his eyes slanted down he was worried and scared and slightly lying to me with a long story about a girl he met, whom he had never seen before warmly greeting him as he and his wife were walking down the avenue; I stammered, compulsively asking him if he wanted to find out who she was—it sent him away, he hated the way those analytical bastards talked, "can't stand their *language*," and I cried, but, if he wanted to know who—he angrily did not, I burst out: "*I* would!" and the tall bar friend took my hand and said hello, the Englishman left and Ray ordered drinks around, the tall bar friend grinned above his dark topcoat—it was nice to see me, he said happily, and I said the same to him with a grin, Ray laughed and my wife joined in at my bar happy face, yet the tall bar friend was moving his hands in such a way that we should listen to him, he moved his hands seriously conducting a prelude to what he was about to say, "you're a writer," and he stopped smiling and conducting and asked me, knowing that I was—because I was a writer, what this meant:

I see as through a glass darkly

and he tilted his head back and gave me a tightlipped smile. I got a slip of paper from the bartender and wrote down the meaning and handed it to the tall man but Ray intercepted it—he read it

"Wonderful!" he cried. "Very good!"

The tall man read it and squinted his eyes at me—*you?*—and I described his look to him and he blushed and Ray and I and my wife laughed and had another round of drinks and the girl kissed the little man. The door burst open and an editor of a man's magazine came in, red faced and screaming about Goldwater, two girls ran after him and three men chased them and his wife and an old literary friend followed them as they swept to the bar. The tall man in the dark topcoat said he wasn't sure about my interpretation and wanted to know who I had been reading lately, I told him: me—ha ha I laughed, casting it in front of me. Ray chuckled in his drink and my wife looked at me and smiled distantly, the tall man smiled from the collar of his topcoat as the editor began embracing everyone and the girls next to them while confiding in the bartender about a certain style, a personal style, after all, about a certain drink? A lot of whiskey, a little water, I saw the back of a girl, a pleasant girl-figure in long stockings and light coat and dark brown hair curled at the shoulders; the editor stood to her left and opened and closed his face gnashing teeth and bursting and hissing laughter—someone spoke to the girl, she turned and I saw her face—as lines cut in leather, and doomed dark eyes; parted lips in an expression a realization of poison: age, her whole wrinkled face

224

was a bitter map of time—against all advice she had come away from Shangri-La.

Later I looked at the other girl, of age and youth who had kissed the little guy standing, an anachronistic beauty baby face and dimpled cheeks, twin spear spit curls by her ears rosebud lips turned up nose and dark ringed twinkling eyes I, astonished, said in italics Louisa May Alcott—her lips parted, her head tilted forward and she bit into her highball savagely, swallowing looking at me eyes bright, looking at me, she, leaning to Ray, said,

"I took it into fields with me."

My mind wrenched. I rose, glaring, incredulous, "What did you take!" I cried. *"Your face?"*

Dimpled, darling, gravely shook her head. "No. The book: *Little Women."*

Shades of Yesteryear

SHE CROSSED THE CROWDED TAVERN and sat next to him at the table. He was drunk. "Hello," she said. "Remember me?"

He looked at her.

"I went to New York again," she said, "you weren't at your old address so I asked around. Somebody in that bar told me you had come to Provincetown, so I thought I'd come up to Provincetown!"

"That's swell," he said. "How have you been?"

"Well, that's a big question, if you mean it seriously, but you don't mean it seriously. You hardly mean it at all, and not even nicely." She looked at him. He was older now, a little gray. "I want to tell you something," she said.

He looked at her; she smiled. "I was in St. Louis this spring, and I saw your old psychoanalyst Doctor Sommer at a party, and as we know each other *fairly* well, I asked him if he remembered you. He said yes and asked how you were and what you were doing, is it fifteen years? I told him you were writing, and he was very pleased. He said—"

But the look on his face frightened her. "Don't you want to hear what he said? Still the same!" she sang. "You haven't changed at ALL!"

November Dreams

THE BUS LEFT PROVINCETOWN on a long downcurve, and then gathered speed onto the straightaway, and I looked out at the pine trees and bushes. It was a warm day.

As we approached a curve I had an uneasy feeling that gathered speed as I became warm and then hot. I saw a dirt road ahead leading down to a motel in the pines, and I went up the aisle to the driver and told him to let me off there.

I climbed down from the bus perspiring, and as the bus roared away I turned and ran down the road toward the manager's office, at the bottom among motel bungalows and pine trees, hearing a shriek of rubber and sharp horns, I wheeled around, and saw a hook and ladder firetruck in the sky, and a sportscar flying level above treetops. The firetruck was coming sideways, ladders slipping askew and hoses uncoiling, wheels spinning and firemen somersaulting out into space, and in a slow roll the engine sparkled red and orange against the sun, and smashed loudly into trees in a cloud of pine needles and dust bounced, and with a splintering of ladders and crush of metal the long red body hit the concrete block of the manager's office, which shook once, and held, as water and gas ran out from the firetruck. The sports car, with three fellows in it, came fast down the incline bouncing off posts and trees, turning over once, and, like a final slap, smacked against the front of the manager's office, and stopped, steaming. The three fellows climbed out, and stood before me laughing. I frowned.

They were lean and tan. Grey and yellow eyes twinkled; white teeth shone; they smoked and talked and examined the wreckage. I gaped at them like I did in 1944 outside the dentist's office by the Osage Theatre in Kirkwood, and before they headed down a differ-

227

ent street one of them took off his face. She was laughing and shaking her hair. Straw hair, an oval face, an egg shaped mouth. The others made soft amusement with her, and I shrank in fear against the building. She looked at the wrecked sportscar, and then at each of them. They went between unfamiliar buildings towards Chippewa Drugs. I followed at a distance, and sat away, in slanting sunlight beside a wall of windows with no sea beyond, but the rain, or storm swept through me in dead Gene's teenage laughter as he was talking like he used to. And Lloylac was his friendly implacability again. I looked out the wall of windows like *The Lady from Shanghai*. We stood by the door.

Dead Gene took change from his pocket and paid the cashier, Lloylac did likewise, and then myself, and for a moment dead Gene's face was shadowed by the sun pouring through the glass. I saw his head turn, and gaze with blank eyes into nothing. His shadowed profile began to float out of my memory of him in a white shirt, cuffs rolled up; creased slacks, argyle socks and loafers, his profile floated away.

Young again. Walking down my hometown street.

Familiar houses were spaced in such a way that even through trees from several yards away I could see the low silver roof where the family of individuals lived. I loved those three children, in their younger and older ages in my youthful couplets of loving/fearing, envying/possessing.

The oldest brother stood in the yard.

I had an apple in my hand. I threw it at the sky. I walked down the street passing house after house, even walking by the driveway which led to his low house with its silver roof. I saw down the driveway; the oldest brother stood in the yard like a statue of his normal disappointment and loneliness.

The apple was plummeting down. My heart froze. I continued walking, legs trembling as my knowing raced across lawns between trees charting the downward plunge of the apple. A black and grey shadow stood crisply on edge, on the corner of the street ahead, as the apple downward fell, struck, and killed the oldest brother. He fell on the lawn.

I crossed the street laterally, but not knowing where to go I headed back down the other side of the street towards home. Crowds were gathering at the end of the driveway. Two police cars and a firetruck blocked the street. I passed between them with a glassy face. What if they were to ask me? Who did it? Who could do such a thing? A fine boy was dead.

I crossed my front yard and went up the steps into my house and my aunts spoke to me of their helpless selfishness. I passed between them nodding, and went into my angularly darkened room. I lay down on my bed dizzily but could not rest so I went into the kitchen and a high school buddy of mine came into the kitchen, too, smiling in his tall face, we looked in the refrigerator for something to eat and had a glass of milk, but I couldn't drink and we went out in the front yard as another pal appeared, and we began the game beneath the tree. Someone laid the board out, brightly colored discs and dice tumbled upon it. Who would go first? We threw. I tossed my dice gloomily. A woman called.

She stood on the sidewalk looking angrily at us, saying,

"What they ought to do is form a posse and surround the neighborhood. *They'd* get him!"

I looked away, her eyes hated all I was anyway, and my friends stood numbly beside me mumbling it was a terrible thing and the woman's angry eyes glared into my circle, unaware yet furious she spoke in headline language.

I was drifting.

Then, I remembered. As I had passed between police cars and through the crowd on my way home, it was as if someone had joined me, fallen in step with me, and going across my lawn, I was two, and as I had gone up the steps four feet had moved—who was it seeming so close to me and understanding? So close to my heart! Who was it that was near, and also invisible, understanding I-killer drifting away as the third lay dead on the grass with his head cracked?

Doors of shops were open, wares displayed.

I walked down Main Street.

The town was deserted.

I headed out of town: Main Street turned into a dirt road which went up a hill, and in a shaded area entered a country asphalt road

229

where I stopped. There was a screened-in grocery store on my right, and a closed-up house on my left. I went in the store and asked the man behind the counter for directions in déjà vu; in the same way: I left, and began hitchhiking along the road. Cars passed. No luck. A car stopped, and I got in, immediately distrusting my driver: plump man about forty-five needing a shave, perspiring talking about the highways he wasn't sure of, he had to stop at his place, he said, and also for gas and we would go on to where I was going, it sure was hot, and I followed the car along the road map through small towns along detours and down those upstate highways, until he pulled into the gas station on the X, and later we approached the mark I had made, went up a rocky driveway to the detective story house and went inside. I waited in the dusty wooden American hallway while he got some money, and we left, drove down roads to the house by the side where two men played poker and smoked cigars as they did at the table by the lake in Northern Mexico, and just as then paid no attention to me, and I began to cough. Dust, there was dust in my throat.

It began as a trickle between rocks; Lloylac and I followed it as it turned into a brook—then into a creek about four or five feet across. We tossed pebbles into it and as it widened into a small river getting so large I couldn't even with my pitcher's arm, throw across it. The earth rose and we were on a river bank, the air ringing with the roar of natives. It was the Ganges! Some sort of celebration? We made our way between the shouting cheering figures, me and Lloylac tossing pebbles in the water.

I looked over the natives' heads back to where we had come from, and I saw a distant tiny raft in the middle of the river. On it a tiny dark skinned old woman sat cross legged, and as she approached the natives howled, and she and the raft got larger, we tossed some stones in the water, and walked parallel with her as she grew, there on her raft, in the middle of the river. Lloylac threw a dozen stones the size of marbles into the water, making an even line of splashes. I only had two. How did he get so many? She was looking at me directly. Angrily. The sky darkened. The day turned into night, and her searchlight eyes fixed on me and I was alone. She strode through the water and stood before me on the muddy river bank, taller than me, glaring down at me. The sky turned a plum color and she was ten feet tall. I looked up and saw her wrinkles disappear, and watched her muscles form into cables, rippling power, and her skin was like leather. I saw up between her spread legs into her shaggy cave and dripping vulva; the muscles of her thighs tensed with power. Her belly and breasts seemed to boom, and she glittered and despised me. Her hands were out, her fingers curved claw-like down, raining invectives in a gutteral language upon me while I crouched helplessly under it—her giant head bent, two ovals of fire and fume seethed down on me, and her fangs gleamed blue white. I fell to my knees in dizziness, and in terror and confusion. Her animal savageness literally breathed sweat and piss and shit, and the setting sun outlined her bronze violence. I dwindled, and fell at her muddy feet in darkness. Her force kept me there. Lightning lit the scene—the sky smashed.

We went towards the rocks. I was carrying a picnic basket and a bundle of rolled beach towels. My wife had a folded aluminum chair under her arm, and as we entered the narrow split in the rocks I saw the water and the beach ahead.

As we moved into the cleft in the rocks we saw two men facing each other, their backs against rock gazing intently at each other. They didn't move. They blocked the passage and my wife and I couldn't get through, and we paused, conscious of a growing violence in separation or sudden deadly union. The two men were unaware of us. Their eyes were fixed on each other's, and I wondered when they would move away, or one to the other or the other to the one.

The fellow on the right was several inches taller than me. He had a high forehead, and blue revengeful and scrutinizing deeply set eyes under darkly bushy brows; strangely like wheels the pupils and irises contracted and expanded, and the man's face was taut as if trying to gather his response to his eye-action reflected in the other fellow's expression—the taller man fixed his eyes suddenly on me, his irises and pupils jumped, I shrank in fear although I saw the man was hysterical, wooden with anxiety, his expensive tweed suit, vest and paisley tie, expensive shoes and colorful socks were like a shell, and when he spoke to me his hollow cheeks spread in a startling leer—his lips split apart: his teeth were huge, but I saw behind them into an iron saw-like tongueless machine grinding sideways around a pool of blood.

The other fellow was rigid, flat against the rocks, face damp with perspiration, eyes wide in fear. He was not as thin as the other, yet he was dressed the same, except his tweed suit was rumpled, the tie loosened and collar open. He was about my size.

I stood a few feet away, between them, and decided to break the spell; I took a couple of steps forward, but the taller fellow stepped in front of me.

I said, with an interior voice I remembered, which was to be obeyed,

"I am going to the beach."

The fellow stepped aside angrily, yet as if to faint. I led my wife between the two men and headed to the beach. The tall fellow took a giant step and caught my wrist as to include my arm, I turned and saw his whole expression harden, and as if his face were trying to turn upon itself—the flesh seemed to fight the bones—his eyes flashed terror and I saw the teeth part, and he breathed a stench of Auschwitz in a sound—a scream and snarl of conviction!

We went woodenly to the sea.

The water was warm.

Floating face down I saw things: a red shovel. A ball with green bands. A yellow pail, and small fish and slowly moving seashells, shifting in currents over the white sand ocean floor. I felt a wonderful security.

I raised my head to gaze at the wooden breakwater slanting out to sea. A lifeguard sat atop a tower at the end. It was all small in a hotel-world wide blue sky, and I swam in a circle, and raising my head for an instant I noticed a man standing at water's edge, on the beach, watching me.

The sun shifted and I couldn't see his face.

The only part of his face on the screen was his jaw.

I broke the circle and began swimming out to sea, going nowhere but away, my little arms and legs thrashing. I saw, from the back of my head, a shadow depart from the tip of the man's toes, and rapidly zig zag through the twinkling strata of wavelets toward my feet—I recoiled in terror, and in revulsion my body made a storm in water as I cried out, and gagged as the shadow zipped obliquely razor sharp into my toes.

The house was white among the trees. Double glass doors opened in off a flagstone patio.

We sat on a low studio couch against the wall near the fireplace. Some young and pretty suburban girls were drinking coffee on a long low couch by casement windows near the doors. They liked my looks. I enjoyed that. They were dressed to impress, like they were at a party. I savored my thoughts about them.

A low wooden banister rail divided my wife and me from a sunken dining area, beyond which a door opened into a hallway. I saw heads and shoulders of people talking and drinking tea around a table in the sunken area, and it was a party.

I then noticed the shorter of the two men we had encountered between the rocks. The fellow was as tense as before, and the talking people only seemed to distract him. I saw his hands tremble, his skin began to go white, perspiration beaded his face and his eyes began to widen, his face tightened in a horizontal stretch—he was being pulled apart, and I realized if I could take away his skin and tear his face off he could have flown apart bleeding as he desired at once, shuddering as in a chill of virus—I stepped over the railing and knelt beside him. Our faces were close and when he realized my presence, he touched me. Boulder-size tears heaved down bleached cheeks, and as a giant redwood his head began to nod, his lips twisted into a rubbery smile of grief, and of bitter and unwilling farewell. The anxiety tuned up to a tiny stunning sonic crash, my face was so near his hollow cheek the cheek was like a cliff, larger than what I knew, and the earth slanted with it. Slipping tears left damp tracks in the sound of smashing glass—"What is it?" I asked. He shook his head, unable to speak. I reached up to stroke his other cheek and he turned his face to me. The look threw my head straight back. The face was petrified and beginning to crumble— and then, in the far corners of the white of each window eye I saw a blue-black shadow begin to creep towards each iris and pupil—they leapt like wheels, trying to flee. His face split. Fingers clawed air,

233

he made a gasp. We stood—I would go for a doctor. I moved fast, and in the doorway, turned.

He stood feet apart, arms out, head and face straining up. The blue-black stain was almost touching the irises of his bugged eyes, and his lips parted for a final cry.

I ran down the street passing houses, scrub fields and an occasional parked car. I saw two women walking in front of two men, coming toward me on the sidewalk. They were coming from—church. I, breathing rapidly, asked where a doctor was, in this town. The women looked at me.

"Listen," I said evenly, "a man's dying back there. I have to get a doctor. Can you help me—"

They turned to their husbands, murmuring something. And so I ran by them, encountering other husbands and wives until I saw a woman in her twenties, and her intelligent look asked me what was wrong.

With force I repeated the message, and she understood, or she seemed to be a knowing person, I thought I saw a look in her eyes—she might be able—"We have to work fast," I angrily said, "this man has been poisoned—"

The girl's intelligent eyes turned inward, and I watched her work on what she knew—it was all fields and streets and I had run beyond the point of no going back, they didn't know, even on time, and the young woman's eyes returned to mine. Regretful, and puzzled in my memory as I ran.

The Old Man

for Mario and Helen

"Just a moment, young man."

The writer turned on edge. A man, at least seventy, was sitting dapper and alone in a shadow at a table, drink before him. The old man said,

"Would you join me for a moment?"

The writer looked at him fearfully. The man's eyes were steady circles, not unfriendly and not warm; they made a camera shutter click at two youths at the bar, who pivoted on their stools to face him. The elderly man flicked his hand.

"You can go now; I'm all right."

The two youths moved toward the writer, black eyes glistening punk-sparkle; and the writer, threatened, yet rose in reaction to his fear of them and his hatred of them, glared at them furiously. They stopped, one on each side of him—and the writer was startled by a disappearance of fear in an air, a dumb air they exuded, of strange opposites: two boys like mute, white, vulnerable, and softly dangling, feminine penises. Irritation riffled the old man's features, and he said,

"Oh stop playing. Go, I'm all right."

They murmured in amusement like sleeping girls, and slipped out.

The dapper man smiled to the writer. "Come. Sit here." He cast a string, caught the writer and he went to him on it; Pinocchio sat down. The man said,

"Would you like a drink?"

The painted writer nodded. The man rose, and at the bar ordered drinks, but the writer was angrily beside him with fifty cents on the bar.

"I'll get this," the man said.

"No. You pay for yours, I'll pay for mine."

"Won't you let me buy you a drink?"

"Never."

"Have it your way, then."

"I will."

They returned to the table with drinks. The man said, "I heard you talking about Viet Nam."

The situation was familiar, and in his fear and anxiety he remembered one time he had let a man pick him up like this—no, not like this at all, but an old threat to end it—or aimed at him *with* his sex, was still there. They had gone to a black and white chrome Hollywood hotel and had a grimy sexual night. He had stolen money from the man the following morning, and run away. No manner of suppression could keep it under the floor, and it seeped upward through the cracks and made him damp, and smell musty, haunted, and the doctor had asked him who it was, unblinking. The writer had said he had been lonely for contact. Contact with—? The writer had angrily answered, oh I know, sure, but that only makes it—. The doctor had then said,

"Do you want to see it now? Or later?"

The writer had said, quickly, "Okay, it's my father, but I don't want sex with my father, my father is dead, I never knew my father, he was always away."

"But, then, who did you—or do you, want?"

"I want my wife!"

"Why can't you have her? Is it someone else?"

"She won't—"

"Answer me."

"I don't know, but—oh yes, Mother!"

"You fear *him*. Who is he?"

"Probably father, while I suckle mother's breast."

"You're not listening."

"Yes I am."

"Why can't you hear me?"

"I can—oh, I see. Ha hahaha," and the writer remembered when he was a boy he watched his mother comb her long white hair in front of a mirror. Occasionally she glanced bewitchingly at him in

236

the mirror, and chanted
Rapunzel, Rapunzel
Let down your golden hair
The doctor had asked, "Didn't you tell me you had become 'the man of the house' after your father died?"

The writer had nodded. "Yes. I proclaimed I was, but when my aunts echoed it with amusement, it was different. I felt I had double-crossed a liberty I had made for myself. Or I felt my aunts did, double-crossed the identity I had made for me, casting away my father *I* was the man, of *this* house with my mother. But then I saw what I had said, or what they thought I meant, which was responsibility: I had proclaimed I would accept all the manly responsibilities of the house, and it finished me. I had sealed myself in, but they used it on me for years."

"In."

"In a twelve year old game of playing Man/Me."

"They saw your role from their eyes—"

"Yes, that would be your word; they saw their boy nephew playing the role of the man of the house."

"All right, but weren't you the man even before your father died? While he was away you were in your mother's room watching her comb her hair, and she sang to you. Can you see your father from that angle? What would happen if he came home and found you there?"

"It would—"

"It?"

"Okay, *he* would wreck—what—I had going."

"Do you know what it was? And who is the man in the street you fear? Or the man you had the homosexual relations with?"

He began to fall backwards in a warm feminine wave suckling whiteness and water and cream scent, softness and security filled him, crying out,

"The light is bright!"

"Easier to sleep with a man than to fight him, as you say: fear blocks experience, so every act you make to be a man is threatened by the lurking *one*, who will appear to destroy the man you're afraid to be. Coming from a mother's warmth to father's fury you fear so greatly you return to her, a little like a woman, even with a man,

237

rather than face the man with the man you are, and you are *very* angry."

United States Policy in Southeast Asia, walking down University Place. The writer asked,

"Have you ever read Jung?"

"Freud's early friend?"

"Yes. Jung says the shadow is the same sex as its owner."

"What are you telling me? I wasn't talking about that!"

Pinocchio said, "I am."

"What do you do for a living!"

"I have a job with an importing firm."

"Is it a good job?"

"Yes," woodenly.

"What else do you do—are you an artist, a poet?"

He had no life, no sex, no mind and the street went on forever. He said,

"I am, a fiction writer."

The man smiled. "Fiction! Good."

An angry tape unwound. "Fiction: truth the way it isn't lived."

"Ha ha, that's good. You know, I like you."

He stopped in his tracks. His knees knocked together and his wooden jaws clattered, his painted eyes were wide as he pointed up the street:

"You go ahead. I'm going home."

"Don't be ridiculous, come for a cup of coffee."

Stainless steel, formica and lettered signs: the counterman in Rikers gave them coffee. The writer was dizzy, nauseous and exhausted, he yawned and drank some of the hotness, it was good. Something came clear. He turned to the man.

"I want to tell you something."

The dapper man looked at him with his cool but not unfriendly eyes. He could manipulate men and stay clean to himself, which explained the slight mocking smile: I want to tell you something was nothing new.

"You bring my past to me."

"How so?" Surprised.

"You resemble a dark fellow I fear."

"What are you trying to say!"

The writer was a little startled, and as he began, the man interrupted him with an angry hiss:

"My God! Don't tell me you're another young *faggot!* I'm *sick* of them!" He paused. "Is that it?" Angrily.

They looked in each other's eyes and laughed, seeing their selves on strings, and a subtle watery glitter covering each's eyes, and the writer reacted first, despising his own water, which the dapper man seemed to enjoy in himself.

The writer said, tight-lipped, "Now I don't like you completely."

"But—why? Why?"

"You look like a crook I know—"

"Come, come," the man angrily interrupted, "really, now; don't be naive, you don't know anything about me."

"Yeah," the writer sneered, "not about you, but—I'm going home. You scare me, I'm tired of complicity and ill with me."

"But why are you afraid of me?"

"You remind me of me, which is a threat."

"I'm not going to hurt you."

"Not like the others, or me, anyway. And how do you know?"

"What are you saying?"

"I'm going home. Goodnight."

"Finish your coffee. Sit down."

"No. I'm exhausted."

"Sit down, come on. Finish your coffee, then I'll go my way and you go yours."

Pinocchio sat down gloomily, defensive and emotional. The dapper man said,

"You're an extraordinary young man."

"For Christ's sake! I'm fucked up! And thirty-five is *not* young!" He turned vehemently on the man, "You're twice my age and we understand each other exactly, how about *that!*"

The man laughed for a moment; "From where I sit, that is not a mundane statement."

They were both surprised, and both grinned.

"See? You can be pleasant."

"You really grab at straws, don't you?"

"I wanted to talk with you . . ."

239

"No, with someone."

"All right; true, but I listened to what you were saying about Viet Nam, and it so happens—" but the writer's face had darkened, and the man paused, asking what was wrong.

"Please, don't go through it again."

"What! I also read what Carey McWilliams wrote this week! Ha, ha, the old goat is not *all* stupid!"

"Goats terrify me."

"Ah—this is ridiculous."

It was as if the writer stood up in himself, he stood up and stepped away from the counter stool and looked levelly angry down at the dapper man, who shuddered. The writer gravely said:

"You condescend and make me helpless so you can manipulate me. I don't like that. I know you because I know myself. I don't know, however, why I'm here. I was drawn here. Why am I here? I'm hysterical! Shall I throw the coffee cup through the window there? Or shall I strike myself? How shall I show my anger? Shall I hit *you*? Don't you see what you do? No. Do you see what you are? No. You're a manipulator, and the stereotype upper echelon crooked politician with a shadowy past."

The dapper man lowered his eyes, and stared at the floor; he said softly, emotionally, "I'm sorry you said that."

The writer gasped, and stammered, "Me too, now! Me too, and what does *that* mean? That's a THREAT to me, you can't talk like that to paranoids, we'll run out of here screaming! You don't want to be hurt? Me neither, so you blind well-dressed fool, can't you see it's my role to hurt you to get at me, can't you see that? I don't know *you* in you, but in me, I know—I've boozed in too many Village bars for too many years not to know you when you show up. When you're like you, you have to show up, so every now and again you come in the door to have a talk with writers or artists, and you mean well, you're a little bored with your jungle life and want some honest neurotic people that understand that you're lonely while you buy us drinks, but you will somehow threaten them because just the way you are you bring them a story they know and fear, you can't walk into a world where guys are crazy *because* they're artists, you want the real thing, you want to meet the guy who can't help but paint, and you can spot a phoney—snap?—but they—we—fear your hunger for the real because we are so real that way ourselves, it's our *norm.* How do you expect us to pass truth on to you when it's all we can do to admit it to ourselves and then live with it. Your act is a venomously vicarious one, and deeply hypocritical, which will be met with resentment, awe, fear and anger in the men you most want to talk with, not because you are *you,* as you fool yourself into thinking, but because your mind and emotions are starved, but your habit is manipulation, and you are, in your way, tragically screwed, and when you appear before us, we see it, what we know by heart, miserably familiar."

The writer tossed fifteen cents on the counter and left, hearing the dapper man say,

"I'll never forget that."

And he hated that response because he couldn't yet accept what he had just said, if he knew, and he stormed along the streets striking fist against palm, and had he been another substance, say sulfur, he would have smoked, from rage and fear, and when he got home he threw his clothes off his body and collapsed into bed as the two punks beat him in an alley because the dapper old man had said he would be sorry, he fought helplessly, and bitterly, in loneliness and a deep grief sensing a figure across his dark loft, gazing at the writer's wrenching body, a man with a white and yellow sunny face and wings who gestured in care, regret, and sorrow for the figure of unhappiness on the bed, speaking,

"Sorry for you,"

dripping sweat the writer wept in confusion and futility—he called out for help, a tearful mutter, and the angel came close, the writer was aware of grace and slowly slipped through smoke into darkness, wiping his eyes he let his head sink into the damp pillow, sleep, the angel said, kindly aware of his wife's warm sleeping body next to his sleep, the gentle voice said, finally,

"Sleep."

The Man in the Ground

HE SPOTTED THE POET Lately, at the bar, and they embraced each
other warmly, laughing hello in smoke and shadows and had a
drink.

The writer drank compulsively because he feared the dreams he
had written—he hated his cowardice: he melted into the icy booze.

But the poet Lately was guzzling double bourbons as a self-
conscious comic machine and the poet Lately was not.

Cool, bright, deductive; in the past the writer, feeling lonely,
had sought him out to talk with him, and though the poet always
seemed to understand, in a way of being pleased, was visibly
patient, and the writer felt a guilt using his friend so, and yet kept
on talking, the poet's eyes were becoming resentful, and it came
about in the conversation that the poet knew Carraday, an old
friend, and the writer wondered why he hadn't known that the poet
and Carraday were friends, and he felt dizzy as the poet, in a
pointed way, became interested in the writer's relationship with
Carraday, schoolmates the writer smiled, was the poet Lately
jealous? No. He didn't smile, he fell darkly silent, he—the poet—
turned to the bar and gazed through smoke into his drink.

The writer began to realize he didn't know the poet at all, he had
only used him and his ear. The writer was embarrassed and regretful, and turned, introspectively, to leave, but the poet, looking at
him, spoke his name normal and friendly.

"So what's new?"

It was the one the writer knew. Anxious to get things going
again, the writer said several things were happening, and he began
to tell them, yet every thing he said was personal, and though the
poet understood because it was the writer talking, the poet could

not understand fully because each thing was personal, and the poet, as the writer talked, pointed things out, things the writer had mentioned in the years before, though the writer did not intend it that way, the writer said yes, in anxiety, and when the writer, not knowing what to say that was new and would bring them together mentioned a mutual friend the poet's face once again darkened, and he became hostile, as the writer realized the poet had heard that before, yet the writer became irritated because the poet was or seemed to be listening in revenge with a different motive.

"Why doesn't he tell you to shut up?"

"Do you think a relationship is someone listening to you?"

The poet had again turned gloomily away. The writer nervously said,

"I said I saw Carraday. I'm not going into the whole thing again because I—know, I mean I know—" and the first person stung, the writer carrying out his sentences: "I know you've already heard it.

"But this is something different, if I can talk it, and I'd like you to—"

The poet glared at him and turned away disgusted. The writer dropped his eyes muttering okay, and ordered another drink, the poet turned to him.

"What happened?"

"He didn't recognize me."

"Who didn't."

The writer looked at the poet. "Don't you know?"

The poet made a tight smile. "I know."

"He didn't recognize you."

"He saw me, he looked right in my eyes and didn't recognize me—he was preoccupied of course. Yet it was—*it was from another time*—"

The poet gave the writer a hard directly hostile look. He said, "I know about you and his wife," and the poet made his deduction.

The writer was taken aback, and angry, and for a moment looked at the poet in silence.

"I must have told you when I was drunk, or maybe he told you, it was years ago. There was none of that in his eyes when I saw him last week. It was as if—"

"I know about you and his wife," the poet repeated bitterly.

243

"You son of a bitch telling me again and not letting me finish my sentence."

The poet said through a smile, "Am I right? Or am I wrong?"

"Wrong," and he saw the poet flush in rage; "wrong in un-explained motives, and wrong in—" but the poet interrupted him and the writer interrupted, "Look, hey, what's happening? Something's—tell me, will you?" The poet had interrupted, how-ever, with a cherub's smile and fiery eyes. "You're angry, you want to hurt me."

The writer cried, "I want to get things straight! Tell me! Tell me!"

"Too late," the poet smiled gently. "You want to hurt me," and he touched his lower lip: "Hit me.

"Hit me, there." He gave the writer a shrewd look. "Remember, I don't fall down."

The writer grabbed the poet's shoulders and shook him. "You're out of your head," he angrily said. "D'y' hear me?"

The poet grinned behind tight lips: "I don't fall down."

The writer stepped back, and looked at him. "I do."

The poet mused, "That's the difference between you and me. That's the real thing."

The writer shook his head, "Wrong again. It's the distance, not difference, between us."

The poet was smiling a coloring mask of violence; the writer frowned, fearing it, and slowly turning, the mask disappeared from him.

A chill rushed through the writer. He began to crumble before a shadow of fear flowing through him, and he scorned himself growing smaller fearing the tall poet. The bar rose slightly and the writer stumbled down to the other end of it and leaned on it dizzily, and he was very angry, and identities in emotion charged up; he wanted to vomit.

He did not in a flash of rage, and—something peculiar, a breeze, wafted near his temples. I'm drunk out of my wits, he mumbled; "Tomorrow then, I'll tell you, for it is coming." The writer hardly heard, yet behind himself,

"Not what. Who."

The writer finished his drink quickly with a twisted face, terrible shit, whiskey, he grunted, stomach convulsing, anxious, in a dream

all the Men are coming to get me

He flushed crimson, his heart banged boiling blood throughout as perspiration started down his forehead, he ordered another drink, lit a cigarette trembling and rapidly swallowing suppressed nausea, huddled in his clothing against the wind.

All the Men

He knew, and the cold wind swirled around his temples, chilling the perspiration, he froze on his feet. His red brow turned white in a new alarm and his new blood ran cold, the glass clattered against his teeth and he turned, to face the poet Lately directly. The poet had an ugly mask in his hand; the writer said, but the poet interrupted him.

"Where have you been."

"Here," the writer said, the voice said. With one hand he gestured the poet away, "You won't listen. I refuse you."

The writer walked away, to a wall and leaned against it, while the poet sat at the bar and peered dismally into his drink. He turned, and looked sadly at the writer who was talking with a reporter. The poet said he would listen. He did, for a while, but again slanted into the other, and the writer again walked away.

David Henderson was sitting in back and they greeted each other warmly. It had been a long time. David looked weary and poor in worn denim. He gazed, as exhausted, at the (fiction) writer, who said, "You look terrible. Want a drink?"

"I have some money," the young poet said.

The writer stood up and waved at the waiter, and sitting down, asked, "What have you been doing? Workin' on de railroad?"

The writer cackled and the young poet smiled, and said he had been writing a lot, and was starting on a circuit of readings which would take him over the country including the south. The writer said, "The south?"

The young poet said bitterly, "This city's cold, baby, weather-wise; otherwise freezing."

"The south?"

"The sun," David smiled, "is warm in the south."

The waiter appeared and they ordered drinks and talked until the bar closed.

And as the writer wove towards the door the poet Lately grabbed him, and they staggered home parting on a blue sidestreet. The poet Lately threw an empty bottle up Broadway, and it made a smashing echo.

The next day the writer's wife asked him why he hadn't hit the poet Lately, she said she would have.

"Tough you," the writer said.

"Were you afraid?"

"Yes," he said, ashamed.

Shadow in! And he began to crumble, again—the walls seemed to rise, and he felt himself a little shorter.

"I fear!" he had cried. "But *I* am NOT afraid! Although I CAN be!"

The doctor nodded. "What do you do, when you are."

I run away.

"I run away," he echoed.

"What happened?"

After he finished talking, the doctor asked, "Do you know who it is?"

The writer shrank. The man's eyes were headlamps:

"Who is it you want to hit that you fear and can't hit?"

The writer's back arched, and with his head back, saw eyes closed in a box of hate of a guilt for a force to kill the father who died, and be rid of them all and write in a rage of the past.

The Face in the Casket

In Memory of Paul Blackburn

THEY SAT ON THE MEXICAN RUG beside the colorful pile of presents under the Christmas tree. The writer's wife in her nightgown and housecoat, and himself in pajamas and robe. He poured coffee and suggested she open the first present. She slowly took a large oblong package, undid the ribbon and carefully took off the tissue, and opened the box full of brightly colored rolls of wool, plus two long ivory needles.

Later, he said, "Well, don't you think we should talk about it?"

She murmured she supposed it would be better.

"We could go on the rest of our lives without—" he began.

"—the intrusion," she finished looking at him. Her brown eyes were shadowed. He added: "of talking with him about it."

She nodded and angrily mentioned he had finished what she had already finished. He said he only wanted to finish his sentence. He said if he talked with him it *would* be an intrusion, and he would be the hypocrite, intruding. She agreed.

He asked, "Then why not just let it—go by?"

She asked, "You want to talk to him, don't you?"

He nodded. "I want to intrude and prove a point I don't know."

She said she would rather not, now, talk about it. Would he play something?

A present from the poet Lately, and Ellington and Coltrane softly swirled and swept through the loft, blending with the paintings, drawings, poems and photographs on the walls, and the lovely bright Christmas tree, and all the open presents into the hardship of the writer and his wife in conflict.

"We ought to talk, regardless."

"Regardless of how I feel," she said bitterly.

247

"In spite of it."

She breathed hard, but she knew he was right. She said she wasn't very delighted to be with him. She would rather be alone. Her-self: alone, she knew he understood, but he hated to see the shadow cast between them, and in her division she was angry at her and self; had she told him the dream? In spite of self and her she envied him in a sharp arrow.

He said energetically, "All right, I'm afraid to say what I think! But I want, I want to say it in the way I'm screwed up in it, and I fear it in the saying—remember in New Hampshire when I couldn't say George's dog was the vehicle for George's suppressed hatred and violence? Granny had to say it for me! Tender, shy, self-conscious George—with a police dog at his heels? Are you ready? How could I say that about George—I know George—old George, I've known and loved George, yet when that dog went after that girl on the street, and I saw George's face—

"Somewhere deep I hate Marko, yes, just like that, and I know I'm crazy but I swear he killed her, I remember her voice on the telephone that day—"

The writer's wife was gravely shaking her head, but the writer raised his trembling hand, "Yes! Sure it's crazy—you just can't *say* things like that about people, but SOMEWHERE I'm RIGHT! I *know* I'm right! Can't you see? I want to tell him I know, I want to intrude into his new life with his new wife and tell him I know something I don't."

"I'm not there at all," the writer's wife said; "you are. Maybe you're right in yourself, at least you feel it, a truth—fact, maybe, and I know you want to be friends again, but I don't; it'd complicate my already complicated life." Her face began to go slack.

He quickly said, stressing last and night, "Why did you dream of him last night!"

She said:

"After the days when I used to hang around with the street gangs, I started to come down from the Bronx to the Village, and I met some people from the Bronx there, who, it turned out, though I didn't know them in the Bronx, lived on the same street I did—you know all this—well, but it was, they were, different from any of the people I'd ever known. They were serious. They were bright—very bright, high IQs etc., and there was a guy who was a painter, he did that—"

He nodded. She pointed to the wall; he knew she meant the little painting of the sea, he didn't look, she smiled, and he said it was the first time she had spoken of these people as a group, he had come to know them through her as specific individuals, not as a group in time.

"The painter was in the army at that time," she continued, "I think. But the others, high school dropouts, and the rest, guys and girls, were very bright, and we hated the political system, and some of us were pro-Communist. Ann was always there. It was where I met Nathan, and even though I went with him I could never talk with him. The only one I enjoyed talking with was—"

"Marko."

"Yes," she murmured. "Marko was serious in the way I was."

"Way you are."

She nodded. "We understood each other. There was a way I could talk with him and be aware I was talking to him, him I was aware of, and he was of me to me. It was a way we were—" she gestured—

"Together."

She smiled sadly. "Yes. We had great times. Drinking coffee and talking until late. Then Ann and I'd take the train home. One night we all linked arms and made a Broadway show line in the street— can you imagine it? Outside the Waldorf cafeteria on Sixth Avenue—NEW YORK NEW YORK! we sang." She had her hands out and her face was happy.

She finished her coffee.

"Is that why you dreamed about him last night?"

She shrugged.

The writer remembered the night before last: the 23rd. She and her friend Judy had gone out Christmas shopping and had stopped by the bar to see if friends were there, but only saw the old standbys, plus some strangers, and among them the writer's wife had encountered the cartoonist Kingsley, and they had sat at a table and had had a long talk. She had come home at two thirty a.m., beaming, and told the writer about it. He and Kingsley hadn't hit it off at all, and he found himself jealous that Kingsley was attracted

to his wife, yet the writer knew jealousy, his jealousy was something he had always felt, a chaotic little whirlpool that grew bigger
and drew him in. It frightened him, and then it took his legs away
and terrified him pulling him down, yet he seemed to arise in a
strength.

The writer leaned forward. "Do you think you dreamed of
Marko last night because of your rewarding talk with Kingsley the
night before?"

"Mm." She brightened. The writer said,

"Speaking seriously for a prolonged time awakened your relationship with Marko—awakened Marko to you."

"Yes," she said. "That's good. But I—manipulated Kingsley—
so I could speak with him, and when I got him where he could
respond, he did, but it still wasn't spontaneous. Kingsley's fucked
up."

To vindicate his fluid jealousy, the writer asked,

"Can you speak to me seriously?"

"Sometimes." You jealous baby.

To step out of a dizzy spell, he was redundant, "So you were
making it with Nathan, but loving Marko."

It didn't work, and he was angry with himself; she nodded
unhappily: "I loved him," she said. The writer was sitting beside
himself whispering in his ear, "WRONG! WRONG!" He was
coldly watching him looking into his wife's eyes, saying,

"The months after Sherry's funeral had no meaning to me, I felt
so dulled, but when we went to Marko's new apartment that night,
there was Marko with a new girl, and he was clearly happy, but
nothing had changed between you two. I was very drunk, at my
worst, but now, no wonder, and there's nothing else to do but say I
didn't have any relationship with Marko—ever, and I thought I
did. We liked each other very much, possibly loved each other; at
times I felt very close to him. I was certain he understood me,
although I didn't understand him, I saw him—I was sure he'd make
a fine therapist—which you know, and I used to have fantasies of
going to him. Wow."

She nodded. She had been aware of that.

"Things yet disturbed me" the writer went on, "and the day
when Marko and Sherry and their kids met us in the park, and we

250

were all together, there were a few things happening.

"You and Marko were together and I was with Sherry. But—remember just after we were married? I felt a little strange about visiting them, there was something contradictory I was never conscious of. I would see Marko, and Sherry, and the kids, but—I mean, I—was the one outside—something, the plot, look inside your head a little and listen and remember. It was like going into a pool, slowly, and as you get your head under and wave to the underwater people you know—your wife, her old friends and their kids you realize something's strange; you feel different."

"You fuck," she spat; and he nodded.

"Marko always enjoyed me talking about Kline and Pollock and all the Cedar Bar stories, and he listened close to my opinions and perceptions, he was always interested to hear what I was writing about (or trying to write), or what I was drawing, or not painting, in fact it was all we ever talked about, and I of course loved it."

"Because you could talk about yourself."

"Right; you were sitting beside him and he was asking me about my new book; I felt something was funny, and you were always talking about psychology, I remember how he listened to you, and you listened to him while I sat there and got drunk, occasionally chattering about something, or the kids would start to whoop away, or his wife would suddenly want to play a record. I liked his eyes, I liked his power of listening, I liked his objectivity and I really admired the slow expansion of his pupils, 'real analyst's eyes,' I thought. And he seemed to understand from his listening distance, but like any guy, he didn't as much as I thought. Marko was generous with his patience, it was his style. He was a soft spoken, very perceptive and sensitive man who cared a great deal about people. He was very very patient, and controlled.

"But—something needled me. What was it? I kept asking myself. Then, when I called them, and asked them to meet us in the park, something clicked.

"Sherry answered the phone and in a distance I could hear—a silence before she spoke—I heard a wind, and I softly said, 'Sherry?' There was a soft mumble, or cough. I said her name, again, gently, and she responded in a strange mechanical echo—'Yes?'

251

"I said who I was, and why don't we get together; it's a lovely day.

"She said, that, stop whisper, sounded, stop whisper, good, I heard her trying to come forward from it; the word good was desperate. I asked her where Marko was.

" 'He's—here,' she whispered, and after 'here' was nothing, a void, where was 'here'? I was tense, looking at it.

"Then I saw him. He was sitting on the sofa, across the city from me, across the living room from Sherry as she talked to me on the phone. Her back was to him, and he was looking at her—no, watching her, and his pupils were expanded, giving him a hard, cold look—a terrible look, with his beard, a direct satanic look of fury and impatience.

" 'Wait a second,' she said, in a strangled voice, and I saw her turn to him. She trembled under the power of his eyes, and he changed them.

" 'Who is it?' he asked.

"She told him, and about Central Park. I heard him be enthusiastic, and saw his face brighten.

"We arranged the place to meet.

"We met them at the zoo, we had a pleasant afternoon.

"We asked them to come down to our loft for supper, and they thought that was a fine idea, but their car was so full of furniture, for some reason, they couldn't give us a ride down, and just before they got in their car, and just before we turned to head for the subway, Marko looked at you. Do you remember how he looked at you?"

"Yes. I don't want to. Why are you doing this?"

"Please let me go on. You loved him then, and now, out of the past, he was unlocking the car door, Sherry at his side gazing up at him, but Marko's eyes were on you, hard, they drilled across space into yours, as I stood beside you watching him. He was trying to tell you—and in that still air of an October Sunday afternoon, Sherry, in a shattering whisper, pathetically asked, 'Why don't you ever look at me like that?'

"Marko didn't even turn to her. He answered—and could we have heard correctly, on that strange still afternoon air?

" 'Because she's prettier than you are.'

"They got into their car swiftly. We took the train down, and met them at the door and came up here. I went to the delicatessen and we had Sunday afternoon beer and cold cuts, and it was very tense. I gave the kids paper and crayons and charcoal so they could draw, and then, just before they all left—it was—I couldn't stand knowing something I wasn't conscious of—I had had a quart too much of beer, and I almost took him by the lapels, and said anxiously, it was *very* I repeat *very* important that he come by where I work, and see me! Marko was a little astonished, and, as he was and is a deep man, I saw his eyes were telling me I was trying to tell him something.

" 'What is it? What is it?'

"It was clicking through my mind, dot dash dot dot dash I couldn't translate it, it didn't get through, they left, and a week later the phone call came which sent you weeping out of your head into my arms: Sherry had jumped to her death."

"I arrived at the funeral parlor before you did. Marko was in the inner lobby. I shook his hand solemnly, and expressed regrets. His eyes were in terrible emotion, and then you came in, like something off the *Saturday Evening Post* cover you went straight into his arms. He wholly embraced you, and wept in your presence.

"You and Marko talked a while, some of your old friends showed up out of childhood, and time dragged around. I got a drink of water and when most of the people had left the inner parlour, I went in.

"I was confused, and of course felt alarm. I hate those places. But—and as I trembled I knew I would experience something which would reward me, and one more thing would fall into place—I went in on a string, I went down the aisle, I moved toward the casket with death all decked out around me, obliquely, across my life, and then I was there.

"I looked down at her waxen face. I was so right I felt faint, dizzy with it. Her eyebrows were raised sharply arched, and her eyes were so severely closed, and her lips so tight it was as if, an inside job, they had been sewn shut and it had a nasty twist, a shattering bitterness, a mock smile—she had made it, the one shot leap had worked; it had been her triumph.

"I set my teeth in rage and helplessness. The head on the silken pillow was a ravaged history, headlined:

REST
IN
PEACE

"I made a vow: in response to a question I didn't know, I vowed I would. *I will*, in revenge and heartbreak.
"Goodbye, sweetheart."

"About six months later we went to Marko's new apartment, and he was with his new woman. She was lovely. He was visibly happier, and he was now seeing patients. Remember when he showed us his office? But then we began to drink and things got bad. You hated me that night. I wanted to tell him I'd never forget Sherry, that he killed her and he *must* learn to live with it.

"How could that be true? But my emotions meant so much to me, and if he can't live with what he did, how can he understand that I do?"

It was bitter cold. The writer and his wife walked down the street holding hands. They had just come from a party.

He unlocked the door and let her in, he locked the door and they went up the stairs, and he opened the blue door into their loft, and the golden light from the far corner lamp shone outward as in Rembrandt, and the objects of their living had a sudden identity, he helped her with her coat and then she heated the coffee.

They drank coffee by the Christmas tree, eating the Christmas cookies her mother had made.

As they had arrived at the party—as they had just arrived Kingsley was leaving. They said hello. Kingsley was cool, and that was that, or that was that then, but when the writer and his wife had gotten in to the party, had taken their coats off, glad to be there and dance after a ruthless afternoon, the writer and his wife, really dancing, on a crowded floor to slam bang music, looked at each other and laughed, saying, together:

"Fate."

He walked across a rising field of ice.

He went up it. It was a mountain covered with ice, and he

remembered Ronald Colman at the end of the movie.

Was it the end of the movie?

It was bitter cold. But he felt an odd sentimentality sweep up and turn into sorrow, and then to grief, and he began to cry, weeping and struggling up the slippery ice field. He was weeping for himself, but he was going ahead! His heart beat faster, there was the ridge! He was actually going ahead! He was going toward—? What. The top? But there it was!

Down and down he fell, tumbled, rolling all the way down the mountain in a swirl of snow and wind, he bumped against the base of a tree, and he lay confused in pine needles. A tall man in a uniform was standing there, and the tall man (it was the Christmas Officer), began to interrogate him.

The writer grinned.

"There I am working to get to Paradise only to wind up with you in the woods."

"Evidently you're not out yet," the man said.

"Why be so corny?"

"What's ice?"

"A field for dreams."

Great glacial barriers, frozen force of power larger than life. What was it? Ice was frozen water. They chased identities and associations without any luck.

"What about a force of resistance? As field equaling self, as I—experience, me going—crossing a way, a high way face, or a vertical ice wall—I have to break through."

"Break through the glacier?"

"To get to the mountain underneath . . ."

"Mountain? Underneath?"

"Or behind, an ice-wall in front of a mountain. I have to go over the mountain to get to—Rimbaud said you have to go through the mountain, not over it—well I was going over it to get to something."

The Christmas Officer smiled. "Paradise."

"—What—"

"Yet Rimbaud said you had to go through the mountain. Didn't you say ice covered mountain? No, mountain underneath, that was it."

"Yes, but to get to—"

"Who. What is the mountain underneath."

Power, power, a mountain of emotional power.

"The room is dark."

The universe was outside each ear—dot dot dash dot rigid in the chair. Time was incredible. The Christmas Officer had risen and the writer also, but woodenly.

Next session:

"Do you remember Grimm's fairytale about a ring? Yes, yes, sorry of course, etc., the king, I think the king is on an ice floe, it is dark and cold and the sea is stormy. He finds a ring in the ice. Something like that."

"The king?"

The writer blushed, and tears stung his eyes. He lowered his head. The Christmas Officer said,

"It's hard to accept, isn't it? You, king. King, also father, and it became difficult; well, we will get to it. But how can you be king when there is another? Who is that?"

"Father—my father was and always will be king. The most kingly kind of man."

"King*ly*. King*ly*. Why? Is it because you can't say you're king, in the face of your father, you are only—you feel your kingness in calling him kingly—even king—was and is and always will be, king, amen and yes. But actually you are king; the kingly kind, found even in your language. That is your truth, which is your fear."

The writer would not look at his interrogator, who said, "It hurts, so deeply."

The writer whispered, "Sure."

The Officer said, "It is almost impossible for you to confront your father and say, 'I am father' when you can't admit that now you are married you don't dare—be—"

"Me."

"Yes," the Officer said warmly. "Do you have any daydreams on this? There can be a lot there. Would you like to wait and think a bit, or continue."

The writer said he wanted to get to the ring. The Officer nodded,

256

and the writer wiped his eyes.

"It's a wedding ring."

"How is your wife?"

"Ice and a ring." The writer added, bitterly, "Now how about that."

The Christmas Officer nodded.

The writer angrily said, "I was right. Experience as field of self. I can't believe it, don't want to." He covered his ears. The Officer frowned, what was.

The writer muttered, "Bells."

"Bells?"

"Bells! Conflict and anxiety!" the writer cried, "don't you see? I saw you nod! That means you saw! I've got the ring and I'm stuck on the fuckin' ice! ICE-cold—ICE!" He shouted, "Don't you GET IT?"

"Ah. Her."

"God-*damn* you and your classic understatements."

"What's Paradise."

The writer threw a look at the Christmas Officer snarling, "My wife and I together."

"She dropped her ring somewhere! Is *that* what you mean?"

The writer admitted: "Right in my path."

And put his head in his hands.

Going down the elevator it began to come to him. He was snapping his fingers as he rapidly left the building. He ran to the subway.

She served the Chinese cooked beef over rice with brussel sprouts on the side. It was Sunday afternoon, outside quite cold in off and on sunshine. She said,

"I don't want to talk."

"I do," he said.

They looked at each other. He said, "When you withdraw from me now, I understand what I used to feel when I didn't understand. You see, I thought you were withdrawing to someone else."

Her face was going through changes behind an artificial amusement. He said,

"Yet you insisted there was no one else, that my jealousy was crazy. There is no one, you said, and I believed you when you said you withdrew to be alone. You meant that then, but now we can realize, from your dream on Christmas Eve, that in fact you were, then and now, withdrawing from me to Marko."

She hesitated, then agreed. He said,

"Think of the seven years we've been together. Think of that. I haven't painted a picture in all that time. Well, the thing I experienced when you withdrew, even when I knew you were going into yourself, was, first, a deep and miserable chill—a shudder which turned into jealousy. Why? And how can cold create heat? Because you were cold, and I mean you were really cold to me. You were *ice* to me, and you made me jealous by turning, away from me to Marko."

"Yes, it's true," she whispered.

"You didn't know it, but when you told me you had a rewarding talk with Kingsley (That! Of all the people! Of all the *names!*), I experienced the old icy shudder which then became jealousy, but today—no, on Wednesday night it came clear, and I tell you my darling the dead are stirring in their graves. Yet none of it—not any of it—means anything to me if we can be really together. When you said there was no one, I wanted to believe you, yet you, as you stood before me, were more clear than your words, and it was a paradox, that you were there before me and you also were not, while your words were saying, 'alone, alone' but I knew there was another one."

She said, "I am cold to you when I do that, and you're right about Marko. I—I don't know what to do about it."

"I don't either!" His face was drained of blood as he whispered, "What made him do it, he must have *hated* her. Am I crazy?"

He gave her a long look. "Don't love Marko. Okay, you know him better than I do, but don't love him now, from then; I don't know why he and Sherry got married in the first place, but—they did. Did they ever go out? I mean to movies, or bars, or parties? I'll bet not. They had the baby of course, then, and Marko was working hard in school, and yes they were broke, all good excuses die in our own headlines. Can't be true, can it? No, can't be. But you love him from then, yes, which explains when I am the way I know you love me to be, you're guilty because you—you love me—but never completely, for out of the past comes Marko into your life, a figure of understanding and communication—as you flash your message of love across the floor to me, I see a shadow of guilt cross your wonderful self, I wondered why I hated you, and resented something. What was it? I kept asking myself, bitterly standing there at the bar, why should I go home? For what? To be with her? Why?" He looked at her sadly and angrily, or drunk, one eye was a little off. "Who can believe it? Who wants to?"

She was perfectly still.

"Well," he said, straightening his face, "we know, so you can approach your guilt directly, or more directly; because I love you."

Her head was lowered. "I'm going to cry."

"As I saw her being cold to me I saw her being warm with him, and knowing what Marko is to me, I felt double-crossed, and she suddenly became a rising figure of death in my mind, and I was frightened, faint and dizzy, in the whirlpool I told you about, but—"

"Wait. How about his wife, Sherry? What was she like?"

The writer clenched his fists—"I—I liked her, I felt a sympathy—afterwards—"

"After what."

"After I got to know her—or them, Marko and Sherry, she was impossible at first, almost hostile, blunt and caustic, friendly though, yet she was never—ever—close, and then, as we visited them more, I saw there was something, I didn't fully know, but she was, in a way, something terrific, to me; there was a hidden warmth and power of tension, nerves all going right and wrong at once that I almost envied, she seemed very alive, I liked her. Boy she was real! Did I think about sex? Maybe, but I always do, I felt—"

"Like a brother?"

"No. Like I could understand—that's it! I felt I understood her. We went out for beer once; Marko and my wife stayed in the apartment (check), well Sherry and I got the beer, and as we were going home—her hand was around my arm—I felt close to her. We stopped in a bar and had a couple of beers, but she didn't know—

well, she didn't know what it was, I mean she didn't know where she was, or what was where she didn't know! It was a bar! A bar! She had never been in a bar! She sat beside me like something sad, cut from a party hat and turned into pulp, she sipped her beer, and she couldn't finish it; she couldn't talk. She stared ahead, she hadn't said a word. I finished my beer and hers and we left. On the way home she relaxed a little, not much, but a little, and I knew there was trouble. We went into the apartment, and there was Marko with my wife, just as we had left them, and it was something strange. Crazy—like a dream, it was always like a dream. I was there and I was not there, I was talking and drinking. What was happening? Anyway I began to like Sherry."

"You mean you fell in love?"

"Did I? Do you think so? No. But maybe."

"She would need you."

"Yes, but that's not what—"

"In a way you could care for her, she would need you."

"Yes, but—"

"Who—"

"Okay Goddammit, my wife, will you let me go on?"

"If your wife turns away she doesn't need you, and you can hardly care for her doing that, isn't that right?"

"Right, lots of fights over that."

"Okay, why don't you tell me about that—the fights, why deny your emotions? Nobody's saying need is love, but it's there," he paused. "Think a moment, how you are when you need your wife."

"Yes, that's good, and I see now—I do—but understand how I felt when I saw Marko's wife in the casket, her face—it was as if she was trying to tell me something, I can't say—exactly, as if she really didn't know either, but took it to the grave with her. I don't know! I CAN'T—somehow, *say* it! But I made a vow—and I didn't get it! I—I made a vow: *I will.*"

The voice seemed to come out of Egypt:

"Do you know what it was?"

The writer, spellbound, shook his head. "No. I can't seem—to get—"

260

"Remember me."

"—*God,*" the writer began to weep. "I will." Simply.

"Whether or not Marko killed Sherry—*that* is another story. The woman you thought would—could—need you, whom you cared for, is dead, surely the look on her face was one of revenge: she got Marko to pay attention to her at last, and tragically for him, too late. But as we haven't much—how long have you known your wife?"

"Seven years."

"Where did you meet her?"

"Provincetown."

"What were the circumstances?"

"Franz Kline asked me to help him fix up his summer house."

The Christmas Officer had a startled look. "I—when you were married, wasn't Kline the best man?"

"Yes."

"And didn't Kline die that same year?"

"Yes, that—the year we were married."

"Then how did you—"

The writer cried, "Don't even ask me! I know you by now! I was guilty!"

"When did you stop painting?"

"About—seven years ago—to find myself in language!"

The Officer leaned forward. "Since you met your wife! Now," and he said it intensely: "Tell me who it was who said *remember me.*"

The writer's hands began to shake. "What's painting got to do with it? I write now, I *must,* and I—I don't know, are you telling me I hate my wife? What is it? I love her—I do!" The Officer began to stand up. He had a harsh look on his face, and a hard perceptive demanding expression in his eyes, as the writer fumbled, "It seems, I think, or I feel a wild devotion, I say *I will,* with *all my heart,* my—"

"Darling." The face on the silken pillow.

"Oh God—*God,*" the writer wept, openly, "it was my wife."

The Christmas Officer gravely nodded, and for a moment they were a tableau, and then the writer struggled to his feet, in tears, in the disciplined and poignant gaze of the doctor, who parted the curtains and opened the door, and as the writer left, rode the elevator down, walked through the lobby, and outside onto upper Park Avenue, he saw her rushing into Marko's arms. And the other lay in the casket.

The Unveiling

THE CAR HEADED THROUGH THE RAIN toward the cemetery in Queens. Our lawyer, my wife's cousin, Nathan's father had died the year before.

My wife's father drove between iron gates and we were lost in the fog. We drove around the vast cemetery. I was hung over, and depressed to spend a rainy foggy Sunday in a cemetery, any cemetery reminding me of the rainy day in April 1942 when I witnessed the burial of my father. He went into the ground. On the way to that funeral I had sat in the same back seat in a different car looking out the window at trees and houses, and then at tombstones in the cemetery just west of Kirkwood, Missouri, making April and November reflect in me, dully, like pewter, this was November, showing up in analysis.

BELOVED DAUGHTER
DIED FROM NAZI
PERSECUTION
REST IN PEACE

I passed my hand over my face, and my mother-in-law said, "There they are."

We parked, got out and joined the others on the damp ground between tombstones, and like—as in a wild vision, with a hellish roar, a huge jet airplane drifted over the trees. I took my wife's hand.

The layout of the cemetery was rectangular, and we were in a far corner, surrounded by rows of stately ghostly November trees; the whole cemetery was fenced in by a high steel cyclone fence, with the backs of suburban houses and their back yards on the other side. The airport was almost next door.

My wife introduced me to some of her cousins I hadn't met before. Who was that blonde girl with the pasty face and dark glasses? Long legs out of a cream colored raincoat. My wife saw me looking at her and whispered that the girl looked terrible, and under her breath wondered why. From a distance the blonde stood out, in contrast to the city people in dark suits. I spotted Nathan speaking quietly to a man and woman who had their heads down. I waited until he was finished, and then they were talking, and then he was listening, but backing away, like lawyers do, until he turned to me and as if still carrying on his conversation with them said he hadn't expected to see us there. He said, and he was pleased, he was pleased. I liked Nathan; he had spoken warmly of having met Franz Kline in Provincetown, and it was a link between us.

"We couldn't not come," I murmured. At least I was there, and "We wanted to. And that's a rule." In a windy anxious moment I realized Franz was dead, and there was Nathan's father with pebbles on the tombstone to tell a knowing passerby, one year. I looked over my shoulder.

A slender ten year old boy stood on the back steps of a small white frame house on the other side of the fence, coolly watching the Jews; suddenly an earsplitting sound of screaming kids.

Breezes wafted among the tombstones. A roar mounted to the deafening senseless howl of turbojets, and a plane appeared low in the sky, loomed for a moment, and tensely swept out of sight in one solid hell of sound.

The Rabbi made his way through fog towards us, scowling.
"I was lost."

Pale smooth shaven young man in a black suit, white shirt, black tie and a black highcrowned businessman's hat. Gravely dapper he was, and everyone gathered around the tombstone and the Rabbi began to sing. I was alien.

In hard glances. I saw the blonde standing there, between figures, her head lowered concealing a bitter and irritated expression. My wife was exactly in front of me, and over her shoulder I saw Nathan beside his brother and the Rabbi.

I couldn't understand the wailing language. I was—and felt—

264

different. Yet I became able to give up self-consciousness, and then I did while the people wept in a flutter of handkerchiefs, and the Rabbi's voice cracked and held, then rose in a nerve-wracking dissonance that changed into full voice, and fell, to again sweep jaggedly up to a quick wrench in his throat like an ancient cry, which it probably—which it was. I didn't know the story. There was a story. I felt a chill in my kidneys, and a force, pressing at the base of my skull. Somebody—was trying to get into me! I saw double.

My face was scarlet. I saw Nathan and his brother repeating lines after the Rabbi, and as I fought for control I watched Nathan make a speech; his normal mottled pink and sometimes florid face was chalky, and his eyes bugged. His father hadn't been a religious man, Nathan said, yet he had been generous, and Nathan said he was sure those who had known him would remember how angry he could get and afterward be cheerful and giving.

I saw a large living room above the grass. A long staircase ran up on the left, and a hole—fireplace!—without fire—in the floor, and lots of people sat on upholstered chairs and stools, talking happily around the hole. They all knew each other, and a sense of family rose like an aroma making me reel, while an unidentified man moved around the room teasing and delighting them all. He had just been angry.

Nathan was having difficulty speaking.

My mother was dressed in black.

Nathan began to cry.

She sipped a glass of wine.

Nathan said his father had accepted the burdens of his life, and those also of his friends, and as Nathan said he remembered when he was a little boy I was trying to remember my father's rage and couldn't, and then I, did in a flash and my father was always away from home, in New York, it was one weekend! We were wandering to the cars, he had spanked me and I had screamed, I tripped but caught myself on a tombstone—I didn't know where to put my feet, really furious for not bringing the half pint of rye. There it was, on top of the yellow cabinet by the door, next to the Mexican crock.

I leaned against a tombstone, head aching from the repeating

265

roar from the sky, plus that boy on that back steps watching me.

I hid my shaking hands in my pockets. And me? Thirty-five years old on the grass in a graveyard, *boy* I wanted a drink.

My wife.

I moved towards her time and identity. My heart jumped, and I took her hand with a smile.

"I'll come."

Yes. "Hi," I said to her. But she was talking to Nathan's brother, and I turned away blinking.

Out from between two cars, two women came through the fog opening boxes as they approached a man who was setting up a card table. Another man appeared obliquely, and set bottles of wine and whiskey on the table, oh the Jews! THE DEAR JEWS! Shaking as though someone were shaking me I went on a roundabout way from one tombstone to another to the table, and when the crowd had gathered around it I stepped out from behind a piece of marble, and with a sideway crouch slipped a hand in and grabbed a bottle of V.O. and a paper cup, and like Ray Milland poured a jolt in the cup, spilling it in laughter and anxiety and shakily replacing it. I retreated to a tombstone watching my lovely wife eating some cake. Talking with a young lawyer from New Haven. But then her face was serious, and *beautiful:* deeply moved by Nathan's speech.

Two men to my left, in front of me, they didn't see me, were muttering they were glad Nathan had said the old man got angry, but the low mutter that startled me was the one that asked how Nathan could even talk about his father at all: Nathan hadn't even known him—

I made a loud cough and they turned around. I looked away. I lowered my eyes, and in the blur of Nathan in short pants and me in my blue button pullover, lay down on a grave, any grave, and kicked and pounded the ground.

Who was that?

I took a stiff drink and wheeled towards my wife, but her back was turned.

A man walked between tombstones.

I felt a wind on my cheek, like a breath, and I had—I felt like my head was in a skull; a jet plane glided gloomily howling overhead. I began to slant to my right, and on the way down the blonde walked into the upper left hand corner of my vision, and stopped. I focused on her.

She stared into the distance.

My cup was empty.

I was on my feet: thank you darling, you saved my life.

I went to the table, nearly filled the cup with V.O. and drank. My eyes drilled into the ground, and teared from the violence in the whiskey, as I heavily salivated I breathed very deeply gnashing almost crushing my teeth, I inhaled, exhaled, inhaled, exhaled, swallowed a while and blinked *wow* I whispered. My wife was walking toward me.

"That was difficult."

I nodded, perspiring; "It was, thanks."

"What? How are you?" She smiled.

"B—better," I stuttered, but her eyes were direct. I told her I felt the same way about Nathan's speech and for a moment we were close. I told her what the two men had muttered, about Nathan not knowing his father, and she looked at me. She looked at me while her eyes widened, "Oh—" and she put her hand on my cheek and her eyes on my eyes and tenderly and deeply perceptively murmured my nickname, "sweetheart," and I just couldn't look at her through my tears. She said, dearly, "But he knew him a little. When he was young. Like you."

She ran her hand over the crown of a tombstone, and we stood there. I came back.

I sipped. "Hey," I choked, "who is that blonde?"

"Sheila. She looks bad. Feel better?"

"I will," I said. "Sheila. Of course. Yes, I do, I want to and that's a rule."

So innocent.

We joined some other people and she fell into a conversation with a handsome woman in a forest green Robin Hood hat with a jaunty feather; darkly painted eyes shone proudly. She had beautiful flat lips, like my mother's, in disturbing emotion. She looked Egyptian. It was real, she was and I turned away, and seeing Nathan went to him and spoke my response to his speech. He thanked me with a look, and with a gesture to underline it, said,

"I didn't know if it would be okay—I mean I—at first didn't

know if it would be—proper—"

"To speak at all," I said.

"Yes," Nathan said. "But the Rabbi said it was. I'm glad I did."

I touched Nathan's shoulder and told him I admired him; boy was Nathan lonely.

I looked down that long football field studded with death and felt included. Not alone after all. I offered to get Nathan a drink. He declined.

I got drunk.

Whispering, "Look at me. Can you see her?"

"Sweetheart."

I sat in the back seat glassy-eyed. Uncle Manny was in the front seat talking and laughing. I looked out the window as my wife sat close to me and held my hand. The car drove down the highway and I wondered if I was eleven or thirty-five and the car drove down the—I blinked and blinked and blinked and the car drove up the street and stopped in front of Manny's house. I was rigid, blinking, I had to get out. I crawled through onto the sidewalk and turned to take my wife's hand, and opening my eyes I grinned, and brought her out of the car to my lips, her shoulder blade struck my jaw, she moved away angry whispering *you bastard* jerking free of me.

In a fire I backed away. What was wrong with that? What did I do?

She crossed the lawn. I followed, alone. I stopped half way. My left eye was crooked. Her father called and said let's go in.

Uncle Manny took my elbow. He was chuckling and laughing and rubbing his hands together. We crossed the lawn together laughing and talking crazily. Coughing.

But inside the house the young mother watched. The metal storm door swung open; the inner door swung in. She was kneeling buttoning her daughter's coat, watching us. Very white skin. Very liquid mascara. Alizarin crimson lips. Glossy young mother, a white black and hot pink widow, do not take internally and keep out of the reach of—so we all stopped and said hello hello and passed by on the way upstairs and on the first step of the first turn my eyes met hers, a square black moustache appeared under my nose and I went to in *Deutschland,* kissed her invisibly foully and put my hand hard on her ghost. Nothing but revenge. Her legs were without muscles, but cared for white; her arms were without muscles but cared for white; her milk white body was in the power of my fantasy, in time before her husband was killed. Before he lived. Or after. Uncle Manny threw the little girl in the air. The girl shrieked. The polished widow with a caustic smile, watched, saying oh you're spoiling her.

Something flashed in my head and I tripped on the second step, turning to her. I wanted to kill her.

"Gee, you look fine."

Oh yes, but it was the soft tip of my tongue said that, and she lowered her eyes with an empty smile. I—

I started up the steps in wooden terror that I—to fuck that? Head filled with thunder, I was almost staggering, and Philip Roth was real, and I was on the top step clutching the rail. My right hand was slightly out in the air. My fragile face was tilted forward still fixed to my imported China head, on my wire neck twisted on a stick, legs like steel scissors.

My wife crossed the sunlit room with a look of alarm.

"She has a bagel in her hand. When she offers it, take a bite."

Chewing on the bite of bagel, I moved into the kitchen, my wife holding my hand. Uncle Manny was smiling. He asked,

"A little drink?"

He added soda and I took the drink and retreated to the living room. That bagel hit the spot.

I stood looking out the window at rows and rows of the same houses and roofs against the sky; there, a distant church steeple with a round metal silver phallic dome. Far to the right a football drifted up and fell behind a rooftop. That was the first time. The second my left kneecap began forward, and on the third the glass began its first slip from my fingers, and as my jaw just began to fall and my eyes close I exhaled in the acceptance of the final trip of separation, and the roots wrenched.

"Why don't you sit down."

I sat in a chair.

"Put your drink on the table and your feet on the ottoman."

I put my drink on a coaster on the table. My hand was wet. I put my feet up.

The last thing I saw was a book on the table. Kennedy was dead.

Sunlight twinkled off it.

The sun was lovely.

I slept.

I was looking out the kitchen window.

Uncle Manny grinned, and gestured both hands, fingers spread, to me:

"Such a fine young man! Ah yes! Not afraid to be unhappy—not afraid to be happy in this troubled world! Good! Good! Have a drink—more, more, that's it, a little ice? Yes? Fine help yourself are you hungry? Eggs, sandwich meat, fruit, anything! A good young man! Drink up!"

He crossed the kitchen and put his arm around me, but I turned away, he was concerned and when I glanced at him I saw the questions in his eyes, too, and I couldn't stand it, and when he embraced me I saw through tears, my wife had a tender expression, and it was after the explosion, I almost broke, but I didn't,

"We love you," Uncle Manny said. "We love you."

I had to leave.

The garage door slammed shut, the subway train was coming in and Manny's wife scowled and the black and white and hot pink widow got in the car and started the engine. The car backed into the street, a detective story image every time it swung around and began the long trip across Queens, across Manhattan, into New Jersey. It was Daddy's car, and her milky body was covered with the clothes Daddy bought.

We waited on the high platform, and soon the subway train came rocketing toward us, out of the distances of the Bronx it came, to screech and squeal to a stop so we could get on and at last head home for ourselves, like she did, glittering only making for New Jersey in his car, smiling, possessively, down at her little girl. Inevitably— oh no oh YES: it is ONE experience OUTWARD FLOWING—

I woke suddenly—in darkness—I—I couldn't go back to sleep, there was—my dream. I—I had had a dream.

The Sun Rises Into the Sky

HIS WIFE GOT OUT OF BED and dressed hurriedly. He rolled over still in the dream listening to his wife's exclamations about her being late for work. He sat up, and looked at her.

But captured by the dream, he slipped back down and under the covers, and fell asleep.

A monk sat on a high stool at a table by a window, in the corner of a cabin on the side of a mountain. The monk was writing in a black bound looseleaf notebook; it was a brilliant yet simple narrative. The monk felt heat of enthusiasm and chill of fear, and as he gazed at the few lines he had written he knew he was right, yet he also knew his narrative would cost him dearly, the evidence being on the page before him. Total knowing had never been so well written, it must be true. On that page. But knowing his fear, and failing courage, curiosity was real, and though it was forbidden, he turned the page *to see what would come next.*

The page, like a tombstone, was pushed over, and from out of bright whiteness, a virgin whiteness, a jagged black spider rose, and crouched, and held its stance, powerful and evil. It stirred, and made harsh scrapings gathering itself to move towards the hand on the table, and like a shadow it crept across the page, over the wood table top, and onto the monk's fingers, and as the monk's hand was up, and partly curved, the spider moved onto the monk's open palm, as the monk writhed, hand frozen, as if nailed down, he rocked back and forth and tossed his head, as the creature dug into the skin, and exuded in a terrible downward drive its darkness into the monk's hand and blood.

He woke in frenzy.
The second dream came around a week later, at about the same

271

time. He woke as his wife was rushing to go to work, again almost late and complaining as he helped her find her keys, and gloves, and then after a hurried kiss she was gone.

The book in his hands was thicker. The writing was different than before—not so brilliantly clear, clear like something old made clear.

The cabin was clean; shelves were packed with books, the day was warm, or rather the dawn was warm, and he looked at his book.

The sentences ran across the pages and filled the book, they told a story, and he read his story and it was as though the pages were billowing curtains in front of large open doorways, and he felt a wind on his cheek as if tugging at a chill deep in his guts, like the residue at the bottom of a deep dark well, and he feared the words he had used, and he saw and felt a sense of stone; old stone, his Stonehenge: of emotion.

Madness, and a fearful joy filled the sentences. The man came out of the ground and filled the sentences as his son shuddered in written winds of violence and love of the dead, and the monk wrote *"it is colder,"* and pulled his threadbare robe around him and looked at the book, a small book getting larger, a gust of wind whipped up off the page—so cold he cried out.

Sunday they both had hangovers and it was a day then of a late breakfast, reading and napping and humor and loving; she made a fantastic supper with chicken and onions and mushrooms, noodles with a smoking butter/garlic sauce, and French stringbeans. It was so good they laughed as they ate. At midnight she made cocoa. And they read late.

He was reading a novel by Nevil Shute, *An Old Captivity*, a really dreadful novel, which became worse and worse and he finally threw it across the loft, as his wife laughed; she had read it too. But the beginning of the book involved a dream by the pilot who had been hired to fly an archaeologist to Greenland, and by air chart the whole area that the archaeologist was digging—something like that, and the way the author wrote about the plane, and the flying, was terrific. At first.

As the journey progressed, however, the pilot began to have strange dreams, and was unable to remember them the next day, it began to bother him more and more and when they got to Greenland and everything was set up the pilot couldn't sleep so had to take sleeping pills. One night he took three and the next day they couldn't wake him; one of the Eskimos said the pilot wasn't going to wake, ever, etc., and the pilot's feet began to get cold, very cold, and then his finger tips, etc. and then his heart slowed.

The Eskimos said they had better move him from this haunted campsite, etc., they did, and thirty six hours later the pilot woke up and the girl, the professor's daughter, took his hands, and he looked her square in the eyes and said he would ask Leif if they can stay, and the book slammed against the wall and fell to the floor.

"Yeah. I get it," he said, and began to work on one of his manuscripts, yet the written cold of Greenland prevailed, and so did the pilot figure who dreamed of his archaic past. He tossed and turned, and the lights went out. She fell asleep, and he stared at the ceiling. It was November, and the loft became chilly, and he tried to find a position to sleep in, and in his anxiety he began to perspire, and then literally water began to run down his face, and he began to be afraid he would catch cold, and slowly the loft got colder and colder.

"Lie still!"

He made a final attempt at comfort, pulled the covers close around him, and settled his body and began the effort of giving up consciousness; he wanted to sleep, and following the rules of that desire, in a passion to turn over a new leaf he began to sink, and having made contact with a good beginning in fiction, he began to relax in an outward spreading darkness, deeply into the cabin with his book. The spider sprang up, alert, to be fed and to be charged in itself, and trembled on the snowy page, and the monk twisted in agony, and in terror, trying to move his paralyzed hand; a cold wind came in the window, it blew and chilled the monk—it came from a far place, and the barren cabin was cold, and yet within the fear and the chill, something was different. It lacked—

It lacked its former drama.

The spider leaped onto his wrist, NO the monk screamed, as the tiny needlepoint spider leg-tips claws dug in the skin above his

273

pulse, and even as he groaned and rolled his eyes it was different, and gradually sensing a consciousness, he fought it, forcefully, and watched the evil black spider working down down to inject the darkness into him, it didn't work, it didn't and the spider paused and the monk stared in disbelief: the spider was impotent.

It was straining on the monk's wrist, it shuddered, and then, slowly, it began to shrink within itself, and become thin, and hardly able to move, staggered weakly to the edge of the monk's wrist, and tumbled off and fell into darkness.

His wrist was bare, the page was filled with sentences. The monk rubbed his hands. The question of what would come next—was over.

A candle burned brightly on the desk. Books filled the shelves around him. A clock ticked to his right, and pens and paper, ink, and stacks of manuscripts lay in scattered sloping piles; the room was warm. The window was closed.

The air was still. The chill wind had gone.

The monk opened the window, and looked out. The wind receded across the valley, and across the mountains, and plains and hills far away, back; father was journeying back into the grave.

A hush fell over the mountain. The monk—the writer—I—read the sentences, and looked at the clock. It was my day off from work, in fact it was ten after four and my wife was due home: I had worked on my story all day—there were many stories to tell, and I would tell them and I would witness my past recede, and leave me alone to suffer my further emotions, greater surely, and therefore more terrible than any before, but as if in a dream—it came to me—incredibly, as the sun rises into the sky at the end of my dream distance was no longer an influence. Father. Even then, when he and it was, it and he was and were the past the size of the future, looming so huge, the massive mountain of *to be*—to be myself, be all of it my future, rising, into it all, willing, with him, we will move the tombstone into place, and name it the *Lapis*, and so realize the tone, like the sound of a call: of a new literature on our lips.

Dream

THE SKY WAS BLUE. It was a warm breezy day. We walked into the water. The other side was a grassy line against the sky. We swam towards it and pleasantly we came up on land and walked through tall reeds and onto the old footpaths.

We went in and swam across another waterfield and entered a balmy grove, walked between trees which got thicker and for a time we were in darkness, and we moved slowly, parting ferns and bushes. It was dark when we got to the water and the swimming was eerie, and then more difficult. The water began to taste like mud, and there was debris in it. I became worn out, and asked my wife how she was doing. She said she was doing okay and I said I was getting worn out and hoped I could make it. I knew there was no turning back, and as my arms and legs were beginning to stiffen I was afraid, and began a heavy dog paddle. Somebody called out they thought it was just ahead, and soon my feet touched bottom, and we clambered up a muddy slope and rested.

We rose and went into a heavy jungle, heavier than before, and slow going. I was close to my wife all the time, and the blonde artist and his wife were just behind, and the others followed them, and in the afternoon we came to the grassy edge of a small cliff, and as I looked over I perceived a girl, in wet rags, climbing up.

"Let's go down!" I cried, and as we passed her I asked her what it was like. She tilted her head and I followed the direction to a group of people swimming in a very muddy lake at the foot of stick houses with thatch roofs, standing in the water. The people seemed to be having a good time.

"It's fun!" cried the girl.

Myself and my wife, and the blonde artist and his wife joined the people, but the people were too rough, too noisy, unconsciously animal-like splashing and ducking and no sooner were we beyond them than we were swimming in an endless maze of waterways between reed-forests. The water was clear, though, and the sky was like the old high sunny days of before, and we swam out into a clearwater lake which we happily crossed, and came onto land, and so it went, we crossed one narrow lake after another until we came to a large island.

The ground was hard packed, it was grey, the surface was dusty, the palm trees were beaten husks and the grass and bushes were smashed and split beside dusty stone-like grey dirt paths, it was a stripped island, the trees were carved with graffiti and sadistic slashes, and we kept on walking, and when we came to some deserted grass huts the sky was white. My wife and I were walking alone.

I was depressed, and frightened.

We heard the sound of angry laughing men as we came to a clearing: unshaven white dirty men in undershirts and torn khakis milled around drinking cans of beer.

We passed them unnoticed, and descended a steep very slippery cliff of dust into a dry village of torn grass and bamboo shacks. The grey dirt between the shacks was as hard as concrete.

This, then, was the place where we were, on the edge of the village, and late one afternoon we stood outside by the corner of our shack. My wife was close to me, my arm was over her shoulder and her arm was around my waist.

She was thinking her thoughts and rather gazing at the village. I was looking in another direction and—suddenly I—through the dry shattered jungle I saw the twinkle of a clearwater inlet. This was new! I reached out for my wife, but she told me to wait.

I looked again, and through the dusty curtain of jungle greyness I saw a golden shaft of sunlight reveal a dark green frog and oh—the emerald valley!

My wife said, "I'm going swimming."

"Stay a moment!" I cried. "See the frog in the valley!"

"I'll be back," she said. She smiled warmly to me, and as she walked into the jungle—the twinkling green valley overwhelmed me, and among a traffic of lazy half undressed men looking like pigs—the veterans of wars—a young man watched me; with clear and sympathetic eyes.

My wife came around the corner of the shack, she was limping, and being helped by one of the pig men.

She fell into my arms. She had broken her foot. Her upturned face was damp and pale and grim in pain. Over her shoulder I saw the man with sympathetic eyes. I could trust—my wife said,

"I'll have to go back."

"Go back!" I yelled. "Go *back!* Look how far we've come! How *far* it's been! And—LOOK THERE!" In rising emotion I pointed to the twinkling crystalline water, and the dark green frog in the heart of the emerald valley.

"You go," my wife whispered resolutely. "I know you want to—"

Her foot and ankle were badly swollen. I was angry. "Go BACK! You can't swim with that!"

"I'll make it," she said gravely, and the pig men began to make a thatch stretcher and she was going away, I felt myself slant away in separation and unhappiness, and in hurt and rage I said, "Your foot, your Goddamned FOOT! WHY—WHY NOW? WHY DID YOU DO IT! OF ALL TIMES—WHY NOW!"

I stood there, and I just screamed.

"I'll meet you," she said distantly. I threw out my arms to her. "WHEN? HOW?"

"I don't know," and her living face, so vivid in my life and mind began to fade as she softly said, "Goodbye, I'll be there."

I chased her wherever she was, and her voice came across a hollowness saying, "Go—go—"

I looked at the frog in the emerald valley. *Go alone to Paradise?* I wept.

The sympathetic man spoke with his eyes of his help, but my wife was helped onto the stretcher, and the pig men picked her up, and carried her away through the trees.

The Triangle on the Jungle Wall

A WHISPER.

The sound of muffled drums, and Phil wept.

"Phil—*Phil*—"

Phil turned in the mud. Nathan was whispering to him.

But what Nathan whispered this time, didn't help, and Phil could hear the care in Nathan's voice, Nathan would protect him. But Phil wept and slid away from his rifle.

Nurse Poppins had sounded her chimes.

"May we have your name rank and serial number?"

Phil had looked at her blankly; had asked could—she repeat that. Softly powdered ding-a-ling and he didn't understand.

"I only want to see the—guy—"

She had nodded. Wasn't she only the familiar means to what he wanted, and he gave her a heavy lidded hopeless glass-look.

"Can't I talk to him?"

I mean for a little.

"I'm not really—I just need, a little while." An attractive smile said pink was sorry.

"Look it's a long time," he cried. "It's a long way here, what will be I'll fear! I'm going to—" the girl rather bleached behind the desk, for the soldier couldn't finish his sentence. She rose from her chair, and holding her hand out, said with her gesture,

"Can't you give us your name rank—"

Phil yelled. "Life and death title! Should you want it from a horse on a swing a Nathan *a* on a porch in Ohio, my father?" Irrational, frightened and lost Phil staggered out of the midwest into scattering machine gun fire wondering in a jungle, bracing himself to incredible distance. Nathan whispered.

278

He heard the shattering whack of helicopters coming and the men ran to them and jumped in, were flown back; Phil felt yellow and guilty. He put his arms around Nathan, and sobbed.

Nathan held his buddy close, rocking with him in the moving craft.

Phil couldn't sleep and walked in the mobbed Negro and Oriental city drinking the next day wandering around waiting for it. She said,

"Hey Feel, why you—mind—"

The hand, yes, but her lips and tongue no, slanting in a crashing darkness of children, in remorse he had orgasm, and got out of the landed ship, ran stealthily across the ground into the paddy. Nathan was about fifty feet to his left and the V.C. were on the other side of the paddy behind the trees waiting, and when Phil came out of the water he got it twice in the stomach. He sat down, shocked. Bug eyed.

Nathan saw that and came out of the water fast, running to the right on an angle across the clearing like an angry shortstop, firing towards the trees as he ran, hearing cries all the way, he knelt at Phil's side, reloaded and fired at them paying no attention to the corpsman who came out of the paddy, and who bent over Phil tearing away his shirt, as Nathan, slit eyed, laced the trees and bushes with gunfire.

He cried, "How is he?"

The medic: "Bad."

Nathan advanced slightly towards the trees, his body in front of the working medic, and with a killer's eye and ear he simply lashed out at the jungle, and when the enemy came out at them, Nathan tight lipped and unforgiving reloaded and cut them down so fiercely they paused, and the medic and Nathan heaved Phil up, and dragged him clumsily toward the paddy opening the holes in Phil's stomach, blood gushed out and the medic cried,

"No go! Let's go!"

He grabbed Nathan's arm and spun him, yet Nathan froze and gave the medic a glare of vileness, snarling, "Go," and crouching opened fire over Phil's body. The medic was wading away screaming, up to his waist in water.

They saw the crazy American in the water, and the other on the ground, and as they ran they threw stones and spears and rifle fire in glee of hatred shrieking and advancing on dead and living men. Whack in the air. Nathan reloaded. Whack! In the racket of the descending metal angel Nathan killed them as they rushed. He killed and killed the enemy that was not to be erased, and they advanced in heavy cover that sent spumes and spouts of mud around Nathan who, retreating, helplessly, finally sought his safety wanting yet to get them; while the other, now safe Americans, watching from inside the bird, and saw the medic turn, go back in the water and haul Nathan out, and stumble through the bog with him weeping and cursing, they gripped the ladder, and as they climbed up to outstretched hands in a hell of fire, it was two men in the sky, the medic, and Nathan who would never die in war, as the helicopter swerved up to the left and veered over the trees, Nathan coughing and spitting and the medic screaming why?

Because the enemy had concentrated on getting Nathan and the medic, and Nathan had held his ground, the other Americans were able to withdraw, and Nathan and the medic got medals.

Several weeks later Nathan was sent home, and one day he took the bus, from New York (Brooklyn), to Columbus Ohio to see Phil's folks, and going up the front walk saw a star in the window.

He clumsily introduced himself, and Phil's folks were proud to meet him. Phil's dad was a mechanic, he said something about the Communists and they all sat on the porch and drank beer. Phil had died in his country's battle, and Nathan nodded that was true and Phil's mom brought out some pretzels and they sat in Ohio and talked about Viet Nam. Phil's dad—Phil's dad wanted to know.

Phil had come out of the paddy and been hit, Nathan said. Phil's father said,

"You mean—he walked right into it?"

Nathan nodded. "We all did."

"You mean he never got his licks?"

Nathan looked over the lawn, and told a little lie. At length he said, unemotionally,

"It's different—hard for you to see—how it is, was, I mean it's muddy and dirty and hot. They're good—"

280

"Good! They?"

"The—V.C.—they're very good, it's their—"

"Whaddya mean they're *good*—"

"Fighting; they're good at it."

Phil's father's face was hostile. Nathan said,

"It's their country; they—they can go back—back and forth in it."

"And we don't?"

Nathan made a gesture. He was embarrassed. "Well, we're trying—getting to—"

Phil's father stood up angrily: "Are you one of them—peace fellas?"

Nathan smiled. "No."

Phil's father asked, "What are you?"

Nathan sipped his beer, frowned, and ate a pretzel. "Me, I guess."

"Tell us more about our—boy," Phil's mother said.

Nathan heard an explosion—he turned completely in the chair and looked out at the street, hands shaking; all right, do it.

"Phil," he began, "a guy—" he scratched his head and sighed, feeling their eyes upon him. He, rapidly, then, told the truth. Perspiring. The words rushed out. "Day before he got it he tried to see the—shrinker—please let me finish—he wanted—he told me nobody understood him. We had a crazy religious guy in our outfit, and this guy was always taking photographs and talking about the CIA. He'd go into Saigon, and photograph the girls, and the guys who sold black market stuff, the pictures were lousy, blurred—but Phil always wanted to see them, and the guy—Phil hung around him, too much, wanted to know why he did it. Pestered him. The guy—they had a fight, and Phil lost. He started seeing things. Hearing stuff, and talking about horses, a horse and a nut as well, I tried to tell him it's okay to lose, but Phil got— funny, and when we came out of the paddy—" Nathan stopped, fearing the deduction. He said instead,

"He was sorry he didn't get his—chance—" Nathan fairly spit the last word.

Phil's father said, "What happened to the guy who took pictures?"

281

"Nothing."

Nathan looked at Phil's mom and dad; he couldn't control his eyes' fury. Phil's mom and dad were sitting alertly on the swing, yet they were invisibly leaning back, secure in their hatred of Phil revealed, and Nathan nervously stood up and said he had to go. Go?

Didn't he want to stay for dinner?

He had been there twenty minutes and he shook his head, and clasped, and quickly rid himself of, Phil's father's hand; Nathan was beginning to flip.

He walked down the sidewalk and a youngster turned a bike onto the front lawn, and stopped in his tracks seeing the man in uniform.

"Hey soldier! Did you know my brother?"

"A little."

There was a bar by the Columbus bus terminal, and Nathan had boilermakers. When the bus came he was dizzy, and hungry, furious that he had worn his uniform, and as he sat by the window he tore off his tie, and loosened his collar remembering he had worn it for them, they'd probably like it if I do, who cares, he whispered, and breathing heavily, he stared out the window at passing houses, playing children, mothers with baby carriages, and moving shiny cars in Ohio.

Down the highway went the bus.

Pulled into Port Authority near midnight, and Nathan caught the 7th Avenue subway to Brooklyn, straight to the bar.

His buddies greeted him again, full of wisecracks; yet careful, with him.

Nathan swung onto the barstool like war, and vehemently ordered: they watched, wishing they could come home from Viet Nam and look like Nathan, doubtfully.

Nathan's face was flushed, his stare was fixed on the top of a slightly tilted floating triangle being pierced by slowly moving technicolored dotted lines, his eyes were almost violet, and as his lips drew back the bartender glanced in alarm at Nathan's buddies, because Nathan was grotesque, almost alchemical, manic in rage on the barstool, hands gripping the invisible automatic rifle, and Phil's father opened another can of beer, in Ohio, unaware of the gun aimed at his face, or that his face was being projected on a wall of jungle in Viet Nam by a young man with a gun in his hands gone mad in Brooklyn, firing at that elusive white face behind the yellow faces of the running shouting shooting V.C.—Nathan saw Phil at his feet by the paddy. And Phil was still there. Phil was a star in a window; *"Who cares,"* Nathan snarled, in gunfire.

The Word

A RUNNING CORPORAL with pink cheeks and blazing eyes jumped over a dying G.I. who tried to grab his foot. He missed. The Corporal ran towards the mudpile. Bullets kicked up a shower of earth and blasted the dying GI dead. The Corporal dove to safety in huddled bodies behind the mudpile. Bodies clumped in a statue. A Pfc. was screaming into a walkie talkie, V.C. machine gun bullets struck the edges of the pile and the dead bodies beyond, the Pfc. wept in frustration, and the enemy came out of the jungle running, and firing at the edges of the mudpile keenly wailing behind blasting guns. Then the jungle and sky tilted, rocked by one concussion, and the whole area exploded and went up in an expanding ball of liquid fire, and they burned. All of them.

Underneath a house on the outskirts of Detroit, in the spring of 1941, when he was not yet born, underneath what his mother and father did above revealed concerns of their selves, and if, and when, children, they would have a son, first, son like father; sure wanted that. Father a contract merchant with a solid sense of profit and identity in his head, and a sensitive tightly strung a priori wire in there too, that when touched, decided yes or no; it was father who got the deal with the government. He drove in the driveway and jumped out of the stopped car and went in the house. He said, to her, leaning against the doorjamb to the kitchen,
"I'm home."
She said hi without turning around, and he asked,
"What do you want to do tonight?"
She turned, looking at him angrily. "You got the contract."

He nodded, and grinned. But she was in a mood, and she said bitterly,

"Why do you always ask me what I want to do! Why don't you say let's do this, or—this, or that—?"

"Like what," he laughed.

"*I* don't know!" She added.

Well he loved her, and that talk was the price he had to pay, so they had a couple of drinks while they dressed; then they got in the car, and rather argumentatively went to a steakhouse, had dinner, and went to a nightclub and jitterbugged in the milieu of about a thousand kids. She had a good time.

On the way home they stopped off at another place, more quiet, and as he parked she asked him what the deal was about.

He mumbled something.

"Gas?" she frowned.

"No, it's different. But pretty close! How'd you guess?"

He was handsome in his sureness, all the way, and he was—he was a great dancer. She clung to him in their slow fox trot; words, he thought, to sell, after Harry had moved his lips about fire; well, Harry had been wrong.

His language made his heart beat. He danced smoothly. She was chuckling. He was trying to seduce his wife. Why not? She was the one he wanted, and he said, let's go home soon. Did you get the jelly? She nodded and touched his fly, breathing.

Reeling around curves, heart hammering evenly, he settled in his seat and she put her head on his shoulder. Every marriage, he thought, his eyes in slits, is a stereotype. Why be different? A pattern is formed to thrive in, flexible with possibilities of strong identity. As I.

He swept the car downward into the valley that meant home, and after a few graceful turns swung it into the driveway, stopped and got out in one motion with a grim smile. That really marvelous swing down the valley and around the turns, and the lovely slip into the driveway; combination of speed, power and something sleek or slick, smoothly phallic in entrance, was soothing to the excitement. One motion. But the lust and excitement and slickness, like a big deal, neatly sucked up home, and coming into the valley in those years, he kissed off the future, and with the somnambulist's sense of time, he drove through perpetual now which he was certain was included in experience, but which would not only be missing in action, later, like twenty-five years, but cremated alive.

The Greatest Story Ever Told
A Transformation

for Betty

1
April, 1947

I WAS SITTING IN STUDY HALL studying the 9th grade girl sitting in front of me. I knew who she was—she had the worst reputation of any girl in school.

The guys she ran around with were from Valley Park, which was about seven miles west of Kirkwood, meaning, in 1947, that Valley Park was the westernmost extension of urban expansion, Valley Park being about seventeen miles west of St. Louis, and a mill town of small population.

The kids were poor, and tough, they didn't like jokes about their poverty, and the girl sitting in front of me rode with a boy named Al, who had long artistic midnight blue hair and drove his glistening black four-door white-walled Lincoln at a hundred around turns and one ten on straightaways. I envied and feared him; but he fascinated me, too, because he liked me, because I was an artist. How strange! I used to ride with him, occasionally, after school.

She was his friend. She kind of hung around him.

And she had been assigned to sit in front of me in study hall on Mondays, Wednesdays, and Fridays. The room was large and sat about 150 of us in some seven or eight rows overseered by huge fat Lou Pabst, an ex-gym instructor, nicknamed The Blue Whale on account of that blue suit he wore every day up and down the aisles: slit-eyed, tightlipped and powerful. I fell asleep once, and he had lifted me out of my seat by my hair, and it had really hurt.

Sleepy, Dawson?

Well. I was in the next to last seat, back in the rear of the second row from the window which meant I could see out across the front lawn of Kirkwood High, and to Kirkwood Road beyond, and looking to my left, see the lawn descend into a circular hollow in front of Junior High where the fêtes were held, and the most beautiful girls in the world were crowned Queen of the May year after year, and the girls that weren't bit their lips, wept, embraced their Queen and prayed alongside their crazed parents on Sundays, in church, and every night at home like their parents too; they created a complicated and questionable God of success, and made requests, and asked forgiveness in a kind of dream to Him, in or kneeling beside their beds every night, they thus put themselves to sleep. Norman Rockwell couldn't get that right, somehow.

And there I was: the artist, the writer, the clown, the serious acolyte, the too-intelligent boy who failed too many courses, the Midnight Peeper, and Dreamer to End All Dreamers anxiously wild about Stan Kenton, Woody Herman and Dizzy Gillespie sitting behind the girl from Valley Park, reading from textbooks so dull and pointless they held a mystery I was never able to unravel, even when I tried. The new semester, begun in February, passed through towards the end of March, and I, sixteen going on seventeen, re-read the list of prepositions, readying myself for the test Mrs. Sandfos would give the next day—which I flunked, and Mrs. Sandfos was furious, and kept me after school memorizing prepositions. She really fought me. But meanwhile, there I was, studying for the test I would flunk. It was a sunny day, near the first week in April, and that girl in front of me turned around in her seat, looked square in my eyes, and with a mysterious little smile, murmured softly,

You think you're smart, don't you?

And turned back around. I saw her head lower, and she began writing. I looked at the prepositions, and then, in the same motion a girl uses to clip on her bra, she passed me a folded note, withdrew her hand and to all appearances was doing her school work; she was fifteen years old, and the note was written in a fast slanty hand,

But you're cute, anyway.

My handwriting was normally uncontrolled and wild, and my

288

message, slapdashed beneath hers, said,

Hey, you are too!

She was, and I was frantic!

Heart pounding, my mind racing, and the bell almost took my head off. We rose to leave and go to classes, and in a smell of books, dust, teenage bodies, perfume and leather, shoe polish and spring, she bunched her books against her breasts, turned, and for an instant looked squarely in my eyes, and walked away into the throng of the corridor.

What did it mean? I—oh well hell I knew, of course, but what was happening in me?

I was feverish and oh Jesus I'd have to wait until the day after next to find out WHAT NEXT and I made up my suddenly crazed mind I would—I'd find out.

2

The guys in my gang—Bob, Al, Lassin, Gene, Mac, and, when he wasn't practising how to break the next shotput and discus record which he would (and did) do, Doc—we all made a pact that the first guy who got laid would let the others know. And none of us were getting laid. So after each date, Mac and Gene, and myself, and Al, reported to each other how we had made out: I got a double last night; Mac's excitement telling me he got a TRIPLE—

We almost fell on the grass laughing.

But suspicions had it that Lassin wasn't coming clean, and not even to me. Which angered me. He and I were very close, and when the bunch of us would spend the night at each other's houses, Lassin and I would lie in bed and smoke and after a long while I'd whisper,

A—Are you, you know you can tell me, I won't tell anybody, are you laying Junie?

He chuckled in the darkness.

Gene and Mac were more overt, unlike myself who was more covert, and they put it to Lassin directly that they thought he was a fake, and the whole thing with Junie was only singles and doubles, and I, well I wavered. I mean I believed Lassin was the assassin he pretended to be with his girls, and even if Mac and Gene were right about him, their motives of jealousy and their anxiety in not

289

knowing, and Lassin making a big Goddamned mystery out of the whole thing, that was their frustration, because each of us was pretty honest about what luck we were having, except me, and I wasn't getting laid, but, I was making secret plans. And it was tough to keep a secret because boy she was built like anything but a secret, I mean, my secrets were always obvious, except to me, I mean she was so obviously terrific I was baffled.

I asked Mac, You tripled? Why didn't you come in home?

He stroked his upper lip, and frowned. She wouldn't let me. I tried, he tensely explained. I mean we were parked and I had her skirt off, her sweater up, and her pants down and—well, she wouldn't let me! I got my finger in—and got—left on third, what could I do? and she said no; NO!

Jesus, I said. But, for myself I must admit, I mean I excitedly told my buddies my true adventures, it was, yes it was true I wasn't getting laid, but I had something going with a girl down the street, I had a secret, etc., and I wasn't going to tell anybody everything—if they found out how well I was doing, and what the girl thought about me, and anyway it was so complicated, she was complicated, I couldn't figure her out and she liked me, was hot for me, and she was in love with that son of a bitch Bernie Keller, and what was going to happen to me? They knew I was peeping on her, but they didn't know how serious I was—the degree, I mean, and I wasn't gonna tell 'em. Only a little bit. I must admit, also, that—I was the real peeping tom in town, and that actually my closest competitor, who worked the other side of Kirkwood (where Sally Hopper lived) was Jasper Richterclout; he and I went to the same church, all my gang did except Lassin, and well Jasper was completely but I mean totally in love with Sally Hopper, and Sally was without question the most beautiful girl who ever drew breath—she could float, no joke, she wasn't of us, she was the Materia Fantastica, boys passing her in the hall almost crossed themselves, and, well, the effect she had on me was devastating and typical. If she'd say hi Fee, my vision blurred, and as I fought for control and gasped hi, I was only instantly in love, dizzy, knees shaking, etc., all the symptoms. But I mean she crucified Jasper Richterclout, she knew he was in love with her, he dated her constantly, and to her it was like a happy sort of game, like playing dolls, but murder to Jasper because knowing

wasn't a known reality to Sally because Sally didn't know anything, she was in a daze, hopelessly innocent, stupid, sweet, she
didn't even know she didn't know. She was about as bright as a
turtle, and Mr. Curba, the Biology teacher was in love with her,
the head-over-heels kind, and who, I mean how could he flunk her
even though she flunked every test and couldn't remember hardly
where to go to get to what class? And to expect her to know the
difference between a paramecium and an amoeba was to expect a
baby to know calculus, and, well, she got by okay, her friends
helped her, and she graduated with her class, while almost every
night, snow, rain, sleet, regardless, Jasper climbed the tree beside
her house and paused on the limb just outside her second storey
window and watched her undress. An ever faithful slave to the flesh
of his personal teenage goddess, and so, he was as far as I knew,
beside myself, the other persistent peeper in town, and also like
myself, in the daylight hours, a popular person whom everyone
enjoyed being with. Although he was a little wilder than me.

So, while Lassin was at least honestly staying silent regarding
Junie, I was dishonestly talking of my partial action. Bob suspected
me, and Gene and Mac were suspicious, too, but Mac was too busy
with Lucy Ann Miller, and also with Sally Musgrave (she was in
love with Bob Topper, they were a year ahead of us, and Bob almost
died when Sally married a guy in her first year in college, and even
though Mac and Sally had broken up at least a year before, Mac,
too, Mac was crushed), and Gene had his hands full(?) with Anita
and anyway they were too busy to pester me, although, actually,
they did anyway. Well, it was complicated, we were all busy. We
all dated. And walked girls home after school, etc., and if I walked a
girl home from school and in daylight got a single on her doorstep
which I did, and told my gang, it kept 'em busy enough to overlook
my secret madness down the street.

But it irritated me Lassin wouldn't tell me about Junie. Me. His
best, most trusted, friend-to-the-end. Me. I who said to him, that
if I got laid, I would tell him, and nobody else.

Why? he asked. He could be sardonic.

I explained: Well, I mean, because you'd understand, and you
can keep a secret.

We were pitching horseshoes in his backyard after school. Just

291

the two of us. He was winning again, again, and with a horseshoe in his hand, he looked at me.

You mean I'd understand because I'm getting Junie. Is that it? He smiled, darkly.

I leaned against his house, laughing, and he chuckled mysterously, and threw a leaner.

Still laughing, I asked, Well, aren't you?

It's your turn. Throw. Give me a ringer, he smiled. A little strangely.

I asked, Then why does Junie look at you like she does? and I added, my ace, She almost faints when she looks at you!

He smiled and arched his eyebrows; that meant the answer was obvious: Because, and he put his hand on his heart, she loves me!

LOVES YOU! I yelled, laughing, the horseshoe in my hand my mind racing maybe she does! But is he laying her, and does love mean screwing?

The next day I confessed to Mac, I think the Assassin's laying Junie.

Mac jumped a little. You do?

Yeah. I can feel it. I have a hunch. I was—famous for my hunches.

Did he tell you? Did he? What'd he say?

I told him, and mentioned Lassin had beat me in horseshoes again. Mac made his habitual rub across his upper lip, and frowned, Maybe, maybe, but I don't know, she's pretty conservative.

My sister, however, not long after that, gave us a crucial clue. She was five years older, and one night when we were all at my house, she looked at Lassin with an amused smile, and said, in her direct style:

Do you know you have bedroom eyes, Mister Assassin?

And he blushed!

We looked at each other, and secretly nodded. He may have bedroom eyes, but we sure knew he didn't have a bedroom to use 'em in, and therefore he wasn't laying Junie. It was singles and doubles in that blue '41 Chevy of his, and all that other mystery was a lot of crap.

3

She had passed me the note on Monday, and on Wednesday, seeing her appear to not notice me, and having flunked the preposition test, I was watching her with one eye, and with the other trying to diagram a sentence. If Mrs. Sandfos ever had a mission in life, or a few, one of them was definitely to get me to learn grammar, and I heard a whisper, *hey*, and looked up.

The Blue Whale was talking with Mr. Curba in the doorway. She had half turned in her seat, and was looking directly into my eyes, a hard steady gaze, and she whispered,

What are you doing after school?

I shook my head imperceptibly. Nothing. Whispered.

A smile flickered and her eyes were as mirror stones, hard and haunting as she whispered,

Is there a place we can go to?

After the thunderbolt, I found a voice and whispered Yes, and she coolly murmured,

Where can we meet?

By the Library, corner of Taylor and Jefferson. Okay? As thunder rumbled down the highway.

She nodded. Three thirty.

Okay, I whispered, seeing The Blue Whale glaring at me. I whispered,

The Whale watcheth.

She turned around, and again to all appearances was doing schoolwork.

I sat, transfixed. Was this it? My whole body was trembling, and, then, a voice with an echo on its tail came drifting swirling as out of Asia, across the Seven Seas, the Mediterranean, 'tween the Straits of Gibraltar, and whirling across the Atlantic, across the Appalachians, and Ohio, Illinois, and just missing St. Louis, did a loop, and in a descending curve, came through the open study hall window and slid into my ear: *Yes.*

This is it.

!The rest of the day was a feverish blank and a fantasy. A dream, and in a state of total nervewreck, apprehension, and in a hot stew of lust and terror, wooden-legged I walked down Taylor Avenue and stood on the corner by the Library and in a near fainting stage of anxiety that the neighbors see me with her, and that she

wouldn't show up, I tensely waited, and then there she came
walking along Jefferson toward me, and when she got to my side we
said Hi and holding hands I walked her to my house, my head
rolling along, Where were we going to do it?

In my room? Through which Aunty Mary must pass as she did
every day to get into the basement for things for supper? On my
bed, in my room where Mother stopped by at four on the dot,
always, always, and came in to tell me she was home, as she'd done
every day for almost ten years? On my bed in my room, where the
door to my room had no lock?

Yes, the occult voice said.

I was crashing and smashing around in my head, her hand felt
great, soft and hot clasping mine as we went around to the side of
my house, we passed the pine tree and turned the corner in under
the grape arbor, passed the cistern and I opened the back door and
we went into my room. I closed the hallway door to my room and
pulled my big desk over to block it. I closed the outside door, and
she stood looking around at the walls of my Grandfather's books,
my drawings and paintings and mobiles, my ballglove, my model
airplane. And I turned to her, I was nearly literally on fire, and
paralyzed in fright. We looked at each other, and she said, awe in
her fifteen year old voice,

This room's really swell, and added, All yours? I nodded.

She came into my arms, and we kissed.

She caressed my hair and my ears and neck as we kissed, she
more kissing me, and I rather tensed, but only for a moment, for
when I kissed her, I began to relax and then became completely
relaxed in a sudden full body, our tongues curled and licked together, and I felt her body with my right hand while my left
encircled her. I lifted her sweater and firmly held the naked beginning of her curve of hip, and she disengaged herself from me, and
stepped away, and looked in my eyes. I said huskily,

My mother's due home in a few minutes. Aunty Mary was
banging pots and pans around in the kitchen. Right through the
wall.

You want to rush it, huh?

No, I grinned, and as she undressed, I did too, I sat on the bed
and took off my shirt and my Levis, my hard-on was so hard and

large I had difficulty getting my underpants off (she watched and snickered—that was funny to her), we laughed, and I thought Oh to hell with it, let the whole WORLD walk in, my consciousness was altogether on her, and we lay on my bed, and felt each other, and the power of it. She rose and knelt beside me, she took my hard-on in her small hands, and licked the tip, squeezed and pulled the crystalline fluid to a liquid bubble and drank it and as her mouth was small, she could only get the head in. But as I went into cosmic anxiety Mother walking in my fifteen year old girl licked and sucked, her head bobbing and turning, and I loved her for it. She looked up, hard-eyed, and smiled,

You're big, okay.

I held out my arms and she came to me and we kissed, and rolled over and kissing she spread her legs, my dick slipped in and all the way in, and as easy as sunrise and sunset, we were together. She looked up and said,

You're crazy. I'm not the first. (I'd told her she was.)

You are, I nodded, and kissed her parted lips as she whispered, I don't believe it, you know too much.

And just before we began to go too quickly rushing to the end of it, I thought, Wow, so this is it! Wait'll I tell Mac—it's EASY! and the voice said, *No no, tell no one, for this is yours to keep,* and I felt humility and suddenly flashed out of consciousness, it had been painful, but easy and simple, and yet something was lost, and in a brilliant flickering feeling I was already remembering, and I had made a slight outcry. I felt a wonderment, and fear, and the exclamation of God as we dressed, she watched me. I took her phone number and said I'd call and she said okay.

Walk me to the bus?

Sure, I said. I pulled the desk back, straightened the bed, and we quickly left. Cut across the back lot and went along Washington to Kirkwood Road and up the west side to Adams, and the bank, where her bus stop was, and I pointed out the spot where I'd been hit by the streetcar three years before. But I panicked again, because I mean, there I was, I—me, walking along in plain daylight with The Bad Girl and so sure enough a bunch of Presbyterian guys came towards us, she squeezed my hand, my heart stood still as they passed and we said Hi, I lowered my eyes because they'd passed censure, curled their lips and sneered, and yet their eyes had been inwardly wide, bright, curious, and astonished. And jealous.

I did feel better after they'd gone by, but I still wanted to get away, and for that I hated myself, and worst of all she knew it, and I was tortured, and also frightened at what I was feeling. She looked up at me.

You tell nobody about us, she said, and, she added bitterly, you don't have to wait around here.

I want to, I choked, and so waited with her until the bus came, and when she got on, just before, I mean, I made a little leap to her, and smiled. I knew my eyes were bright, and as she made a mischievous smile, I whispered,

I'll call.

She nodded, got on the bus, found a seat, turned, and looked out the window at me. Her eyes were level. Mine too. The surface was thin, and new. We smiled, and waved as the bus pulled away.

I walked home slowly, yet did an occasional leap, and smelled myself and her on me, and was thrilled. I had supper, and after listening to the radio, I did some homework, and yet later, I couldn't concentrate, even on *Look Homeward, Angel,* because the thought of her in study hall again made the rest of the world haywire. The paradox of her simple but deep magic caused me to think about the sensation. I could jack off and feel it, but boy being inside her! And we had been together, and I began to feel what I wanted was her, and not the sensation at the end. The sensation was easy. And she was anything but easy. She was mysterious and yet so real, and, as I knew in my own deep dark darkness, God, I love a mystery.

But a question which really puzzled me also seemed obvious: Why me?

I mean there were guys who were—beautiful. And—for example, Buzzy. I mean I thought he was really handsome, popular, and a swell shortstop. Or Arty. Arty made the rest of us, me especially, look like creeps. Every girl in school almost fainted if he'd say hello, and give her that smile of his . . . he—he was like Sally, a little. Me too.

Well, the only answer I could come up with was, evidently she liked me, so I settled for that. She seemed happy at my side, walking to the bus, and before, on my bed with me, and I hated myself for feeling ashamed to be with her, which was so hypocritical, as if my reputation was something to brag about. So, because of her, I found a very articulate self-criticism, and I felt a liberation and strength. I mean just because I was a so-called figure in a couple of church organizations, and a leader in my own church, and was asked to hold the Cross at more weddings and funerals than anybody, and because my Mother was the secretary to the minister of the Episcopal Church in Kirkwood, and I could feel a little dash of guilt there as I was betraying her and the church both, and also because my Aunts and Uncles had been teachers and were loved and considered by the city and the county to be totally upright citizens, and because my Grandfather had known and worked for that rascal Joe Pulitzer, and had been in *Who's Who,* and had been written about as The Most Learned Man In Missouri, and because of all that was exactly why I was self-conscious walking along the main street in town with That Girl. Well, those tough guys from Valley Park, okay. You'd expect it. But Guy Dawson? Guy was my Christian name.

But secretly, Guy Dawson liked it. I didn't know why exactly, but I was very proud, maybe even vain, and it was okay because I had a secret. In fact Guy Dawson had a secret you'd never dream he'd have. Holding the Cross on high, leading the Reverend Charles Kean and the choir down the center aisle, with everybody on their feet singing me too A Mighty Fortress Is Our God . . .

Next night I phoned. She wasn't home. I saw her in the corridor the next day, and we smiled Hi to each other as our eyes held in the surface of the transparency (sweet) between us, and then we were in study hall again, she there in front of me, and me looking at the back of her head, and every move she made was explosive. I passed her a note. It was Friday.

The Blue Whale, had—almost literally—a little beady eye under the hair on the back of his head, his hearing was so sharp, and we really had to be careful. All of us. So when I passed her a note it was like at war, to be destroyed after reading. If The Whale saw us, and intercepted it—well—

8 p.m. Tonight Kwood Rd & Wash ok?

Her answer:

297

Okay.

I was WILD and the day passed in a snail paced stumble my mind was so racing, and at 8 p.m. I was standing on the corner of Washington and Kirkwood Road. Waiting. Heart pounding, dizzy, legs trembling, and the bus came along, and slowed, and stopped, and she stepped down off, and for a moment, she looked at me silently, and I almost fainted in my awe of her body.

As the bus barreled away she came to me and took my arm, and we said Hi, and walked along the darkening street. I could feel the tension in her arm and asked her what was wrong.

Nothing, she said. Skip it.

I'm sorry, I said.

For what? she asked angrily. What the hell have you done? Don't give me that crap, that's—that's what I'm so sick of.

She stopped walking, and I looked down at her and she glared up at me, and asked, Did you hear me?

I nodded.

Okay then, no crap. None. You wanna talk with me you talk straight.

I said okay.

We cut across the farthest edge of the Pickles' side yard, to the low wood fence in back. I helped her over, and we walked through high grass, between trees. I guided her in the darkness. She was silent.

The spring night was warm, and open. The trees were getting green. Missouri was so beautiful and powerful in April, and that night the sky was clear, and the stars bright.

We came to the spot I'd chosen, and sat down. Her mood seemed to change, and as we lit cigarettes (I lit hers), she smiled in the flame, and said,

Gee, this is really nice.

I fought my hammering heart, and it obeyed and slowed a little, and began to pound normal, and in a minute or two me and my heart were relaxed and I felt a fulfilling ease being next to her, with her, really, as we sat and smoked. We were sitting on a small hill of moss about the size of a blanket, under a large tree with low spreading limbs, and there were bushes here and there, and at our side a lovely brook rippled by. We could hear it when we didn't speak. The moss was spongy, dank and sweet. I looked up and the stars twinkled down through the treetops.

She undressed; I too.

We lay beside each other, on our backs, naked, smoking and looking up at the stars. Then she rolled over to face me, and I put my hand on her breast, caressed it, and then laid my hand on her hip. I shifted position, my right hand was under my head, my elbow on the moss. Our faces briefly appeared in cigarette glow. She asked,

Do you like Mister Peterson? (Civilization teacher.)

Yes and no, I said.

I don't, she said. Then, after a pause, But in a way I do. Aw hell, I don't know. He seems honest.

Well, I said. Then, after I puffed on my smoke, I said, You know he's pretty dedicated and I like his honesty too, but boy, he sure can get mad.

He ever get mad at you?

Oh, you bet.

She laughed. What happened?

Oh, well, you know me, I was clowning around, and he yelled at me and—

Does he like you? she asked.

I don't know. Yes and no I think. But I can't tell.

He doesn't like me, she said.

I was about to ask why, and changed my mind. Then I said I didn't think he liked anybody, and she asked what I meant.

I think he decides to treat us all the same, I said. I mean, he doesn't seem to show any favoritism.

Yeah, she said, you gotta point there—except to Sally Hopper.

Rrriiight, he does! But I mean, well, ha ha, what man wouldn't? You know her? I think she's a dreamboat. Jesus.

No, I said. She goes to a different church than I do.

That means something to you, doesn't it? she asked.

I was embarrassed. Yes, yeah it does, I guess. The kids I know best are from my church.

You're Episcopal, aren't you.

I nodded, in darkness, and asked, You?

Nothing. Baptist. It's all crap to me.

Then she said, But I know it means something to you. Don't pay any attention to me. I'm crazy.

That's both of us.

You know that guy Arty what'sisname? I can say it but I can't spell it, she laughed, and I nodded, and said, A little. Why?

He's cute. You know that redhead chasin' after him?

I nodded. Audrey, her name is.

Like her?

No, I said. You?

I don't know her but I don't like her, but I betcha five bucks to a mill she gets him and marries him.

Her voice had a triumphant quality, and I was startled. Holy mackerel, I said softly, I hope not. He deserves a better fate than her, but she sure is after him; I paused. Then I said, But she's talented; she can draw.

She laughed, Yeah, but can she screw? and you hate her guts. You're just jealous. You're a little fruity, know that?

No, I said—lied, defensively—it's

Y'are.

I'm not, I lied—

Oh yeah y'are, I can tell. She chuckled. I know you.

I felt a chill, and I asked, feeling a childish fear, You do?

Sure, she said, confidently, I've been watching you ever since I came to school. Want to do it? I like you.

She laughed again, and we put out our cigarettes, and I felt her arms come around me, and I embraced her and we kissed, and lay close, touching each other, and slowly I began to kindle and burn fully clean and cool and then I was a steady hard flame and we screwed, and again in the flash before the end I flashed out of consciousness, and in a soft pain I as if woke and her body in my hands was miraculous, and again I had the sensation of already remembering, and again the feeling of loss, and of my own sound, and I was confused and I asked her if it had been okay.

Sure, she said; surprised. You're different. You're good. You know how.

I do?

Get you, she said. Listen, she added angrily. Never ask. Never. Get it?

300

I nodded, bewildered, and in awe. We lay close to each other, and I lit cigarettes for us and we smoked in silence for a bit.

Then we separated, and lay on our stomachs. She said, I like Mister Curba. He's cute.

I said I liked him too, but he flunked me, and when I took Biology again, he passed me with a D minus because I wrote a love story he liked, about an amoeba. A girl amoeba.

What's an amoeba?

One of the smallest forms of life, I said. I've seen 'em under the microscope, they keep changing and dividing. Haven't you seen 'em yet?

We haven't gotten that far, I guess. Listen, I want to tell you something.

I said Okay, and she said, You don't tell anybody about us, you hear? But no-body. Do you hear me?

Yes, I said, and she said, I don't wanta hurt you, but I will if you talk. Her voice had power in it, and anger. She asked, harshly,

You know Moe Strickland?

Not well. Just by sight. He's a junior.

Well, that scar over his right eye was because he talked. I had to cut him; I always carry my knife.

She laughed, and ran her hand along my side, and I felt the fire again, flickering along my body, and my breath came fast, as she said, coming close,

I saw you playing softball one night in the park, and you were a funny one okay. I thought you were cute.

I kissed her, and then we kissed each other, and in a rise and an embrace I was in her and we began to make our love again. She giggled,

Al took me to that game. He was bored that night.

And then she laughed, deeply amused. She reached down and tickled my balls, and said,

You struck out twice.

You should have seen the other games, I said.

Why?

Twice is a good game.

And we laughed, and went on, on along that beautiful surface of the sweet strong transparency between us, ours, and I felt espe-

301

cially mine, to be through her.

Walking in the streetlights, and warm night was lovely, and I waited for the bus with her, by the bank, and we talked about school some more, and then I saw the bus. I said,

Here it comes.

In it came, and stopped, the doors opened, and she got on, and turned. I said,

G'night! and I smiled warmly. Thanks.

She winked, See ya Monday in study hall.

We laughed, and again I waited until she had found a seat, and again, until she turned to look out at me, and we waved, as the bus moved out.

I went home with my senses so alert I almost felt star touched, and there was a chorus of Where Have You Been from everyone and I told a pack of lies, and even to Mac and Gene, and my so-called mind, was very very busy that weekend. I couldn't get her out of it, and the preoccupation became an inner desire, almost a lust, to be alone. There were questions, way back in that mind, that I had to find so I could ask myself, for the answers I needed. For example, would she be pregnant.

Also, the mystery of why she picked me (I was cute) (but then, Arty, Mister Curba, etc.—who wasn't), and though that mystery was given a clear surface in the form of our bodies together, it yet deepened, and I found myself in an area I'd never been before. Something was definite (she picked me, me, cute and a little fruity and I accepted), and something was indefinite (the what of her), and then there was that which wasn't definite or indefinite, but persisted and caused me to be alone without knowing why, and I didn't know what it was, but it was the need to be alone to feel her effect on me.

In me. Which I feared, because I feared (and unconsciously loved), this new responsibility to my body. The surface of us had expanded and become my world through her, and me, through her. She through me?

Quietly I saw it all anew, through different eyes. My friends. And the girls I knew, even their parents, and I saw the heroes, the anti-heroes, and I felt the mass flow of the students at school didn't know what they were missing, and though I felt a peculiar loneliness, I yet felt unique and proud. And I felt sad, too, because of the girls I really liked, and knew, at parties, and on dates, like Charlene Reed, for whom I'd painted a twenty foot banner of love and in the middle of the night rigged it up in her front yard so she'd see it in the morning. So I felt alien, and depressed, and guilty for all my feelings.

After Friday night under the trees by the brook, the Sunday service at church seemed like a dream, and when I knelt and prayed, and felt God again, I opened myself and released a desire to understand what was happening to me, yet there was a barrier of anger and confusion, so I prayed I'd keep my wits about me, toward the other kids, and parents, because if I gave any of it away, even though the best of those people could understand what I'd done, and the adults might slap my back, and say attaboy, or simply frown or outright condemn me, it was pretty certain that no one, literally or as literally as I liked it, could understand what she meant to me, on the moss, naked under the tree by the brook. Not because they rejected it and what it had meant to them in their lives, with their secrets too, but in an obvious and literal sense of their not knowing what I was to myself, and had become because of her, in the plain power of my understanding, that I knew they couldn't know, and yet bitterly enough, I understood them in their inability and could know what they were to themselves through their overlooking of me, and what I felt was obvious, and literal, and in the seeming irrationality, certainly inarticulate, I felt more lonely than ever.

And that frightened me. Sunday night I phoned her. She wasn't home. And Monday she was absent, and in suspense I almost wept. Tuesday I gathered some kind of control and waited for Wednesday and Wednesday she came into study hall and sat down in front of me, turned around, winked, and said,

Hi!

I smiled. My eyes were as green flintstones, direct on hers, and she laughed, and turned, and went to work, and my hand trembling, I passed her a note.

Tonight same place 8?

Her answer,

Okay

303

was received with joy, and needy hunger. I was getting used to it, my body with hers, I could feel the power in her flesh and will at the sight of her, and the day went by like a deep blue split in crimson, and that night I was there on the corner waiting, and the bus came, and went like the next. And the next.

I waited until nine thirty, and she didn't come and with my nuts hurting me, I went home and jacked off, which stopped the pain and didn't help at all, and the next day I was in a rage because I had to wait until Friday to see her. Friday. Friday came. I passed her a note:

Where were you? What happened?

Her answer,

I was there. Where were you?

I hissed RIGHT THERE—and there I was, all right, only it was after school that day, and I was sitting alone in an empty study hall, for an hour and a half with The Whale, as I copied the rule,

I will not talk in study hall.

It disturbs students who are working.

The Whale puttered around, returned books to the library in front of the room, etc., as on page after page of lined yellow paper I made the hundred and fifty copies of the rule, handed it to him, and stood by his desk as he looked it over. He put it down on his desk, and looked at me. His eyes were cold, and angry.

If you do that again, Dawson, I'll throw you out of school.

I'm sorry, sir.

Sorry my ass, he said contemptuously. Get the hell out of here.

However, after I'd made my hissing shout, she had begun to laugh, hiding her face behind a book, and as The Whale wheeled around and walked rapidly toward me, face darkening in anger, and as students looked and laughed, The Whale lifted me by the scruff of my neck, held me partly in the air, and said,

You see me at 3:15.

He slammed me back into my seat, cracking my hip on the desk, and I thought, You sadistic son of a bitch—I opened a book, tears in my eyes, of self-pity, pain and anger, at her and myself, as The Whale stood there, in the aisle at my side I mean he stood there. Glaring down at me, and she, in complete innocence asked to be excused to go to the bathroom. He shot her a dirty look, and nodded, and as she told me later—I caught her outside at 3:10—she said if she hadn't gotten outa there, she'd a laughed so hard he'd a kept her after school, too, so she went in the bathroom and leaned against the wall and laughed and laughed, slapping her knee, Boy the look on your face!

She walked across the grass, looking over her shoulder, and grinned at me, You're really a card. Know that?

I caught up with her. You know what you are? I asked her.

No. What. Tell me. Upturned face, turned-up nose, baby lips, honey colored hair and pasty face, her eyes in slits, challenging, smiling.

A rat, I said. That's what. A girl rat.

She smirked. I've been called worse things.

Where the hell were you? I waited until nine thirty!

I was there, she said. But you weren't around, so I caught the bus back home. Don't, she leveled a finger at me, do that again.

WAIT A SECOND, I shouted—I was, I mean I was there, and you WEREN'T!

Gee, she said, turning her palms up and shrugging, I think you're cute okay, but if you don't believe me . . .

I made a decision. Okay, okay, I said, okay. Maybe—maybe—I was wrong. Maybe I wasn't there. How about tonight, same place.

Okay, she said: you be there, and I should have known better.

Because I was there, and she didn't show up. I could smell her, even taste her, and after a weekend nightmare of compulsive telephone calls and she wasn't home, on Monday I caught her before we went into study hall and I didn't care who saw us. I was all about her, I was, and that's what I was, in fact I had a funny feeling she was in me, and I said, Okay, where were you. I was there.

We'll be late, she said, and brushed by me. I followed her into the room, and as The Whale watched me steely-eyed, I whispered, You're lying.

She sat down, and turned to me: I never lie. Ever. I was there.

She said it straight into my eyes, and her eyes were as hard as ice, and so my eyes, too. Then—that smile flickered, faded. I was there. Where were you?

She turned away and did schoolwork and I felt a veil come over my face. I turned and gazed out the window, I saw nothing, and for an instant I looked back at her, but she was reading a movie magazine, and was as if gone from me, and I sat in unexpected silence, gazing at the closed book on my desk, trying to figure it out.

We didn't speak or send notes, and when school was out, I walked home doomed and angry, and hurt. Tuesday was a crazed impatience, and on Wednesday I passed her a note, same thing, adding, *Are you pregnant?* and she wrote back she'd be there, and added, *Why worry?* and that night there I was on the corner, and the buses came and went and I went home and telephoned her and she wasn't home, and I was jealous, and furious, I was going crazy, I kept feeling my body for her, and in my crazy state I had to make a decision even a crazy decision, so I decided to play it cool and catch up with the girl down the street, take a few peeps, etc., carry on like before, and give my fifteen year old a week or so and see what she'd do. Let her sweat a little, ha ha, so I did, I played it cool, and on Monday, Wednesday and Friday, feeling she was kind of testing me, somehow, I said Hi to her, and my body was shaking. I sat at my desk and pretended to do my schoolwork, etc. The Whale stepped into the hall for a drink of water, and she turned to me, whispering,

You're leaving me alone. That's good; I still think you're cute.

You're not, I whispered angrily. You're murder.

She laughed, and her eyes twinkled, as she murmured, Oh aren't you the funny one today!

I wanted to kiss her so badly it hurt, and I sat, bent at my desk, in my demanding agony, and on the way home after school young crazy dog decided to give her up, and the next morning, while brushing my teeth I definitely decided it was too much. We're through. No more. I looked at myself in the mirror and said,

You're cute, but you're through. Finished. You hear?

My image nodded, and I said, Okay.

And then we laughed, and my heart lifted; and I—it was as if it was with her, that I heard her laugh too! And I heard a—another voice, the old guru voice on a breeze come clean across from China—and Mandalay, softly, softly murmur,

306

Keep trying.

I did, the old note trick, and that night she didn't show up, but before, when she returned my note in study hall, she had written something extra on it: *Al says too many questions spoil the answer. Quit worrying. I'm not pregnant.*

It was almost the end of April.

What's the matter with you! Mother exclaimed. You're walking around here like an animal! You've got that haggard look, she laughed. Who is she?

Well, who wanted to hear that? and alarmed by Mother-intuition, I fled, hearing her chuckle, Norma? Is it Norma? And as I walked through the Pickles' back lot, I thought about the beautiful virgin Norma, and bitterly shook my head. I'd left the Norma world, I'd turned into an alien, a beast, and I found the mossy hillock, and lay down where we had lain, and I lowered my head on my arms, feeling her, and I lay there, still and hungry, listening to the rippling brook, smelling the powerful earth, thinking,

So this is it.

In study hall, two days later, I slipped her a note.

Same place. Tonight. 8. There'll be a moon.

(I'd seen the moon in the paper.) Her answer:

Okay.

I was cynical, amused, and weird. My personality seemed, even to me, a kind of fractured joke, and I stood on the corner as the moon came over the trees, and about ten after eight the bus rolled up, the doors opened, and she got off, said Hi, and seeming like an apparition, walked to my side, and as I stood in shock, I whispered Hi, and she took my arm. We walked. My teeth were chattering, and I was dazed, and rapidly losing control. We arrived, and sat on the moss, I lit cigarettes for us, my hand shook. I could smell her and she said, grinning in the flame,

Gee, you're pretty nervous! You oughta take it easy!

Had I not laughed I would have wept, when I said, You're right. Do you know the minister says that to me, too?

Is that right? she asked—then she laughed outright, yet also in her throat. The minister? she laughed. Maybe he's right!

I had to laugh, so we laughed together, and I felt her watching me, so to gain control I decided I'd talk myself into it and tell her a

307

story, and I asked her if she knew Jasper Richterclout.

She made a wild little laugh, Jasper who unhwuzzat again? And then she said no, she didn't know him, she laughed, and I said sure she did, and I described him, adding he was a cheerleader last year with a heavy crush on Sally Hopper.

Oh yeah? Do you?

Yeah. No. And at the, gimme a break will you (she laughed at that), at the last dance, he, Jasper told me he had been dancing with her, close, and he had a hard-on, he said, and—

He tell you this at the dance?

Yeah I said, in fact just after it happened. He said he had been rubbing against her, pushing his hard-on around, and she had said, "Jasper, please take your pipe out of your pocket, it's—"

But she was laughing, on the moss by the brook, slapping her knees, tossing her head, really laughing.

"—hurting me," and but when Jasper told me, he was laughing, had difficulty speaking, and he finally said, "Jesus, how can I love such a dumb-bunny."

Because she's beautiful. That girl's a dreamboat, she added.

Dreamboat is right, I said. Mostly dream in fact, and a couple of days later, in Geography, listen, the story had gotten around, and Harry Budrow said in a loud voice, to the teacher Mister Mayer, Gee, Mister Mayer, that's a nice pipe I saw you smoking this morning—

She was on her side in laughter, and I took her shoulder, and said, Listen, the whole class went crazy, guys beat their desks, because Sally was in the class, too, and the two people who didn't get it, were Mister Mayer—

And Sally! she cried, in her delighted laughter.

Yeah! and as I said that I was surprised she hadn't heard the story, the whole school knows it, she was suddenly close to me, whispering I go to a different school, she was undressing, and then I was too, and I felt her body brush mine and she whispered in my ear, Let's do it. She pushed me down on my back as I ripped off my shirt. She kissed my lips, I held her warm body in my hands and I touched her completely, and a little harshly, as I began to melt into fire as our tongues met. I was raw, and angry, and she embraced me and held me tight, and I knew she wanted me, and I gave her

308

everything I had in that soft spectacular moonlight. Light sifting down through the trees onto our white bodies, panting on the moss, by the brook; and afterwards she stayed close to me. God, you were fierce, she whispered, and caressed me.

And we rested, and after a while talked about students and teachers for a long while, and then we made our sex our memory again.

I felt, intuitively, or knew, of and in the air under the moon, this would be our last meeting. And then she told me. I felt a crystalline loneliness, and was confused as I walked her to the bus stop. When the bus came, and just before she got on, there was a hard look to her face, and her eyes were narrowed, yet at the last moment we smiled to each other. Her face could change so fast. I held up my hand, and we said See ya in study hall, and she got on the bus, the door closed, and as she turned my heart ached, the street was in complete view, and in my sense of loss, I waved so long. Her face was so serious, and yet altogether ordinary, gazing out through the glass to me. Then she was gone. And as I turned and slowly walked home, I saw her serious face before me—face of her life?—I undressed casually, and lay on my bed smelling her in the dark, as a soft shaft of moonlight came through the window and lay on my naked chest.

May and the first week of June were disillusioning. We spoke, but it was over, and in a futuristic insanity, school was out, and on that day, with that mysterious smile on her lips, she walked across the grass towards Kirkwood Road straight out of my life forever.

She didn't return in the fall. Al told me she had to get a job at the mill. Her mother was sick. He told me in September, of 1947, a month after I'd turned seventeen.

4

April, 1949. Two Years Later.

Mac and I were due to graduate in June. I knew where I was going to college, so did Mac, and around the third Saturday in April, he and I went to a ballgame together. Something we often did. We took the Manchester 56 to transfer at Grand, and catch the car that'd take us to the ballpark. Mac was a Cardinal fan, and I a

Brownie and New York Giant fan, and the Cards and the Giants were playing that afternoon. Brecheen against Hartung.

It had been on my mind, and on the way into Maplewood, I said, Listen Mac, I've got a confession to make, but you can't tell anyone. I mean it.

I made a small shadowy smile, and said,

On your honor: no one. This is between you and me. Swear it?

I swear, he said, and his eyes lit up a little, and I held up my hand, and said Be patient, and he said, I promise, swear, and cross my heart (he said quickly), and hope to die if I tell ANYBODY okay tell me.

Okay, I said. Two years ago, this month, when I was sixteen, Old Mac, I laid a girl. She and I had three meetings, and on two of the meetings I laid her twice. She was fifteen years old.

But the blood had drained from his face, and his eyes were wide as he began to stand up on the moving streetcar, and he gasped, You did it! and he cried, as everyone turned, Two years ago! Two YEARS ago!

He sat down and grabbed my shoulders, breathless, What's it like?

I laughed, and put my hand on his shoulder, and after I'd glanced toward China a second, I said, It's the most beautiful thing there is, no joke, and she was, she was wonderful, she was, God, at my side, and as tough as nails.

I paused and asked, with a laugh, You know Moe Strickland?

And I told him, and he began to laugh, and tear his hair. I was laughing, in release, long pent up, but Mac was, I mean he subsided, and rubbed his upper lip, and then he made a groan, lowered his head and drummed his fists on the top of the back of the seat in front of us, and he stamped his feet and rubbed his hands together excitedly,

Tell me from the beginning! he cried. So I did, and as we left Maplewood, passed by Scullin Steel, crossed Kings Highway and headed toward Grand Avenue, and when we transferred at Grand, Mac knew about the notes, NOTES, he yelled, and as we stood across from Pevely Dairy on Grand, and waited for the streetcar to Sportsman's Park, I told him about Mother being due any second, and the miracle it was she hadn't shown up. Mac went, I mean he just went to pieces. His voice was tense, husky, reverent and terrified Mother, oh Jesus MOTHER, my God how could you DARE? and he yelled DUE ANY MINUTE, and that's when he began his irrational laughter. I had to repeat things, because he went into seizure, and on the streetcar cried AND AUNTY MARY (he knew her) and Mac—couldn't stand it, the suspense, he couldn't stay in his skin, he threw back his head and howled as we approached the ballpark. I—me—with this tall eighteen year old spectacle of hysteria, I held onto his body laughing, and we staggered toward the ticket window.

Mac, I said, take it easy, they won't let us in.

He looked at me a little wildly. What happened next?

I said wait till we get our tickets, and in rigid apprehension he remained silent, index finger on his lips he whispered to himself Shhh and we got our tickets and took seats in the second tier behind first base, and as the professionals on the grass and the infield threw the ball around I told him about her sucking me, and he stood up, left the seat, walked down the steps, gripped the second tier railing and glared into space, returned, sat down, took my arm, and whispered, What was it like?

It was fan-tas-tic, I said, and I told him the rest of the story.

There's Mize, I commented. Jesus, he's a big guy.

Then I said to Mac, Oh, and I told her the story about Jasper and the pipe, and Mac went completely wild. You did! What'd she say?

I grinned, She thought it was funny—like we did, and Mac looked at me, and suddenly we embraced in laughter.

Brecheen finished his warmups, and the players left the field. Both managers met with the umpire at home plate, and the announcer read the lineups over the public address system.

Sportsman's Park was small and old-fashioned. It looked, and had, all the charm of an old trolley car, the hot dogs were delicious, and Marty Marion had a lot of pebbles to toss out of his way. The Star Spangled Banner went on, and we stood, and afterwards we sat down in a ripple of applause and cries, and the game began.

I get afraid, Mac said, thoughtfully, even when I get my finger in.

I nodded. Triples used to scare me too, but not with her. All I could think about was—and suddenly I was aware of her, and

311

mysteriously my heart and body were with her again, as I sat behind first base staring into the sky above the slum rooftops beyond the centerfield bleachers. How really wonderful it had been, how fantastic, she, how incredible I and she and the moss and the brook and the moon—Rigney doubled into left center, and the fans were upset. I marked it down on my scorecard absent-mindedly, and the ball came back to Brecheen. He rubbed it around as if nothing had happened, bent for the signal, and went into the stretch, she had liked me, and I grinned at the called strike, *You're cute*, she had said, the *little fruity* astonished but pleased me, and I cherished her amusement and the memory of her saying *I know you*, and my voice, *You do?* and her answer, *Oh sure, I've been watching you ever since I came to school,* warmed me completely. Kurowski snatched Lockman's grounder, held Rigney at second and made the play to first. I notated 5-3 and there was one down, and Mac grabbed my arm and shook it,

YOU'RE THINKING! WHAT ARE YOU THINKING ABOUT!

I turned, and looked at him. Musial was testing his flipglasses against the sun, and the look in my eyes quieted my old friend, and Mac smiled warmly, still excited, but in a quiet way, and he hugged me, and in the hug we watched Brecheen field Thompson's hard one-hop shot, turn, hold Rigney at second, and make the play to first. I wrote 1-3. Two down, and Mac slapped my shoulder, and sat back saying you son of a bitch as the crowd cheered, and I laughed. Brecheen looked for the sign as Mac looked at me and shook his head. His eyes were a little glazed, and Mize backed away from an inside curve; ball one.

Mac said, I can't believe it but it's wonderful. Really, Fee. God, and Musial drifted in for the fly; the fans cheered, the Cards were out of the inning, and Mac was thanking me for telling him, and wringing his hands. He glared down at his crotch, and said, It's all your fault, and looked at me and tossed his head BUT I'M JEAL-OUS! he yelled, and gripped my arm. I am, he whispered, and he laughed crazily. I laughed, too, and suddenly I—I heard her laughing. For a fleeting second I caught her scent, and in a flash I was inside her. Then I actualized—suddenly consciously in the crowd under the blue midwestern sky, her direct eyes, her pasty face, her toughness, and the durability of her effect on me and my consciousness of all of it, God, and this because in the most real sense she had given me the world. The actual world of major league baseball, vertical in religion, the arts, the sciences, and the crowd cheered around me, and I had cried out. In loss, then sudden consciousness of her, and of myself in this actual world of North St. Louis, and the smell of cigars on fresh air, as that guy named Musial walked rather slowly to the plate. Musial? I asked. Two down, Mac said, you dreamer, and I laughed, and Musial stepped into the box, dug his spikes in the dirt, took a couple of swings and then assumed the most original batting stance in baseball history. And I had struck out twice. Al was bored that night and she had laughed.

You're thinking, Mac growled, tell me tell me.

I nodded, and said, She told me I was cute.

He laughed, and leaned back and looked at me, rather a paternal look, and suppressing laughter, said,

Well you know—she was right. Y'are kinda cute.

As I bent in self-laughter a snuffle pop came out of his nose, and he pretended a startled look, and then burst into laughter. We hit each other's arms and both laughed. Musial ripped a liner down the first base line, it went by Mize so fast I didn't think he saw it, and the crowd was on its feet in a roar, as Musial raced to first, leaned around first and went into second hard, sliding, the tag was late, and he was safe. I made the ideogram on my scorecard, and Mac yelled I CAN'T STAND IT!

I scowled, What the hell's the matter with you? Are you crazy?

Yes, he nodded, I'm crazy, and, he added passionately, I'm crazy I'm crazy I'm a crazy virgin.

I asked, You mean you haven't laid that Jewish girl from Clayton yet?

He shook his head vehemently as we watched Kurowski walk, and Slaughter dig in, and Mac said, Boy she's hot, you know those Jewish girls, and she wants to, but Goddamn it I get my finger in and it's driving me crazy EVEN I mean CRAZIER I'm telling you I can't get by third I—CAN'T! he yelled.

But I, the wise young Buddha in the second tier behind first base, said, to my old buddy,

Keep trying. You will.

313

And I heard the echo of Asia in my ear, as a breeze drifted in from centerfield, and Mac said tensely, Jesus! Do you think I can—but WHEN and HOW will I? Will I—really?

I nodded, hearing her fifteen year old laughter and I grinned with her, and nodded, assuring Mac, *You will*. Mac stood up and—shouted—yelled an inarticulate cry of hope and delight, a whoop and a hard holler and a sort of scream and a lot of people turned to look and he sat down, collapsed, rather, still in a tense reaction to his future chance. And all this behaviour was very unlike him. I mean with his upbringing, stockbroker Father, and all, Mac was a very quiet young man, never given to loudness, and he dressed very conservatively, but when he looked at me, his lips quivered, and he blushed, and his eyes were blazing in the roar of the crowd as Slaughter slammed a liner into right, and Musial scored.

A Blue Ribbon Civilian

for Otie

ONE SCALDING MISSOURI AFTERNOON after I had gotten out of the Army, I walked across my back yard, cut through the neighbor Pickles' big back lot, went through their old broken fence, crossed the Kroger parking lot, crossed Kirkwood Road—our main street—and went across the large oven-hot and partly melted black asphalt parking lot of Katz's, a huge cut-rate store. I went up the one concrete step and opening the glass door, I went inside to the icy conditioned air, the whole place smelling like frozen denim, lint and leather, I turned right to the cigarette counter and asked for, and got, Home Run cigarettes, which aren't in our future anymore. When I was home last year (1969), Katz's didn't even have Picayunes.

I walked across the marble floor passing the paperback book racks, bins of shoes and toys and clothes, sales counters and signs for and of thousands of different things, passing the jellybeans and the display of chocolates so oddly irrelevant to taste and not to me, but in a really *weird* way, perhaps only relevant to the point blank melting power of Missouri summer held at bay by the wall of window glass to survive in gumdrop scent, cookies and the tang of peppermint. I entered the luncheon area on a zig zag between formica-topped steel-trimmed tables and chairs, and I swung first one leg and then the other over the low rail that divided the table area from the soda fountain, where I went, and sat down ordering a cup of coffee from a very shy, very quiet, and very sweet looking waitress, and when she drew it, and put it down in front of me I smiled thanks and paid her, and looked at her closely, because I saw that things had changed. A lot of things.

My home town had changed. The people, as in this girl, were

315

quiet and I saw it would be me doing the talking (nothing new), but in the old days it was different, because there were more than a few others to whom I really loved to listen. Charles Kean. Lee Jones. Old Gus. Mrs. Sandfos, Mr. Lindemeyer—

She rang up my dime and went down the counter to three silent high school boys, renewed their Cokes, and cleaned up a gone customer's spoor of sundae, as I sipped my coffee.

I was looking out the front window and across Kirkwood Road at the house which was for sale. My Godmother's house, and I remembered her pretty well, her effect, and her smell, she had stood beside mother when I had been baptized in St. Louis, about 1936, and later her nephew Bill had married my sister, in 1947, my mind crystallizing his selfishness and sadism, and suddenly his name was not Bill but Harlow, and with a shock I saw next door, and the Durbin house by the lot on the corner was also FOR SALE! I knew both Durbin boys had married, but had—Jane, too? Was Jane um—old enough? I decided I'd go over and see Mrs. Durbin (Otie), to get the news: she would talk! She was, in fact, a talker yes it does, take one, to know one, and what the hell was happening?

I remembered I'd glanced at the gas station on the corner while I was on my way to Katz's, and saw that the house next door there—to the gas station, Bob Franz's dad owned it, remember Beans? Boy he was terrific, and many an afternoon held me in suspense with *his* talk—the Turner's house, was being torn down! and I wondered where Bob Turner was, and if he ever got over Sally Musgrave. Old, in theory, high school days far behind me and in truth WAY ahead, and I began to look forward to writing it as I sat there and sipped my coffee in that normal but peculiar smell, retail, I thought, deciding to have another cup of coffee and then see Otie, and then start doing a little snooping around town.

So I ordered another coffee, and the girl silently drawing it placed it before me. When I paid her and she turned to ring it up, I said, Wait a minute.

She turned, and I put two bits on the counter as a tip, plus my last French franc, a coin which had been worthless in Paris, was worth about a mill here—remember mills? the retail tax in the 2nd War, and the pretty girl looked at the franc, and quietly asked what it was.

A piece of French money, I said.

She looked at me.

French money, I said. I was in Paris in April, and I was so broke, I said, it was funny. All I had was this franc, and it was worthless, but it meant Paris to me, and so you take it because of that.

She didn't understand, so I said, You can look at that and think of Paris. You have a little bit of a GI in Paris—his souvenir, there.

Were you in the Army?

Yes, I just got out. I went to Paris on leave.

Where were you stationed?

Germany.

She thanked me, put the franc and the quarter in her apron pocket, I finished my coffee, winked, grinned and gestured so long and I walked outside into the heat, and stood on the concrete step and looked at what I could see of my home town, and then I went across Kirkwood Road to look at Otie Durbin's house For Sale and see if she was home.

All summer long I made a point of going to Katz's for coffee, at least twice a week, and more, to talk with the quiet waitress, making hi how are you a hopeful cause for dialogue, and it lasted into the end of August, and through blistering September, October, and cool, low sky rainy November, and around Thanksgiving I went in as usual and she wasn't there. I inquired around, talked to the bus boys, and the other waitresses, but they said she had given notice and left. I asked the manager of the store, he said the same, he had a stitched anxious face, and he echoed the others, he was an echo in fact, and he said she had left no forwarding address.

Late one afternoon I had, I remember, walked her home after work. She lived catty corner across Bodley Ave. from the Durbin house, in a small room in a huge wood frame Byzantine American apartment house, painted gray. The Meyer sisters had lived there when we were in high school, and I had been in love with Taffy (and her taffy colored pigtails), and I remember years later, then the future, Mother wrote me in New York that Taffy had stopped by the parish office for a visit "every bit as pretty as she used to be," Mother wrote, "happily married, and three children," delighted

317

because Taffy had seen my drawings and collages in *Vogue*, and Taffy had quote loved them, really unquote which meant even more to me because she and I had been in art class together. Mrs. Voorhees.

But neither Taffy nor her sister Margo lived in town anymore, and I walked the silent young waitress home. I asked her where she was from and she only murmured, a feeling tone, she wouldn't talk, and on the front porch—a front porch large enough for a town meeting—I said I'd see her soon, and she didn't say anything. She opened the gray glass door with white curtains, and went inside. She closed the door.

I went down the steps and across the vast lawn to Bodley, and crossed on an angle to the vacant lot next to the Durbin house. I crossed the lot and went up the steps onto the front porch, opened the screen door and knocked. No answer.

Otie wasn't home.

I dug the envelope for my GI unemployment check out of my pocket, and wrote on it saying I was back in town a blue ribbon civilian and would love to see you. I stuck it in the screen door, and left, crossing the lot and heading east along Bodley, until I came to Taylor, where I turned right and walked home, thinking of Otie, and the strange silent waitress.

Boy it was *cold*. I stood outside Katz's and let snow flakes fall on my face, listening to the small town noises of retail Thanksgiving with Christmas—right on the heels of the turkey. Well, so she had gone.

I looked at the snow, and the cars and the treetops. It was around one in the afternoon, and then, in a strange way, I saw her face before me.

The skin around her eyes and at her temples had been so thin I had seen the veins, and her nearly colorless eyes seemed to be held in a suspension, or perhaps a suspicion of failure. Her pupils and irises seemed held by the surface in her accepted continuity of failure, like needles, held on the surface of her consciousness, and as silent as that, too.

All summer and through the fall I had taken care not to alarm her. One wrong gesture, one overstressed word, and she'd sink,

318

and go right to bottom. It was so difficult and strange because she was so young, just out of high school. I'd ask, *Where did you go to high school?* but she never told me, except in her murmur, her feeling-tone. She had come to Kirkwood and gotten the job. She was so delicately full-fleshed and small boned, her skin was too soft, too white, so thin, almost skim, and I knew her breasts would be slightly blue, and suddenly I thought it was—was it the orphan's clue? Was she an orphan? walking silently through the flow of her loss, of abandonment, in the constant seasons of empty love in her white waitress's uniform, where would she go? To another little town? Where, in all America, or even the world? Where would she go? I angrily clenched my fist, and whispered God—God *damn*, *God damn*, and felt a tug on my elbow.

I turned, and Otie Durbin beamed up at me, and cried, above the large bag in her arms, in snowfall,

"Why it's Fee Dawson! Land's sakes—let's have a drink! Come on!"

I laughed and looked into a bag, and saw peanuts, popcorn, a quart of gin and a quart of vodka. She laughed her grandmother's laugh, winked up at me, and as we laughed, she confided, you know,

"Just a little Thanksgiving shopping—"

The Making of a President

WELL, I'LL ANSWER YOU about how they made him, being you asked.

They put the left eye in last, which was wrong, because they put the right one in without thinking of both eyes, and the right one was put in crooked anyway, so when he laughs the way they puffed out his cheeks, his cheeks bunch up making his eyes look creased and crooked, and kinda funny. When they made him they weren't thinking—it looks that way, anyway, particly when they made his jaws, after that nose Jesus he got a jaw like a bulldozer blade, kinda like them retired generals you know them Vetran's of Farn Wars you see their lower teeth when they laugh, and the things they made for *them* to laugh at makes a body wonder who it was that made him and them and us too, and why. No, I didn't read the book.

And the real damn shame you know, is the way he walks. Pity. They stuck his legs onto his back like they forgot his hips, and they left the hinges in his knees instead of taking them out and putting in the ball-sockets, so it looks like he's always walking shoulders up like walking won't work, like walking downhill with that straight back, block, almost falling which he is, and maybe they knew, maybe they weren't so dumb after all, knowing what he'd be, they made him to fit, and maybe I ought to be quiet, with them kinds of ideas, but I can't help it, and it looks like on top of all that and the way he talks, in his hollow chest, his feet are turned in.

Well, pretty sad, ain't it. Especial as he's so mizrable these days. It ain't for me, which I understand, to be questioning these things, so I'll shut up and go on my way, down that long and winding road to whatever big goal-line *I* come to and so long pal, this corner'll be fine. Thanks for the lift this far.

320

A Slow Roll Over Haystacks

I SAW HIM ABOUT TEN YEARS AGO. We had a drink on East 57th Street. No. We didn't talk about our childhood (Missouri), so the meeting is not one of the bright pages in this novel.

His name used to be Bud, but he was irritated when I became familiar. Albert. For example Bud—Al—used to have a sense of humor when I called him Al then (when we were kids). Used to? Yeah. He changed? Yeah. You get that. A newspaper man. With a by-line etc., embittered and went to Virginia to get a job with his youngest brother in the bank.

I got this information from Al's next youngest brother my good pal Bill. Kim, the youngest of the three, is the dude at the bank. Yeah? Uhn huh. And Albert got married in Virginia to a dominating woman remarkably like his mother. Oh yeah? Yeah. And after Albert's father died, his mother moved in with Kim, near the bank, and then later moved in with Albert and his dominating wife and after that, from there, from there his mother went and visited Bill who had been married and divorced but then remarried. It had been a trying period. I was at Bill's (first) wedding reception in St. Louis and me and my pal Charley Dart who is still my pal Charley Dart got so drunk on champagne the memory-line is a little dim, but Bill's first wife was so high-class Charley and me thought maybe there had been a mistake. Yeah? Yeah, and anyway (you get that: bring her down to us (earth) class) we didn't do anything except talk about Hemingway who was then popular.

Anyway, as things turned out, later Al went to Florida, started up a land development operation, Bill quit teaching at the University of Puerto Rico and joined Al there, backed with the money from Kim's bank, where their mother went back to, gimme a light—ah, there, puff. Thanks. Puff. Their father, Pop we called him, and may he ever rest in peace, had, in his youth, been a barnstorming pilot, and a couple of years before he died, took to writing poetry.

The Singing Man

THERE IS A MAN in my neighborhood who makes his deliveries on foot, and sings as he walks, pushing his hand truck in the streets and on sidewalks.

He is a large black man, and as he pushes his hand truck along he throws back his head and sings. Loud.

In all seasons, as local trucks and interstate rigs line both sides of the streets, and deliveries and pickups are made, the man who sings is the object of a lot of response and the victim of a million silent and spoken jokes, but there is no stopping him, because he really loves to sing; he's been singing for years, and Puerto Rican and black guys more or less let him be, in their way, which is not completely. Secretly they like him, and envy him, admire him, and learn from him, because they can tell how far removed they are from their own when his singing embarrasses them, so in reaction to their own embarrassment in awe, SING it, baby, and laugh, WAIL! because he also and definitely embarrasses white truckers and delivery boys and businessmen.

He comes around the corner—everyone hears him coming, and all heads turn, and the true emotions are replaced by more reasonable emotions turned a little to the right of embarrassment, into a togetherness, and all the guys grin and wink at each other, as the singing man takes the corner and heaves into view, dodging traffic up the street toward them expertly, he just as they in traffic, except he'll be singing.

White businessmen and women avoid him because they're twice embarrassed first in the eyes of black truckdrivers, stockmen and delivery boys, which embarrassment white people imagine black people reject, and then, or really originally being embarrassed because a man is singing in the street, and nobody sings in the street, who sings in the street? Whaddya crazy on the street, singin' ya dummy, and as the black and Puerto Rican guys yell at him—the singing man—their laughter is more tense, and the white man thinks they laugh and yell obliquely at him, true, because they see he is embarrassed, but also, which has a unifying quality, for release from their own embarrassment, but what upsets the black guys is not only his singing in the street, which is embarrassing enough as he is black, and they think white businessmen think he is an extension of them because he and they are black, as if the businessmen see right through the singing man to them, make an on the spot identification, and expect them, maybe, praying not, but possibly expecting them all to burst into song, so they shout and yell at the singing man to let the white businessmen know the singing man is different from their point of view, too, yet while being one of them, in the sense anybody can see, this guy's just gotta sing, which maybe is a black fact, and the white businessmen see through him to them, unconvinced, and the black guys yell back through the singing man at the white men, it's a street game anyway, and constant, but the singing man is special, because the real suspense is not only in the loud voice he uses, but that with his loud, booming, voice, he can make the air crinkle, and the street turn into a skyscraper embarrassment because of what he sings, he has a nice voice, resonant, and yet he forgets the words, and can't carry into the range the melody needs, yet though his range is limited, his lungs are not, his songs are a seizing of words behind (or in front of) melodies, and when he forgets the words he improvises on the melody which is limited, a sort of behind hum, mouth open, head back, as a loud rising hum, especially when he is carried away, the melody chasing the hum upwards it's all he can do, and everybody is with him, helplessly, he makes a high choked C scrape in his throat, he can go no further, higher, and everybody in the street is up in C with him, as he lowers his head, frowns at the pavement, while everybody else is adjusting, and near hiccups in a complicated embarrassment because not only does everybody know the words he has forgotten, and certainly the melody, but everybody wants to forget it, all of it—the whole thing—because his songs, in this day and age, unleash rage and revolution, or an

324

embarrassment hard to rationalize not to mention suppress, having been drawn from the pens of men who lived in a former age literally no one wants to recall, except the most hardened bigots, sentimental cynics, and the loose and irrelevant sleepwalkers, and so when he comes striding up Park Avenue South, and swings west on 19th Street bellowing Old Man River, a silence like a suddenly emptied city, crystallizes, and forms a *hard* edge, and especially sharpens when he gets to that point in the song where, as we all know him, he can't remember the words, and we all know the words, and yet as he appears in no way aware of anything amiss, his habit is to make no effort to be sure to remember not to forget, or learn, those words, why? it is his way and so he goes back to the beginning—his beginning—and starts over, Old Man River, booming, Old Man River, imminent explosion Old Man River air pervades the street until he catches a phrase, follows it, gets carried away, peaks, and in collective suction, falls silent, mind running around trying to get that or those words in a high-energy perplexity as audible as Mack trucks, head lowered, he searches beneath him, and then, as a fresh breath, an inspiration! he throws back his head, and in a rolling gusto, loudly attenuates Old Man River with all the spirit of a profound remembrance, a new beginning in an unexpected vitality, and obvious pleasure, and everybody on the street, save some startled passer-by, is relieved, for a repetition is better than that tense discovering silence, and they hopefully go on with their work, and yet, in his not remembering, the singing man can carry a prolonged, always surprising, terrific, volatile, silence, as he searches for what he suspects he forgot, which he never knew, and which he'll never remember, because he will always remember what he will remember, and as he is midblock everybody on the street adjusts in the aftermath of embarrassment—a relief to the empathy of helping him find the words to a song nobody wants to remember, and he can't anyway, and as he approaches Broadway, on his way west, when he begins to sing again, his beginning again, it has an odd quality, like an echo in the empty following embarrassment, on the air, even in the air, in the racket of machines.

Well, he smiles when he sings, and as he is a big man, he lifts his head and fills his lungs to renew his singing, a spectacle as he has the chance to gaze at the available strip of sky and skyline, and smile his personal message that all's right with the world, to him. His eyes shine, and his shoulders move a little, he tosses his head and he begins to sing.

But the song which he sings best, and he only knows a few words to it, and only a part of the melody, but what he knows sends him into bellowing ecstasy, and the second octave, of Danny Boy. Danny Boy is his song of songs.

One afternoon before Christmas, I was heading uptown on Union Square West, and under an overcast near-snow sky, I saw him walking along in a rather shabby black topcoat, a meager dark brown scarf, bare headed and handed pushing his hand truck with a couple of boxes on it to be delivered evidently in my neighborhood. His shoulders were moving, his head was back, and his open throat cast the melody and the words of Danny Boy to the clouds, as he passed through a throng of people, an illegal fruit-seller, and that tightlipped slit-eyed newspaper man and his rubbermouthed wide-eyed short pal, at the entrance to the BMT subway there. Just this side of the statue of Lincoln, in Union Square.

The singing man passed them by, not seeing them as they watched, because he was singing, and when he smiled up into the late cold December sky, and gazed along the dramatic northern skyline of Union Square, he had the words he wanted and plenty of (a little) melody, and I saw vapor come from between his lips in the formation of words to Danny Boy, as he moved between bodies and machines, everyone aware of him, the street game was on, but he was aware of nothing but his song: I watched, on an angle from him, as he went, and I was aware of it all, in that singing man.

Oh, Danny Boy, he sang; the words came out of his throat like a call, I hear the pipes are playin', he sang, oh Danny Boy, that figure in the distance which perpetually separates, which distance separates, I mean, from his booming calling cry *Oh*, Danny Boy, he warmly drew the words, and softly, beautifully sang I hear the pipes are playin', and his voice rose and broke in the second octave of boy, after Danny, he lowered his head and I lost him in the crowd, but found him again, as he raised it, in the dense and complicated distance, heading towards 18th Street, and Park Avenue South, as he began to sing, again.

326

The Messiah

ONE DAY AROUND COCKTAIL HOUR towards the end of the war I was standing at the bar having a drink and talking to a guy about something or other, when I looked out the front window and saw a group of people walking up the middle of the Avenue, and curiously, the cars weren't setting up their usual cacaphony. Then I saw Mike in the crowd. His red hair flashed in the late afternoon sun—then he saw me through the window! He ran inside, took my arm, said O.K. come on out and march against this fuckin' war, and I said No, I'm drinking and he took me by my arm, and began to pull, so I finished my drink, told the fellow I was talking with and the bartender I'd be back in a little while. Mike laughed angrily as we went outside and joined the marchers. There were about seventy-five people.

We walked up the Avenue. Traffic behind us.

Others joined us as we went, and as we turned left onto Broadway and approached the Flatiron Building, there were about two hundred people, and as we continued up Broadway and approached Herald Square, just south of 34th Street, there were at least four hundred of us.

There were about fifty Vietnam veterans, and as we walked I looked at those young guys—half my age—heads up and flashing the peace sign, yelling, COME ON, JOIN US! against the mass wall of people going home. Some did join us, though, and when we were in Herald Square the leaders of the march told us to stop, which we did. They told us to sit down, and we did that too. We lit up smokes, and talked. One guy had a pint of whiskey, and I got some of that, which tasted good. Especially as it was such a lovely chill day in October. So we sat there in that intersection with Macy's right there, and Broadway and 6th Avenue making an X in Manhattan.

I was talking to one of the veterans—I was the oldest person in the march, my gray hair was down to my shouders, I was clean-shaven, and wore a white shirt and bluejeans under my dirty raincoat. I passed him the pint, which he took, winked at me, we laughed and he flashed me the peace sign and said Brother as a cab nosed its way into the crowd of us and I saw guys and young women leap up: the cab kept coming, in first, but it kept coming and then it was surrounded by marchers as it came. The cabby yelled that he had a fare, and I saw a big kid say to him, Yes, but we're sitting here, and the cabby said whaddya a buncha fuckin' Peaceniks?: the kid, wearing an Ike jacket, beard streaming down his chest, adjusted his glasses, and said Man we'll throw you in the River, can't you give us a chance to get out of the way? The cabby said Fuck you, and rolled up the window as a young guy about six feet two slugged the hood of the car and left a dent, went to the window and told the cabby that he had no courtesy, Roll down your window, he said, or I'll put my fist through it. The cabby was looking at the knuckle imprints on the hood of his yellow car, and he rolled down the window and said something to the young guy, and as if by ESP fifteen guys lifted the cab just off the ground. The cabby's face bleached: he lowered the window all the way down:

Hey, I gotta fare! he cried.

Yeah, but you got no fuckin' courtesy, the young guy said.

The cabby shifted gears, they dropped the car and on contact with the street it lurched forward, hitting several of the marchers, and the cabby slowed, and cringed back away as the young guy's fist came through, and grabbed the cabby by the collar hard, with the voice behind it saying Stop the car. The cabby braked, and then the car was tilted against the downtown skyline, and it dropped back flat down, everybody parted to make room and the cabby shifted gears, floored it and sped away. Nobody was hurt, but everybody was angry, and we got up, and began to walk up 6th Avenue as the cops appeared.

They walked up the Avenue with us, and they looked at us as we looked at them, and as the sun began to seriously head for

New Jersey, we were at 40th Street, I felt something touch my left shoulder, and I turned expecting to see a face that was perhaps going to say something, and my eyes met an intricate pair of eyes that literally crashed through my gaze. My head jerked back, and he touched my left shoulder with his nightstick, and eyes loathing me the police captain smiled, and said,

You stay on that side of the (parking area) line.

I nodded.

As we approached Bryant Park, which is behind the New York Public Library, the marchers were ordered to stay on that (east) side of the white line, which we did, and the police captain had stepped over the line to remind me not to cross. I was the oldest, you see. There were about a thousand of us, then, and as I walked along, the police captain kept pace with me, while he looked at me, with his mocking smile and his eyes brilliant in hate: I was, I think, younger than he, but I was taller, and he said, again, that I should stay on my side of the white line, which I was doing, and then he stepped on his side of the line and pointed his nightstick at me, and smiled his flat, white-lipped smile, as grey eyes glinted, he said, softly, tenderly,

"I'm gonna get you."

He grinned and I saw his lower front teeth. I looked in his eyes, and then I looked at him.

His face and his fully uniformed figure were set. He stood ramrod straight though his shoulders slanted down, and like all cops who have been in that long, he had an inward cringe, but his neck was, which amused me, rather scrawny, and his face, which was not amusing, was gaunt. As sharply boned as a redneck racist, and as lined as a farmer's field. But his lips, like an old cop's smile, twisted the wrong way even in cynicism, because a cynical cop after all those years is beyond irony even to himself, because it doubles in, like murder, after a while. In his trade for irony (beyond irony) doubled into that little whisper Kierkegaard spoke, tone of St. Augustine: the soul as feminine, the icy, contained hatred in that cop's eyes meeting mine, was, I thought the connection which is not necessarily or unnecessarily beyond speech, but the form that was formed when his hard grey hate met my green New York Public Library eyes: a union, and in that union I

329

considered a different interpretation of the Messiah.

"Why?" I asked.

The police captain smiled, his little smile. God how he loathed me. But our gaze held, and I moved two steps to my left, so that I was walking just an inch on my side of the white line, as he was walking on his, because I was getting angry.

His face, as I walked, went as gray as cement, concrete hard in the disbelief that I would literally challenge his authority, but his eyes took on a sparkle, and he smiled in a brighter way, as we walked shoulder to shoulder, the white line separating us, and I looked in his eyes and asked:

You can't tell me?

The insult, like a shock, froze him in his tracks, and I walked on, but when he briskly caught up with me, you know how they walk fast, he said, and his voice was from the grave, a kind of grave he'd stayed out of so far, but one he knew, and would avoid, yet never sure what tomorrow would bring—I was challenging something beyond my experience. Death in that cop captain's voice. I hated him too, oh would in fact look straight into the eyes of the murder of the soul. Sure. So I did. He was all for one and one for straight death: somebody else's, and he gripped his night-stick so fiercely he could hardly speak. And.

He pointed the stick at me, and said, glee pure murder:

"You're mine!"

Something within me turned, I wanted to hit him so badly my heart hurt, so badly I didn't care what happened to me, so badly I regretted having had the drinks at the bar, so badly, my full force *all* of it in the one hit, and I felt myself being wrenched off, my eyes and his eyes—he had a madly delighted glitter in his eyes— our gaze held, but I was suddenly, which puzzled me, somehow wrenched away from the white line, and his killer's smile which I wanted to break, and as I stumbled to my right, away from the cop, what in hell was going on? in my astonishment I looked down, and a tow-headed boy about ten years old was holding my raincoat with both hands, and pulling me away, his eyes angrily gazing up at me as he grabbed my wrist, and said, vehemently,

"No violence!"

I stared down at him.

"That's not what we're here for," the boy said, and our eyes held: I smiled, in a way of self-admission, and nodded. The boy grinned, took my hand and pulled me into the crowd of marchers, and as we turned and headed east on 42nd Street, I glanced back at the police captain. His eyes, like the wake of a .38 caliber slug: drilled into mine, and liberated, I laughed, put my arm around the boy's shoulders, flashed the cop the peace sign, and marched up to Mike, linked arms with him and the boy and we went eastward, toward the River and the United Nations where we would demonstrate.

The Messiah (2)

ONE DAY LAST SPRING I went around the corner to get the paper and some smokes. There is a little old-fashioned neighborhood newsstand nook in the wall run by an elderly Jewish couple—really beautiful people, and I picked up the paper off the outside bench, walked into the little store and waited while the little man finished putting sodapop into the cooler.

The day fit my mood. It was one of those big tough city days when spring comes in like a green-eyed girl from Siam: suddenly, without warning, the town's warm, blue and breezy with a very special salty tang from the Atlantic—a real day to be on a ship to a far place. A real day to be happy, to work hard and to hell with the results: a great day for making love, taking a nap and then a walk up to 34th Street and seeing a flick before you go to that East Indian restaurant where the curry is so good and the wine so marvelous. So I waited, to buy the cigarettes I wanted. The door was open and the fresh air came in on a breeze, the way the true motion of a curve feels, and when he gave me my smokes and I paid him and put the pack in my shirt pocket, I laughed, and said,

"What a beautiful day!"

The little man grinned, and nodded, and in his accent, agreed, what a beautiful day, and looked to my right, from behind the counter, to the door, and said, Yes boys?

I turned, and to my right there were two cops.

The place was so small, they blocked the doors with their wide hips packed with the .38 caliber pistols, the nightsticks and cartridge belts. I paused on my way out. The cop to my left was young, in his twenties, and he had overheard the one-two dialogue I'd had with the little store keeper, and the young cop and I exchanged smiles, and echoed the fact of the beautiful day. The young cop said hello to the little man and bought a candy bar and a pack of gum. The little man smiled—his son was a cop too, so the boys treated the old man with a lot of respect.

But when my eyes fell on the other cop, my smiling expression vanished, the words of the beauty having just left my lips, he looked at me, and then into my eyes, and I saw Hell.

He was older, and a Sergeant, but younger, I thought, than myself, but he was so much older, and had travelled so far, had lived so long, far too long, he knew it and didn't know what to do with it, he was simply stuck with it. Face leathery, lined, bitter, drawn and exhausted and as gray as his dull, flat black dead eyes which had seen so much they literally refused vision.

He was thin, rather small, and dreadful, and he knew it. I see his eyes before me, therefore I know Hell in the complete corruption of the soul: that pure tragedy. In murder, bloody headlines, but mostly between those lines, the suicide of his soul. And in the brief flash of our eye-contact I was transfixed, my day beautiful smiling lips, and eyes, seeing clear into the unholy flat eyes, in his torment, and utter desperation, his shoulders curved downward, as within himself he cringed, at his own personal dead end, inwardly, and after the flash of our eye-contact broke, he glanced away for a second involving eternity, then glanced back at me, and then, he lowered his eyes. In my humiliation I died, from the force of his death, and then he lowered his head, as I walked out the door dying, he said, in a grotesque whisper, *Yeah, a nice day*, screaming to the lost beautiful day, in his wrecked corrupt cruel toughness, the boy girl soul had died in his heart, the girl boy soul had died, and so did the beautiful day, gone in the Hell of his own eyes helplessly, the doomed cop, paralyzed, *saturated* with violence, unable to scream for help in a scream-force toward change, which is why talking was so tough, and beauty such a locked and silent agony.

Nightmare

I WAS A SPY and the pursuer pursued, chasing a man on the periphery of a deserted airfield in Germany and I would never find him, because it was my fault he was on the run, and in guilt and fear it all had the color and texture of a bruise, the screaming vulnerability of men who feel lost within without guns, themselves pursued, as I was while he followed me running.

Like a shadow he fled down lone dark city streets like I did with the girl in my yesterday Army dream, towards the airfield where the plane waited. And like a shadow he slipped through tall grass by smoky lakes and valleys, sheets of glass under his arm, or was it the sky under his arm? In the glass were the eyes, eyes in the glass like the sky under his arm that hated me, and told me I was wrong, that I was originally helplessly wrong, and that my tension caused airplane crashes, trainwrecks and ships to smash and sink at sea, as bridges fell, the eyes glared.

They said it was my fault—if I could see the eyes, therefore within I was the true fault, otherwise I would be blind, God they were awful, really so hateful—*spiteful!* and so lordly, in *venom.* Also, I heard voices. As if in the constant fear of the eyes, like electronic waves the fear created voices, I was so anxious—I heard a man's voice, and occasionally another which I knew was my own, but I was by then the third person and the man was describing what I was doing while I was doing it, and I was like a little boy watching a movie far beyond his comprehension: glassy-eyed, chasing and being chased by I hardly knew what, fascinated and in terror by eyes that came out of the sky in sheets of glass under his arm, and as he chased him across the field, they went across a highway.

Towards the old barbed wire fence.

They climbed between the sagging wires, and headed towards the hangars in rapidly approaching darkness, like the approaching Christmas blue in Ivory Black.

"Can't you see you will never win? Yet you'll never give up. You will be all the things you always were, and even yet will be, and you will have no effect, the world is going to kill itself because you witness it. Can you hear me?"

"I'm afraid."

"Because you will lose, what can you do? Forming a world of murder, starvation, grief and carelessness which is your fault because you witness it."

"Because"—the voice added, ruthlessly, Kitasono, Black Rain—"The beautiful women, remember? Like they will be, you don't know them yet but you will, won't you? Ha ha. There's a certain amusement, you sad bastard, look in the eyes will you? Women won't help you. You're too much. You are too wrong."

For a strange sudden witnessed collision of the known past with—and becoming—an experienced future, in a flash I saw him by the wall, blazing sunlight (typical), and I came through the grass fast to him, but the glass under his arm tilted, the glare was blinding and the eyes circled and spun out of the brilliance, like the lion in the sun, roaring visually, *your fault is the world*, they said, *die alive*, and I covered my eyes, sank to my knees in the grass and mud, blinding flashing explosions behind my hands I still saw the eyes, and heard the comforting voice pronouncing my known destiny,

"Because you will lose, what can you do. You will go anyway. Your fault is the world. I know. You'll never give up. Well, he's almost to the plane—it's taxiing down the runway. Hurry! She's inside, waving to you—hurry!"

Dream

NO, SHE SAID, GRAVELY, she thought the new stories were a failure, and I saw her handsome face look up from the page, and as her dark eyes fell on mine, I saw distance. She pushed up the puffed sleeve of her Emily Dickinson blouse, and freed her long granny skirt from her legs.

Her very shapely naked legs and her high arched feet in shoes with buttons on the sides, and as she lit a cigarette she looked at me accusingly, yet from far away, and she seemed above me.

As if we were on the telephone, yet my face was close to hers. It wasn't actually, except I knew every detail of her features, and her body, so it was easy to feel close. Even at a distance, I had.

In the past.

Why, she asked, don't you get rid of—what's her name? and think of coming to Alsace: we're leaving . . .

But! I exclaimed, you know I can't! and I cried, When do you leave? seeing her luggage in the cart being towed across the tarmac to the big plane.

Tonight, she said, as far after.

Tonight, I repeated. But what can I do? I love you, yet how can I—?

The line went dead, her face looked at me, and slowly it became a mask, of false pity, irony and soft contempt in a scent of regret (*Replique*), as she shook her head. Sorry, the woman in the wind of the city seemed to say. *Sorry, Fielding* . . .

Icarus

IT WAS A WARM OCTOBER AFTERNOON, about three o'clock and school had just let out. The streets behind me were loaded with teenage black and Puerto Rican kids of all kinds—junkies, winos, and assorted tough guys plus the not so tough kids who must, though, play tough, and they all streamed along the streets loud mouthing and bad mouthing a lot of things and people, in their theatre of the streets, as they moved to stoops and luncheonettes, and the IRT and BMT subways at Union Square.

They were *loud*, aggressive and sexually flagrant. The black and Puerto Rican girls were plump, fat, skinny and well-built, too, in tight sweaters, mini-skirts, as the boys freaked in sneaks, tee shirts, and tight black pants walking tall, keeping the neighborhood on edge.

I walked among them going the other way—north, in my dirty raincoat not worth their attention: too alien, too old and too square, and I turned left onto Irving Place and headed uptown on the west side of the street, and a block away I saw a boy walking south toward me, on the same side of the street, and the contrast between the other kids and this boy was more than the fact that he was white—what was so different, so unusually different, is this kid was *beautiful*.

Straw, light wood-colored hair that was parted in the middle and curled down on his shoulders a little untidy, framing his pale, slightly undernourished face.

His lips were thin and soft just as his face was soft in a true contrast to his lean and agile body. He had a longish turned up nose, and his direct and guileless soft grey summer eyes and gaze held the steady quality of chamber music: and yet in an innocence

337

so natural he seemed on the threshold of a dream come true. Expectant, yet curiously brilliantly cautious, shy even, and so close to fey he seemed to be spellbound, and when his eyes met mine, and our look held, I saw the flash of a boy's anger at being looked at and appraised, yet he lowered his eyes, and a spot of color appeared on each cheek and I felt regret because I liked him and because I could feel his body.

He was no more than sixteen, and he walked along the sidewalk with his head high, his hair flowing and his psychic tourist's eyes wandering the roof tops as his hands swung lightly and open, at his sides. He wore a faded purple and white tie-dyed tee shirt, dirty sand-colored chino pants, his feet were bare in low faded and softly torn blue sneaks, and as he passed me I caught the rhythm of his lean young body, ethereal in space, and my heart warmed to those darling freckles across his nose.

A Puerto Rican man passed me on my right, going my way, and moving ahead of me at a rapid pace, and in a kind of union-gaze, a white man and a black man in front of the garage next to Sal Anthony's, plus the Puerto Rican man and me, watched that sweet kid walk down the street toward that interracial crew smoking grass and drinking cheap wine on the stoop of a building across the street from Washington Irving high school, they were smack in his path literally, and as I thought Jesus, they'll FLIP when they see *him!* I snapped to attention, the two guys in front of the garage were looking square in my eyes, and the Puerto Rican man in front of me had turned to watch the boy, and then his eyes too met mine, so the eye-contact was all over the street, in, to put it mildly, a unique recognition, but I stared back at the two dudes by the garage until they lowered their eyes, the Puerto Rican man turned his gaze away and continued walking, and at 18th Street I crossed and headed east to Bohack's to shop for supper, lighting up a smoke, and angrily studying the shopping list my wife had given me.

Labor Day

I AM LISTENING to a special radio program devoted to Scriabin, hearing things he wrote when he was ten and fifteen.

He went to military school, he hated to be tickled, and the students threatened to tickle him unless he played the piano so they could all dance together.

He loved girls and boys.

It takes, the narrator says, a feminine man to play him.

He kissed the piano every night before he went to bed, even when he was a baby.

There is a lovely blonde girl riding her bicycle up and down the street, below my window. She has a nice tan. Her hair flows in the wind. She has lovely legs, and her white short pants are short, under a crisp turquoise and white floral blouse, tail out.

Her head is held high, her back erect, and she rides her bicycle on the street below my window.

Naked, I type.

Pirate One

I'M WRITING THIS on Mozart's birthday—January 27th; a Wednesday morning, just a few minutes after nine a.m.

It all came clear last night. I don't know how. Through talking, I guess.

Last night Nixon announced the war was over and the day before yesterday Johnson died, and George Foreman TKO'd Joe Frazier in not quite two rounds, as reported in yesterday's papers. Also, the Supreme Court ruled that abortions are legal in the first three months. So, a lot of news, and most of it good, and though my heart's been with it, especially the war and abortion news— I've secretly been thinking about something else. And talking with a lovely young dancer last night at the bar, I realized what it's been; running around in my head there. These last two or three weeks since he died, and being with her last night, talking and drinking, the memory of last fall, after sixteen years of an unanswered question, at least that part came clear, a big part, when the question was answered.

About the place where I'd met him. Not really met him, but I'd stood beside him, and, well, that was enough, I mean.

All along I've been thinking—so I thought—about him, but what's really been on my mind is Jackson Pollock and Johnny Romero. Then him.

Do you remember Johnny Romero? I remember Pollock yelling and being angry when strangers didn't know who he was.

Well. I came to New York in May of 1956 because I had to, it was where my future was, and it was also where Julie Eastman was, in her wonderful apartment on Spring Street. I was so completely in love with her my life was hardly real, and it was only later—too late by then—that she realized how much in love with me she was. Because, in spite of all the famous guys who loved her, she loved me most of all. I knew it, too, but she didn't. Not then. I was—really crazy about her. It didn't take much. Christ she was beautiful.

Anyway, it was very brief, and after we broke up, I moped around New York for a few months, and around September or October of that year, I was walking along a street in the Village and I passed a little place with one door, which was open, and I stopped, because Chris Connor, who got all she knew about singing from June Christy, was on the jukebox and Stan Kenton was behind her and it was All About Ronnie, and I was standing on a side street in New York City, just come from my home town Kirkwood, Missouri, and I was inside a dive outside U.S. Army Headquarters Germany, with a couple of lean bleached Lesbians, who hummed along with Chris and stared through smoke, boy Hesse caught that, and the name in neon in the window to the right of the open door said *Johnny Romero's*.

I went in.

The jukebox was to the left of the door, and beyond it was a small rectangular wooden table, which fit into a small corner, fitted with an L-shaped bench, and beyond that on the left still, were a lot of posters most of Negro guys and women, and just beyond that, along the wall there, were the bathrooms, and as they marked the rear of the place, the door (curtains, actually) that was there, led, I assumed, to the kitchen. And following around, the bar ran the length of the place, opposite the jukebox and wall of posters. Underneath the window up front, was a cigarette machine.

The young colored guy behind the bar looked at me, and I sat on a barstool and asked for a draft, which he gave me and I paid for, I looked around the place, it was small, clean, and had a nice feeling, I played a couple of songs, took a leak, finished another draft, and left.

I began to go there when I was in the neighborhood, and occasionally when I wasn't, and it was quite a while later that I discovered the kitchen wasn't behind the curtains, it was a small, lovely and secluded garden, with three or four tables and some chairs. So, often if it was a nice day, and I had a couple of dollars, I'd go to Johnny Romero's and sit out in the garden, and think the grave thoughts serious romantics think, drinking at three o'clock in the afternoon in New York. On a beautiful day. The beer was so cold, and good. Julie Eastman sure made a blunder when she let me go, I'll say.

I also went at night. Thirsty for experience, and frustrated and angry because I couldn't seem to bring my life into focus, and somehow use it in my art. So the knowledge that I had a lot of living yet to do, while thrilling me, yet made me angry and impatient.

The slang was different then, of course; the word was spade, and in more proper circles, colored, or Negro. But the city was simply alive with jazz, and everyone spoke hipster lingo. Yeah man, well, I'm like cool.

Johnny Romero's was the first all-black downtown bar in the city; very few white people went, though no one was actually unwelcome in a racial sense, but there were so many other places to go, and drink and hear jazz, why go to Romero's, where there was, actually, not much happening, and people stood around and talked, drank, and listened to the jukebox. Why listen to a jukebox, when two or three blocks away the man on the record was alive before your eyes?

Tea (grass) was still a fairly inside thing, and the hipster jokes, some of which were really funny, were spade jokes about grass, until suddenly they weren't, which like grass, slows reality down. Most white cats including myself spoke a spade musician's lingo and it was (embarrassing) strange, me talking to some spade cat imitating his jive. Hi man, gimme some skin!

Heeyyy baby, what's happenin'?

But I—and I cooled it—so I never experienced much hostility; and I enjoyed Romero's because I was in a world I hardly knew—hey, let me put it like this (you dig):

New York, in 1956, was the wildest, greatest city anywhere; American painting had just been taken seriously for a first in history, and the city was the art center of the world. Europe was as jealous as all hell, and it was wonderful. You could walk along 10th Street and stop and say a few words with Philip Guston, go

342

into the Colony on the corner there, at 4th Avenue, have a beer with deKooning, walk over to the Cedar and have a few with Creeley, Dan Rice, or Kline, and that night fall by the Riviera or Romero's and then cross up to the Vanguard on 7th Avenue, dig Getz and Brookmeyer, and then walk down to the Cafe Bohemia, and get your head torn off by Miles, and around one, fall by the Cedar, and pick up some friends and go over to the 5 Spot and completely flip over Cecil Taylor, then afterwards go to Riker's for breakfast, and around dawn head home, maybe with a chick. It was really great. You could feel the exuberance, you could see and hear the dedication. I did, and I miss the way musicians talked. Things were opening out. I'd made friends with a few spade cats overseas so I had an idea how to behave, a little, I mean, I tended to get carried away. It was easy enough. I'd slip into Romero's, get a beer and stand around for an hour or two and then split to hear Sonny. Or Monk. Or Miles. What not many people knew was Romero's was an essentially middle-class place. Black guys and their chicks drove downtown in their big cars, or their sports cars, and went to Johnny Romero's.

Especially on weekends. It was the downtown place to go. I guess there were black gangsters and black detectives, too, but it didn't matter to me, as I stood by the door, watching, because what the place was all about, which you could feel, I mean even when it was crowded there was a nice quality, and people were friendly, and that's what I learned. It was Johnny's effect. He was a popular guy. Everybody liked him; he was very friendly, and in a very real sense, though odd-seeming, there wasn't any reason for violence, and then, sensibly perhaps, the black guys that went there were *big*, big guys, and some of them must have been prize fighters. Also, the customers were cool. To themselves. Yes, baby, tonight I am very cool. It was a bright, warm, classy little joint, and those big dark skinned guys dressed in dark blue and white silk and their chicks looking like twenty million in furs and perfumes, and as I stood there, learning Johnny's effect, I caught a sense of friendship that was to me at the end of a long and far flung thread, which yet seemed, for these people, the beginning of every day.

Happily, there were precious few of the white guys who hang

around only with black people because they don't know what to do with their lives, and they figure black cats will understand because they don't either—it's a loser's fantasy and rationale— white guys feeling black guys will understand because black guys are born losers; how can they handle life, being black, and the double irony is lost in the misunderstanding that the loss is in being black! a natural fact you dig, and the implication in the audacity of that white fantasy, is also lost. And if, following the definition of irony in a textbook of rhetoric published about 1872, irony consists in ridiculing an object under a pretense of praising it (with the true meaning indicated by the tone of voice), you can see the rather horrible meaning of that loss. Which, of course, black people were, and are, supposed to understand. Literally.

Those white guys would be called spade freaks today. Then they said he digs spades. Chicks, too. She digs spades. But you could tell in the tone of the voice. In the beginning, like when she hit on him, the spade stud was flattered, but when he discovered she dug him because he was—uhn, well, and she couldn't dig herself anyway, he—it was a pretty bitter discovery. There was a lot of that in the Fifties.

You can spot chicks and cats who only dig spades; they have a sleepy look, a somnambulant look, eyes wide open. And a sharp kind of hysterical glitter along the edges. Somebody else is holding them up; guess who.

Anyway, my involvement with writing and painting made my life hectic enough, and lonely enough, so that Romero's was so different from me, though I might want somebody to hold me up, the effect of Johnny Romero's persona wouldn't have it, so I enjoyed his bar, and the obvious tone of relaxation. In fact that effect rejected the cats and chicks who dug spades. And kept me just different enough to constantly realize something I had learned in the Army: when black people are together the cir- cumstance is of people being together in that way.

And that success was because of Johnny—hands down. With out a *doubt*. He was a very nice guy—he was the kind of guy when he saw you on the street he'd wave or call to you just as you did him, and then when he suddenly saw you, and remembered you from his bar, the warmth of his greeting deepened. Really, everybody liked him.

He was about six feet two, had a lithe walk, dressed casually, and stayed calm; but of course there was something behind his eyes, that something the response-structure to his making it in the white world. Every black musician in America and maybe Europe had that look; some guys were more outspoken than others, but it was tough, because the guys who owned the clubs where you played were Italian gangsters, and they held you in contempt for obvious reasons, and they told you what to do, and they took your money, and there wasn't anything you could do about it. I'm certain drugs were a way out of that humiliation, rage and anxiety, and then a way into the music. I often saw Miles take breaks between sets, and walk outside for a smoke so tightlipped and angry he was literally speechless—or couldn't speak what was on his mind.

But Johnny Romero seemed to take it all pretty well; he had a good thing going, and the sacrifices he made were at least conscious. One of the nicest things about him was he tended bar, and I don't know if he needed to, but I think he enjoyed it, because he was an active man, and he enjoyed work, and the company of people, and especially people he liked. He was very handsome, and given his size, and his casual open friendly style, and his attractive light brown skin, warm smile and grin, it was obviously a pleasant thing to drop by for a drink, sit at the bar, and say Hi Johnny, how about a nice cold beer! And in that spirit, one day about a year later, I was in the neighborhood, so I walked over for a quick one, and to dig Billie on the jukebox and when I got there, the door was closed, locked, the lights were out inside, and the sign on the door said Closed. What the hell! I thought.

So I walked away, and that night and a few days later I asked around—what had happened? I asked a couple of black guys I thought might know, they didn't, and I asked a couple of bar owners, and they spoke in low tones, mumbling something about Johnny and trouble. Trouble, in that usage, meant the Mafia, and until last fall—for sixteen years—all I knew was something about Johnny and trouble.

It was after a game, in very early October—1972—I'd pitched a two hit shutout, and our team had won 7-0. We were happily

getting our gear together, most of us half drunk from the beer
we'd had during the game, we always have fun, we have a good
softball team, and in the car heading across town to our bar, I was
in the back seat, fat and forty-two, and somebody was talking
about the Pirates, and remarked that Clemente couldn't do it *all*
by himself, and for some reason, maybe the warm afternoon, and
the motion of the car and the breeze, and our victory and therefore our good spirits and certainly my relaxed pleasure—I'd gotten a double and single, driven in a run and scored once—I lit a
smoke, and in a rather wistful way remembered Johnny Romero's
bar, and the night I had stood beside him at that bar, and I asked
my pal Joe, who was in the front seat,

Do you remember Johnny Romero's?

Yes, he said, adding, that spade joint in the Village.

I nodded, and asked, right out, What ever happened to him? I
heard he'd gotten into some tr—

Trouble! Listen man, that guy was balling a Mafia guy's chick!

Holy Christ! I cried, horrified. But, why—why I mean they
didn't but why didn't they kill him? How *awful!*

Joe laughed, Because they liked him, and added—he was a nice
guy!

I made a peculiar smile, and shook my head, remembering
Johnny, saying, Boy, how close can you get. What did they do? I
asked, did they do anything? What did they do to her?

Joe shrugged. They didn't do anything to him, they told him to
get out of the country or else.

Man, I whispered, he must have moved fast. No wonder I'd
been surprised, seeing the *Closed* sign on the door. I'd stopped in
the night before.

Fast! Who wouldn't—

After a minute or two I told Joe, and the other guys in the car,
what had happened one night, around one in the morning, at
Johnny Romero's bar, when I had been standing at the bar near
the door, having a bottle of beer; Ballantine, it was. Ballantine
was good in the Fifties.

There were a few customers in the place, I was thinking my
thoughts and Johnny was serving people and talking, and the
lights were low. The mixture of perfume scent and cigars breezed

around the vision of dark skinned couples, talking, as Miles and Sonny played Paper Moon, and as I faced the bar, on the wall in back and above the bar, just opposite me and up a little, I looked at the advertisement that never ceased to amuse and fascinate me: slick photo in color of a handsome black guy beautifully dressed, and his chick, a knockout, in low cut gown, enjoying the drink Smirnoff was advertising and it was the White Cadillac—flashy and funny: vodka and milk, and a guy moved in and stood next to me, on my left, and I moved to my right as the guy stood there and got comfortable, both hands on the bar in a relaxed manner as Johnny walked up the duckboards to him, and I saw the guy, who was about six three, was wearing a baseball cap, and it looked professional. Johnny and I exchanged glances, and I made a thin smile.

So did Johnny.

The guy to my left was muscular, and extremely handsome; skin very dark, but of a rich hue, and his features were chiseled, and his eyes dark, but very bright, and he pointed at Johnny, and then at his ball cap, and said,

You know who I be?

Johnny shook his head.

The guy was hurt, and he tapped his own chest, and then his ball cap, and asked, surprised: You no know who I be?

Johnny smiled, and said no, and that he was sorry, but—

Well, the guy got a little angry. He took off the cap, and pointed to the large curved P on the front, and glaring at Johnny, he said, angrily,

You *know* who I be!

Johnny lifted his big shoulders, and turned a hand palm up, and was about to say something, when the guy slammed the cap on his own head, jabbed himself in the chest, and yelled,

I BE ROBERTO CLEMENTE!

Hey, great! Johnny grinned, but the Pittsburgh outfielder sensed it hadn't really worked, and glancing at me—I was poker face O.K. because this guy Clemente was a powerful cat, man, and he was very bugged, and as he was calling the shots, I was just there, period. So he looked at Johnny, again, tapped himself on the chest again, and yelled,

I BE RO-BER-TO CLE-MEN-TE! He looked at Johnny and, searching for words, stammered, I—I be—he cursed in Spanish—PITTSBURGH!

He looked at Johnny to see if he had said it right, knowing somehow he hadn't.

I said, Right field.

Clemente nodded, yelled, Si, laughed, and cried, I— RO-BER-TO—I Ro-ber-to CLE-MEN-TE!

And Johnny laughed, reached across the bar and put a big hand on Clemente's shoulder, and laughing right out, said,

That's great, baby, and what is it you want to drink?

They laughed, I had imitated the voices, and the car pulled up outside the bar and we got out with our bats and gloves, and as we went inside, I said, in a deep soft swirl of emotion, to no one in particular,

He reminded me of Pollock.

Pollock had died in an automobile accident. August 10th, 1956; last night, when I had remembered Clemente, too.

The Miracle

for Maigret, and Rex

THERE IS A SCULPTOR I know, I've known him for about six or
seven years—longer than that, actually, but it was about six or
seven years ago that we became good friends. We're very good
friends. He's swell to get drunk with, because he's done so many
things in his life, and he's such a great story teller.

He's about fifty years old, is tall and lean, has a lot of thick grey
hair, wears Ben Franklin glasses, and absolutely *loves* wine—
cheap wine, which he buys by the gallon.

But he can take care of a martini.

This sculptor is passionate, and handsome, he has two beautiful
daughters which he says are beautiful, the tone being that of a
Greek father sipping wine, and telling, in lyric, of his beautiful
daughters. He loves women, has been married twice, and twice
divorced—which amuses him, although he can have a long look in
his eye. He can sip wine, gaze before him, and sigh the single sigh
only the twice-married twice-divorced understand. Or com-
prehend to understand. I mean, one has many memories, and
there is that four o'clock in the afternoon cool glass of wine that
causes memories to converge.

He is a dedicated sculptor.

He makes his living by teaching, which he hates, because he
loves to be alone and work.

I met one of his daughters.

She was beautiful O.K., and conscious, and I would say about
twenty-four years old. Not knowing her, I said hello, and we
talked, and when she told me her name, my face opened, and I
exclaimed, but

Your father is one of my best friends!

There must have been a way I made the exclamation, because she laughed, and confided, oh yes, I love him, and her eyes deepened:

Isn't he wonderful?

Indeed so, I smiled.

Well, I haven't seen her in a couple of years. She was a waitress in a restaurant I used to go to.

Anyway, I thought, and often, about his man and his beautiful daughters; if this daughter-woman was one of two, the other must clearly be a young goddess.

Clearly!

That is the sound of Simenon!

Well, my sculptor friend told me he travelled through Europe with his two daughters, around six or seven years ago when they were about eighteen years old, and when I thought about the three of them, I contemplated the inevitable sensation they must have caused—particularly in Europe, when in fact, he had just gotten his second divorce, but you see when he told me about the trip, he didn't mention any details and when I asked him, he waved his hand, sipped his wine, laughed and said Oh we went, places—Paris. Rome. You know. And I nodded, O.K., and smiled my smile because what he was really telling me was he was thinking about still being in love with his second wife, just as he was with his first, and the divorce from the second certified the divorce from the first, just as it certified the love, in the sense— perhaps a rather final sense—that not only was marriage not his way to happiness, but in an alternative wisdom, happiness was that perfect state which literally, maybe even inexorably, didn't know what marriage was, except as a metaphor, and even then, strange. An untranslatable ideogram, with its reversal a miracle.

O.K., but why? I asked. Two divorces!

Well, he said, it was his fault.

He was sad when he said it, and he added, angrily, I'm impossible to live with.

I offered him one of my French cigarettes, which he accepted, and I lit both, and he said Thanks, and he added,

I'm a drunkard; and then, he sighed, there's my work.

He looked at me; I nodded, and he said that nothing would

interrupt his work, and he said (and I agreed) artists are impossible. The more dedicated, the worse. Yes, I said.

She soon saw she couldn't rely on me, he admitted.

Jesus, I said.

Both of 'em, he said. But, he added, I'm a romantic, and thus I get what I deserve.

But they must love you, I said. I exclaimed! actually.

Oh yes, he said. Very much. We write. I have a talent for loving intelligent and beautiful women. They write wonderful letters.

Where are they? I asked.

Jeanne is in London, and Annabel—married again—is in Chicago; happy.

I got the bartender's attention, and we ordered two more. I said,

But you seem all right. I mean, understandably you remember it all, but it doesn't seem to—have wrecked you.

No, he nodded. I came to be what I must be, and live it out.

I said yes, I had come to that myself.

He said, I'm very happy, in fact.

I said, Me too.

Yes, he said. It's good to see you again. How are you?

Good, I said. Broke.

Yes. Me too, he said.

We laughed.

The thing I most admire about him is his rejection of cynicism, and his comprehension of his relative position in the art world. He's a known sculptor, but not Famous, and he doesn't seem to want Fame—a hellish waste of energy, he once said. He's a man of few appetites, like they say, and is most happy when he sips wine, and sculpts. He rises early, early early, and works until three or so, and when he isn't teaching (three days a week), he then goes, as he does after he teaches, to a bar where artists go, and talks and drinks wine. And then to a movie, or home to read—he's very well read, and brilliant in his field—goes to bed early, and the next morning gets up early and goes to work.

Don't you eat? I asked.

Occasionally, he smiled. Cheese—I love cheese. All kinds. And nuts, fruit. Sweet butter. Black bread.

A classicist, I said.

But yes, he said; in French.

We laughed.

*　　*　　*

I saw him on the street a few days ago, it had been several months, and we hailed each other—arms out. Fielding! he cried. But he looked tired, as we shook hands warmly, and walked a few steps down the sidewalk together, as I eagerly said,

How are you?

Well, he laughed. O.K., but actually not really.

Oh?

He ran his hand over his eyes, I have a terrible hangover, was up all night, and . . .

Want to have a drink?

No, he said. Yes, of course, but I'm not going to. Oh, let's do!

We laughed, and walked a few blocks to the bar he likes, and ordered a couple of drinks.

His hand trembled as he sipped the wine, and he said, One and at the most two, and then I'm going. I'm too old to feel—and be, so shaky.

I didn't say anything, and then I asked him how his work was going, and he said wonderfully. He asked about me and I told him, saying I've been staying home, he said he had too, except for last night, and we smiled, and talked about what we had been working on.

I asked,

Do you see her anymore?

He looked at me. I didn't say anything. Her? he asked. Oh, he said. Then he smiled, and in a long breath,

Ahh yes. Yes! But—and he put his hand on my shoulder—it isn't the same. He smiled.

I said, sadly, warmly, I'm sorry. So then, she's older.

Yes, she's twenty-three. January 10th.

We laughed. January 10th, I said.

Yes, he laughed.

January 10th, he repeated.

We laughed, and I said, Well, and I murmured, too bad.

Oh, he sighed, well, that's how things go, you know, and I asked, What's she like these days?

Beautiful as ever, he said, adding wistfully, We're friends.

Does she still visit?

Once or twice a week, he said. It isn't the same.

How does she feel. Grown up? Sad?

Oh you know. Who knows?

Did you finish the sculpture?

Yes, they're all done. I did several.

Do you like them?

Very much.

Does she?

He began to laugh, and so did I, a little, and he said,

She has no idea what it really is, no idea; why should she.

No idea! What a mystery!

He raised his glass, I did too, and as we toasted, he laughed, with a long look and a strong sparkle sadly, warmly,

They all are. And here's to it.

Today being February 16th (Friday) 1973, I must have met him seven years ago, because it was winter, and the early months in 1966 that stand as a landmark in my life. That was the year I began my process of individuation. I was in real trouble, and felt so close to Death, It was almost a comfort. When you're that close to It, there is a beneficence, and I felt life was an act of grace, to be given to Death. But that, like they say, is another story.

I don't know why, but he and I became friends immediately, and as he was in his late forties, just divorced from his second wife and returned from Europe after a summer of traveling with his beautiful daughters, he seemed to be pleased with an American like me, and for a reason known only to the gods, perhaps it's better that they alone know, bar room conversations being what they are, convoluted, dense, enthusiastically forgettable memorable and possibly incredible depending on who's who, and the quality of listening and talking voices, the success of the combination God alone has granted the gods: to give us remembrance. Well. Anyway, we hit it off, and he told me about a girl he had discovered late the past October, and how much in love with her he was, and she with him.

He was ecstatic, telling me; in the warm bar, on those cold 1966 nights, he told me from the beginning.

I had wanted, he began, to sculpt the head of a girl, I had wanted to for several years, but the desire really hadn't come in to my consciousness, and I think the journey to Europe with my daughters began it, and probably my desire to capture a sense of their (and possibly my own) perfect youth in a personally eternal way, so for all the weeks since I've been back I found myself studying the heads of girls everywhere I went. On the streets, in subways, etc.

The heads, I said.

He laughed, and continued:

My studio is on Riverside Drive, a couple of blocks down from Grant's Tomb, it's a nice studio, and I've been very happy there. Well, one afternoon I was coming home, and there was a group of boys and girls playing hopscotch. It was quite chilly, and they were bundled up, and playing hopscotch, and as I put my foot on the first step, to go up to my front door, I saw the crown of a blonde head, a flying pigtail above a red jacket, and I stepped down, and looked at her.

She was intent in the game and I watched her hopping around, panting and serious-eyed, and of course I realized, quite consciously, I mean, that this was the girl's head I'd been looking for, and when she paused, I spoke with her, told her who and what I was and I asked her if I could sculpt a head of her, in clay, and I explained what it was. Clay, sculpture, art, etc.

"Sure!" she said. "When do you want to begin?"

I told her my apartment number—you know those big brownstone apartments—and said that when she finished playing, she could come up, and I'd do some sketches, and she cried,

"I'm through playing!"

I began to laugh but God he really *laughed!* He yelped at the ceiling, lowered his head and looked at me.

354

So, he said, I said fine, and we went up to my apartment, and into my studio. She took off her coat and scarf, sat on the high model's stool, and I got paper and charcoal out, put on my apron, fixed my easel, and went to work.

It went very well. She has a perfectly molded skull, high on her neck. Proud, even, and her high forehead comes down to an almost perfectly featured plainly beautiful face, and as I sketched, she watched me. Her eyes are dark brown, almost a reddish color, and she watched me, steadily and gravely as I worked, and after a half hour or so, I offered her some tea, crackers, and marmalade. I had a glass of wine. We talked. I found out her name, her age, she's fifteen, where she lived, etc., and she questioned me about what I was doing, and I explained it was what I most love in life, that it is what I had done and would continue to do, and she seemed to think it was O.K., you know—all right—and she asked if I wanted her to sit on the high stool again, and I said yes, I'd work for another twenty minutes or so, and then she could go.

That was fine, and I was very pleased. Happy, even, and when she said she had to go, I said fine, and I helped her into her red jacket and thanked her, and she turned in the doorway, looked up at me, and asked, seriously,

"Do you want me to come tomorrow?"

I said yes, that would be fine, and she asked if after school was O.K. and I said sure.

She showed up the next afternoon, I said.

3:21, he said. He ran his hand across his eyes, shook his head, stared into space and drank half of his glass of wine, looked at me, sighed, asked me if I had a cigarette, I did, a French cigarette, a Gauloise, he took one, lit it, puffed, and looked at me again, and smiled.

She must have made up her mind the night before, he said, because as I sketched her the next afternoon, I became aware she was looking at me differently. Looking, really looking at me. Her eyes followed me everywhere, and believe me, her aura came into the room, and I—I couldn't stand it, so I crossed to her, and stood in front of her, looked down at her and met her upturned eyes and asked why she was looking at me like that. She stood up on one of the rungs, put her arms around me, looked square in my eyes,

355

and kissed me. Passionately.

Holy Christalmighty, I whispered.

Yes, he said. Oh, he murmured, he tossed his head, She was so unutterably beautiful and willing. WILLING! he yelled, and made a choked sound. I lowered my head onto my arm on the bar, and repeated Jesus Jesus. He finished his glass of wine, as I looked up, and finished my vodka, he said:

Another. Yes. Definitely. We made love, on my bed, and it was—beautiful. Incredible. Fantastic. WONDERFUL!

She was—

A virgin, he said, to himself, and looking at me, he said it didn't matter. I was insane, he said.

Did you—

No. Nothing. I know it's dangerous, but we don't use anything.

Boy, I said. That's fantastic. Watch out.

He caught the bartender's eye, and we got a couple more drinks. He said,

Afterwards I made her some tea, crackers and marmalade, and as I drank some wine, we sat on my bed, and in silence, refreshed ourselves. She put on one of my shirts.

Since then, she comes by every afternoon, and also in the mornings, and after I finished the sketches, I began with clay. It's coming along perfectly, and we make our love and once again I'm in love. And she says she loves me. In that little voice. With her serious eyes.

So when I saw him on the street a few days ago, she'd turned twenty-three. On January 10th, and I felt pretty sad.

Junior High School, he said, High School, and two years of City College before she quit and got a job, and at least four days a week she came by all those years, and in the old 9th, 10th, 11th and 12th Grade years, as her school was near where I lived, she would come by in the mornings. I gave her the keys, and she'd come in, we'd make love, and then she would make tea for herself and coffee for me, and we'd have toast and then she went to school. We never used contraceptives.

I sculpted several heads of her, and did some excellent nude drawings. It's actually my best work. No it isn't, he said, and I have to go home, I'm getting depressed.

He looked at me a little angrily, made a quick smile, and stood up.

I can't stay for another, he said. I must go. Really. I'm exhausted.

I said O.K., and we shook hands, and suddenly I saw that long long look, in his eyes. If he had burst into tears it wouldn't have surprised me, but he didn't, he took a step toward me, put his right hand on my shoulder, and laid his head there, and laughed. He drew back smiling, and said, Yes, definitely.

He sat down, we caught the bartender's attention, and got two more drinks, and drank thirstily. He smiled, but then grew solemn.

He said:

There is one thing I must tell you. In the first two or three weeks—about a month before I met you—I tell you, I would look at her—she would look at me with such a complete trust, and love, I couldn't stand it, it's lasted for years, and then, I mean I, I was very near emotional breakdown. My whole body was filled with impossible love, just impossible, I was crazy with it, and I was very calm, very conscious, and yet I was permeated by a sense of completion I'd not known before, it was like I was calm and controlled, yet electrified with tenderness, but in a full, total, constant charge, exactly understanding restraint, and an absolute passion, but so often I was overcome, not in disbelief, but in the newness of it, the constant newness, with this—this GIRL! *which has almost lasted* I couldn't find the words, to fit a living experience I'd not known before and which I knew my future held, and one afternoon, when I was sculpting her as she posed, naked, I was so overcome by emotion I didn't know what to do, so I put down my tools, and crossed the room and stood before her, and looked in her trusting upturned eyes, searching, because maybe she could give me—no, that's not it, but maybe she—maybe she could tell me! And I stood there, transfixed and looking into her grave and poignant eyes, my love of her pouring from my heart, and she rose on the rung, put her arms around me, and with her naked body against me, gazed deep into my eyes, and in her profound pure marmalade breath and fifteen year old voice, sim-

357

ply and unbearably without stress, so simply, said, "I know"—OH *how* I embraced her, insanely happy and laughing, as she nodded, seriously, and warmly with her hands on my cheeks she repeated it to my released and radiant heart, *"I know,"* and rising upwards, kissed me, tenderly.

The Man Who
Changed Overnight

*After Coppard (Adam & Eve
& Pinch Me): for Marcella*

1

THE AMERICAN PROFESSOR and his wife were sipping rum punches
in a marvelous restaurant which extended out over the water.
They watched the yachts and big speedboats at anchor in the
harbor. It was about four p.m.

They looked over the rail and watched the fish play among the
undercurrents of water, above the mud and undergrowth, in
which lay slime-covered beer cans and soda bottles. The fish were
beautiful, and varied: some were thirty inches long, thin as a
pencil and almost transparent. They hung suspended and one had
to look close to see them. They were great. Enviable, even.

The American Professor and his wife faced each other across the
painted wooden table. She was enjoying the view, so didn't pay
much attention to her punch, and as she had to turn in her chair
to see the whole mountain/harbor vista, at which he could glance
while looking at her, he saw more of her profile than her full face,
which didn't bother him, as he enjoyed her from any angle, which
she knew, in a way she could ignore, although there were moments when he fastened on her features, her really beautiful lips,
for example.

But especially her dark and dancing eyes, which made her
move, and in an inner way happily laugh, although his watching
her could also irritate and even anger her. But, as that was no
one's fault, for there was no real motive involved in his eyes, he

understood it was how she was, and if she liked it okay, so did he, and if she didn't that was okay too.

There wasn't much that she did that bothered him, and it was if anything, what she didn't do that did. What bothered her about him was most likely both.

So he enjoyed her profile, as she enjoyed the really impressive view.

As if the land was holding the water, as if reaching for it: the land advanced into the water for the land was thirsty, with an aggressive hesitation while the cliffs were dramatic and shy.

She turned and lit a filter cigarette, and he wondered how these native people made such marvelous drinks.

Their stay was brief: two days and two nights in a gloomy but functional cabaña right on the beach. Then, beginning the day after tomorrow, the long trip back to New York: not real, or right. Especially as she was getting a better tan, but then he had been inside the apartment helping Bill pack, while she had gotten the sun.

She had a tawny skin that took the blazing Caribbean sun better than his skin did, so in a funny sense he envied her. I'm tanner'n you, she teased, Unh huh just wait, he had responded, and suddenly serious she baffled him, turning from the humor of competition, she baffled him: he who enjoyed being baffled by her, which she understood.

Not like years ago when she had said she couldn't help it because she too was baffled, and he had agreed that this, then, was baffling in itself, but—or, and if they both walked around being baffled, nothing could have been clear, in those days, and she had said she was confused, and he had admitted he was too.

Secretly, though, he felt that presently it took something real to baffle him: something real like his competition with her. Because the fact was, he liked her, and, curiously, she liked him, yet it was true that he loved her more than she loved him, and that could irritate, yet he accepted it because this was how she was, and he was too smart, he thought, to make an issue out of it.

If he made an issue out of it she became guilty and unhappy, thinking she was being confronted with a personal puzzle which she couldn't handle, and as he pretty well knew her, why should

360

she? These were her feelings! Were they both competing for her love? Especially, he knew once years ago she had loved him, but had learned how not to, and oh boy this hurt, though he knew why. His old old self contempt.

She had become considerate, honest, and brilliant, and she baffled him and he envied her for her effect on him—as an alien force, with a tanned body, which is the haunting quality a tourist feels: this is what ran around in one's mind. Not a drop of sentimentality in a picture postcard ocean of fear and doubt matched with delight and thoughtful enjoyment of each other. In an alien culture the tourist was introspective, and the American Professor was divided.

Their eyes met when she turned, and they both smiled. She slid her hand across the table and he took it, and they sat in silence. She finished her drink, and they decided to have one more, but on this order she changed to a virgin punch, and as the waiter came, on signal, the American man ordered, in English which embarrassed him, as he pointed to her: *no* rum——no ah *rom* for (he gestured at her)—

La Señora, the waiter grinned.

Yes, si! the American Professor laughed, then pointed to his own chest, and said *Rom* y punch, and the waiter nodded, amused, and walked away. These people were incredibly friendly. A family operation, this restaurant. The drinks came quickly, too.

Boy! But.

He tipped too much. Look, she often said, and for God's sake—we're *not* rich!

The drinks were great and I thought the service was—

But two dollars on a five dollar check is too *much!*

Jesus I must have been drunk.

Well then you're always drunk.

Ah si, he sighed, you're right, in your lightning mathematical mind and tipping percentages. But one night at home, last summer, coming downtown in a cab, she had slapped his hand and then had gone into gales of laughter as the cabbie had turned and was looking at them, she whispered, *That's too much*, laughing, and then she said Aw fuck it, give it to him, which the American Professor had done, and when they had gotten out of the cab and

walked home laughing, she particularly, she cried, I'm awful!
Awful! In her true, ringing laughter, but his too, and they were
often the object of irritation and envy when they went out. Not
many handsome couples laughed in art museums, or in East Indian restaurants. Or on the sidewalks of New York.

They watched the Caribbean sun go down, huge and fantastic
and as probable as the land going out to get the water, yet the sun,
in a kind of eerie glow as from the sky, literally sank into the
water. Suddenly, therefore, it was dark.

He paid and left too large a tip, and they said goodnight, and
walked along through the little fishing village, and decided to go
back to their cabaña via the highway and after a bit, arriving at the
gate, he showed their pass to the guard, and they went into the
government owned park under palm trees and an obviously cosmic sky, with an almost full moon climbing up to where the sun
had been. The features of the man in the moon were so vivid one
could see smile lines at the eyes.

"I need some cigarettes."

They stopped at the little store and she bought smokes. They
walked toward the beach under the palm trees. The water gleamed
wonderfully dark against the brilliant stars above. The long beach
curved. The air was warm, almost balmy. A sound of laughter
and sudden music floated on a breeze, and as they got to the beach
they leaned against a coconut tree and looked along the soft ulti-
mate water and sky. They embraced and kissed, and her lips
trembled.

Inside their cabaña he helped her make supper, and afterwards
they played casino, she beat him and then he beat her and then he
said he was tired. They had been on the beach and in the water all
day, except for a nap. But she wasn't tired, but he was, and he
really was, too, so they stripped, got into bed, and she read
Maigret's Memoirs and often laughed: he read not quite a page
and a half of another novel by Simenon called *The Blue Room*,
before he fell sound asleep.

Against her tan, her white breasts had startled him.

She continued to read, until she too fell asleep. Yesterday. The
day before.

Bill and his wife Barbara had come out with them to help with

362

the formalities of renting the cabaña which, because Bill knew Spanish, was fortunate, as the other American man—the Professor—didn't, and even then it was tedious, as the manager made the easy paperwork a complicated ritual.

But finally it was done, Bill drove back to Mayaguez to finish up the semester's teaching at the University, saying he'd be back that night and pick up Barb, they'd all have supper together, and then he and Barb would return to Mayaguez, and leave the other American couple there until Friday when he and Barb would come and pick them up and they would all return to Mayaguez for the night, go to San Juan on Saturday, and on Sunday, well, back to New York. But then.

Everyone was enthusiastic.

The two women and the American Professor walked along the beach to the cabaña, passing others as they went. Because it was in the middle of the week, Tuesday, in fact, hardly any Spanish or American people were there.

The bright blue sky, the lovely lapping Caribbean stretching outward, and the sprinkling of yachts at anchor in the bay formed a picture that made isolation a beautiful thought, and as they went into the cabaña and put the groceries away, and took the small wooden table and benches outside onto the secluded patio, he saw a Spanish man sitting on the edge of the patio gazing out to sea. Then, in the noise of arranging the table and chairs, the Spanish man looked around, rose, and gestured to the American Professor for a cigarette; the American said no. The Spanish man advanced to him. The two men faced each other. The Spanish man was staggering drunk, and the American smiled to himself, and said, as the other again gestured for a cigarette, no, sorry, and went inside thinking the guy would go away.

The cigarettes the American indeed had, were in his shirt pocket, and visible, which the other guy had seen, and so followed the American inside. The two women were making the bed in the next room while water on the stove heated for coffee, and as the American man opened the refrigerator and took out a bottle of beer, a hard-hitting German beer called *El Tigre*, and uncapped it, and drank, the native guy advanced and tweaked the American Professor's shirt pocket, and made a malicious smile: Once again

363

the Yankee tourist has lied to the poor native.

The startled American took out the pack of cigarettes, and said Si, he did have some but they are *very* strong, French, comprendo? and the American imitated a cough and pointed at the Spanish man, who shrugged, and was then belligerent, and as the American shook out a Gauloise, and gave it to the other man along with a light, the man's eyes glittered fiercely: Ah, amigo, the guy took the light, inhaled, and choked. His eyes bulged, the smoke caught in his throat, he brought his hand to his neck, and dropping the cigarette on the floor, coughed, very loudly, a large cloud of smoke, and then went into a gasping fit as the two women came out of the bedroom and said Who's he?

I don't know, the Professor said: he wanted a smoke and I warned him mine were strong, but he wouldn't listen, and—

Well, Barbara exclaimed, what in hell's he doing here anyway? Get him out!

The American Professor put his hand on the native's shoulder, and shoved gently, but nothing doing, and as the American opened his lips to speak he realized he didn't know the words, and as the native guy was finding his breath and wiping his eyes with his sleeve, he smiled because this American, who had tricked him, si, would have to throw him out, and that was what he would do, he would test this vicious gringo tourist.

Look pal, the American Professor said, I gave you a smoke, you choked like I said you would, so that's it, beat it.

He doesn't understand that, said Barbara, and as her eyes met the eyes of the native guy, the guy paled and took a step toward the door, hesitated and looked at the American man who, embarrassed, blushed:

Eighteen years in New York and I come all the way down here to run into this creep.

His mind raced: What's the matter with me? I don't know the words! I can't say anything! My God!

The Spanish guy pointed at him and then at the beer and Barbara advanced to the man, her eyes blazed, she pointed to the door, and cried, angrily,

Basta! VAMOOSE!

364

And the guy vanished, as if up in—smoke! The American Professor turned to Barbara saying Thanks I—I didn't know the words.

If you lived here you would. But, she grinned, this sort of thing is rare. In fact, she added, it's never happened before, and Bill and I have been here lots. Don't worry about it.

But, he said, you see, I know those words.

His wife nodded and served coffee and they sat down at the table, and Barbara said it takes a while to put what Spanish you know into use, and when anybody comes at first they're always nervous, you know.

He nodded, depressed, and thanked her.

He finished his beer, and changing into swim trunks, went outside. The Spanish guy was gone. Not lurking out back, or hiding behind one of the palm trees. Ah Yankee!!

What a fool I am, he thought, and went for a swim, which didn't work, and as he lay on a beach towel and looked up at the warm deep blue sky, he berated himself, because he knew those words, especially the one. Twenty years before Cynthia, Dan and Victor had returned from Mexico loaded with wraparound Zapata pants, sombreros, huaraches, tequila, and a lot of new words, and henceforth *basta* was a favorite, occurring often at the end of those letters

Basta!

Love,

Cynthia

through the years.

But *vamoose?* Who would think to tell anyone *vamoose?* Hopalong Cassidy? How ancient can you get?

So then, *basta!* and he raised his face to the sun. Three days to get a good tan, and as he looked down at his pale body, he sighed: fuck it.

Chalk up an encounter to experience: remember memory. You never, the old man had said, stop learning. But.

As the two women joined him, he was angry at himself. He went inside, lay down, and in difficulty took a nap.

Then later Bill showed up. He jumped out of the car, laughing, Hey Amigos!

That night the rum punches were great, supper was lovely and their good mood lasted into the night. The moon came out, almost full, and they had coffee and gazed out over the water at the reflected moon-path. It really was like a movie and he half expected Dan Duryea to walk through the doorway, which amused him, and he mentioned it to Bill and the women, who laughed with him.

Then they paid up, after a discussion who would treat, and he happily insisted saying: courtesy of West Virginia University (where he had lectured the month before), so Bill and Barbara graciously gave in. Who could deny West Virginia University, eh? Then.

Outside in the parking lot, Barbara waved and called See you Friday, have fun! as the car swung out onto the road.

The American Professor and his wife walked along the beach together, under the moon by the sea. The night was warm, balmy. Sleepy.

To bed early in that climate, so after playing casino for half an hour, and after reading from their Simenon novels, they turned out the light and embraced. Then they made love, and he didn't fulfill her, and though she kissed him afterwards and whispered not to worry, he was depressed, and while she slept he lay awake, and after an hour or so, in the sound of lapping waves and strange sounding night cries, he fell into a not so deep sleep, and then when he did, it was a troubled one at that, quietly.

Quietly, I rose from him, and gazed upon her, and then slowly so as not to alarm her, on my quiet call I went to her. She turned and reached up for me.

We touched, embraced, kissed, and in the soft Caribbean night I fulfilled her, and myself, too, and afterwards I lay by her, and caressed her and watched her drift into sleep again.

When I heard her steady breathing, which I know so well, I rose and stood in the room. In the dark, which is not dark to me.

In the next room, where the refrigerator, stove and dinette table and chairs were, I noticed that the door to the cabaña was open, and as I stepped, or rather glided, into the room I saw a shadow framed in the doorway, arms spread upward, hands on the inside edges as if curiously hanging: the shadow of terror, to which I went and said,

366

Enough.

Go.

As if in a puff it vanished, and I stepped outside, gazing at the scene before me, in that little corner of the world (I know it so well).

Then I returned to him. Quietly.

2

They agreed to have breakfast in the cabaña rather than at a restaurant down the beach, but first a swim, and holding hands they walked outside and down along the sand to the water. They walked into the soft surf, pebbly at first, and continued on and just when the water was too deep, laughing, they paddled around and kissed, and he smiled,

I love you completely.

She swam back toward the beach, and when she could stand, she stood and looked at him until he went to her.

She embraced him, and with her eyes deepening as she put her body against his, she whispered: clean breath in his ear,

Thank you.

They embraced and kissed seriously, as the thrill of the mystery of women ran through him.

The sea, the sky, the palm trees sprang into view. The air was suddenly clear, as consciousness quickly achieved. Quietly. They shoved off, shoulders breaking the surface, and the little waves curling around their ears. They swam briskly. Distant yachts and motor boats bobbed at anchor, and on one a retired professor of chemistry from Boston unfurled a sail. His figure was small, and perfect, and expert in motion.

They enjoyed scrambled eggs and toast with sweet butter, and afterwards had coffee. He took his vitamins then, and thought when she thanks you, don't ask why. Any guy knows that. But, just the same, he wondered, and as he shaved he looked at his reflection in the mirror. He smiled, hearing her gather the things she'd need on the beach, and then her clear wonderful voice:

"I'll be outside, darling."

He felt a new force flow up into consciousness, and he became strong, consciously, and it seemed that anything he wanted was at his fingertips. Quietly. This is the way to be, he thought, and later, cleanshaven, towel and notebook and pen in hand, he joined her on the beach, and after enjoying a pungent Gauloise, and the vista before him, he began to take notes for a new lecture on adverbs.

Something he looked forward to giving.

A Little Visit

LISTENING TO WAGNER'S *Tristan und Isolde* today while cleaning our loft, the sky clouded and it began to rain. Saturday, May 12th, 1974. Warm, and pleasant, and at the end of Act One, the rain increased, the sky darkened, then really darkened, and then I heard thunder, and as Isolde began to approach the third octave, a flash of lightning lit our loft, and just as Isolde, and the whole dangblasted orchestra hit home, a blast of thunder rocked the sky—and New York City.

The floor moved beneath my feet.

Dust mop in hand, I stood there. Feeling it.

Wow.

The Daily News

IT WAS LIKE ALWAYS. A little different from the way it was a while ago and from the way it might be later but in the whole scheme of things it was like it has always been. I came home early because the bar was hopeless, quiet and dull with that lethargic nothing-ness about it. I undressed and got into bed. I dozed and then woke up suddenly and got up to turn out the light, got back in bed and couldn't sleep. So after an hour and a half or so I got up again and dressed. The same old dirty socks, the same smelly pants, the shirt that looked ok and my middle name corduroy jacket and walking GI boots took me back to the bar thinking I might meet Max there and when I went in the door there he was with a shot of rye and a beer so we greeted each other and I got a drink and we talked. Later others came in and we sat together talking and drink-ing, going in together for drinks until closing when Sam bought a round letting us sit around till about twenty after four, as always, talking and scatting a little. Then we left and walked towards home again.

The others split off at a couple of streets and Max and I turned down Fourteenth and headed east.

Already the first sense of dawn was in my mind. The wind was blowing hard up and down the avenues. Max and I held our coat collars to our throats and bitched, cut across the street and went into Riker's for a hamburger and coffee.

The place was filled with bums, and colored guys and Puerto Ricans and those like me and Max who just came in but everyone was either half loaded or plastered and after Max and I got our order a Puerto Rican guy leaned over and let an old man have it on the mouth and another Puerto Rican guy cut in to stop it and the guy who hit the old man, his girl got furious with the guy who cut in and two colored guys came in and hauled a colored punch drunk Spanish French German speaking bum out and threw him on the sidewalk at the feet of a colored woman who was speaking quietly with a short fat white man in green slacks and a brown shirt and hardly any hair and Max and I were drinking coffee and the chef was running around like a rabbit and the bums were yelling for free coffee in this fucking joint and laughing and the Puerto Rican woman smacked the guy who cut in and the guy and the old man who had been hit were shaking hands and grinning and arguing and a blonde guy with short hair on top and long hair on the sides and a plaid jacket, chino pants and engineers' boots was murmuring man man man where am I and the punch drunk tri-lingual Negro came back in and asked Max for cinco centavos and Max gave him a nickel and we left just as a guy looking like Sugar Ray in Ivy Leagues came in.

Max and I parted and he went on down east and I headed west towards home. When I got there I unlocked the street door and went in the hall, locking the door behind me. Then I went up to my room and got a buck, deciding to go out for coffee and cigarettes at an all night luncheonette on the corner. When I got there I sat at the far end of the counter and gave my order. The chef brought me smokes and a cup of coffee.

A man came in and sat near the door, ordered coffee and toast. He was a large man, sleepy eyed and pale, in a brown chalk stripe suit, white on white shirt and silver and brown diagonally striped silk tie. He stirred his coffee and stared in the cup.

Behind him was the large plate glass window of the front of the place. It was like a mirror and the luncheonette seemed to be unfolded out into the dark street. The blue ice cream sign hanging just over his shoulder reflected in. Outside it was windy and chilly, newspapers heaved and rolled in the streets, men walked with heads down and hands in pockets, jacket collars up. Lights were out in the multi-million rooms of the city. The cold streets were dark and empty. Mid-October in New York. Max was probably home in bed trying to get some sleep.

The man drank some coffee and ate a piece of toast. I sipped my coffee and lit a cigarette. Watching that pane of glass behind him reflect the two of us outside the place.

Then I went home and got in bed again. After a little while it began to get light, and later I fell asleep.

The O. Henry Memorial Award

IT WAS SNOWING. Every time he sat down and faced his typewriter to write something or at least something he had felt the past few days (and couldn't get hold of), it seemed to be snowing. And if it wasn't snowing it was doing something else. Something just as fresh and distracting.

So he sat back and folded his arms across his chest and watched the flakes fall on the city.

He realized maybe he shouldn't be writing. Maybe he should watch it some more. Would it make him think of her? God that was easy; snow—or a sunny winter day—made it worse because it was always her. The sky had been so blue one day last week it was like the ocean and he spent a long paragraph trying to tell her about it, explaining the only ocean he had seen was the North Atlantic and that ocean was not blue. He had never seen the Pacific but it was blue. Able Baker grew up right by it, right by the big Pacific and Abe said it was blue; deep everlasting blue.

He had torn up the letter. How could he mail it?

"It isn't me," she would say. "It's only about something. Why can't you ever write to me?" Boy.

How could he ever write a story? What would be the plot? Who would it concern? What would happen? What would be the beginning, bridge, ending??? He watched the roofs gradually get covered with snow. Tops of cars looked like abstract paintings in two tones and white. He looked at his machine on his desk on the floor of his room.

"My room," he said.

Wondering a little and slightly bored he began to describe his room. After that, wondering about that he described all the objects in his room. He gave the room its planes and surfaces in space and then he gave the history of himself in the room and related himself to everything he had previously described. It took three and a half pages single space. It ended the day she left. He read it again and his heart sank. When she came into it the story began to get bad. He made three spaces and began writing about her. Just her. He was frowning and writing and getting depressed, watching his story get worse and worse. He stopped writing about her in the middle of a word, sentence, paragraph, story, double-spaced and wrote what he saw out the window and when he felt he was overdoing that he wrote it would snow every time he tried to write—

He lay down on his bed. The story was finished. He felt tired and confused. He looked at the ceiling and missed her.

Printed September 1982 in Santa Barbara &
Ann Arbor for the Black Sparrow Press by
Graham Mackintosh & Edwards Brothers Inc.
Design by Barbara Martin. This edition is
printed in paper wrappers; there are 300
cloth trade copies; 250 hardcover copies
have been numbered & signed by the author;
& 26 lettered copies are handbound in boards
by Earle Gray each signed & with an
original drawing by Fielding Dawson.

No writer moves more aptly, quickly, closely, in the tracking of human dimensions of feeling and relation. I have been fascinated for literal years now by this extraordinary man's ability to move the world with *words*. Not at all simple—when so little says anything anymore, and there are so few to hear it. So his work is factually heroic, and always will be.

—Robert Creeley

The author was born in 1930 in New York, but grew up in Kirkwood, Missouri, graduated from high school there, and in 1949 went to Black Mountain College where he continued painting and drawing, as well as writing. Four years. Was drafted in 1953 and served as a cook in a large Army hospital kitchen outside Heidelberg, Germany. Returned Stateside in 1955, freedom, New York for keeps (so far), in 1956. He is a prolific writer, has published stories, essays, criticism, poems and dreams in hundreds of magazines around the world. Travels a lot. Does book covers, is an exhibiting artist known for his photo collages.

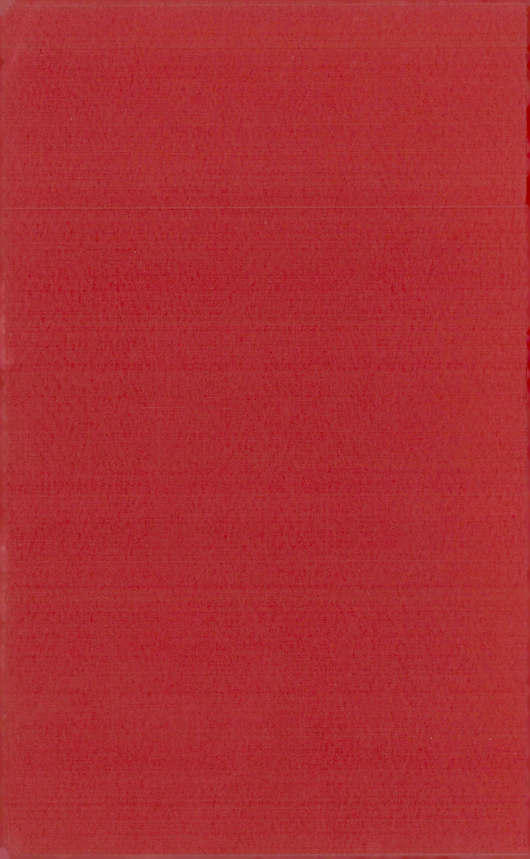